W9-BYK-417

PRAISE FOR *THE BIG SECRET*

"Earley's knowledge of the internecine machinations of Washington in general . . . give the book verisimilitude. . . . A cut above the popular thrillers of John Grisham and Tom Clancy." —*New York Sun*

"Chillingly believable, *The Big Secret* is a fast-paced yarn that's all fun. As always Pete Earley's writing is superb and engaging." —Nelson Demille

"Earley effectively tweaks the novel genre, beginning as a conventional chase thriller that grows deeper and more relevant as the story progresses." —*Kirkus Reviews*

"Readers learn a great deal of information about, among other topics, investigative journalism, U.S. Senate politics Mississippi's social strata, soul food, racial bigotry, identica twin studies, bipolar personality disorder, creation of false identities, college social clubs, friendship, lust and love." —*St. Petersburg Times*

THE BIG SECRET

Pete Earley

TOR®

A TOM DOHERTY ASSOCIATES BOOK
NEW YORK

This is a work of fiction. All the characters and events portrayed in this book are either products of the author's imagination or are used fictitiously.

THE BIG SECRET

A Tor Book
Published by Tom Doherty Associates, LLC
175 Fifth Avenue
New York, NY 10010

www.tor.com

Tor® is a registered trademark of Tom Doherty Associates, LLC.

ISBN 0-765-34692-3
EAN 978-0765-34692-6

First edition: June 2004
First mass market edition: May 2005

Printed in the United States of America

0 9 8 7 6 5 4 3 2 1

Dedicated to Tony Francis Luzi

"Life is but an empty dream!
For the soul is dead that slumbers,
And things are not what they seem."

—Henry Wadsworth Longfellow,
"The Psalm of Life"

One

I'm watching a man who thinks this is going to be one of the happiest days of his life. I'm about to make it the worst.

Information is power, especially in politics, especially in Washington, D.C. But it's only truly powerful if you know how to use it. My boss, United States Senator Leslie Homer DeLong, taught me this. In the decade that I've worked for him, he's taught me plenty. He's a Texan. A die-hard Democrat. And he's been a politician nearly all of his life. He first ran for election to a city council job in Tyler, Texas, after he returned from killing Germans in World War II. From there, he climbed the ladder to the nation's capital quickly. He's been a senator for seven consecutive terms. That's forty-two years! He likes to say that he learned everything he knows from another Texas Democrat: President Lyndon Baines Johnson. You can say what you want about this country's thirty-sixth president and the mess that he made in Vietnam, but early in his political career, Johnson was the youngest majority whip ever to serve in the Senate, and he was shrewd and tough enough to guide a civil rights bill through Congress at a time when the word "nigger" was still being spoken without embarrassment at fashionable Georgetown parties. My boss quotes Johnson all of the time. "Nick LeRue," he says to me—for some reason he always says both my first and last names—"if you want to survive on Capitol Hill, you've got to remember what LBJ used to tell me: 'I never trust a man unless I got his pecker in my pocket.'"

Which, in a way, is what today is all about. My boss was double-crossed by another senator. The man sitting in front of me right now had nothing to do with it. He's a pawn, but it doesn't matter. He's about to pay the price.

The man is wearing a charcoal gray pinstripe suit, tailor-made and pricey. His wife and their two kids—a boy about six and a girl about four—are sitting in chairs directly behind him and are also well dressed. The woman is the man's second wife and the kids are his second set. I know this about him, and much, much more. For example, I know his wife got caught stealing when she was thirteen years old. She's never told him. Her two best friends pressured her into stashing a bottle of Revlon's Fire & Ice fingernail polish in her purse. It cost ninety-five cents and she was stopped by a sales clerk trying to leave the store. I know these details because an FBI agent who interviewed the shop's manager told me about them.

The man's name is Daniel Hertell and he has been nominated by the president to become a U.S. District Court judge in Mississippi. He and his family are appearing before the U.S. Senate Judiciary Committee this morning for what should be a largely ceremonial confirmation hearing. The U.S. Constitution gives the Senate "advise and consent" powers over the president's choices for federal judges. It also reviews the president's nominees for U.S. Attorney and U.S. Marshal jobs. It's all part of the "balance of power" that our forefathers put into place. Remember high school civics? Three branches: the executive, legislative, and judicial. Checks and balances.

The Judiciary Committee meets on the second floor of the Dirksen Senate Office Building. Politicians like to name federal buildings after one another. The Senate has three office buildings and each is named after a former senator: Richard Brevard Russell, Jr.; Everett McKinley Dirksen; and Philip A. Hart, respectively. The words "Senate Office Building" are always tagged onto the address. Our committee meets in Room 224 Dirksen *Senate Office Building*. Since that's cumbersome to say, everyone uses the acronym *SOB*. That makes the committee's legal address: 224 Dirksen *SOB*.

I've always thought adding *SOB* after a senator's name was fitting. But then, I've been accused of being a smart-ass.

The committee hearing room in which we are sitting was built to impress. The ceiling rises fifty feet tall. A plush green and white carpet covers the floor and the walls are made of oak panels. Slabs of dark green marble line the base of the walls and the room's lighting comes from antique brass fixtures made in the shape of large Roman torches. The committee members' rostrum fills one entire end of the hearing room. It's a half circle and resembles a judge's bench. In spite of its size, it's not big enough for the ten Democrats and nine Republicans appointed to our committee. There's only enough room for twelve to sit, not nineteen. Luckily, this hasn't been a problem because my boss prefers to work behind the scenes. By the time our committee meets, he's already resolved most of the controversial issues, so we rarely draw a full quorum. On most days, our members keep busy by attending other, more volatile hearings where they can be seen on television.

The senators' swivel chairs behind the rostrum have thick cushions that make each senator look several inches taller than he is. My boss has a cushion twice as thick as everyone else's. I sit directly behind him and my chair doesn't have a cushion. I'm not an elected official. I've never run for office and never have wanted to. My title is Chief Investigator, Senate Judiciary Committee. But what I really am is a political detective whose specialty is investigating people's pasts and uncovering information that they would prefer to keep hidden. I have a top-secret security clearance and I can subpoena both records and witnesses—as long as my boss approves. That gives me virtually unlimited access to just about any record in the government and private world, and anyone living in the country.

I began my career as an FBI agent and a lawyer. In Washington D.C., being a lawyer is essential because politicians, federal prosecutors, and federal judges prefer to speak to other lawyers. It's snobbery, but that's just how Capitol Hill operates. I can't think of another place in our nation where the virtues of the common man are praised more by people who have never thought of themselves as being common and make damn sure whenever you meet them that you quickly realize just how special they are.

But I'm getting off track.

This is how the nominations process works. After a new president is sworn in, he sends our committee a list of his nominees for federal judgeships. Most are attorneys who either have given big contributions to his political party or have worked in his election campaign. Some are state judges who are banned from engaging in partisan politics, but are buddies with the local Democrat or Republican big-wigs. It's all part of that ancient "to the victor belong the spoils" process.

Now, if a president is savvy, before he sends a single name to our committee, he'll meet with all of the senators from his political party and toss them a bone. If a state needs four new federal judges, for example, a politically wise president will let a senator fill one of those spots. It's called trickle-down patronage.

But our Republican president didn't do that. He never bothered to meet with a single senator. None. So several of them complained to my boss. The result: The first batch of judge nominees from the White House is still waiting for our committee to approve it. The "paperwork" has been lost and I'm guessing it will never be found. After a few months of waiting, the White House realized what was happening and the president woke up and met privately with several Republican senators. He offered them a peace offering and that led to a second wave of nominees being put before our committee. Most have sailed through.

My job begins after the president sends over his list of candidates. By that point, the White House should have already investigated each of its nominees. No one there wants to embarrass the president by nominating someone who once got caught cheating on his federal income taxes. As soon as I get the White House's list, I contact the FBI.

Over the years, I've developed a tremendous admiration for the bureau's ability to burrow into a person's past. Okay, I'll admit I'm biased since I used to be one of J. Edgar Hoover's boys. But the bureau has vast resources. It not only uses all of the computerized federal records at its disposal, including limited Internal Revenue Service tax information, it also sends out agents to delve into your past. Remember that second-grade teacher who was your first crush, the camp counselor who caught you smoking in your cabin, the fraternity brother who got sloshed with you? The FBI finds them.

By the time the bureau finishes its background check, it's collected hundreds of pages of personal information. I call it the "This Is Your Life" file and it's delivered directly to *me*.

I'm responsible for warning my boss if I think there's anything politically damaging in the FBI report. Most of the time, there's not. But when there is, I take charge. My boss likes to handle skeletons quietly. Generally, he'll have a private chat with the senator from the nominee's home state. They'll agree to use what's called a "blue slip." It's a piece of blue paper that I send to each senator whenever one of his constituents has been nominated. If the senator conveniently "forgets" to return it, the nomination is lost forever in a paperwork netherworld. After a few months, the White House will quietly pull the nomination and submit a new name. Chances are, the media will never notice, and even if they do, there's no one to blame. After all, paperwork gets lost all of the time on Capitol Hill.

Which brings me back to today's hearing and Daniel Hertell. This is not one of those quiet, lost-paperwork nominations. About a month ago, my boss handed me a slip of paper with Hertell's name written on it.

"Do some digging," he said.

I didn't ask why. If he'd wanted to tell me more, he would've. I pride myself on my sources and ingenuity. If a senator has too many shots of Jack Daniel's in an Old Town bar, I hear about it. If a senator's top aide pressures a congressional page for a blow job, I hear about it. If a senator's spouse buys two hundred thousand shares of a blue chip stock on margin and the stock jumps the next day by five points, I hear about it. My sources always have a reason for talking. Mostly it has to do with partisan politics or revenge. I always examine their motives for leaking me gossip. It's important to wonder: *What's in this for them?* Otherwise, you could get burned.

It didn't take me long to figure out why my boss was curious about Hertell. The White House had given Mississippi's senator, Nehemiah Peterman, the right to pick a new Mississippi federal judge and Hertell was his choice. As soon as I realized Peterman was behind the nomination, I understood.

Peterman is a brash know-it-all who arrived on the Hill less than two years ago after defeating a Democrat who had been a senator since the late 1960s. The old bulls don't like it when one of their own is slaughtered. It scares them. To make matters worse, Peterman had run an anti-Washington campaign. It's a popular tactic, but what folks like Peterman don't realize is that those nasty anti-Washington television ads that they run really do piss off the Washington establishment and, like it or not, the Washington establishment is still in power when a newly elected senator arrives in town.

But what got Peterman into real trouble with my boss was a double-cross. Another senator, George Mathias, a Michigan Democrat, had introduced a bill that would have given auto workers an upper hand in their upcoming labor negotiations in Detroit. Everyone understood the bill was a publicity stunt. Mathias was simply kissing up to the auto unions. His bill was sent to a rather insignificant subcommittee for review and Senator Peterman happened to be on it. When Mathias asked the subcommittee to hold a public hearing, so he could get even more beneficial publicity, Peterman balked. That's when Mathias came to see my boss.

At this point, I need to explain how the U.S. Congress actually works. First, forget most of what you were taught in civics. Instead, rent the movie *The Godfather*. Picture my boss and other powerful Senate leaders as the mafia dons of the Hill, just as Vito Corleone and the other godfathers ran the mob's five families. The only difference is that my boss and his buddies cut their deals in the private steam room of the "Members Only" Senate gym or during eighteen holes of golf at the Congressional Country Club rather than over a plate of steaming linguine at Umberto's Clam House.

I realize this may seem melodramatic. But it's true. Politics is the "art of compromise." Or, as Vito himself used to say, making an offer to someone he can't refuse.

My boss had cut a three-way deal. Senator Mathias did a favor for my boss. In return, my boss did a favor for Senator Peterman. The next step was having Peterman help Mathias. But he didn't reciprocate. He promised that he would and then didn't.

I'm watching Senator Peterman right now. He's seated next to Daniel Hertell in front of the committee at the witness table. He's delivering a prepared speech about his nominee.

"Not only is Daniel Hertell a legal scholar, he's also a Christian, and a solid family man with a loving, and might I add really attractive, wife," Peterman said. He paused and glanced over his shoulder at a blushing Dana Hertell.

I've noticed that senators from the Deep South can get away with sexist comments like that. It's part of their cultivated Southern charm.

Peterman continued: "Daniel and Dana Hertell have two

beautiful and talented children. This family makes all of us proud to be Mississippians!"

I could tell from Peterman's confident manner that he didn't yet realize that he'd walked into a trap. I'm certain part of the reason he feels cocky is because my boss isn't at today's hearing. The session is being chaired by Senator Harry Bannan, a Republican from Ohio. And right now, he's the only committee member seated at the rostrum. Everyone else stayed away. Being absent gives them "plausible denial." I love that term. It's so Washington. Translation: a believable lie. Later in the day, my boss will make certain that he "accidentally" bumps into Peterman. "Sorry," he'll say innocently, "to hear your nominee got jammed." Translation: "Hey, smucko, I'm the guy who stuck it to you!" Then he'll add: "If I'd been there, I'm certain I could have prevented you from being stymied." Translation: "Next time, don't double-cross me, you jerk!"

So far, everything is going according to our plan.

Peterman, still unsuspecting, finished his speech.

Bannan said: "I have consulted with my fellow senators and none of them has any questions for Mr. Hertell."

Peterman and Hertell both grinned. Home free. At least, that's what they thought. And then Bannan said: "But our committee's chief investigator has given me a few questions to ask."

Peterman's smile vanished. No other judgeship nominees had been asked questions this morning.

"Excuse me, Mr. Chairman," Peterman announced, almost leaping from his chair, "but I'm due at another hearing, so I'm afraid I must leave now."

Peterman shook Hertell's hand and hurried from the room. *Coward,* I thought.

Bannan asked my first question. "According to the résumé that you gave the committee, you identified yourself as a Vietnam combat veteran. Is that correct?"

"Yes, I served in the Army during the war," Hertell replied.

I looked for a sign that he was worried, but there wasn't any.

"Were you wounded?"

"Yes, during the Tet Offensive. It's embarrassing because I was hit with shrapnel in a spot I'd rather not mention, since there are ladies in the room. Let's just say I was on my stomach with my head buried in the dirt because of incoming mortar rounds and, well, I couldn't sit down comfortably after I was hit."

The spectators in the hearing room laughed. It sounded to me as if he'd told that joke before.

"In addition to a Purple Heart, you were awarded a Bronze Star, according to your résumé, is that correct?"

"Yes, but I didn't get it because of Tet. I really don't like bragging, because all of us who served in Vietnam are forgotten heroes. However, I was awarded the Bronze Star because of an incident in the Quang Tri province. The enemy killed the man loading the M-60 machine gun that I was firing. But I just kept shooting somehow and I was told later that I was responsible for keeping the enemy from overrunning my platoon."

Someone began to clap and soon everyone was. Bannan rapped his gavel.

"The Army called me a hero," Hertell continued, "but I don't think of myself that way. I was simply doing my job."

"Really?" Bannan replied. If you listened closely, you could hear a touch of sarcasm beginning to rise in his voice. Bannan continued: "Isn't it true, Mr. Hertell, that you purchased your Bronze Star at a garage sale in Montgomery, Alabama, nearly twenty years ago?"

Several onlookers gasped.

Bannan didn't wait for a reply. Instead he said: "After you answer that question, perhaps you can tell us how you were able to participate in the Tet Offensive when your military records reveal that you first arrived in Vietnam on April 28, 1968—two months after the Tet Offensive already had ended?"

Hertell was now breathing fast. Beads of sweat popped from his forehead.

Bannan moved quickly to pound in the final stake: "You

might also like to explain why medical records that our chief investigator found reveal that your buttocks were cut when you slipped in the barracks while mopping a floor and landed on top of a metal bucket. There is no record of any shrapnel wound. Nor is there any record that confirms that you ever saw combat. You spent most of your career as a 'motion picture operator' at Subic Bay, Philippines."

Hertell looked nauseous.

In a flat voice completely devoid of emotion, Bannan concluded the attack that I'd scripted for him. "Is there anything you wish to say? Please remember you are under oath."

Hertell shook his head, indicating that he didn't.

"Then I believe it would be in the best interest of our committee to table your nomination at this time," Bannan declared, rapping his gavel. "We'll now take a short recess."

I watched Hertell's dumbstruck wife. The couple's children didn't understand but knew something had gone terribly wrong. A shell-shocked Hertell turned to face them while I exited through the door on my left that led into the committee's offices. Senator Bannan was waiting there. "My nephew was killed fighting in Vietnam and I hate those bastards who pretend they saw combat," he said. "Good work." Then he asked me: "Didn't you lose a brother in Vietnam?"

"Yes, Senator, I did," I replied. "He was older than me and my only sibling."

"How the hell," Bannan asked, "did the FBI miss Hertell's fake medals?"

"Records dealing with Vietnam are difficult to check," I replied. "I don't know all of the reasons why. But there's even been a book written, called *Stolen Valor,* that exposes dozens of guys posing as Vietnam war heroes. One claimed he was a Medal of Honor winner!"

My cell phone rang. "Nick LeRue, talk to me!" It was my boss. "Does Peterman's nominee sleep with the fishes?" Besides quoting LBJ, my boss loves Mafia-speak.

"Yes," I answered. "But Peterman jumped ship before Senator Bannan went in for the kill."

"Was the media there?"

"The only reporter was from the Jackson, Mississippi, *Clarion-Ledger,*" I said, "but Judith is calling Hartson now." Judith Delagold is the committee's public information officer. Ted Hartson covers the judiciary committee for the *Washington Tribune,* the most influential newspaper in the city.

"That'll teach that son of a bitch to betray me," De Long replied. "It was JFK who said: 'Forgive your enemies, but never forget their names.' I admire that. But personally, I live by what LBJ said: 'I demand real loyalty. I want someone who will kiss my ass in Macy's window, and say it smells like roses.'" He chuckled.

"Did you already know that Hertell had lied about Vietnam before you asked me to investigate him?" I asked.

"No, but I suspected it. A pal of mine overheard Hertell bragging at a veterans' meeting about Tet and what he said didn't jibe with what my friend, who was actually there, remembered. Gotta go." He hung up.

The rest of the judicial nominees breezed through the committee that afternoon, although I noticed each one eyed me nervously. We finished around four o'clock. It was a Thursday, early June. When I returned to my office and looked outside, I noticed it had rained. Pedestrians were sidestepping puddles that would soon evaporate thanks to an oppressive summer heat wave. I love the smell of Washington D.C. after a hard rain. The air seems crisp. It's as if God reached down, grabbed this city, and scrubbed it clean.

Maybe I'm getting too old for this job, I thought.

For me, the glamour of Capitol Hill had waned years ago. The Hill devours starry-eyed innocents. Yet, there's never a shortage of fresh faces. The best and the brightest arrive in a never-ending stream.

I blame Heather Cole for my cynicism. She left me two years ago. Of course, I've always pretended that the breakup hasn't affected me. Call it macho pride. But it did and has and still does. If I'm not working, I'm sitting in my apartment, eating take-out Chinese, and watching C-Span. *Pitiful.*

In contrast, Heather appears to have fully recovered. She's a newspaper reporter for the Style section in the *Washington Tribune,* so it's easy for me to keep track of her. Political profiles are her speciality. She can cut off a puffed-up politician's *cojones* and hand them to him before he even realizes he's been emasculated.

Recently, she's been living with Andrew Middleton, another writer at the *Washington Tribune.* Actually, he's much more than a writer. Middleton is one of the most famous investigative reporters in the nation. In the early 1970s, his reporting led to the resignation of a U.S. president. Since then, Middleton has written a half dozen insider books about Washington. Every one of them has been a blockbuster. He's broken lots of important stories. He's famous for his scoops. He's rich too. Few journalists in America are as powerful. I loathe him.

It is nearly five and I'm scheduled to have dinner tonight with a good friend: Phillip Shurman. He's the FBI's congressional liaison officer, which means he spends his time prowling around the Hill trying to keep everyone happy with the bureau. He asked me earlier if I'd take him to eat at the Senate dining room, which is in the U.S. Capitol and exclusively reserved for only senators, their families, their top administrative aides, and the media. I'm not officially on that list but I still get in whenever I wish. Shurman has just returned from a family vacation and wants to catch up. I'm supposed to leave on vacation tomorrow but I really don't have anywhere to go.

I used to walk from our offices in the Dirksen SOB to the U.S. Capitol, which is just across the street, but now there are too many waist-high concrete barriers around the Capitol property and too many security checkpoints. I use the underground trolley in the Dirksen's basement. It's one of a series of tunnels and trolleys that connect various congressional buildings. Tourists used to be able to ride the trams, but not anymore. September 11 changed that.

I headed downstairs and strolled down a long corridor. For some reason I was thinking about how Daniel Hertell had looked when he had turned around in the hearing room and faced his family. I'd just reached the trolley's entrance when I heard a woman's voice call: "Nick LeRue!"

I instantly recognized the voice. It was Heather. She was walking toward me. She looked magnificent. In her early thirties, she was short, fit, with high cheekbones, thick brown hair that's cut shoulder-length, and a killer smile. She seduces you with that smile. It makes you feel comfortable. She's the sort of person who always reminds people of a best friend, sister, aunt, or favorite neighbor.

I'm still in love with her!

For two years, I had imagined this moment. Lying in bed, unable to sleep, I'd rehearse dozens of lines: some clever, but most just mean. We'd lived together five years and I'd thought we'd always be a couple. I'd asked her to marry me and a month later, she'd moved out. I'd scared her, I guessed. I'd convinced myself that it was her damn career. Workaholism is a disease in Washington. I wanted to move to the 'burbs, have kids, own a house. The American Dream. Apparently, she hadn't wanted any of that.

As she stepped up to me, all of my clever one-liners went blank. I couldn't remember even one of them. All I could muster was: "Hello, Heather."

She stuck out her hand to shake mine.

"I'm not Heather," she replied. "I'm Melanie. Melanie Cole. Her sister. I guess she never told you she had a twin. I'm not really surprised."

She hadn't and I was. *Flabbergasted!*

"I need your help, Mr. LeRue," she said. "Heather is missing. She's disappeared and someone is going to kill her!"

Two

Is this some sort of a joke?" I asked.

"No," Melanie replied. "I'm her twin and Heather is in trouble."

I led her along a basement hallway into a cafeteria reserved for Senate employees. En route, I called Phillip Shurman on my cell phone and told him that I was going to miss our dinner. A few people were eating in the cafeteria, so I found a table away from them and asked Melanie if she wanted something to drink.

"I'll get my own," she answered.

I bought a diet Coke. I drink them instead of coffee, averaging about eleven per day. Melanie filled a cup with water and then took four slices of lemon from a plastic container next to the iced tea. She twisted three of the slices so their juices dripped in. She added a single packet of Sweet'n Low and then twisted in the final lemon slice.

"Your sister makes that same drink, the exact same way," I said. "Heather calls it 'low-budget lemonade.'"

"I didn't know that," she said.

"You've never seen Heather make lemonade by squeezing three lemon slices, adding Sweet'n Low, and squeezing in the last lemon slice?" I asked incredulously.

"No. It's embarrassing, but we really haven't spent much time together since we were teenagers. Back then she used to drink Fresca."

"If you'd never seen her make lemonade, how were you able to make it exactly the same way?"

Melanie shrugged. "It's a twin thing. We do lots of things the same and neither of us can explain why."

This "twin thing" bothered me. I was now sitting across from a woman who appeared, sounded, and was acting exactly the same as a woman whom I had hoped to marry. Part of me wanted to kiss her passionately. Another part wanted to wrap my fingers around her neck and choke her. I stirred my diet Coke with a straw and tried to seem nonchalant.

"I spent most of today at the *Washington Tribune* talking to Andrew Middleton," she began. "He suggested that I speak to you, although he said you aren't friends."

"Your sister dumped me for him," I replied.

"Did you know she left him too? She moved out three weeks ago."

I shook my head.

"Heather has taken a leave of absence from the newspaper. She left town on Monday to begin doing research for a book."

"What sort of research? Where'd she go?"

"I received a letter from her last week. She said Mr. Middleton had given her a book idea. It was about a lynching in Mississippi that happened in 1955. Mr. Middleton said—"

"Can we drop this Mr. Middleton crap?" I interrupted.

"Oh, ur, I'm sorry. Anyway, ah, in her letter, Heather said Mr., ur, Middleton had suggested that she investigate this old lynching."

"Investigate it how?"

"You know, find out why this black man had been hung and discover what had happened to the five white men who had hung him."

"How'd he know five white men did it? Were they arrested?"

"No one was ever charged, but the lynching took place in a small town where everyone knows everyone else. In her letter, Heather wrote that discovering the men's identities was going to play a key role in her book. Middleton had told her that the men had carved their initials in the tree trunk. It was a clue."

"Wait," I said. "They carved their initials in the tree after they lynched a black man?"

"They were proud of what they'd done. Middleton told Heather that the locals called it the 'trophy tree' after the hanging. He convinced Heather that the lynching had all of the makings of a great real-life detective story. Who were these guys? Why did they do it? How did the hanging later affect their lives? That sort of thing. He felt there was a chance some of them might even still be alive."

I had to admit it was an intriguing idea for a book, but I wasn't going to give Middleton credit for being clever.

Melanie continued: "Only it was odd this morning. When I met with Middleton, he acted like the book really hadn't been his idea. He told me Heather had learned about the trophy tree from a book publisher. He made it sound as if an editor in New York had contacted her directly, and that's not what Heather had written to me in her letter, although I guess it really doesn't matter whose idea it was. I mean, the end result was that Heather got a hundred-thousand-dollar book advance and left for Mississippi."

"Did Middleton tell you why Heather had broken off their relationship? Why she had left him?" I was curious.

"No." She paused. "I don't know if I should tell you this, but I'm going to. He said that he had encouraged her to write a book and had helped her get the hundred thousand dollar advance because he hadn't wanted them to end up bitter about each other—the way that you and Heather had ended up."

Bitter?

I thought about the night when Heather had told me that

she was leaving. Had our final conversation been nasty? Oh, yes. It had. Very nasty. I'm not the sort of man who lives with a woman for five years and then gives her a soft peck on her cheek and wishes her a cheery tally-ho after she announces that she's leaving for another man.

"A hundred thousand advance is a lot of cash for a first-time author," I said. "But it's not much if you aren't around to collect it."

"What do you mean?" Melanie asked.

"Ever heard of Medgar Evers?"

"Of course. He was a black civil rights leader who was murdered."

"He was shot in 1963 by a member of the Ku Klux Klan, a man named Byron de la Beckwith," I replied.

"What's Evers got to do with Heather?"

"Byron de la Beckwith was tried twice, but both times, juries couldn't agree on a verdict. For twenty-five years, de la Beckwith strutted around bragging about how he'd gotten away with murder. And then a reporter began digging, uncovered new evidence, and in 1994, Beckwith was put on trial again. Only this time he was found guilty and sentenced to life in prison for a murder that he'd committed thirty-one years earlier."

Based on her confused expression, I knew Melanie still didn't understand why I was telling her about de la Beckwith.

"Not long after de la Beckwith was convicted," I continued, "two white men were tried in Alabama for a 1963 bombing that killed four girls in a Baptist church in Birmingham. Once again, a reporter dug up evidence against them and they were convicted. You see, there is no statute of limitations for murder. No matter how many days, months, and years go by, a murder remains an open investigation until the guilty party is brought to justice."

"So if Heather identifies the white men who carved their initials on the trophy tree and they're still alive, they could be tried for murder?" Melanie asked. "Is that what you're telling me?"

"Yes. White prosecutors in Mississippi in the late 1950s

might have been eager to look the other way. But not today, not now."

"But wouldn't a prosecutor need witnesses? It seems like a 1955 lynching would be too old of a murder case to pursue."

"Tell that to de la Beckwith and those two white bombers."

Melanie paused. It appeared as if she were taking a moment to think about what she wanted to say next so she could say it exactly right. "Andrew Middleton never mentioned anything to me this morning that suggested Heather might have been walking into a dangerous situation. In fact, he laughed at me when I told him that Heather was in trouble and needed help."

I suddenly realized that she hadn't told me when and how Heather had contacted her. "Did she call you from Mississippi?" I asked. "Did she find one of the white men? Have you phoned the FBI?"

Melanie took a long sip of her homemade lemonade and again thought for several moments. "How much do you know about twins, Mr. LeRue?" she asked.

"I know there are fraternal twins, who are born at the same time but don't look anything alike. And there are identical twins. If I remember my high school biology correctly, it has something to do with the mother's egg."

"Out of every hundred human births, about one or two are twins," Melanie said. "Fraternal twins are born when two different sperms fertilize two different eggs. Identical twins happen when one sperm fertilizes only one egg and then, for a variety of reasons, that egg later splits into two babies. Because there is only one sperm and initially only one egg, the result is two babies who each have the exact same genetic blueprint from their parents."

"Sounds as if you've given this speech before."

"When you're a twin, you don't have much choice. People ask you stupid questions, like, 'Are your birthdays on the same day?'"

I noticed when she smiled that she had perfect white teeth, just like Heather. "'Identical' is really not an accurate description," she continued, "because identical twins often aren't true carbon copies of one another. There are lots of theories about why two people born from the same sperm and same egg can end up different. Maybe it's because of the location of the embryos in the womb, maybe one baby gets zapped with radiation from an X-ray and the other doesn't. Who knows? But because of these minor differences, identical twins are divided into subgroups. The most identical of all identical twins are called 'mirror image twins.' Look closely at my face, Mr. LeRue."

I already was looking. I hadn't stopped since we had sat down.

"Do you see anything different about my face compared to Heather's?"

I used to stare at Heather in the mornings before she woke up. She is not a morning person. I am. I would watch her and marvel at how beautiful she was. I don't think there is an inch of her body that I don't recall perfectly in my mind. Now I looked at Melanie's face and compared it to my memory of Heather's face. The entire time we had been together, I hadn't noticed any difference between the two twins, yet I had sensed there was something amiss. I spotted it.

"The mole on Heather's cheek—the one just under her ear," I said. "It's on the left side of Heather's face and on the right side of your face."

"Very good," she replied. "That's mirror-imaging. When we were children, Heather and I could stand in front of each other and move our arms and legs in sync. You would have thought there was only one person in the room, posing in front of a mirror."

"That must have been a sight."

"In its simplest form, mirror-image twins have opposite birthmarks, moles, and dental patterns. In rare cases, one twin's internal organs will be located on the wrong side of his or her body. Some scientists believe that the longer a woman's fertilized egg remains together, the more physically alike the twins will be when that egg finally divides itself."

"Does that mean the egg that produced you and Heather remained together a long time?"

"Yes, much longer than any other known twins at the time. Doctors at the nation's most prestigious twin research center in Minnesota got permission from my parents to study us. They'd never seen mirror-image twins as identical as we are—to the point that even our fingerprints are the same, only reversed."

We'd been talking for twenty minutes and Melanie still hadn't told me why Heather was in danger. Still, I wasn't in a rush to leave.

"The researchers studied us for ten years," she continued. "Twice a year, we'd fly to Minnesota for various tests."

"What did they discover?"

"Heather and I are unique, even among mirror-image twins, Mr. LeRue," she said. "As infants we developed our own language. It was gibberish only we could understand. I later learned this is common among twins. Doctors even have a name for it: cryptophasia."

The image of Heather and Melanie chatting in baby talk flashed through my head.

Continuing, Melanie said, "Mirror-image twins often can feel each other's aches and pains too."

"I've heard of that," I said. "One twin gets a toothache and the other's tooth will hurt."

"Yes, but once again, researchers discovered that we had a much more heightened sensitivity than other twins. When we were five years old, our parents took us skiing. Heather and my father started down a ski slope. My mother and I had already made the run. Suddenly my nose began bleeding. Heather had fallen and had gotten a bloody nose."

This was beginning to sound creepy. As a former FBI agent and a lawyer, I've been trained to study facts. Simultaneous nosebleeds seemed iffy.

She said: "The most unusual similarity first surfaced when we were six years old, and it involved dreams. We began appearing in each other's dreams. This has been reported before by other twins, but with us, there was a slightly different twist."

"I dream about other people all of the time," I said. "My brother died years ago in Vietnam and I've dreamed about him several times. What made your dreams so unusual?"

"One night, researchers locked us in different bedrooms to make certain that we couldn't talk to each other. The next morning, we both described our dreams. We had dreamed the exact same dream. This was something that no one had ever done before. The next night, we did the same thing again. Both of us had the same dream. The doctors got so excited that they told *Life* magazine and it published an article about us. The magazine called us the dream clones—mirror-image twins who were so identical that we even dreamed identical dreams."

By this time, she had finished her lemonade and was now twisting a paper napkin with her fingers. Heather had that same nervous habit.

"The researchers began focusing on our mutual dreams and they soon made another startling discovery. Even though they kept us in separate bedrooms at night, we not only continued to have identical dreams, we were able to communicate with each other during them."

"What do you mean? Talk to one another?"

"Before Heather went to sleep, the doctors had her write down a number on a piece of paper. The next morning, they asked me if I knew the number. I did. Heather had told it to me during our mutual dream."

"That's impossible!"

"That's what the doctors thought. They decided it was a fluke. So the next night they told her a seven-digit number that they had selected. There was no way I could have learned that number in advance."

"Did you know it the next morning?"

"I told them a seven-digit number, but it wasn't correct."

"So that first time—when you were correct—had been a fluke, a coincidence."

"No, it hadn't," she replied. Lowering her voice, she said: "Mr. LeRue, I knew the correct seven-digit number. Heather had told it to me during our mutual dream, but I intentionally gave them a different number."

"Why?"

"Because we were tired of being freaks, of being pinched, poked, and studied. We were done being laboratory rats. When Heather appeared in my dream that night, the two of us discussed it and we agreed that I'd intentionally give them a bogus number."

"You and Heather discussed all of this in your dream?" I replied sarcastically.

"That's right, Mr. LeRue. We had a spontaneous conversation in our mutual dream. It was no different from how you and I are talking right now."

I didn't believe her and it showed.

"Mr. LeRue," she said, "you asked me earlier how I know Heather is in danger. Last night, she appeared to me in my dream and she told me that she was terrified. She'd identified one of the white men who'd taken part in the lynching. She said he'd threatened her."

I noticed that her hands were trembling. "That's it?" I asked. "That's how you know Heather is in trouble? Because she appeared to you in your dream?"

"Yes," she replied.

"Heather didn't telephone you from Mississippi? Didn't send you an e-mail?"

"No," she said softly.

"When was the last time that you actually spoke to your sister?" I asked.

"We've not spoken in several years. The truth is that I was shocked when I got a letter from her. We're estranged and she wrote that she wanted to resolve our differences."

"Whoa!" I said. "Let's back up here. You haven't spoken directly to Heather in several years, yet you know she's in trouble because she tells you in a dream?"

"I know it sounds far-fetched, maybe even ridiculous. Mr. Middleton reacted the exact same way as you when I told him. He said that he had spoken to Heather twice in Mississippi this week and she is fine."

"I assume the two of them spoke on the telephone," I interjected, "and not in some mutual dream."

She ignored my jab. "I know Heather and I know what she told me last night in my dream."

"For once, I've got to agree with Middleton," I said. "If Heather was in trouble, why didn't she tell him when they spoke on the *telephone*?"

"I'm not sure Middleton was telling me the truth this morning."

"Why?" I asked. "Because he was skeptical when you told him that you and Heather had been chatting it up in your dreams? What reason would he have to lie to you, especially about Heather's safety?"

"I don't know."

I became blunt: "Why are you and Heather estranged?"

"A fight—over a man."

"Now, that *is* something I do believe!" I replied.

She looked hurt.

"Maybe you're worried about Heather because of your own conscience," I volunteered. "Maybe you're simply looking for an excuse so the two of you can meet and make up."

"I didn't fly out here from South Dakota this morning because of guilt," she snapped. "Heather came to me last night and told me that she was in danger. This is real!"

"You caught a flight from South Dakota to Washington D.C. because you had a nightmare?"

"No. I flew here because my sister's life is being threatened!"

"Why didn't you go directly to Mississippi? Why'd you come here? Did Heather tell you to contact me?"

"No," Melanie said. She hesitated and then added, "Actually, Heather told me to contact Middleton. That's why I came to Washington."

"If she wanted you to recruit him," I said, clearly irked, "then why are we talking now? Why'd you even bother to contact me?"

"That was his idea—Middleton's. He suggested that I ask you for help."

"Don't you find it odd," I said, "that a man whom I personally abhor has recommended that you ask me for help?"

"No, because he knows that you still love Heather."

"What about him? Doesn't he still love her? Why isn't he dropping everything and running down to Mississippi to save her?"

She had twisted her napkin so many times that it now was frayed and knotted.

"Mr. LeRue," she said, "will you go to Mississippi with me? Will you help me find Heather? You're an investigator. You know how to find people."

"Let's review the facts here, shall we?" I replied sternly. "Your sister dumps me for another man. She destroys me emotionally and completely undermines my self-esteem. She doesn't call me or even acknowledge that I'm alive. Now you show up unexpectedly from South Dakota and ask me to put my life on hold and run down to Mississippi with you. Why? Because you had a nightmare and think your sister is in some sort of danger."

"I don't think Heather is in danger," she interrupted. "I know she is."

"What if you're wrong? What if we go dashing off to Mississippi and find Heather sitting in her motel room, perfectly fine? Do you understand how stupid that would make me look?"

"Heather wouldn't have contacted me unless she really needed my help."

"Sorry," I replied, "but you're asking the wrong former boyfriend. Andrew Middleton works for one of the most prestigious newspapers in the nation. He's a famous investigative reporter. He's rich. If he thought Heather needed rescuing, I'm certain he would rush down to save her, especially if he wanted to win her back."

Melanie's eyes filled with tears, but I didn't care. At some point during our conversation, Melanie Cole had disappeared. I was now talking to Heather—the woman who had broken my heart and shattered my dreams. Two years of frustration, sadness, and anger bubbled to the surface. "I think you need to know something about me," I continued. "I don't believe in ESP. I don't believe in magic, witchcraft, voodoo, fairies, angels, demons, the devil, UFOs, astrology, or any of that New Age mumbo-jumbo that everyone in California seems to swallow. I don't believe in ghosts, don't think that animals can talk to one another, and I'm not even really certain there is a heaven or a hell. Now, since I don't believe in any of these things, why would I believe that you and your sister can chat it up during your dreams? I'm sorry, but if your sister needs my help, she can call my office and leave a message with my secretary."

She rose from the cafeteria table. "I know my sister hurt you," she said. "Heather does that. She's hurt me too. I also understand that it's difficult for you to accept what I've just told you. You can't possibly understand what it feels like to have an identical twin—another human being walking on this planet identical to you. But I know my sister better than anyone and I know she *is* in danger. She *is* being stalked. She *is* going to be harmed unless we help her. And despite the horrible things that have happened between the two of you, I know my sister would have dropped everything and gone to Mississippi to find you if she had learned that you were in danger!"

"Nice speech," I replied coldly. "But your sister ripped out my heart and never showed any sign of regret or guilt. The only reason she would come rescue me is if she thought it would get her a front-page story in the *Tribune*."

Melanie Cole walked out of the cafeteria, leaving me alone at the table.

By the time I got home, I was exhausted. But I couldn't fall asleep that night, so I decided to watch a cable television movie and drink some wine. That usually helps. A half bottle later, I still wasn't drowsy. I thought about my father. I often do. As a Pentecostal Baptist preacher, he was strongly opposed to the consumption of alcohol. Hallelujah! Praise the Lord! Repent or burn in hell! It was as simple as that. My brother and I went to church services every Wednesday night, Sunday morning, and Sunday evening. We moved from town to town. There were always souls to be saved somewhere down the road. My mom used to fix me a cup of hot chocolate when I was a child and couldn't sleep. I'd dunk a piece of toast in it. She's dead now. But my father's alive. We haven't talked in years. Just like Heather and Melanie. We're estranged. It has to do with my brother's death, but I don't want to think about that now.

I popped an Ambien tablet. An hour later, I was still staring at the television. I was tired of thinking about Heather and her sister, but I couldn't stop. I began tabulating all of the reasons why I was making the correct decision in turning Melanie away. Logic was on my side.

The doorbell rang. It was 4:10 a.m. The hall lights outside my apartment stay on all night for security reasons. Melanie Cole was outside. I saw her through the peephole. You had to give her credit for being tenacious. I hadn't told her my apartment address but she'd found me. I opened the door.

"I've just had another dream," she said, stepping inside. "Heather has been kidnapped! He's going to kill her!"

It was ludicrous. I wanted to kick her out. Heather wasn't my problem. Let Andrew Middleton deal with this. But, instead, I said: "I'll need a moment to pack."

How could I say no?

I was looking at an identical copy of the woman I hated, but still desperately loved.

Three

How many times had he hit her face?

She couldn't remember. She'd been asleep.

How did he find me? I covered my tracks. How did he find out where I was staying? It's impossible! I only told one person! He wouldn't tell!

She couldn't open her eyes. She gently touched her swollen eyelids with the fingers of her right hand. Something crusty had sealed her lashes shut. She picked it slowly. *Blood. Dried blood.* She felt its trail along the curve of her nose, up between her plucked eyebrows, onto her forehead. A gash. A scar? More dried blood. She forced her right eye to open. Then her left. Darkness all around her. *No*, she could see light. *Daylight?* Perhaps. Thin slivers slicing through long, straight cracks. In rows. Like lines on school notebook paper. She reached out and felt around her. Dirt. On both sides. She swept her arms and spread her legs. A snow angel in dirt. Her movements stirred dust. Gagging. She stopped moving, froze, and thought. There were no chains, no ropes, no handcuffs. She forced herself to sit up and spit. More blood. More dust. She was wearing her nightclothes. A T-shirt. Panties. Nothing else. She reached up toward the slashes of light.

"Ouch!" she cried out loud. "Damn it!"

Her hand had struck something hard only inches above her head. She had raised her hand too quickly. Now she raised it gingerly, palm up, until it touched a rough barrier. Wood. A splinter confirmed it. Her mind processed the details. Cracks of light. Wood. Straight lines. Boards. A floor! She looked to her right and then to her left. Darkness. She was locked under a house. Inside a crawl space. But where? Why?

She turned over onto her stomach and felt an immediate pain in her chest. A cracked rib? Maybe two? She gasped for breath. Her head was exploding. Despite the pain, she crawled across the dirt, following the cracks of light. *Keep straight,* she told herself. She reached a wall less than four feet away. Cold. Hard. Smooth. Concrete. She ran her right hand up its face and came to a different texture. Moist. It crumbled in her fingers. Rotting wood. Something moved, scampering across her hand. Another followed. And two more. Quick, desperate scurrying. She jerked back her hand and slapped at the still-unseen creatures. But there were more than she thought. They were crawling on her hand. They moved quickly up her arm. Scattering across her skin. She swatted them. Still one reached her neck. Another, her face. She grabbed them, crushed them between her thumb and forefinger. Rotting wood. Insects. *Termites.* It had to be termites. She scooted backward.

A sound. Footsteps above her. A metal bolt sliding open. The snapping sound of a latch. The squeak of rusty hinges. Light. Bright. Gushing in. Flooding down through a trap door. A square opening. Two feet by two feet. Directly above where she had been when she had first awakened. She pushed herself back against the wall, against the termites. The light was more alarming than they were.

"Show yourself, bitch!"

It was a man's voice. His.

"Hey, nigger-lover," he continued. "I'm talking to you!"
She didn't reply.

"Want me to starve your sorry white ass? Show yourself!"

A red flash. Thump! He'd dropped something through the trap door onto the dirt. A red tub. Plastic. Splashing. Water was being poured through the trap door into the tub. An old towel tossed down beside it onto the dirt.

"Wash up and if you piss and shit, bury it in a corner. Can't have you stinking everything up."

She inched closer but not enough to be seen or grabbed. She peered upward. She wanted to see a face, but saw only boots. Black. Pointed. Cowboy. Old. Thunk! A plastic bottle of water fell through the opening. Thunk! Thunk! Thunk! Three more dropped onto the dirt. Whoosh! Something bigger. Something white. Her eyes focused on the paper carton with its bright red and white lettering. An old man's face. A beard. Glasses. Colonel Sanders. Fried chicken. Food.

"You like fried chicken, don't you, bitch? All niggers do! Chicken and watermelon. Be a good bitch and maybe I'll get you a slice!" He laughed.

An arm appeared. Thin. Hairy. A faded tattoo. Blue ink. Reaching down into the darkness. His fingers grabbed a chrome ring on the trap door, pulled it upward, sealing her inside once again. Total darkness, except for the slices of light. It took her eyes a moment to adjust. A snap. A bolt sliding into place.

"That's two days' worth, you nigger-loving cunt. This ain't no Holiday Inn."

Another laugh. Footsteps. She followed them with her eyes across the floor. A door opened. Slammed shut. Locked. Silence. She felt termites on her legs. She scooted forward, slapping off the bugs.

When she reached the area under the trap door, she arranged the items in a line. Bottles of water. Chicken. Plastic tub. Towel. The water in the tub was cold. She splashed it onto her face. Used the towel to wipe off the dried blood. Her skin was bruised, sore, tender. He hadn't spoken during the attack. She'd awakened with the first punch. At first, she'd thought she was dreaming. She'd been asleep. There was no explanation. Just another blow to her face. Then more to her abdomen. Her last thought before she'd passed out had been: *I'm going to die! He's going to kill me!*

She felt inside the warm, moist bucket of chicken. He'd already eaten several pieces. Left the bones. She felt for one that hadn't been contaminated by him. There weren't any. He'd taken a bite from them all. *Bastard!* She rolled over on her back and took an inventory of her pain. The worst ran through her ribs, although her head was still throbbing. She bit into a half-eaten chicken leg. *How did he find me?* She tried to focus. But her head hurt too much. *I was so careful. I covered my tracks. How did he know where I was staying?* She prayed. But not to God. "Melanie: Come save me! Please! Hurry! I need you! Rescue me!"

Four

Melanie and I caught an early flight at Ronald Reagan National Airport, but Delta Airlines didn't fly directly into Jackson, Mississippi, so we had to land first in Atlanta, where we waited an hour before boarding a second aircraft. There's something about flying that makes me sleepy, especially when I haven't slept the night before, especially when I'd drunk nearly a bottle of wine and gulped down a football-shaped Ambien tablet. I dozed during our flights while Melanie flipped through pages and pages of magazines. By the time I picked up our rental car at the Jackson airport, the cobwebs in my head were starting to clear.

The computer-generated directions that the perky car rental clerk gave me said it would take us two hours to drive to Pushmataha, Mississippi, which is where Heather had gone to investigate the 1955 lynching. Most of the trip would require us to travel along Interstate 220 north. There wasn't much traffic, so I figured I could make the drive in about ninety minutes. If I drove about twenty miles per hour above the posted speed limit.

"Hungry?" I asked.

"Sure," Melanie replied, but she sounded unconvincing. I think she was too nervous to care, but I was famished. After standing up Phillip Shurman last night, I'd never gotten around to eating dinner.

"What I really need is caffeine," I said. "If I don't get a couple of diet Cokes each morning, I get headaches."

"I've never met anyone addicted to a soft drink," Melanie said.

I didn't reply. She didn't know it, but Heather and I had argued several times about how many diet Cokes I drank each day. Although Melanie was not Heather, it seemed pointless to argue with someone who looked and sounded exactly like a person with whom you already had had that same argument!

I drove past the gauntlet of a McDonald's, Burger King, and Wendy's that lined the interstate, and instead exited when I spotted a one-story eatery tucked in the woods with six pickup trucks parked in front of it and a badly weathered sign hanging over its front door that identified it simply as SCOTT'S CAFE. The words HOME COOKING were painted in giant letters on the building's side.

"Must be where the locals eat," I proudly proclaimed. I had rented a Chevrolet TrailBlazer SUV, which was a good choice, because the road was pockmarked with deep ruts. I parked next to a mud-caked red Ford Bronco, a reminder that I was no longer in the Capitol Hill world of Beemers and baby Benzes. Blackflies hugged the outside of the screen door, which was the only barrier preventing them from swarming in. The café's wooden front door had a chipped brick holding it open, a sign to me that there was no air-conditioning inside. It was 103 degrees outside and staggering. Spotting the flies and knowing there was no respite from the heat inside should have been enough to make me reconsider, but my declaration that this was clearly a favorite hangout for locals had been tossed out with a sense of adventure. Put simply, I was too stubborn to admit that we were both about to make a big gastronomic mistake. I tugged open the screen door and Melanie and I raced the flies inside.

It was dark and cooler, but not that much cooler. The café reeked of deep-fried food and human sweat. We were the only white faces in the room, which had about twenty diners.

"Welcome to self-segregated Mississippi," I whispered.

A waitress wearing a white cotton apron over a sleeveless white blouse and faded cutoff blue denim jeans asked if we preferred a table or a booth. I said either was fine, so she led us to a booth near the back of the room next to the café's only bathroom. Flies were guarding its door too and I could hear a toilet running. There was an old-fashioned metal Coca-Cola tank on this side of the partially closed bathroom door. The tank was waist-high, there was no lid, and it wasn't plugged into an electrical outlet. Instead, it was filled with water, ice, bottles of Coke, and other sodas—submerged just under the surface.

"Our special today is chitlins," our waitress declared. "They come with hot sauce, a slice of ham, a couple spoonfuls of macaroni and cheese, collard greens, and sweet potato pie."

I glanced at Melanie and saw what I thought was an "I dare you" look.

"Okay," I said. "I'll take the special."

I returned Melanie's look.

"Not me," she announced. "Make mine a barbeque pork sandwich with a side of baked beans."

As soon as the waitress left, Melanie said:"Do you like chitlins?"

"Actually, I don't even know what they are. But life's an adventure, right?"

"'Chitlins' is an abbreviation for 'chitterlings,'" she said, "which are the large intestines of a pig. Slaves used to eat them because they were the parts, along with the pig's feet and ears, discarded by their white masters."

I wished she hadn't told me that.

She continued: "Most blacks I know consider them a throwback to the past and refuse to eat them. They say they're demeaning and offensive. How about collard greens? You ever have those?"

"No," I said. "They're not something you'd find on the Senate dining room menu."

"Then this should be a very interesting lunch," she said.

The waitress returned with two large plates and I nearly gagged from the smell of the one that she put down in front of me. I stuck my fork into a white, slippery slice of what looked like overcooked pasta, as Melanie and the waitress watched. I raised it to my mouth and bit down into what was the foulest food I'd ever tasted. Because the women were both looking, I tried to chew the rubbery bite and swallow quickly. But I didn't fool either of them.

"What's wrong, baby? You don't like our chitlins?" the waitress asked loud enough for everyone in the café to hear. I heard several snickers.

"No, they're fine," I replied.

She grinned, revealing a mouth nearly empty of teeth, and left us alone. When I glanced around the café, I noticed everyone else was eating BBQ and wondered if the "daily special" was only offered to gullible white people.

"You seem to know a lot about Southern cooking," I said.

"We had a black cook when I was growing up. She used to love to eat chitlins and hogshead cheese."

"Don't even tell me what that is," I said. For a moment, I thought about Heather. She had told me stories about their family cook. Heather had called her Auntie Rose.

"I find it odd that Heather never mentioned you or told me that she had a twin," I said. "Whenever I asked Heather about her childhood, she mostly talked about your father."

"He was a great newspaper editor and one of the kindest, bravest men I've ever known. Heather idolized him."

"Whenever Heather talked to me about him, I'd get this

image of Gregory Peck in my mind," I said. "You know, playing Atticus Finch in *To Kill a Mockingbird*, standing up to the town's bullies and racists."

"Our father would have laughed at that because he was short and pudgy. He had thinning gray hair. I think he was the main reason why Heather became a reporter. I remember she told me that her goal was to win a Pulitzer prize. There's been a father and a son to win Pulitzer prizes, but there's never been a father and a daughter to both win."

"I read your father's editorials about race relations back when I was in law school. Other journalists referred to him as the 'Sage of Little Rock.' "

"We teased him about that. At the dinner table, we'd say, 'Will the Sage of Little Rock please pass the salt and pepper?' But he deserved that title. He stood up for what he believed was right and he died fighting for those same principles. I remember shortly after he won his first Pulitzer, a mob gathered outside our house and burned a cross on the lawn. My father stood on the front porch and watched them. Heather called me a fraidy-cat because I was too scared to go outside. Not her. She dashed out there and stood beside him."

Melanie removed a pack of cigarettes from her purse. "I've always been more like my mother."

"You smoke?" I said, surprised. "Heather is a health freak."

"When we were teenagers, we searched for ways to be different, to declare our individuality."

"That's why you took up smoking?"

"Yes, and other things," she replied, raising an eyebrow seductively.

"So I take it that you are the evil twin?"

She laughed. "No, not really. We both had our good and bad moments. How about you? You have any brothers or sisters?"

"An older brother, but he was killed in Vietnam."

"Let me guess, he was the much-beloved firstborn: serious, hardworking, type-A personality. And by the time you came along, he had already established himself in that role inside your family, so you chose not to compete with him. Instead, you earned poor grades and focused on exceeding at sports or other things that he didn't do well. Correct?"

"Those stereotypes don't always fit," I said. "But I did compete with him—up until his death. That's when I discovered that you can't win when you're competing against a ghost."

She took a long drag and then blew the smoke out slowly. "Heather and I went through a period when we absolutely hated each other," she said. "She went the cheerleader route in high school. Pom-poms. Pep rallies. Voted most popular. Real high-maintenance. Had the quarterback boyfriend."

"I know," I replied. "Remember, I lived with her for five years. And you—what route did you take?"

"I hid in the library and became the brainy, quiet one— the animal lover. Horses. Cats. Dogs. I brought home every stray. Drove my parents nuts. I told everyone I was going to become a veterinarian and I refused to eat meat. I got excellent grades, but Heather played dumb. I knew she was pretending to be stupid and so did my parents. My dad loved chess and he was good at it, really good. Heather could beat him anytime she wished."

Our conversation was beginning to remind me of what it feels like to be on a first date. Still, I was enjoying myself. "Did you become a vet?" I asked.

"Eventually. I met my husband in veterinarian school."

"You're married?" I asked, clearly stunned.

"Yes. Why is that difficult to imagine?"

"You're not wearing a wedding ring."

"Too dangerous when you work on a ranch. We live in the Black Hills with our two children: Kaitlyn, who's five, and Matthew, who's three."

"Then you really are different from Heather. She never wanted children. Or to be married, at least not to me!"

Our waitress returned and slapped our bill down on the table.

"You didn't eat a single chitlin," she declared, mocking me. It was okay. I'd already decided to short her on the tip. I scooped up our bill and Melanie and I walked to the cash register. But our waitress was busy flirting with four men at another table. She made us wait and made certain everyone in the café noticed that she was making us wait. When she finally sauntered over, Melanie and I both stuck out twenty-dollar bills.

"This check ain't but for nine dollars and fifty-seven cent," the waitress declared. "I don't need two twenties."

Melanie said:"I asked you to come to Mississippi with me. I'll pay."

"I'm old-fashioned," I replied.

"Then we'll split it," she volunteered.

"Lady, I ain't making change for you both," the waitress announced. She snatched my twenty and handed me the change.

"You can buy me dinner," I said. "Trust me, it's going to be more expensive than eating in this dump."

"Y'all come again," the waitress said cockily.

We returned to the TrailBlazer and were soon traveling north again on the interstate.

"Why did my sister leave you?" Melanie asked.

The question took me by surprise. Even more surprisingly, I answered it. "I didn't meet her expectations."

"Heather told you that?" she asked.

"Not exactly. But your father set a high standard and I assume that Andrew Middleton came closer to meeting it than I did." I intentionally changed subjects. "You said earlier that your father was a good chess player. Heather had told me that he'd taught her. Do you play?"

"No," she replied.

Neither of us spoke for a moment and then I said, "What do you know about the 1955 lynching?"

"Andrew Middleton said Heather had called him twice

from Mississippi to report on her progress," Melanie explained. "The lynching was in Pushmataha's city park. The black man was named Lamar Grant. He'd been accused of stealing a mule."

"Had Heather figured out any of the five white men's names?"

"Middleton said she had identified all of the men, but she hadn't told him their names. And Heather didn't tell me either last night when we talked in my dream."

I didn't exactly know how to respond to her dream comment, so I didn't. Instead, I said: "Pushmataha is a county seat according to this rental car map. The town has about three thousand residents. We shouldn't have too much trouble finding Heather."

"I read about Pushmataha after I got Heather's letter," Melanie said. "It's named after the last great Choctaw Indian chief. Most of Mississippi belonged to the Choctaws before President Andrew Jackson forced them to march west and stole their land."

"When I was growing up in Oklahoma," I volunteered, "we read about the Trail of Tears—the forced march from eastern states. Thousands of Indians starved. Choctaws and the Cherokees. Jackson sent all of them into what then was called Indian Territory but later became Oklahoma. If I remember correctly, Oklahoma in Choctaw translates into 'Land of the Red Man.'"

"It wasn't their land for very long," she said sadly. "As soon as oil was discovered, the whites stole the land from them. It was shameful, and what's happening today to Native Americans is just as horrible. We all should feel humiliated!"

"This might be difficult for you to believe," I replied, "but I wasn't around when Jackson was president. I've never persecuted a single Indian, and that rude black waitress back at lunch—I'd never met her before today. My point is: I don't understand why she had a chip on her shoulder or why I should feel guilty about a bunch of Sooners who stole the Indians' land. I wasn't involved."

"The sins of our fathers are always passed down from

one generation to the next," she declared. "There's blood on all of our hands."

"I remember those lines," I said. "They're from one of your dad's editorials. But what do you think?" Before she could answer, I groused: "Maybe if I had been born with a silver spoon in my mouth, I might share your liberal guilt, but I didn't grow up with a black cook and a famous editor for a father. You know what Barry Switzer said once? 'Some people are born on third base and go through life thinking they hit a triple.'"

She stared directly ahead but I knew from her silence that I'd hurt her feelings. I didn't really understand why I had been brusque. Well, actually I did. After a few moments, I said: "Look, I'm sorry. You're not Heather. But you look like her and, well, I've clearly got some issues to work through here. It's not fair to attack you because of her." She didn't respond, so I decided to switch subjects once again: "Was there anything more that Middleton told you about the trophy tree and lynching that might help us find Heather?"

"There was something interesting that Heather had told him," she replied. "On the night of the lynching, Pushmataha was ravaged by a violent rainstorm and a bolt of lightning actually struck the trophy tree. The bolt hit the exact spot where the white men had carved their names after the lynching. Blacks in the area saw that bolt as a sign from God."

"What sort of sign?"

"That the five whites had made God angry. Heather told Middleton that blacks in Pushmataha believed all five of the men were cursed, and not long after that, three of the five were killed in freak accidents."

We had reached the Pushmataha exit, so I turned right onto the ramp.

Melanie said: "Okay, Mr. Investigator, where do we begin?"

"Heather must have checked into a motel, and there can't be that many in Pushmataha. Hopefully, we'll find her lounging by a motel swimming pool."

"You still don't believe me, do you?" she asked. "I've told you that Heather's been kidnapped. This is real."

"Let's not argue. Instead, let's put ourselves in Heather's shoes. The Pushmataha Chamber of Commerce isn't going to roll out a welcome mat for a newspaper reporter who's come to town to write about a 1955 lynching. Heather would need sources and the best place to find them would be in the black community. If I were her, I would've contacted a black Baptist church."

"Why a church?"

"People from around here probably don't move from town to town very often. Even though the lynching happened in 1955, black families would pass that story down."

"What about the police? Shouldn't we tell them that Heather has been kidnapped?"

"Not yet. I'm a bit leery of storming into the local sheriff's office and announcing that you've been talking with your twin sister in your dreams."

She said: "Yes, I guess you're right."

There was a Holiday Inn near the interstate exit and I thought for a moment about stopping, but I decided to drive through Pushmataha so we could familiarize ourselves with the area. It was an old Southern community that had grown like the rings of a tree trunk—with the newest and most modern additions being the first that a traveler encounters. A billboard welcomed motorists with a list of civic clubs and proudly declared: PUSHMATAHA—A PROGRESSIVE CITY. The highway was lined with businesses: two fast-food restaurants, three service stations, Betty's Bridal and Florist Shop, Nu-Clean Laundry, Wagon Wheel Restaurant, and a Piggly Wiggly grocery store. We passed through what used to be the old city limits and suddenly found ourselves in a residential neighborhood of two-story houses, most with wraparound porches. I noticed that the two-lane highway had undergone a name change, going from State Highway 31 to Main Street. It led us directly into the center of Pushmataha, where an antebellum county courthouse sat in the heart of the town square. The courthouse rose four stories high, was made of red brick, and had four white columns at its entrance. An ornate cupola had been built on top of building. Unlike many Southern towns, the Wal-Mart discount chain hadn't yet arrived in Pushmataha, so its downtown businesses were still thriving. I spotted a pharmacy, clothing store, variety store, florist, law office, café, hardware store, photography studio, and a furniture outlet. They occupied three sides of the square. The fourth—the side that faced the back of the courthouse—opened into a city park. I parked the SUV near a historical marker in front of the park and we got out to read the sign.

1830 INDIAN AMBUSH
RABBIT CREEK PARK

On December 22, 1830, on this site, fifteen members of the Choctaw Indian Tribe ambushed a U.S. Army patrol that had been sent to locate and capture the renegades. The Indians had refused to move west as was required by the Indian Removal Act of 1830. Ten U.S. soldiers were slaughtered. All but three of the Choctaw attackers were killed. The Indians that survived were hanged from an oak tree not far from this site along the banks of Rabbit Creek. Afterward, soldiers discovered that one of the hanged Indians was a woman who had disguised herself.

"I'm guessing this is the city park where Lamar Grant was lynched too," I said. "Let's see if we can find the trophy tree."

We followed a concrete sidewalk that was cracked and made uneven by tree roots. It led us to an octagonal bandstand painted green and white. Nearby was a pavilion, two asphalt tennis courts, and three basketball courts. The pavilion was made of brown brick but its walls rose only two feet high, leaving its sides open. The shingled wooden roof was supported by thick steel beams that were anchored in the bricks. There were about twenty picnic tables inside the structure and seven charcoal grills just outside its northeast corner. A sign identified it as the Harry C. Peterman Pavilion, constructed in 1963 and donated by the Peterman Lumber Company of Pushmataha.

"It looks like Rabbit Creek is over there," I said, pointing toward a small bluff. We walked another hundred yards along a footpath worn through the grass. As we neared an embankment, I heard children yelling.

We stood on the creek bank. Rabbit Creek meandered through the park. In some spots it was so narrow that you could leap across it, but here it was at least fifty feet wide and only a few inches deep. A thirty-foot cliff jutted up on the opposite side of the water, casting a shadow over the slow-moving stream. Four boys were wading in the creek next to the cliff's face. They were armed with spears that they had carved from fallen branches. I guessed the kids were probably twelve years old.

"What are they doing?" Melanie asked. "Fishing?"

I glanced down at the muddy edge of the bank and saw a small green frog leap from where it had been sunning itself.

"Frogs," I replied. "Probably sticking frogs."

"Hey, stop that!" Melanie yelled. Her sudden command surprised the boys and me. They turned and looked at her, not certain how to react. Finally, one of them made an obscene gesture with his hand and then all four laughed and turned their backs on us.

Melanie lit a cigarette. "I just hate seeing things killed, even ugly green frogs."

I stepped over to where the boys had left their shirts, socks, and tennis shoes. I gathered up their clothes and shoes, and dangled them over the edge of the water. "Hey!" I yelled.

One of them turned. "He's got our clothes!" he yelped.

The other boys spun around and began sloshing toward us.

I swung my arms back as if I were going to fling their clothes into the stream and they stopped.

"Why don't you fellows find another way to amuse your-selves beside stabbing poor, defenseless, little frogs?" I said. "You're upsetting my lady friend here."

The boy who had made the obscene gesture glared at me and then dropped his spear. It floated lazily along the cur-rent. The other three did the same.

"Just a bunch of damn, worthless frogs," he hissed.

I dropped their clothes to the ground.

"Thank you," Melanie said. I wasn't certain if she was talking to me, the boys, or all of us.

"One more thing," I yelled. "Where's the trophy tree?"

They looked at each other and then the smallest of them glanced to his left.

"You mean where they used to hang niggers?" their leader asked. "We'll show you—for a dollar."

I followed the tiniest boy's eyes along the embankment and spotted six oak trees to our right about fifty yards away. Although the park contained dozens of pine, poplar, and pecan trees, these appeared to be the only oaks.

"No, thanks," I replied. I motioned in the direction of the trees, and Melanie and I began walking toward them.

"Why'd ya look at the tree?" the boys' leader yelled at the littlest youth. He punched the smaller boy in his shoul-der. "Dipshit!"

As we got closer to the trees, I said: "They're black oaks."

"How can you tell?"

"I used to spend a week each summer on my uncle's farm and he had several. He always said that black oaks were the workingman's forest tree. They're neither elegant nor majestic, just functional."

Pushing the limit of my knowledge, I announced that the trees appeared to be older than 150 years, which was the average life expectancy of black oaks. When we reached them, I tried to judge their width by reaching around one of the trunks, but my arms were too short. Five of the trees were more than 150 feet tall and seemed to hover around the sixth oak, which was shorter and more gnarled. It leaned to one side, away from Rabbit Creek. About twenty feet above the ground, its trunk split into two limbs. The biggest of these continued growing straight up but the other had shot outward at a forty-degree angle for about ten feet before returning skyward. From a distance, the tree looked like the letter K but with only one leg. I walked over to its base and ran my hand across its dark gray, scaly bark.

"I'm guessing this is the trophy tree," I said. "At least this is the one I'd use if I wanted to lynch someone."

Melanie walked around it slowly. "Over here!" she exclaimed from the other side of the trunk. "Here's the initials." I moved around so that I was now standing next to her. Our backs were turned toward Rabbit Creek. A section of bark about ten inches long and five inches wide had been stripped from the trunk years ago. Letters had been cut crudely into the tree.

NIGAR HUNG HERE
9/5/55

Underneath those words were initials:

R.E.L.R.
P.R.
J.R.
S.A.
L.

Lightning had struck the final set of initials, obliterating the second letter and cutting a jagged hole directly underneath it.

"Sad, isn't it," Melanie said, as she ran her hand across the letters, "to think that in 1955, a black man was hanged here in what now is such a beautiful spot?"

"I wonder if those three Choctaw Indians were strung up here too," I replied.

"You'd never guess today that such horrid things happened next to this stream."

I heard a crunching noise, the sound of someone stepping on acorns that had fallen last fall but were still strewn on the grass. A black man in a law enforcement officer's uniform was coming toward us.

"Hello Ms. Cole," he yelled. Obviously, he thought Melanie was Heather, which meant he was someone whom Heather had met before. He had a slight limp.

"Play along," I whispered. "Let's not get the local authorities involved until we know for certain what's going on with Heather."

"Hello," Melanie called back.

"You've returned to our infamous tree," the officer said when he reached us. "And I see you've brought a friend this time."

I stuck out my hand. "Nick LeRue," I said warmly.

"Jacob Moorehead," he replied, shaking my hand. "I'm the Pushmataha County sheriff. I know why Ms. Cole is here. What's your story?"

He seemed friendly but I've never met a local cop who enjoyed having someone from Washington, D.C., encroach on his turf.

"Just a friend along for the ride," I answered.

"You an author too?" he asked.

"No, not me," I said with a self-deprecating laugh. I hoped my chuckle might disarm him, but it didn't.

"A private investigator—or a federal agent?" he asked. "Which is it?"

"Why would you think either?"

"You look like a cop."

It had been a decade since I had worked as an FBI agent, and even then I didn't think that I looked like a cop, even though I wore my hair cut short and stayed in good shape.

"I'm an attorney," I said, "but I'm here on vacation and simply because I'm a friend of Ms. Cole's."

He sized me up. It's a habit that cops have. It's something they learn on the street when they have to decide within seconds whether they can physically control a potential suspect. Since I wasn't a criminal, I assumed that

Moorehead's stare was testosterone-driven. "I can kick your ass if necessary" egotism.

Sheriff Moorehead was at least five years younger than me and I'd just turned forty. He was a few inches shorter too. But he had broad shoulders and carried himself like a man who wasn't afraid of much. The fact that he was a black sheriff in Mississippi surprised me. In my mind, Southern sheriffs were white, fat, racist good ole boys who hid behind mirrored sunglasses.

Turning to face Melanie, Sheriff Moorehead said: "Jeb Rogge called my office this morning to complain about you. Said you went to see him Wednesday. I warned you that Rogge is dangerous. He's a racist and a hothead."

"Sorry," Melanie replied. She was handling this charade beautifully.

"Rogge told me that if you trespass on his property again, he'll shoot you. And, Ms. Cole, he *will* shoot you if you try to ask him any more questions about the lynching."

"I'll keep that in mind," she replied.

"You got guts, lady," Moorehead said. "I'll give you that. Not many people around here are willing to mess with Jeb Rogge." He turned to leave but then looked at me. "It was Nick LeRue, right? Is that Le, then capital R? And you said you're a lawyer from Washington, D.C., is that correct?"

"I didn't say where I was from," I replied. "But that's correct."

"Yeah," he said. "I didn't think you had." He nodded politely toward Melanie and added: "Ms. Cole, once again, I want to urge you to avoid Jeb Rogge. People around here are wary of outsiders poking around, especially when it comes to the trophy tree. If you mess with the likes of Jeb Rogge, you're going to get hurt and there's very little I can do to prevent it. He's a very dangerous man. My advice is the same as before: Forget this book of yours, let sleeping dogs lie, and go home."

We both watched Moorehead as he limped across the

park. As soon as he was out of earshot, Melanie said: "Jeb Rogge." She then touched the initials J.R. that were carved into the trophy tree. "I think we've just discovered who J.R. is. One down. Four to go."

Five

We should have told Sheriff Moorehead about Heather," Melanie said as we retraced our walk through Rabbit Creek Park to our SUV. "He's black. He obviously knows about the lynching and I think he could help us find her."

Maybe Melanie was right. Moorehead struck me as a sheriff who kept a close watch over his jurisdiction. But I still wasn't convinced that Heather had been abducted, even though Melanie had persuaded me to fly to Mississippi.

"Let's see what we learn this afternoon and then we can confide in Sheriff Moorehead," I suggested.

"You still don't believe Heather has been kidnapped and is in danger, do you?" Melanie asked. We were now driving toward the edge of Pushmataha and the Holiday Inn. I didn't reply. Melanie said: "I'm scared that when I fall asleep tonight, I'll learn that something has happened— something we could have prevented."

"Listen," I replied, "we're on the right track. We just got

here and we already know the name of one of the white men. We know he's threatened Heather."

The matronly clerk at the Holiday Inn front desk greeted us with a thick Southern accent: "Ms. Cole, how may I assist you?"

I spoke before Melanie could answer. "This is all my fault," I said. "I've lost her room key. She asked me to put it in my pocket for her and it must've fallen out because now I can't find it anywhere."

The clerk looked at Melanie, who raised her eyebrows as if to say: *Men—what do you expect?*

"Why, that's an easy problem to resolve," the clerk said as she pulled open a desk drawer and fished out a duplicate key. "Now, honey, there's a ten-dollar charge for lost keys and I'm afraid I have to collect it before I can give you this one."

"I probably lost it in my car," I said, as I removed two fives from my wallet. "I'll look later this evening for it." I handed the clerk the cash and she gave the spare key to Melanie. It was attached to a large green tag with a room number emblazoned on it.

"You bring me back that spare and I can refund half of your money to you, dear," she said. "The other five is a service charge."

We walked outside through a lobby exit and followed a sidewalk that passed in front of the two-story motel's ground-floor rooms.

"You're getting good at pretending to be Heather," I said.

"I had lots of practice as a child. Even our parents couldn't always tell us apart."

We stopped outside Room 146, which was the number on the green key tag. There was a blue Ford Taurus parked in the space in front of it. A DO NOT DISTURB sign was hanging on the knob. I knocked. No one answered, so I used the key to open the door.

It was dark inside. The drapes were drawn. The double

beds were made. I saw Heather's suitcase on the floor near the doorway to the bathroom. Several dresses, blouses, and pants were hanging from a chrome rod that hung down from the ceiling. There were women's toilet articles on the bathroom counter, but the trash cans in the room were empty—no discarded tissues that Heather would have used while she put on makeup, no wads of crumpled notebook paper, crushed coffee cups, or discarded fast-food containers.

"Something doesn't feel right," Melanie said.

Someone knocked on the door. Melanie peeked outside. It was a maid. I opened the door, startling her. But she seemed to relax when she saw Melanie standing behind me.

"I got clean sheets and towels," she said, as she lifted two bundles of linens from a metal push cart.

"Don't you make up the bed each morning?" I asked.

The maid glanced at Melanie. "You told me not to be messin' with your room, ain't that right, miss? You said, 'Just bring clean sheets on Friday afternoon and fresh towels,' so that's what I'm doing."

"You haven't changed the sheets or towels in this room since Monday—four days ago—when Ms. Cole first checked in?"

Again, the maid looked for help from Melanie. "You said, 'Don't be coming into this room.' That's what you said. I never changed nothing because of what you said."

I took the sheets and towels, gave her five dollars, and shut the door.

"I don't think Heather has ever slept in this room," I said. "When we lived together, she used a fresh towel each time she took a shower. She insisted wet towels bred bacteria. Heather chewed gum and there are no foil wrappers in the trash cans here and the maid just said she hasn't been in this room to clean it since Monday."

I opened a desk drawer and found Heather's car rental agreement. I compared the license number on the paperwork with the Ford Taurus parked outside. They matched.

"She's not out driving," I said. I walked to where Heather's clothes were hanging and looked at the shoes placed in a neat row underneath them. There were several pairs of sandals, some walking shoes, black pumps, and a pair of hiking boots. Heather liked to keep her shoes orderly.

"There're no running shoes," I said. "Your sister always takes her running shoes when she travels. She jogs every day."

Melanie opened the dresser and scanned the women's clothing inside. She removed a pair of purple running shorts and a sports bra. "She wouldn't have brought these unless she'd planned on running."

"Maybe she's out on a jog right now," I said. "If she is, then she's sure going to be surprised when she comes back and finds us here!"

"She's not out running," Melanie said, "and both of us know it."

"Listen, Heather is smart," I replied. "She always carries pepper spray whenever she runs. If she carried it on Capitol Hill, she'd carry it here too."

Melanie looked around the room. "I know what's bothering me. Where's her portable computer? Her tape recorder? Her reporter notebooks? For that matter, where's her cell phone?"

"Let's think this through," I said. "We know this is her room. But we agree that it looks like she really hasn't been staying here. Plus, we know her jogging shoes are missing."

"I've got it!" Melanie exclaimed. "When we were kids, the Ku Klux Klan threatened my father, so the Little Rock police hid us in a hotel. My father didn't trust the police completely because there were cops on the force who belonged to the KKK. So he secretly rented another room in the same hotel—only it was on a different floor—and he rented it under a pseudonym. After the cops dropped us off at our room for the night, we'd sneak upstairs and stay in our second room. That way, not even the cops knew where we were."

I called the front desk. "This is Ms. Cole's male friend, the fellow who loses room keys," I said. "Ms. Cole has stepped out and, well, this is awkward, but I'm wondering if she rented another room in the motel. You know, one for me."

"No, she hasn't," the woman said. "I don't know your name, but even if she'd rented one under your name, I'd know, because she is using her credit card and its number would show up on both accounts. Besides, we're already full up tonight, except for one single. Would you like to rent it?"

"Are there any other motels within walking distance?"

"I'm sorry, sir, maybe you didn't understand. I have one single available."

"Thanks, but I'd like to stay somewhere else—somewhere close enough to walk to."

The phone line was silent for a moment and I thought maybe she'd hung up. Then she said: "The only other motel in town is the Stars and Bars, but I don't think it would be the sort of place that you would like."

"Is there something wrong with it?"

"Well, it's older and not nearly as nice and, well, how can I say this? You just aren't the sort of person who usually stays there."

I hung up the receiver and checked the local telephone directory on the nightstand for the Stars and Bars number.

"Can you tell me if you have a Heather Cole registered as a guest?" I asked. "I'm a friend and she forgot to tell me where she was staying in Pushmataha. We're supposed to be meeting for dinner tonight."

"Did you say 'Cole'?" I could tell from his hoarse voice and heavy breathing that he was an elderly man.

"Yes, Miss Heather Cole."

"Don't got nobody by that name here. She white or black?"

"White," I replied, surprised by the question.

"Then you best try the Holiday Inn up the road. I got a white trucker and a white woman staying here, but we cater mostly to black folks."

"I'm calling from the Holiday Inn and Ms. Cole isn't

registered here. Sometimes she uses her maiden name when she travels," I said, grasping for straws. "She's divorced. But I don't remember what that name is. The white woman who's staying at your place, is she in her late twenties and real attractive?"

The old man laughed. "Son, I'm eighty-seven years old and any woman younger than seventy is a knockout to me!"

"She has thick brown hair, about shoulder-length, and a dynamic smile that you wouldn't forget."

"Could be her, but this white gal has blonde hair. You want to leave your name and number. We don't have phones in our rooms but if I see her outside, I'll give her your name."

I told him my name and gave him my cell phone number. "The woman I'm trying to find would have checked in on Monday," I said.

"Well, now, this young lady did check in then and rented for the entire week," he replied. "But, like I said, she's got blonde hair."

"Are there any other motels in Pushmataha within walking distance of the Holiday Inn?"

"Walking distance? Only if you don't mind walking twenty miles."

I thanked him and hung up. "There's only one white woman staying there and she's a bleached blonde," I told Melanie.

"Did she have a car?"

I felt foolish. I was the investigator and I'd forgotten to ask. I redialed the motel.

"Sorry to trouble you, but does this white guest of yours have a car?"

"Hang on," he said. A few seconds later, he returned to the line. "She wrote down a Mississippi license plate when she checked in. Looks like it's a Ford, a Taurus. But I've never seen it parked outside her cabin here. I don't really know how she comes and goes, come to think of it."

"My friend is a jogger."

I could hear him cover the telephone receiver with his

hand and yell a woman's name. Apparently it was his wife. "My wife says she's seen this white girl running late at night and real early in the mornings along the old highway. Now, listen, young man, I don't generally tell anyone our guests' names. But didn't you say earlier this white woman was named Heather? I checked the registration book and the woman who's staying here, why, her first name is Ashley. Now, that's not the same as Heather, is it? So it don't look like this woman is who you're after."

"Thanks again." I put down the phone and said: "She's been seen jogging early in the morning and late at night, but she's registered under the name Ashley."

"That's Heather!" Melanie shrieked. "That was her pretend name when we were kids. Let's go!"

"Wait, first there's something else I need to do." I looked in the phone book for Jeb Rogge's address. It was listed simply as Rural Route 1, which wasn't any help. But I did jot down his telephone number. Then I turned to the Yellow Pages and ran my finger down a list of churches. I stopped at the Mount Zion Pentecostal Church of Eternal Salvation and dialed its number.

"May I speak to your pastor?" I asked.

"I'm his wife," a woman replied. "The church's phone rings in our house too. My husband is at work at his regular job. But he'll be home and finished with his supper around eight o'clock. You can call back then."

"Actually, I'd like to stop by and talk to him personally," I said. "Can you tell me his name?"

"You a salesman?" she asked.

"No," I replied. "Just someone who needs some guidance."

"He's the Reverend Bartholomew W. Carter the Fourth. But you best call before you come over here because he might be busy preparing his sermon for Sunday services." She hung up.

I checked my watch. It was 6:30 p.m.

"Now let's find the Stars and Bars," I told Melanie.

It was still possible that Heather was perfectly safe. At

that very moment, she could have been sitting inside her cabin at the Stars and Bars poring over notes and planning interviews for tomorrow. But I didn't think so. Not anymore. Sheriff Moorehead's warning about Jeb Rogge, the undisturbed condition of Heather's Holiday Inn room, and the fact that she had felt it necessary to rent a second motel room under an assumed name were making me feel very uneasy—especially when you added in Melanie's clairvoyant dreams.

Six

I *ain't* lyin'!"

"Bullshit! You don't got a bitch under this goddamn floor!"

"Then who's gonna suck your cock tonight?"

Heather heard the two men's voices and their boots as they walked above her, crossing the floor. It was dark. There were no slices of light. She'd been asleep.

"This damn flashlight ain't worth crap! I wanna see this bitch. I ain't letting her suck my dick unless I can see her face."

"You'll want more than a blow job once you see her! For a goddamn nigger-lover, she's got a real sweet, round white ass!"

"What'd you just say?"

"A sweet ass!"

Heather recognized the voice of the man who had beat her. But she'd never heard the other voice.

"This bitch is white?"

"Yeah, so?"

"This ain't a little nigger girl? Like last time?"

"No, I just told you she's white."

"Where'd you get a white woman?"

"From goddamned Washington, D.C. Why's it matter? She's a goddamn reporter who come down here asking about that goddamn nigger who got hisself hung when we was kids."

"Holy Jesus and mother of God!" The stranger's voice sounded genuinely scared. "Don't open that goddamn trap door, you dumb son of a bitch!"

"What the hell?"

"I may be drunk, but Jesus H. Christ, you ain't making me part of this bullshit!"

"She ain't gonna bite you!"

"You've got to be the stupidest son of a bitch in Pushmataha County. Snatching up a little nigger girl is one thing. We can scare 'em into keeping their damn mouths shut. But a white bitch from up north—and a damn reporter! The entire FBI is gonna be coming down here! What's wrong with you?"

"I did what I had to do!" Now it was the familiar voice that sounded frightened. "You still want her to suck your dick?"

"Damn it! Are you hearing anything I'm saying? All I know now is I'm drunk and you're drunk. We was drinking together and you started talking bullshit about how you got yourself a bitch under your hunting cabin. I ain't seen nothing, so I ain't really part of this yet."

Heather screamed: "Help! Please help me! Don't go! I'll pay you! I'll pay you both if you just let me go! Please! I'll never tell anyone!"

"Shut up, bitch!" the familiar voice yelled. He stomped his boot on the floor.

"Damn it to hell!" the other voice said. "Now she's heard me. Damn you for getting me into this!"

"What d'you want to do?"

"What do I want to do? I'm not doing nothing but leaving! What the hell are you going to do? That's the question here."

"I don't know yet. I'm still waiting for instructions."

Heather heard one pair of boots walk away. Then she heard the sound that a metal bolt makes when it is slid. She scooted away from the trap door just as it fell open. *He's going to kill me!* His flashlight beam shot down from above, illuminating the bottles of water—two now empty—the washtub, and the bucket of chicken, all in the careful line where she had placed them.

"Show yourself, nigger-lover!" he screamed.

But she didn't move.

"I'll beat the living shit out of you again! Now get your white ass over here right now!"

She still didn't move. Suddenly a car horn began honking.

"Hold on!" he hollered, but the honking continued. "You goddamn white bitch! You're nothing but a goddamn white, nigger-loving whore. This is all your own goddamn fault! You're just getting what you deserve for writing about niggers!"

The flashlight beam began moving erratically. She quietly pushed herself back against the concrete wall, expecting him to drop down through the trap door at any moment. *I need a weapon!* The next noise she heard didn't compute at first. It sounded familiar, yet was out of place. She recognized the sound as a metal zipper sliding open. Then she saw the arching stream illuminated by the flashlight's beam. He had undone his pants and was now urinating through the open trap door into her bucket of chicken. His urine splattered as he directed its spray onto the water bottles and finally into the tub of water that she used for washing.

"You'll starve for this!" he fumed. She could hear the horn blaring again outside. "I'm coming, damn it!" he yelled.

She heard him zip his pants closed. He reached down and pulled up the trap door. She heard its bolt shoved shut.

"Maybe I'll bring you a present," he said. "How about a

snake? A rattler or maybe a damn dozen rats!" He laughed. "Yeah, rats. A damn dozen rats for the nigger-loving white bitch."

She heard his boots creak across the floor above her. The horn stopped honking. Silence.

She was running out of time. *Think, think, think!*

Earlier, she had crawled across every inch of her prison while it had still been light. She estimated the crawl space was twenty-five feet long, fourteen feet wide. No pipes under the floor for plumbing. No openings except for the trap door. Wooden plank flooring nailed securely onto the beams. Not one plank loose enough to force free, not even when she laid on her back and pushed against them with her bare feet. All she had found during her search of the crawl space was a discarded beer can smashed flat and half buried near one corner. She'd used the can to carve into the termite-infested wooden wall supports but they were too thick and eventually she had been forced to give up. Even if she had cut her way through, she would not have been able to make a hole large enough for an escape. Next, she had attempted to dig a tunnel but the concrete wall footings went down at least twelve inches deep and she'd hit rock-hard Mississippi red clay seven inches below the surface. It had bent the can and broken her fingernails.

She'd checked the trap door for weaknesses and had gotten excited momentarily when she'd discovered that its two metal hinges were screwed into the underbelly of the floor. That's why the trap door fell downward. She had used the flattened beer can as a makeshift screwdriver and had actually managed to loosen one screw, but the others would not turn. Too old. Too tight. Her fingers were raw and cut from the beer can's edge.

What can I learn from their exchange? They were drunk. He'd bragged that he had a woman. They'd come seeking sex. The stranger said "hunting cabin." That's why no one can hear me. There are no neighbors, no one strolling

*down the sidewalk. The familiar voice said, "I'm still wait-
ing for instructions." Someone else knew. Someone else
was calling the shots. But who? And why?*

*There was more. The stranger said, "Snatching up a lit-
tle nigger girl for fun. . . ." They've done this before! Where
is that girl? What did they do to her?*

Heather couldn't stop thinking about her kidnapper.

How did he know where to find me? What did I do wrong?

She didn't want to cry but she couldn't stop herself. She
cried. She sobbed. And when the tears were gone, she
moaned. She curled herself into the fetal position on the dirt.
She could smell his urine. She moaned and the noise coming
from her mouth did not sound like any utterance that she had
ever made before. It was a guttural groan, the sound that a
dying animal might make after it was struck by a car and
sent topsy-turvy into the roadside ditch with crushed bones
and internal bleeding that would soon prove fatal but not
without first causing it hours of suffering.

She felt certain he was going to kill her. Did he really have
a choice? She knew too much about him. The only question
was when. When would he return? She could hear his voice.
You'll starve for this! And then: *I'll bring you a present . . . a
snake. A rattler or maybe a damn dozen rats! Yeah, rats. A
damn dozen rats for the nigger-loving white bitch.*

Think, think, think, she told herself.

What would she do if she were him—if their roles were
reversed? She tried to predict his next step, just like in
chess. Thinking two and three moves ahead of your opponent. But she couldn't reverse their roles. She wasn't a kidnapper. *How long will it take for me to starve?* It wasn't a
lack of food that first killed. It was water. She still had a
bottle and there was water in the washtub, although he'd
just peed in it. Snakes? Rats? Would he really want them
running under the floorboards of his hunting cabin? At
some point he'd have to climb down and remove her corpse
and them. No, that threat was meant to scare. He wouldn't
do that. Or would he?

Think, think, think.

She considered a hundred different scenarios and saw her own death in a dozen of them.

I have to save myself. I have to do something. At some point, he'll have to come down under his cabin to get me. No matter what he says, he'll have to come through the trap door, because I won't come out on my own.

She needed a weapon. The beer can. She felt its edge. It was dull but sharp enough to cut skin. *Can I overpower him? Is there another way besides fighting? What if I act friendly? He wants sex. I could offer to satisfy him?* She visualized it. He would arrive, open the trap door, order her to come out. He'd step back. She'd call out to him. Pleading. Desperate. Accommodating. Willing. He'd beaten her. He'd won. She was afraid. She'd beg for her life. He'd like that! He'd feel stronger. More powerful. Good. Even if he planned on killing her, he'd want sex first. He'd want to rape her. It would be another show of his power. She'd move to the trap door and stand up in its opening. The cabin floor would reach her hips. A problem. She'd have to place both of her hands on either side of the trap door opening in order to lift her legs out of the crawl space. She wouldn't be able to do that if she was holding the beer can. He'd be watching and see it. He'd probably be armed. Wait! A solution! She'd tell him that her ribs were broken and she was too weak to lift herself through the trap door opening. She'd ask him to give her a hand. He'd have to help her. How else would she climb out?

Again, she visualized the scene, trying to see it clearly in her mind as if she were watching a movie. He'd be cautious but he'd step forward and stick out his hand. She'd reach for it with her left hand and look weak and timid and afraid. When he started to help her from the opening, she'd swing her right hand from behind her back with the flattened beer can turned on its side. She'd aim for his neck. He'd jerk back, but it would be too late. He'd be too slow. The can would strike its mark. Wounded, blood gushing from his sliced artery, he'd grab his neck and scream but his profanities wouldn't save him. He'd fall backward onto the hunting cabin, floor with his life flowing from his jugular in red bursts! She'd kill him! And enjoy watching him die!

For a moment, she savored this mental image. But it didn't last. *No! It isn't a good plan. He'd have a gun. He'll shoot me even if I hit him. I might miss too! The can might not cut his artery. He might not come back alone. Or he might not offer to help pull me from the crawl space. He'd stay out of my reach. Or he might demand to see my hands first. Too many "ors," too many "ifs." I need a better plan.*

She heard thunder. It was close. Another boom, this one even closer. She could hear the rain pelt the floorboards above her. *Is it raining in Washington, D.C.? If I'd stayed there, what would I be doing? Covering a State Department dinner party for the* Tribune? *Chatting with an ambassador? Flirting with a congressman? How can this be happening? I don't want to die! Not like this!*

She heard water dripping. It was seeping through the cracks above her. The cabin must have a hole in its roof. Mud. She was lying in it. She felt it with her fingers. It was strangely smoothing. More thunder. More rain. Drips everywhere, coming faster now. Maybe there was no cabin roof at all. She wiped her hand against her leg. She was filthy. A layer of her own blood, then dirt, now muddy blood.

A plan! A solution! That's it! Am I crazy? Or brilliant? She felt her way toward the water bottles, chicken bones, washtub. She collected them, one by one, and carried them to a corner, where she placed them next to the wall. With the beer can, she began digging. She scooped the mud through her legs, as if she were a child playing on an ocean beach, digging a hole. She pushed the mud carefully back, balancing it along the hole's opening. She paused, removed her T-shirt, slipped out of her underwear. Naked, bruised, wet, muddy, she scraped the red Mississippi clay with her flattened beer can. She began to sweat but didn't care. Her once-beautiful hair was matted and clung together in clumps. She didn't care. Her hands were sore and achy. She didn't care. None of it mattered. Not now.

What works best? A hollow chicken bone? A hole

punched in the bottom of the paper chicken tub? *Yes. That would be better.* He wouldn't crawl across the mud to inspect the garbage. He'd be too surprised that she was gone, too alarmed to think logically. With any luck, he'd panic. He'd open the trap door, discover her missing, and then run outside to find her. *Yes. It was a good plan.*

She dug faster, taking advantage of the rainwater that flowed into the hole, softening the red clay. *Dig, dig. Think, think, think. Yes, it will work. Believe in yourself. The first step to success is believing in yourself. I can do this. It will work. I will be free. Dig, dig. Think, think, think. Where is Melanie? Is she coming to rescue me? No! I can't count on her. I can only count on myself. There's not much time left. Dig. Dig. Faster, faster. My plan will work. The first step to success is always believing in yourself. Dig. Faster. Think. Faster. Feel the rain. It will save me.*

Seven

"This has to be it," I said.

The words STARS AND BARS MOTEL were printed in bold block letters across a road sign that was supposed to resemble a billowing Confederate Flag.

"Don't you think it's odd for a motel named after the Rebel flag to cater to black customers?" Melanie asked.

"I'm guessing this place was built in the late 1950s," I replied. "The original owners probably sold it long ago."

I drove past the entrance.

"Aren't we pulling in?" Melanie asked.

"I want to try something," I said. I drove for about a hundred yards and then stopped. "Give me five minutes and then you come into the motel office." Before she could ask why, I stepped from the SUV and hustled back up the blacktop.

The Stars and Bars office was located inside the enclosed porch of an older single-story gray stucco house. It was next to the entrance of a circular drive. Lining the drive were twelve one-room cabins. Each appeared barely large enough to hold a bed. All of them faced the highway. No phones. But the units had window air-conditioners sticking out of the walls on the right side of the cabins' front doors. Faded pink and green rusty metal lawn chairs, one per cabin, sat on the other side of the doors. A sign next to the motel office read VACANCY. There was a yellowed paper index card Scotch-taped to the screen door that said: AFTER 10 P.M., DOOR IS LOCKED, PLEASE RING BELL. I walked in. Blue, green, and black fish, all dead, with their big mouths wide open, stared at me from wooden plaques. There must have been fifteen of them hanging on the lobby walls. Taxidermy decor. The porch was divided in half by a worn Formica countertop covered with pink, white, and blue specks. On the opposite side of the counter, the owners had posted notices: IN GOD WE TRUST, EVERYONE ELSE PAYS CASH! and OUR CREDIT MANAGER IS HELEN WAITE. WANT CREDIT: GO TO HELL-AND-WAIT.

An elderly black man slid open a metal folding door that squeaked. It divided the porch from the main house. There was a television droning behind him and I could see a woman's feet raised up on a La-Z-Boy chair. She was wearing matted pink fuzzy slippers, mashed down at the heels. Although it was still hot outside, the old man was wearing a checked flannel shirt and green khaki pants sagged with fatigue.

"What can I do ya for?" he asked cheerfully.

"I called earlier looking for Heather Cole."

"What?" he said. He fumbled in his pocket, withdrew a hearing aid, and stuck it in his ear. "Now, you want a room?"

"No, I'm the fellow looking for Heather Cole."

He eyed me suspiciously. "This woman ain't hiding from you, is she? I don't want no trouble here."

"She's a friend. I drove up from Jackson but I forgot where she said she was staying."

"There's only two motels in this town."

"Then she must be here," I said. "I thought maybe she was the blonde woman you described: Ashley. Is she here?"

"Don't rightly know. We like to leave our guests alone."

I heard the office door open behind me. I assumed it was Melanie, but didn't turn around to check. Instead, I watched the old man to see if he would mistake her for Heather, as the Holiday Inn clerk had done.

"Be with ya in a minute," the old man said. He didn't seem to recognize her.

"I don't mind waiting." It was Melanie's voice.

The pink scuffs propped up on the recliner suddenly shifted from their position.

"Randall, dear," a woman's voice called out, "you ain't wearing your glasses, are you?"

A rather plump woman wearing a blue chenille robe stepped through the opening behind him. "I thought I heard your voice, darlin'," she said, glancing at Melanie.

I spun around and Melanie said: "Nick, you found me!" She stepped forward and gave me a hug.

The old man started to speak, but his wife cut him off. "Please forgive my husband. He don't like wearing his hearing aid or his glasses. Now, me, why, I can see and hear as good as the day I was born. I especially remember voices real good."

"This gal here ain't no blonde," the old man replied, incredulous. "The Ashley woman is a blonde. Even you said that!"

"Randall," his wife replied, sounding exasperated, "women have a right to change their hair color from time to time. Now, let's stop embarrassing our guests."

"I'm just explaining why I didn't recognize her," he snapped.

"You didn't recognize her because you ain't wearing your glasses," the woman replied. "Even if she was blonde, you still wouldn't see her because you're as blind as a old bat without them!"

Melanie interrupted: "I'm sorry if I confused you, but I stopped in because I've misplaced the key to my cabin." I smiled. Melanie was a fast learner.

The woman lifted an old cigar box from under the

counter and began sorting through a mess of keys with strings and tags attached.

"What cabin are you in, dearie?" the woman asked.

Melanie shot me a frightened glance.

"I put her in number six," the old man declared triumphantly. "I may not see worth a damn, but at least I still got all of my memory." The woman handed Melanie the key.

We walked up the driveway to Cabin 6 and Melanie unlocked the door. The room was in shambles.

"Don't touch anything," I warned as we stepped inside and shut the door behind us.

The sheets from the bed had been pulled onto the cabin's floor. A bedside table was knocked on its side. Melanie spotted blood on the pillow and sheets.

"I'll be right back," I said. I slipped outside and hurried to the SUV, which I drove back to the cabin. I fetched a bag from my suitcase. It contained disposable cameras, blank computer disks, plastic evidence bags, plastic gloves, and fingerprint equipment. Back inside, I handed Melanie rubber gloves and then began photographing the entire room.

"You going to dust for fingerprints?" she asked.

"No, we'll let the sheriff do that. But I want to check a few things before we call him." I picked up a pocket-sized notebook from the floor. It had Heather's name written on it.

"This was probably on the nightstand before it got knocked over," I said. I used a pen to flip through several pages. "Her last entry is dated Wednesday," I said. I dropped the notebook into a plastic evidence bag. There were red drops on its cover, which I assumed were blood.

Heather's running shoes were next to the door. Her running pants and sports bra were folded and lying next to them.

"Look," Melanie said, pointing down. A tiny canister of pepper spray was sticking out of one of the running shoes. The keys to the rental Ford Taurus were stuck in the other shoe.

"Why didn't she put the pepper spray on the nightstand so she could grab it?" I asked.

"She must've felt safe," Melanie said. "I'm guessing she jogged here from the Holiday Inn. She probably figured no one could find her here."

"The person who took her must have attacked while she was in bed, probably asleep—based on the condition of the sheets and blood on the pillowcases. It looks like he dragged her from the sheets."

Melanie pointed toward the northeast corner of the room. "There's Heather's portable computer." It was on a student-style desk that was bolted to the floor. I turned on the laptop and slipped a blank disk into it. Heather used an older version of WordPerfect. While I was downloading all her files, I photographed the desktop. Heather's purse and several file folders were on it, along with several packs of chewing gum.

"Here's her cell phone," Melanie announced. Apparently it had been knocked off the nightstand during the scuffle and had fallen under a chair. She picked it up by its antenna.

I handed her an evidence bag. "Good work!" I said.

I reached into Heather's purse and removed her wallet. It contained several hundred dollars in cash.

"Whoever abducted her left without stealing anything," I said. "She was obviously his only target."

"Here's her wig!" Melanie called from the bathroom. "Her key to the Holiday Inn is in here next to the sink too."

"I think Heather probably jogged here each night from the Holiday Inn," I said. "This is where she did her writing and where she slept. She'd jog back early the next morning."

Melanie walked from the bathroom toward the cabin's front door. There was no deadbolt lock, no peephole to see through, before opening it to whoever might be outside. The only lock was the one on the doorknob, and that could have been easily opened with a screwdriver, credit card, or a knife blade.

As I scanned the room, I noticed a small brown bag on the floor tucked between the desk and a wall. I pushed it open using my ink pen so I wouldn't leave fingerprints and peeked inside. There was a box of nine-millimeter bullets inside.

"Does Heather own a handgun?" I asked.

"I don't have a clue," Melanie replied.

"I doubt her kidnapper would have brought a box of shells with him," I said.

"Maybe that's why she left her pepper spray in her jogging shoe," Melanie offered. "She didn't need it because she had a handgun on the nightstand next to her bed."

I squatted down so I could see across the floor, but I didn't see a pistol anywhere.

A few minutes later, I felt we had seen everything that we needed to see. We went outside, locking the cabin door behind us.

"Melanie, what we just saw scares me," I said. "Do you think Heather is still alive?"

"I know she is. I can feel it. You know, the twin thing."

"Then I don't want to call the sheriff just yet."

"What?" she exclaimed. "We need his help!"

"Whoever attacked Heather could have killed her in the cabin if he'd wanted her dead. Instead, he abducted her. Why?"

"It has to do with the lynching," she replied. "Maybe he just wants to scare her."

"Or maybe he needs to find out what she has learned. That's why he wants her alive. Now listen, word travels fast in a small town like this. If we call Sheriff Moorehead and he seals off this cabin as a crime scene, then the person who kidnapped Heather is going to find out. I'm afraid he might panic and then kill her."

Melanie didn't reply.

I said: "Obviously, there is no maid service at the Stars and Bars, otherwise the owners would have seen her room and called the sheriff. Today is Friday. You came to my apartment early this morning and said you'd just dreamt that Heather had been kidnapped. We know she arrived in town on Monday and Sheriff Moorehead told us today in the park that Heather confronted Jeb Rogge at his house on Wednesday. Her last notation in her notebook was late Wednesday night. That means she either was attacked later Wednesday or on Thursday night. I'm guessing Wednesday."

"How long do we wait before calling Moorehead?" Melanie asked. "I don't want to run out of time!"

"Not long. I just want to learn more about the 1955 lynching and who's who in Pushmataha before we show all of our cards. We've already learned a lot by having you pose as Heather. I'd like to visit the Reverend Carter just as we'd planned. Then we can contact the sheriff."

She thought for a moment and then nodded an okay.

As we drove onto the old highway, Melanie asked: "Now do you believe me? Do you believe that Heather and I can communicate in our dreams?"

I had to admit that the idea of Heather and Melanie talking to one another in their dreams suddenly didn't seem so far-fetched. In fact, I was praying it was something they could repeat, especially if Melanie could get Heather to tell us where she was being held hostage.

"You've been right so far," I said, trying to reassure her. "And that gives us hope because you just told me that you could sense that Heather is still alive."

"Yes," she replied. "Heather is alive. But we've got to hurry."

Eight

I told you never to call me at home!"

"Hey, you left word. You said we needed to talk!"

"I didn't want you calling me here! Are you using a pay phone?"

"Stop worrying. I know what I'm doing. That bitch won't be writing about us! I guarran-damn-ty it!"

"She's got a sister. A twin sister."

"So?"

"She and a man are here in town searching for her."

"In Pushmataha? Right now?"

"Arrived today."

"That ain't good!"

"Does she know about me, does she? Have you asked her yet? Has she made the connection between me and what happened?"

"No, I haven't asked. I've been waiting. Playing with her a bit. I wanted to get her in a cooperative frame of mind first."

"There's no more time. Forget the questions. You know what you have to do now, right?"

"I ain't stupid just because I'm not some big shot like you!"

"Do it tonight, then, okay?"

"No, tomorrow morning."

"Why not tonight?"

"Because it's raining."

"So?"

"It can wait."

"No one knows about her, right? You haven't told anyone, have you?"

"No one who matters."

"Then you did tell someone! This is unbelievable! You're going to get us caught!"

"Hey, you've got no reason to talk down to me! I said I'd do it tomorrow!"

"I'm going to meet you there. I don't want you to screw this up."

"Well, I guess I'm just the luckiest son of a bitch on the entire damn planet, then, huh? Getting you to personally come help me! Should I call a press conference?"

"What time should we meet?"

"Seven. Oh, and I need more money."

"That wasn't part of our deal. You're already getting monthly checks."

"Well, now it is part of our deal. Besides, why d'you care? You have plenty! Rich as you are."

"How much cash?"

"Ten large!"

"That's too much."

"It's goddamn cheap and you know it. This ain't negotiable."

"Seven tomorrow. But after it's over, never call me again. Ever! Understand? Or the monthly checks stop."

"Just be there with my cash. In fact, let's do it earlier. Maybe a bit after six o'clock. Yeah, that'd be better."

"Fine!"

Nine

The Reverend Bartholomew W. Carter IV lived on the northern edge of Pushmataha in a section known as Pushmataha Heights, but usually referred to by the town's white population as the Heights, or by its old name: Colored Town. Unlike most of the aged shotgun shacks and clapboard shanties that lined the potholed streets, the Reverend Carter's house was made of red brick and encircled by a freshly painted picket fence. There was a large magnolia tree with white fragrant blooms in his carefully manicured front lawn. The tree's aroma mixed with the scent of the red azaleas and pink and white Cherokee roses that edged the house, emitting a sticky sweet smell, as if someone had put too much potpourri in a closet which overwhelmed the senses when the door was first opened. The pastor's wife, who introduced herself as Mrs. Bartholomew Carter, escorted us into a compact but comfortable living room. An old family Bible was open on the coffee table. It was turned to the Twenty-third Psalm. A prominent picture of Jesus praying was hanging above the sofa. Next to it was a print of Martin Luther King, Jr. On another wall were more than a dozen cheaply framed certificates which the minister had received after he had successfully completed correspondence classes in religion. In the center of the wall was a document from the state of Mississippi declaring that he was licensed to perform marriages. Melanie and I sat on a bronze-colored sofa. An oak-stained wood shelf nearby held a multitude of snapshots of the couple's beaming children and grandchildren.

"My wife tells me, you've come seeking spiritual guidance," the Reverend Carter announced when he joined us. He was an imposing man with thick hands and walnut-sized knuckles. I guessed he was almost sixty, but could have passed for being younger.

"Actually, we're here because we'd like to learn about a 1955 lynching that happened in Rabbit Creek Park," I said. I'd decided that we needed to get right to the point.

"Why are you interested in it?" he asked.

I explained that I was an investigator with the U.S. Senate Judiciary Committee and hinted that my boss had sent me down, but the minister was skeptical.

"You're here because you want justice done after fifty years?" he asked.

His wife entered carrying a tray that contained a sweating plastic pitcher of just-brewed iced tea and a plate of homemade oatmeal cookies. Melanie and I thanked her, and I picked up the plate and started to hand it to Melanie out of politeness, but hesitated when I saw the stern look that had come over Carter's face.

"Let's thank the Lord first," he declared. We joined hands with the minister and his wife. "Dear Lord," Carter began, "thank you for bringing these strangers into our home. We ask you to give us wisdom to help them not only with questions about the past but with whatever troubles are lying heavy on their hearts . . ." Carter continued praying for ten more minutes before finally saying amen. His wife immediately left the room.

"Why did you come to me about this?" he asked.

"Because you're a minister and therefore a knowledgeable leader in the community," I said. "I assumed you would know the story behind it."

"But who gave you my name?"

"No one, actually," Melanie answered. "We chose your church from the telephone book."

I thought he might be offended but instead he looked amused.

"Are you saying you chose me completely by chance?"

"Yes," she replied.

Carter shook his head, indicating that he disagreed. "You may think it was by chance but it wasn't. God led you here to me. The man who was lynched was my stepbrother."

Melanie and I exchanged surprised glances.

"My father was married twice," Carter continued. "His first wife was Josephine Grant and she had a child out of wedlock before she met my father. She was only thirteen when she gave birth. She named the baby Lamar. My father married her a few years later and together they had four more children. She died giving birth to a fifth child, who was stillborn. My father later married my mother, Sarah, and had another nine children. I was the fourth child and I was nine when Lamar was murdered."

"We saw the trophy tree in Rabbit Creek Park this afternoon where he was hung," Melanie volunteered.

"The correct word is lynched," Carter said. "Lamar never broke any law."

"Wasn't he accused of stealing a mule?" I asked.

"Lamar was the first black man from Pushmataha Heights to ever attend and graduate from college," Carter explained. "He finished near the top of his class at the Tuskegee Institute. Did you know that Ralph Waldo Ellison, the famous black writer, attended Tuskegee?"

Neither of us did. The Reverend Carter saw a chance here to educate us.

"In 1952, Ellison's first novel, *Invisible Man,* was published and it greatly influenced Lamar, who was then a student at the institute. Ellison's book won the National Book

Award a year later and should have been awarded the Pulitzer prize, but wasn't. I was so young, all I cared about was sneaking away from work to go swimming in Rabbit Creek, but I remember how excited everyone was, at least all of the black folk were, whenever Lamar came home from college."

Carter took a sip of his tea. He was clearly enjoying the telling of this story. "Because Lamar was so much older, we never really did much together, but he used to come into the room that I shared with my many brothers and read to us at night. My mother was illiterate, but she had several Bible stories that she knew by heart and she would recite them to us. But I had never had anyone read to me like he did. It was a real treat. Of course, he didn't read us Bible stories. He read us passages from Ellison's book. I wanted to hear something more exciting, an adventure story. But Lamar told me that Ellison was writing about us, black people. There was one story that, even today, I still remember. Ellison was describing how he felt when he walked down a crowded street in New York City. Whites bumped into him and they were polite and apologized whenever that happened. Even though I was a little boy, I couldn't imagine a white person in Mississippi ever apologizing to a black person for any reason whatsoever."

Once again, he took a sip from his drink.

"And then Ellison wrote something that I only understood when I got older. He wrote that even though the whites were polite to him, it didn't mean they cared about him as a person or cared about his feelings. He wrote that they would have apologized to 'Jack the Bear' if they had bumped into him. Oh, how my brothers and I laughed and hooted when Lamar read that passage. We didn't really understand it. All we could see in our heads was a fat, big brown bear walking down the streets of New York bumping into white people and them apologizing to this bear. Lamar got frustrated and tried to explain how we as blacks were, and still are, invisible people."

"Lamar sounds like he was a very intelligent man," Melanie said.

"Intelligent and very, very brave," he replied. "Too brave. Lamar could have moved to New York City or to Chicago or to Washington, D.C., but instead he returned to Pushmataha. Can you imagine, for one moment, the resentment? Here was a young black man in 1955 who had a college education when only a handful of whites in our community had ever earned one."

"Is that why he was lynched?" Melanie asked.

"It's more complicated than that," he replied, "but that played a big role in what happened. Most people seem to think the civil rights movement began when Rosa Parks refused to give up her seat to a white man on a bus in Montgomery, Alabama, in December 1955. But there were several important events before that. A year earlier, the U.S. Supreme Court officially outlawed segregation in public schools, and that's when things really began heating up down here in the Deep South. Lamar was like all college kids—wanting to change the world. The first thing he did when he came home was launch a drive in the black churches to get our people to register to vote. Oh, Lordy, did that cause a ruckus. Not all whites in Pushmataha were racists. Why, the Peterman family—they've owned the big lumber mill here for generations—they've always treated blacks with respect. God bless 'em! Coming from Washington, D.C., you probably know Nehemiah Peterman— Mississippi's junior U.S. senator."

Until that moment, I hadn't made the connection. Peterman Lumber. Pushmataha, Mississippi. Senator Nehemiah Peterman. I'd seen him yesterday. That was when my boss had publicly embarrassed Peterman by having me expose the fact that his nominee for a federal judgeship had lied about his Army career.

"Yes, I know Senator Peterman," I said, without elaborating.

"Actually, he's in town this weekend," Carter said, momentarily sidetracked. "He's speaking Sunday morning to my flock. Now, that should tell you what sort of man he is: speaking on Sunday to an all-black congregation!"

"That *is* impressive!" Melanie exclaimed.

"When all this trouble with Lamar first broke out, Senator Peterman's father came to our house and tried to persuade Lamar to leave town for a while—just until everything cooled down a bit. Yes, sir, the Peterman family tried its best to protect Lamar, but it was too late. In August, an event happened in Money, Mississippi, that caused a national scandal. I'm sure you've heard about it—the killing of little Emmett Till."

"He was a young black man, who was on vacation in Mississippi when he supposedly flirted with a white woman in a store—if I remember correctly," I said.

"Emmett was only fourteen and was from Chicago. He didn't understand that things were different in the South, especially when it came to black men even looking at a white woman."

"We read about it in history class," Melanie said. "Several white men broke into the house where he was sleeping, beat him, shot him, and then dumped his body into the Tallahatchie River. It was disgraceful and everyone knew who did it, but an all-white jury let them go."

"After little Emmett Till was murdered," Carter continued, "even my daddy suggested that Lamar leave town. He'd already found lots of little cards stuck on his car's windshield that warned: THE KLAN IS WATCHING YOU! and my daddy was afraid the Klan would burn down our house. It seems ironic now."

"Ironic?" Melanie said. "How's it ironic?"

"Emmett Till's murder outraged people in the North because it showed the world just how racist Mississippi was. But in Mississippi, it confirmed what most of the Klan members believed: They could kill a nigger for no reason at all and not be punished."

"Did the Klan lynch Lamar?"

"Yes," he replied, "and no. The man responsible was a

well-known leader of the KKK. But he was acting on his own. His name was Robert E. Lee Rogge."

"We saw the initials R.E.L.R. carved into the trophy tree," I said.

"Then you also saw P.R. and J.R. carved there too. Them is his boys, Peyton Rogge and Jeb Rogge. The entire family is racist and proud of it."

"There were two other sets of initials carved there: S.A. and then just the initial L."

"That's Stanley Alfred and his boy, Lester."

"Were they members of the KKK too?" Melanie asked.

"Well, that's a bit harder to answer. The Alfreds always insisted that they were forced into participating in the lynching."

"I thought those five men's identities were secret, that people didn't know who they were," Melanie said.

The Reverend Carter grinned. "Every black person knew and so did every white person who wanted to know. Old man Rogge was bragging about it before my father cut down Lamar's body."

"Why didn't anyone do anything—arrest them?" she asked.

"My dear," Carter said, "this was 1955 in Mississippi. Besides, who was going to testify against them? They lynched him during the night. What proof was there?"

Melanie said: "Sheriff Moorehead told us today that Jeb Rogge is still alive. He warned us to stay away from Rogge."

"That's good advice! Rogge is a very dangerous fellow," Carter said.

"We've also heard that three of the white men who took part in the lynching died in freak accidents. That they were cursed. Is that true?" I asked.

Carter put down his iced tea and leaned forward in his seat. "A man of the cloth such as myself doesn't believe in superstitions and curses. But the Lord has His way of punishing the wicked. And He works in mysterious ways."

"What happened to those three men?"

"Old man Rogge was killed ten days after the hanging. He earned his living by cutting down trees and then selling them to the Peterman mill. He was working with a logging crew when a tree fell and crushed him. That's when all this curse talk first started, because the men working with him were experienced loggers and they all claimed it was impossible for that tree to fall in the direction that it did."

"Didn't you say he was the ringleader of the lynching?" I asked.

"Yep," Carter replied. "His older boy, Peyton, was the next to die, he got drunk and was driving home when he saw a rattlesnake crossing the highway. Apparently he decided to run over it. Lots of men around here put snakeskins on their cowboy hats."

Melanie frowned.

"Peyton ran his truck's front wheels over the snake and then he stopped his vehicle and opened the driver's door. But instead of getting out like any sensible person would do, he simply leaned his head down and looked under the truck. The snake leapt at him and caught him right in his jugular. A motorist found him an hour later. The snake, which had been pinned under the front wheel, and Peyton were both dead in the highway. He was about twenty-eight when that happened."

"That was eleven years after the lynching," I said, "which means that he was only seventeen when Lamar Grant was murdered."

"That'd be about right," said Carter. "Peyton was a teenager and so was Lester Alfred, who was also at the lynching. They were both seniors at Pushmataha High School."

"If Peyton was only seventeen, then how old was his brother, Jeb Rogge—the fellow who is still alive?" Melanie asked.

"Jeb was only seven or eight years old when his father took him to that lynching. Horrible, isn't it, how a parent can pollute a young child's mind like old man Rogge did."

"Who was the third man to die?" I asked.

"That'd be Stanley Alfred. He was driving along a country road one afternoon on his way to deliver medicine to an elderly woman who lives north of town. Stanley owned the pharmacy here and he'd deliver medicines to whites who were too sick to come into Pushmataha. He was a deeply religious fellow and saw the free deliveries as part of his Christian duty."

"But he only delivered to whites, right?" I asked.

Carter ignored me. "Anyway," he continued, "two fellows were out rabbit hunting in a field and one of their shots ricocheted off a rock and it hit Alfred in the head as he was driving by. It was only a little bitty .22-caliber rifle, but it killed him instantly."

"Old man Rogge has a tree fall on him," I recited. "His son Peyton gets bit by a rattlesnake in the neck, and Stanley Alfred is shot during a hunting accident. I can understand how those rumors about a curse got started."

"That leaves Jeb Rogge and Stanley Alfred's son Lester as the only two survivors, then," Melanie said. "Nothing has happened to either of them yet, right?"

"Lester inherited his father's drugstore. You probably drove past it if you went through our town square," Carter said. "I'm not one to gossip, but like I said, the Lord works in mysterious ways. Sometimes a person suffers more when he is alive than when he dies, especially when it comes to sin."

"I'm not quite certain what you're suggesting," I said. "Does Lester Alfred have cancer or some other medical condition that makes him suffer?"

"Well, he's never married."

I still didn't get what Carter was implying, but Melanie understood.

"Oh, he's gay," she said.

"I don't believe homosexuals are really happy, so I don't use the word 'gay,' " Carter replied. "But that is what some town gossips say, and if that is true, then he is carrying around a mighty affliction."

"Where's Jeb Rogge live?" I asked.

"In a compound just a few miles outside of town. I call it a compound because he has signs posted, warning black people not to come onto his property or they'll be shot. And he means it. He and his kids are as mean as they can be. Jeb took over his daddy's tree business but I don't think he's really worked steady for years. I don't know of any blacks who will work with him. You see, around here, a fellow will get two or three men to help him go in and cut down trees. Then he'll split the profits with the landowner and his crew. The best crews are mostly black."

"How does he make a living if he doesn't cut down trees?" Melanie asked.

"He and his wife run some hate group over the Internet," Carter explained. "At least that's what I've been told."

"What about Lester Alfred?" I asked. "Does he still hate blacks?"

"Lester lives in an apartment above his daddy's drugstore. But he's not anything like Jeb Rogge. After his father died, Lester came to see me and personally apologized for the lynching. He asked me if I would forgive him for what he'd done. He was terrified. I think he believed in the curse."

Carter paused for a moment. He seemed to be trying to decide if he wanted to tell us something private. "Are you really from the U.S. Senate?" he asked me.

I fumbled in my pocket, removed my billfold, and showed him my Senate identification card. He examined it closely, then said, "Please excuse me for a minute." He walked from the living room, leaving us alone.

Melanie shot me a "what's happening?" glance. I shrugged. Seconds later, the Reverend Carter reappeared. He was carrying an old manila envelope. He opened it carefully and removed two eight-by-ten photographs, which he rested in his lap, face down, so that we couldn't see them.

"When Lester came to see me," he said, "I was suspicious. But we prayed together. We got down on our knees right in this living room. He'd been sitting right where you are sitting now. We prayed to God for forgiveness. Like I said, I was doubtful, but it's not up to me to look into a man's heart. That's God's job."

Melanie nodded.

"I told Lester that if he wanted to be forgiven," Carter continued, "then he needed to confess and tell me exactly what had happened on the night when Lamar was lynched."

Once again, Carter paused to make certain that we understood the exclusivity of this moment and what he was about to share with us. "Like I said earlier, the Emmett Till murder made Klan members like old man Rogge feel invincible. After Till was murdered, old man Rogge went to the courthouse and swore out a complaint against Lamar. He accused him of stealing a mule. His son Peyton swore in an affidavit that he had seen Lamar take the mule from their barn. Everyone knew it was a big fat lie. Lamar had studied English literature at college. He didn't know nothing about mules and had no use for one. But that didn't matter. It was a white man's word against a Negro's, so the sheriff arrested Lamar. Now some black folks said later that the sheriff was trying to protect Lamar by putting him in jail. But I never believed it. Every white person in town, except for the Peterman family, was scared of the Rogges. They were bullies."

Carter took a final sip of his iced tea. "Here's what Lester Alfred told me about that night. At about ten o'clock, the sheriff went home, leaving Lamar alone at the courthouse, locked in a cell. Lester said the Rogges came to his house around midnight and got his daddy out of bed. Peyton woke up Lester too. He said: 'We're gonna have some fun lynching that uppity nigger!'"

"Why did they go to the Alfreds' house?" Melanie asked.

"Stanley Alfred was a Pushmataha County commissioner, so he had a key to the courthouse. They knew the sheriff would be angry if they broke a door to get inside. Of course, as soon as Stanley Alfred opened the courthouse door with his key, the Rogges rushed inside and grabbed Lamar. Over the years, I've heard different stories.

Some claim Lamar fought and almost escaped, but Lester said old man Rogge held a shotgun on Lamar and walked him over to the tree in the park without a fight. That's when Peyton Rogge began beating Lamar with a baseball bat. Old man Rogge took a turn too and then he insisted that everyone hit Lamar with that baseball bat."

"He made Stanley and Lester Alfred hit him too?" I asked.

"He sure did," Carter replied.

"How about Jeb Rogge, even though he was only a little boy?" Melanie asked.

"Lester said old man Rogge insisted that everyone had to hit Lamar, including little Jeb. If you were there, you had to take a swing. No exceptions. That way, everyone was equally responsible."

Tears flooded Melanie's eyes. "This is horrible!" she exclaimed. "How can people be so cruel?"

"Hate. Prejudice," said Carter. "By noon the next day, everyone had heard about the lynching. Our local newspaper published a photograph of Lamar hanging from that tree."

I couldn't wait any longer for him to show us the photographs in his lap. "Are those copies of that picture?" I asked.

"No," said Carter, glancing down at the photos. "The picture that was in the newspaper just showed Lamar hanging from that tree. They'd put a sign around his neck that said any black person who registered to vote would be lynched. I remember they'd misspelled most of the words on the sign, including the word 'nigger,' which they spelled 'n-i-g-a-r.' Without knowing it, the Rogges had shown just how ignorant they really were."

Carter handed us each one of the photographs that he had been so carefully guarding. Melanie and I flipped them over. They were identical pictures. They showed five white males standing at the foot of Lamar Grant, who was dangling from a rope behind them.

Carter reached over and pointed at the faces in the picture that I was holding.

"This older fellow in the very center, the one with the open-neck shirt," Carter said, "now, that's old man Rogge."

I looked down at the round face, bald head, and huge smile. He was clearly pleased with himself.

"That skinny, dark-haired boy beside him with his shirttail hanging out," Carter continued, "that'd be Petyon Rogge." Again, I stared at the picture. There was a smirk on the teenager's face that made you want to smack him.

"This man here, the one wearing a tie and jacket, is that Stanley Alfred?" Melanie asked.

Carter nodded. "Pretty amazing, huh? Alfred took time to put on a tie and his coat before he let the Rogges into the courthouse. I guess he felt that he had a certain status that he had to uphold whenever he went out in public."

Standing next to Stanley Alfred was a pudgy teenager with thick Coke-bottle glasses and a face covered with freckles. "This must be Lester Alfred," Melanie said.

Carter said, "Yep, that's him."

"That only leaves little Jeb Rogge," she added. All of us looked down at the smallest figure in the snapshot. Although he was only a child, Jeb Rogge already had developed a menacing look, the sort perfected by bullies and bigots.

"What you need to understand," Carter said, "is this photograph is a *souvenir*. The men are standing in front of Lamar like he was some animal they'd just shot and strung up."

"How did you get this photo?" I asked.

"Lester Alfred gave me both copies. He asked me to burn them. He said that old man Rogge had given a copy of the photograph to everyone who had been at the lynching as a keepsake. Then he'd destroyed the negative."

"Couldn't this photograph be used as evidence in court?" Melanie asked. "It certainly proves who was at the lynching that night."

Carter glanced at me. "That's why I never burned them. I promised Lester that I would. He probably thinks they no longer exist." Carter paused for a moment and then said, "I remember how everyone was afraid when Lamar was lynched. Black people felt helpless. No one knew what to do. My daddy told my mother that he was going to ride down in our wagon and fetch Lamar's body. The sheriff had left him hanging there all day. My mother was terrified. She was afraid my daddy would be lynched too. I ran up to him and grabbed his leg and begged him not to go. Then I said, 'If you're going, then I'm going too.' "

Melanie wiped her eyes.

"We rode through town and white people just stared at us. My daddy was crying when he cut the rope. Lamar's body fell into our wagon like a sack of potatoes. We rode home with Lamar. The sheriff promised he'd investigate, but everyone already knew who'd done it. For God's sake, old man Rogge went around town *bragging* about it. I remember going down to Rabbit Creek later and Jeb Rogge saw me and he yells: 'Hey, nigger, my daddy hanged your brudder! And I helped!' Then he let out a loud whoop! He said: 'We all put our initials in that there tree.' I wanted to wade across that creek and bash in his head, but I was too scared. I ran up to that tree and looked, and by God, he was telling the truth. They'd marked it with their initials, like they were proud of killing Lamar."

I noticed it was after ten p.m. but I still had a few more questions to ask.

"How did Pushmataha end up with a black sheriff?"

My question seem to snap Carter from sad thoughts of the past. "Jacob Moorehead is a local hero," he replied cheerfully, "for both whites and blacks. There's one thing in Pushmataha that makes even a racist like Jeb Rogge temporarily color-blind. High school football. If I could get people around here as excited about Jesus Christ as they get about the Pushmataha Screaming Eagles, we'd create heaven right here in Mississippi!" He chuckled. "Jacob Moorehead was the best running back this town ever produced. Ten years ago he broke every record there is in Mississippi for a running back. Yards gained, touchdowns scored, passes caught. He did it all and he got a full scholarship to Auburn University over in Alabama and even made the cover of *Sports Illustrated*. There was talk that he'd win the Heisman Trophy and he was a certain bet to be drafted into the NFL. But in his third year, Moorehead got his leg busted in three different pieces and that ended his career. That's why he came home and ran for sheriff."

"Is he someone we can trust?" I asked.

The question clearly offended Carter. "Jacob Moorehead is a good, decent man. I'd trust him with my life!"

Melanie shot me an "I told you so" glance.

"What happened after Lester Alfred asked God to forgive him? Did he truly change?" she asked.

"With God's help, he certainly did," Carter replied, "at least he changed when it came to racism. The very next day after we prayed, Lester hired a black girl to work in his drugstore. No other business on the town square had a black clerk. Some whites stopped going there and Jeb Rogge threw a fit, but he couldn't intimidate Lester. Even today, every clerk in that drugstore is black. It's Lester's way of publicly apologizing for his part in the lynching."

"May I ask a personal question?" Melanie said. "Have you forgiven the men who lynched Lamar Grant?"

"Yes," he replied, without any hesitation. "I know they operated out of hate and fear. But I've never forgotten what they did and, quite frankly, I'd like to see Jeb Rogge put on trial and punished. That's why I want to give you one of these photographs to take with you back to Washington D.C. I want you to use it to bring him to justice."

"What about Lester Alfred?" I asked. "He was older than Jeb Rogge and certainly should have known better."

"That's true. And I believe he's truly sorry for what he did and that he has been forgiven. But that doesn't mean a person still isn't punished because of his actions. You forgive, but God never demands that you forget. That's why you'll need to bring charges against him too. Now, I'll be happy to testify on Lester Alfred's behalf and tell a jury about how he asked God for forgiveness. It will be up to them, though, to decide his fate here on earth. In my mind, both men should be held accountable for what they did to Lamar."

Carter took back the photograph that he had given to Melanie and carefully slipped it into the manila envelope. However, he left me holding my copy.

"You take that photograph back to the Justice Department and you show it to the FBI," he said. "You tell them that I'll testify against Rogge and Alfred. You tell them that there were only five copies of that photograph made. I'm sure if they search Jeb Rogge's compound, they'll find the other three."

Melanie and I stood, and the Reverend Carter walked us to his front door. "Just remember," he said, "after their trials, I'm gonna need to get that photograph back. I promised Lester Alfred that I'd burn it and I'm a man of my word. Let's just say it's taking me a bit longer than I thought to find my matches."

Ten

It began raining as soon as we left the Reverend Carter's house. It came hard. White jagged bolts of lightning cracked across the sky. Spits of rain made the rented SUV's wipers struggle to keep its windshield clear. I was forced to pull off the road because I couldn't see.

"I wonder if this is how it rained on the night when Lamar Grant was lynched," Melanie said. "The night lightning hit the trophy tree."

Just then a boom of thunder banged closed by, startling her.

"We should call Sheriff Moorehead now," she said.

Unbuckling my seat belt, I slipped to the rear of the SUV and retrieved my evidence bag that contained the items we had taken from the Stars and Bars motel. Heather's cell phone was a flip-model that resembled a black clam when closed. I touched the phone's "Main Menu" key and scrolled down the options until I reached "Last 10 Numbers Dialed." I wanted to see who she had called before she was abducted.

"Your dream—the one where you first learned that Heather was in danger—was on Wednesday night, correct?" I asked.

"Yes," Melanie answered. "Andrew Middleton told me that Heather arrived in Pushmataha on Monday and I first dreamt on Wednesday night that she was in danger."

It was Friday now and I realized I'd only known Melanie for little more than a day, yet it already seemed as if we had spent weeks together. Was that because our last twenty-eight hours together had been so hectic or because she was Heather's clone? I wasn't sure.

"The last call Heather placed on her cell was made at seven p.m. Wednesday," I said. I recognized the number because I had dialed it myself when Heather and I were still living together. "It was to the *Tribune*'s main switch-board. She was probably calling Middleton."

"That's odd," Melanie said. "When I met with him Thursday morning, he said the last time that he'd heard from her was Tuesday night."

"She might not have gotten through. His secretary could have answered. I'm surprised Heather was calling him at that time anyway," I said, "because she always got angry at me if I telephoned the newspaper between five and eight o'clock. That's when everyone is on deadline and doesn't want to be interrupted."

"She must've had something very important to tell him."

According to the cell phone, Heather hadn't made any more calls after that. None.

"We know Heather confronted Jeb Rogge on Wednesday afternoon," I said. "I'm guessing she was calling Middleton to tell him about their angry encounter. I'm also guessing she was abducted later Wednesday night, since she didn't make any cell phone calls the next day."

"She was attacked at four-thirty on Thursday morning," Melanie said.

I gave her a surprised look. "How do you know it happened at exactly four-thirty?"

"On Wednesday night, when I first saw her in my dream,

she didn't have any bruises on her face. But when I saw her in my second dream—the one that I had on Thursday night—her face was swollen and bloody."

"You saw bruises on her face? You saw that in your dream?"

"I saw them and felt them too. They hurt so much I got up and checked my own face in the mirror. My face was bruised."

"I didn't see any bruises when you came to my apartment!"

"That's because I covered them with makeup," she replied, "but they were there. Listen, I went to bed at ten o'clock Wednesday just before the local news. Heather appeared in my dream and told me that she was in danger. At around two-thirty that same morning, someone slapped me so hard that I woke up. I couldn't get back to sleep. I immediately began checking on the Internet for flights to Washington, D.C. The East Coast is in a time zone two hours ahead of my house in South Dakota. That means Heather was hit at four-thirty on Thursday morning. That's how I know the exact time when she was abducted. When I dreamt about her on Thursday, she had bruises in that second dream."

I didn't reply. I was trying to picture Melanie telling jurors at a trial that she knew exactly when her sister had been kidnapped because of her dreams. She correctly read my silence for skepticism.

"You still don't believe?"

"It's just so unusual."

She watched the rain pounding on the windshield. I noticed something on her cheek. At first I thought it was the reflection of rain from the windshield, but then I realized it was a single tear.

"I hate it when I become emotional," she said quietly. "I need to be strong for Heather."

Without thinking, I reached over and gently touched her left shoulder with my right hand, and as soon as my fingers brushed her soft skin, I felt conflicted. I genuinely wanted to comfort and reassure her. But when I caressed her, a different sensation swept through me. Lust. Pure and total desire. The rain, the threat of danger, the roles that we had cast ourselves in, all made me want to make love to her at that moment in the SUV pulled over by the side of the road. It was crazy because I knew that thought wasn't even remotely in her mind. If anything, she would've been appalled. And the truth is that she should've been, because I wouldn't have been making love to her. It would've been Heather in my head. I pulled back my hand and looked to see who Heather had called on her cell phone before she had called the *Washington Tribune*.

It was a local number. I compared it to Jeb Rogge's telephone number, which I'd copied from the motel's phone book. The two matched.

"Heather called Jeb Rogge's number Wednesday afternoon shortly before one o'clock," I explained. "I'm guessing she made that call while she was on her way to confront him at his house."

I hit the cell phone's "Redial" key. Rogge's number rang twice.

"Yeah." The voice had the practiced indifference of a teenager.

"Jeb Rogge, please," I said.

I heard the voice yell: "Mom, is Dad still gone?" A woman's voice came on, probably from an extension phone.

"Who's this?" she asked. "You know how late it is to be calling someone?"

I hit the "End" key, cutting off the call.

"It must've been his wife. Rogge is running around in this downpour just like us."

Melanie asked: "Why'd you just call him?"

I wished I had a professional explanation but I'd simply hit the "Redial" key on impulse. I'd wanted to hear his voice. "Wanted to see if the number was right," I said.

The next number on Heather's cell phone was a call that she'd made to a local Pushmataha number early Wednesday morning. I jotted it down and then continued scrolling through the list, which ranked the calls chronologically and backward through time. The rest of her calls had been made to the *Tribune*'s switchboard or a private phone number that I assumed was Andrew Middleton's Georgetown residence, since it had a Washington area code.

I recorded each number and noted the times when the calls had been placed. Then I used the cell phone's internal menu to retrieve a list of telephone calls that Heather had received. The most recent calls were all from Melanie and me. We'd been trying to reach her. Middleton also had tried to call Heather on Thursday morning, but had not tried since then. This also struck me as strange.

"When did you meet with Andrew Middleton at the newspaper?" I asked.

"It was sometime after three p.m. on Thursday. I had a cab take me there directly from the airport after I landed."

"You told Middleton that Heather was in danger, correct?"

"Of course. I even told him I'd been slapped that morning."

"Then why didn't he call Heather after meeting with you? Even if he was skeptical of your story, he'd want to tell her that you were in town looking for her, wouldn't he?"

I closed Heather's cell phone and said: "What exactly are you going to tell Sheriff Moorehead?"

"You're worried he won't take us seriously, aren't you?"

"Let's stick to the basics: We discovered Heather had rented two motel rooms and when we saw the inside of the Stars and Bars room, we knew she'd been abducted."

"What about my dreams?"

The rain had slowed enough that I could return to the road. "Right now let's just keep them to ourselves." Using my cell phone, I called information and asked to be connected to the sheriff's office. A voice answered: "This is Deputy Shades. How can I assist you?"

"I'd like to speak with Sheriff Moorehead," I explained.

"All calls this late at night are automatically put through to the deputy on night duty, which is me," Shades replied.

"The sheriff is at home and probably asleep. How can I help you?"

I told Shades that I was an attorney from Washington D.C. and that Moorehead had told me to call. But Shades was not impressed.

"Everyone claims the sheriff told them to call him personally," he explained. "Then they ask him something stupid that I could've answered. Now, how can I help you?"

"I used to be an FBI agent," I said. "This is about a possible kidnapping."

That must've impressed him. "Hang on," he replied. I could hear my name being repeated in the background over a two-way radio. Deputy Shades was describing me as a former FBI agent and Washington lawyer. He mentioned the word "kidnapping" and I grimaced. If Heather's abductor was monitoring a police scanner, we'd just lost the element of surprise.

"The sheriff wants to know who's been 'kidnapped,'" Shades said.

"Tell him I'm not going to discuss it on my cell phone or by relaying messages through a police radio. Tell him to meet me at the courthouse in twenty minutes."

Shades relayed my message. "The sheriff will be there in thirty minutes, but he isn't real happy about it," Shades replied.

It didn't take us long to reach the town square. "There's Lester Alfred's drugstore," Melanie noted, as we circled the block. His business was located inside a two-story, brownstone building with two large display windows facing the street and four narrow windows on its second floor. Since we were ahead of schedule, I parked the SUV in front of the store. A sign on the entrance listed its operating hours. Directly beneath it, stenciled in gold leaf, was: LESTER ALFRED, OWNER AND LICENSED PHARMACIST.

"It's pretty obvious that we have two prime suspects: Jeb Rogge and Lester Alfred," I said. "One or both of them kidnapped Heather."

"But the Reverend Carter said Alfred had asked for forgiveness and wasn't a racist anymore."

"And that's exactly why I'm suspicious of him. Everyone seems to know that Jeb Rogge is a racist. He's proud of it. But Alfred wouldn't have wanted Heather digging up his past."

I glanced up at the second-floor apartment windows, which was where Carter had said Alfred lived. All four were dark.

"He's either sleeping or out running around," I said.

I backed the SUV from the parking spot and drove to the Rabbit Creek Park side of the courthouse. A full-sized white Ford sedan already was parked there in front of a sign that said: SHERIFF ONLY. I slipped into the spot beside it even though a sign warned: SHERIFF'S VEHICLES ONLY— ALL OTHERS TOWED. As soon as I had switched off the ignition, a cruiser with its red and blue lights flashing zoomed in behind us, pinning in our SUV. A high-powered spotlight blinded us from behind.

"Step away from your car so I can see both of your hands," a voice ordered from a loudspeaker attached to the cruiser. I assumed this was Deputy Shades.

We did as told and faced the high beam. The next voice I heard was Sheriff Moorehead's. He had been waiting in the courthouse's shadows and had now walked up behind us.

"It's okay," he called.

The spotlight went dark.

"This how you greet all your visitors?" I asked, slowly turning around. It took a moment for my eyes to adjust. Moorehead was cradling a twelve-gauge pump shotgun in his arms.

"When you're a black sheriff in Mississippi and you get a call late at night from white strangers, this is exactly how you do it," he replied.

We fell in behind Moorehead, who entered the courthouse through a side door. I wondered if this was the doorway that the Rogges and Alfreds had used when they forced Lamar Grant across the street and into the park to be lynched. The courthouse smelled of Pine-Sol floor cleaner. Moorehead stepped into his office, which was a modest operation filled with standard-issue metal furniture.

I've always believed you can learn a lot about a person's personality by examining his office. We'd just left the Reverend Carter's house and the fact that he had decorated his walls with correspondence-school certificates suggested to me that he'd never earned a divinity degree from a theological college. Carter was clearly a fundamentalist preacher who'd answered the "call." As for me, I kept my office intentionally bare. Only one picture hangs on the wall. It's a "grip and grin" shot of me shaking hands with my famous boss. There are two other framed documents, one on each side of the photo. One is a copy of my law degree. The other is a certificate from the FBI Academy. Those three items tell visitors everything they need to know about me.

I scanned Sheriff Moorehead's office walls. They were like a scrapbook. The Great Seal of Mississippi hung directly behind his desk. On the wall to our left were framed clippings about Moorehead's football career, including a cover from *Sports Illustrated* that showed him dodging tacklers. The headline read: *Running to Glory*. The wall to our right was decorated with law-enforcement mementos, including the front page from a local newspaper that showed Moorehead being sworn in. *First Black Sheriff Takes Office,* the headline read. Near that clipping was a sign:

THE PUSHMATAHA SHERIFF'S OFFICE DOES NOT DISCRIMINATE. BLACK, WHITE, OR BROWN— BREAK THE LAW AND YOUR ASS IS GOING TO JAIL.
Signed: Sheriff Jacob Moorehead.

Moorehead motioned us toward two gunmetal-gray chairs in front of his desk. He was wearing a black cotton T-shirt, blue jeans, and running shoes. There was a short-barreled .38 revolver tucked in a waistband holster and he had a toothpick jutting from one side of his mouth.

"Who's been kidnapped?" he asked as he settled in behind his desk.

"Heather Cole," I said.

He looked at Melanie.

"She isn't Heather," I said. "This is Melanie Cole, her twin sister."

Understandably, Moorehead looked confused.

I said: "Melanie, why don't you show the sheriff your driver's license?" She did.

"I'm the chief investigator for the Senate Judiciary Committee and Heather Cole is a personal friend of mine," I explained. "Ms. Melanie Cole asked me to come to Mississippi to help find her sister. We found blood this afternoon on the sheets in Heather's motel room."

"Blood? At the Holiday Inn?" he asked.

"No, at the Stars and Bars Motel."

"Heather Cole told me she was staying at the Holiday Inn," he replied.

"She was," Melanie volunteered. "But she was actually sleeping in a room at the Stars and Bars."

"Why'd she rent two rooms?" he asked. "And today, when we met in the park, was I talking to you or to Heather?"

"My sister rented two motel rooms because she was afraid of someone," Melanie replied.

"She checked in at the Stars and Bars under a false name and wearing a blonde wig as a disguise," I quickly added.

"What about my other question?" he asked. "Who did I see in the park this afternoon?"

"That was me," Melanie replied.

"You were pretending to be your sister?"

"Yes, we didn't tell you because we'd just gotten into town and—"

He finished her sentence for her: "And you didn't know if you could trust me?"

Moorehead glared at me and said: "You could've told me earlier that you used to work for the FBI and why you were in town. Instead you lied to me. You saw a black sheriff and you lied."

."This isn't about race," I said. "Obviously I made a mistake, but that's not important now. We've got to find Heather Cole." I quickly recapped how we had discovered that Heather had rented two rooms and the scene we'd encountered at the Stars and Bars.

He asked Melanie if she had a photograph of Heather. "Something," he said, "that shows the two of you together."

It was apparent that Moorehead wanted to make certain that Heather and Melanie were two different people. Melanie took a tattered snapshot from her pocketbook. "We were fourteen when this was taken," she explained, handing it to him.

Moorehead inspected the photograph and then returned it. "Your sister came into my office and introduced herself on Monday. She said she was going to write a book about the 1955 lynching of Lamar Grant. She asked me if I knew who was responsible for his death. Of course I did. Everyone in the black community knows the names behind the initials carved into the trophy tree." He looked at me. "Where'd you find blood in the Stars and Bars?" he asked.

"On the pillows and sheets."

Moorehead turned to Melanie and asked: "And you have no clue where she might be right now?"

"She's being held in a dark place. She's been beaten too. And she's scared. She's trying to find a way to escape!"

"How do you know she's in a dark spot and has been beaten?" he asked.

I braced myself.

Melanie said: "Because Heather told me what had happened."

"She told you she'd been kidnapped?"

"Yes, but not in the normal way. Heather and I are identical twins. Sometimes we dream the same dream. Sometimes we talk to each other in them . . . you know, share things."

"She told you in a dream that she'd been kidnapped?" Moorehead asked.

I interrupted: "Why don't you inspect the crime scene, Sheriff? How Melanie knew that her sister had been kidnapped really isn't a priority. We've got to find Heather before her abductor harms her."

Moorehead rose from his chair and leaned forward, placing his massive knuckles on the desk surface. "Oh, I'll take a look at that motel room, all right, but I'm warning both of you right now, if this is some sort of publicity stunt for a book, you'll be cooling your heels in our jail."

"I was skeptical too," I said, "when Melanie first contacted me, but everything she's told me about her premonitions and dreams has proven true."

Moorehead didn't appear convinced. "Both of you misled me today in the park. Now you've gotten me out of bed and dragged me down here to listen to some wild-ass story about how twins can talk to one another in their dreams. For all I know, you could've spent this afternoon staging her room to look like a crime scene!"

"We didn't do that!" Melanie shrieked. "Heather is missing! She needs to be rescued!"

"Sheriff," I said, "why would we lie about this?"

"Publicity. I don't know. Maybe you're part of some new reality television show that makes fun of Southern sheriffs."

"I'm sorry we lied to you!" Melanie blurted. "But we trust you now!"

"Yeah, but I'm not certain I trust either of you!" Moorehead said, looking directly at me. "If you're so sure she's been kidnapped, why haven't you contacted the FBI, especially since you used to be an agent?"

"The FBI can't just jump in," I replied. "It has to be invited into a case by a local law enforcement agency."

"That's crap!" Moorehead said, slapping the desktop. "The FBI has jurisdiction over all kidnap cases."

"Sheriff Moorehead," I replied in a purposely flat and well-controlled voice, "regardless of what you've been told, the FBI does not automatically have jurisdiction in kidnapping cases unless the victim is a child or the kidnappers have crossed state lines. Now, having explained the law to you, it's true, I could make some phone calls and get the FBI down here. But I don't want to do that just yet."

"Why not?" It was Melanie asking.

"Heather Cole's kidnapping would spark national headlines. No one can keep a secret in Washington, especially if it involves a famous person. You'd have reporters and television camera crews descending on Pushmataha like a swarm of flies on cow shit. Sheriff, do you want Geraldo Rivera doing a stand-up commentary outside the Stars and Bars with its faded Rebel-flag road sign? Do you want Mike Wallace staking out Jeb Rogge's house or bushwhacking Lester Alfred in his drugstore?"

Without waiting for Moorehead to answer, I said: "I haven't called the FBI because freeing Heather is my primary concern. I want to get her back alive." I paused to let both of them think about what I'd said. Then I added: "Sheriff, you know Jeb Rogge and Lester Alfred. They're the logical suspects."

"Assuming she's been kidnapped, what makes you think she's alive?" he asked.

"I can feel it," Melanie said. "But she's terrified."

"We know that Heather placed a call on her cell phone to Jeb Rogge's house on Wednesday afternoon," I said. "When did Rogge call you to complain about her?"

"Thursday afternoon. He threatened to shoot her if she showed up at his place again. I left a message warning Ms. Cole at the Holiday Inn but she never called me back."

"Do you think Rogge is capable of kidnapping someone?" I asked.

"Sure he is, especially if he thought it might scare her. That's how people like him think. They try intimidation, and if that doesn't work, then violence."

"Would he kill her?" Melanie asked.

"In a heartbeat."

"How about Lester Alfred?" I asked.

"He's an old man who made a mistake early on. I doubt he has the stomach for murder, but who really knows? Under the right circumstances, any of us might kill someone."

Moorehead removed the toothpick from his mouth and said: "Now I have a question for you. How do you know that Heather Cole called Rogge on her cell phone?"

"We have her cell phone," Melanie volunteered. "We found it on the floor in her motel room."

Moorehead shot me an angry look. "You contaminated a crime scene?"

I didn't reply.

"I'll want her phone," he said, "and anything else you might have taken out of that room." He started around his desk. "You two can follow me to the Stars and Bars. If it looks like Heather Cole was abducted there, then I'll launch an investigation and we can go see Jeb Rogge first thing in the morning."

"Why not right now?" Melanie asked.

"Because I'm not certain your sister has been kidnapped," he replied. "And Jeb Rogge is not the sort of man you surprise in the middle of the night."

We followed Moorehead in the SUV to the Stars and Bars. As soon as he looked inside and saw the blood on the sheets and pillowcases, he pulled the motel's door closed and locked it. "I'll have my deputy watch this room in an unmarked car until I can get a state forensic team here."

"Sheriff, I don't mind calling the FBI if you want their help," I said. "I'm just worried about the publicity."

Moorehead thought for a moment. "The only persons who might have wanted to kidnap your sister are Rogge and Alfred. We can confront both of them tomorrow. As soon as we do, they'll know we're on to them. So you might as well call the FBI now. I doubt if they can get here until late tomorrow."

"Can we put Rogge and Alfred under some sort of observation?" I asked. "There's a chance they might lead us to wherever Heather is being held hostage."

"I only have four deputies and one of them is sick right now. Another is a distant relative of Rogge's," Moorehead explained. "Let's meet at six a.m. at the courthouse. We'll take a cruiser so Rogge can't claim he didn't know who we are. He lives about a twenty-minute drive from town."

"But what if he hurts her tonight?" Melanie asked.

"Our chances of getting him to lead us to wherever she is will be better in the morning," Moorehead said. "Meanwhile, I don't want you two doing anything more without telling me first. You go back to your motel and stay put. Is that clear?"

On the drive to the Holiday Inn, I said: "Melanie, you can't stay in Heather's room at the Holiday Inn. The forensic team will want to search it along with the Stars and Bars' room."

She waited outside in the SUV while I went into the lobby to see if they had any rooms available. They still had one vacancy, but only that one. I paid and went outside with the key. Melanie had dozed off.

"Hey," I said, waking her. "I get to sleep in the SUV—you're stuck in the motel."

Still groggy, she didn't get my poor attempt at humor. When she did, she said: "I'm not spending a night alone in a motel room in this town. I'd feel safer if you were inside."

I carried in our suitcases while she disappeared in the bathroom. When she came out, she was wearing gray flannel sweatpants and a sweatshirt. Considering it was summer and we were in steamy Mississippi, I wondered if she was trying to send me a message.

"I always wear my sweats to bed," she announced, "because its gets chilly in the Black Hills at night year-round."

"Are you reading minds now?" I asked.

"I didn't want you to think I was wearing sweats because I'm afraid of you. I trust you."

"I'll curl up on the floor."

"No, you'll sleep on the double bed with me. We're both adults here. Besides, wasn't there an old Clark Gable movie where he hung a sheet down the center of a bed after he and some woman got stranded during a storm? Since I'm wearing my sweats, I'll sleep on top of the sheet. You can sleep underneath it."

"So we'll have a sheet between us?"

"Exactly," she replied. "Now, which side of the bed do you want?"

"I'd like the left side," I answered. Actually, I'd always preferred sleeping on the right, but after Heather left me I'd tried to break that habit. It was part of my attempt to get a fresh start.

"That's my favorite side too," she said.

"Then you take it," I replied gallantly.

She pulled back the bedspread. "I'm going to call my husband while you are in the bathroom. It's probably better if he doesn't hear your voice in the background. That way I don't need to explain why there's a man in my room."

I started for the bathroom door, but she called out: "Nick," and I stopped. It was the first time she'd called me by my first name.

"I want you to know how much I appreciate you coming down here with me," she said. "I'm really scared for Heather."

I went into the bathroom and stripped down to my boxers and T-shirt. I'd never spent the night in the same bed with a woman whom I wasn't already having sex with. This was going to be an unusual experience. Melanie had turned off the light, so I stumbled when I came out of the bathroom, but found the bed and got under the sheet. I was exhausted, but couldn't sleep. Instead, I listened to Melanie breathing. She was lying on her side with her back to me. I thought about everything that had happened since we'd arrived in Mississippi. *What am I missing? There's always something. You always miss a clue even though it's right in front of you!*

I thought about an old friend of mine named Eric. He was a magician and a missionary. He used his magic to entertain people while he gave them sermons. He told me once that children were the hardest to fool. Adults always looked for sophisticated explanations. Children saw a woman being levitated and asked: "Where's the wire?"

What am I not seeing here?

An hour passed and then another. My mind wandered. I thought about Heather. Why did she really leave? What had Andrew Middleton offered her that I hadn't? He was rich, but Heather had a fat trust fund. She didn't need his money.

I thought about Melanie. She was taking deep breaths now.

How many times had Heather and I made love? In the beginning, we couldn't keep our hands off each other. We coupled like rabbits. In the morning before we showered. At night, as soon as we returned from work. Once we couldn't wait and made love in her car in back of a restaurant where we had dinner guests waiting. But time had taken its toll. We got busy. We worked late. We were tired. Yet I'd never lost my desire for her. It was normal, right? A natural progression. We didn't have to make love every night, right?

The "whys" hounded me. Then came the "what ifs" and the "had onlys," as in "what if I had done . . ." and "if I had only said . . ."

This is how you torture yourself at night when you still love someone who doesn't love you—which actually was good, because I was already awake when Melanie screamed.

Eleven

Melanie's entire body was quivering. Her breath came in gulps.

"What happened?" I asked.

"A dream! I was in a desert. It was blistering hot. The sand was burning my feet and I was thirsty. There was nothing around me except for sand and the sun. I climbed this hill and when I reached the top, I could see a city."

We were both sitting on the bed now. I was still holding her shoulders with my hands. I had shaken her awake after she'd screamed.

"I need water," she said. I got her a cup. She was covered with perspiration.

"As soon as I saw the city, I was whisked there. Only I was naked. I was standing on a busy sidewalk. Yet no one seemed to notice that I was not wearing clothes. They were dressed and they just kept walking by as if I were invisible. It was a big city with skyscrapers, like Chicago or New York. I needed directions. I kept trying to stop people to ask, but none of them would acknowledge me. Then I heard someone calling my name. I looked around and saw this old man sitting on the curb. He was homeless, un-shaven, and had a crazed look. He pointed to an alley and laughed, and when he opened his mouth, all of his teeth were gone. It was daylight and the sky was a bright blue and there were white clouds above me and all of the people on the sidewalk suddenly put on sunglasses."

She took another swallow of water and asked me to refill her cup.

"I couldn't see their eyes now. I walked to where the old man had pointed and entered an alley. It led to a solid brick wall. The wall went so high I couldn't see where it ended. There were no doors, no windows. That's when I knew Heather was on the opposite side. I screamed to her but the wall was too thick."

Melanie stood and began pacing. She lit a cigarette, took four puffs, smashed it out, and lit another. She spit out her words in manic bursts as if she were afraid that she might forget them if she held on to them any longer.

"Suddenly I was no longer in the alley. I was still nude. But everything was pitch-black—so black I couldn't see where I was or what was around me. I couldn't stand up be-cause there was a ceiling above me. I was forced to lie on my back. I was trying to decide what to do when I heard whimpering, like a scared child. When I turned to my right, I saw Heather. She was about ten feet away and she was drenched with water and she was naked too. Only her body was covered with mud and her hair was clumped to-gether with grime. She was digging a hole like a wild ani-mal and when she saw me, she said: 'Hurry, Melanie: There's no more time!' I asked: 'Where are you?' And she stopped digging and said: 'Under a hunting cabin in the woods.' Then she held up two fingers and said: 'There's two of them, Melanie, not just one!' "

"Wait," I said, interrupting her. "She told you two per-sons kidnapped her?"

"Yes, she said there were two."

"Did she tell you their names?"

"No." She began telling me again about her dream. "I said to Heather: 'Hang on! We'll find you! We're coming!' and she said: 'Who?' I said: 'Nick came with me. He's here.' And she smiled. As soon as she heard your name, she smiled. Then she said: 'Got to dig. Hurry! He's coming back!' "

Melanie went to the sink and splashed cold water on her face. Without any sign of embarrassment, she removed her sweatshirt, used a wet washcloth to wipe off her neck, shoulders, and chest, then reached down into her suitcase and got out a bra, which she put on. She turned and faced me, wearing only her bra and sweatpants. "I've never seen my sister as petrified as she was," she continued. "Her skin was so white she seemed translucent. Her eyes were swollen and her pupils were red dots—like what happens when you take flash photographs. Heather looked at me and she was crying and she said, 'Melanie, they knew where I was staying! Do you understand what that means? He told them!' "

Melanie dashed into the bathroom. I heard her vomit. When she came out, she washed off her face again and sat down on the bed.

"I can feel her fear. Even now. Being held under that cabin was like being buried in a coffin. I was suffocating. I tried to scream but nothing came out."

"Oh, your scream came out!" I said.

"No, the scream you heard came later." She paused. "There was more to my dream. After Heather disappeared, I was in the desert again and completely alone. Only this time I was dressed. I was wearing a black dress, and I had on black gloves. I remember thinking: *Shouldn't they be white?* Then I saw something in the sky, far away at first, but coming closer to me. Closer and closer and closer. It flew until it almost reached me. There was a tree, not a tree with green leaves, but a dead tree. It had only a few branches. It was sticking out of the desert and that's where this creature landed. I saw that it was a bird and I moved closer and recognized it. It was an owl. It was daytime and hot, but the owl was wide awake and it looked down at me with its dead black eyes. That's when I screamed and when you began shaking me."

She lit a cigarette.

"What do you think it means?" I asked.

She thought for several moments and then said: "When Heather and I were little, the researchers talked to us a lot about our dreams. They said dreams were one way our subconscious mind communicates with our conscious mind."

"You make it sound as if each of us has two separate brains."

"In a sense, we do. The subconscious and conscious minds speak different languages. The conscious mind uses words, language. But the subconscious uses symbols. Most dreams are about our fears or troubles. I think this dream was about searching for Heather. I remember the researchers telling us that a desert symbolizes feelings of isolation, of being alone. Being naked is fairly common. It usually means you feel vulnerable. Those people in that big city who were ignoring me, I'm guessing that has to do with you and others not believing Heather and I can talk to each other in our dreams."

"What about your encounter with Heather?" I asked. "Was it symbolic or did she mean exactly what she said to you?"

"Heather was part of this dream, but, in another way, her appearance had nothing to do with it."

"Now you've lost me."

"My dream was a channel for her, a way for her to appear and speak to me. I told you earlier that twins often think the same thoughts, share the same feelings, even get the same symptoms when one has a cold. Do you realize how little scientists and doctors really know about our brains? Take mental illness. The truth is that no one knows what causes schizophrenia. Twenty years ago, psychiatrists blamed mothers. It was their fault. Now they claim schizophrenia is caused by a chemical imbalance. But there are some researchers who are convinced it might be caused by a germ spread by household cats. Can you imagine that?"

I didn't understand what schizophrenia had to do with Melanie's dream and she sensed my confusion.

"My point is that researchers really don't understand how or why our brains operate. This is especially true about twins: Heather and I came from exactly the same egg and exactly the same sperm. We're as identical as two separate human beings can be. That means we have identical brains. Obviously, we have had different experiences during our lives, but on some rudimentary level, we still share the exact same thoughts. Put simply, Heather will always be inside me and I will always be inside her. That's why we can communicate even when we're sleeping. I can't really explain it any better."

She got herself another cup of water and drank it. Now that she had cooled off, she pulled her sweatshirt back on.

"Heather told me that she's being held under a cabin, somewhere wet and dark. That's what she said. She is naked and is digging, trying to escape. I guess she is digging a tunnel."

"She told you that two persons kidnapped her."

"No, she said two were involved. She also said they knew where to find her at the Stars and Bars. That's significant. She was upset. It must mean someone betrayed her. But who?"

I said: "Tonight's hard rain: Could that be why she's wet and muddy?"

"I think so. I think she's being held in a hunting cabin somewhere close to Pushmataha."

"Jeb Rogge wasn't home tonight and we didn't see any lights in Lester Alfred's apartment windows."

Melanie seemed distracted.

"Do you know what an owl symbolizes in a dream?" she asked.

"Wisdom?" I guessed. "Isn't that what owls always symbolize?"

"Not among Native Americans, especially the Lakota."

"The who?"

"Lakota. They live on reservations near the Black Hills in South Dakota where I live," she said. "Have you ever seen a fully grown great horned owl? It's a terrifying creature. It's the only bird that can outfly a golden eagle. Its talons are as big as the paws of a baby mountain lion. It eats fresh meat. It can swoop down from the sky with lightning speed and tremendous force, and stick its claws into a heavy target and carry it off."

"I never thought of an owl as being a fierce bird."

"It is. The Lakota believe in what they call 'power animals.' Each beast represents different skills. The owl has the ability to see the truth; it can see behind the masks that people always wear. But that's not the attribute that caused me to scream."

All of this talk about dreams, the subconscious and conscious minds, schizophrenia, and now Native American symbolism and owls, was becoming overwhelming. "What caused you to scream?" I asked.

"Owls hunt at night and rarely appear during the day. When they do, the Lakota believe it's because they are carrying an important message. They believe the owl is the only creature alive with the ability to fly between the dark, unseen world and our world of light."

"What exactly are you saying, Melanie?"

"The owl means death! The owl in my dream was an omen. Heather is going to be murdered this morning unless we find her first. We've got to call Sheriff Moorehead now!"

I checked my watch. It was 4:35 a.m. We were scheduled to meet him at six. He wasn't going to like being awakened this early, but Melanie refused to listen to reason. While she took a quick shower and tried to calm down, I telephoned the sheriff's office.

"You again!" Deputy Shades said. "Let me guess, you want to disturb the sheriff. You'll be waking him up, you know."

"It's another emergency," I said. "Tell him to call me at the Holiday Inn." I gave him our room number.

"What's wrong?" Moorehead asked when he called minutes later. He sounded more concerned than irked.

"Melanie had another dream," I said. "Heather's going to be murdered this morning unless we find her fast."

The line was quiet.

"Sheriff," I said, "I know this sounds crazy but I believe her. She's been right so far. In this dream, Heather was being held in a hunting cabin in the woods."

"A hunting cabin?"

"That's right. She's under the floorboards. You know such a place?"

"Yes," Moorehead replied. "Jeb Rogge has a hunting cabin and there's a crawl space under the floor."

"How do you know that?"

"I've been under that cabin, in that crawl space," he replied. "How long before you're ready to go?"

I no longer heard the shower running. Melanie had finished.

We'll meet you at the courthouse in a half hour," I said. "And, Sheriff, thanks."

When Melanie emerged, I noticed her hands were trembling.

"What did Moorehead say?" she asked.

"He was skeptical until I mentioned the hunting cabin and the crawl space. It seems Jeb Rogge has a hunting cabin with a crawl space under it."

"I can feel Heather's fear," Melanie said. "We've got to get to her now!"

Twelve

We parked our rental at the courthouse. Sheriff Moorehead handed us each a Kevlar vest. Melanie's was too large. She looked like a baseball umpire. The sheriff led us to a police cruiser. Melanie sat in the front seat while I sat in the back.

"I've known Jeb Rogge all my life," Moorehead said. "He's unpredictable, which makes him extremely dangerous. His wife, Julie, is the one with brains, but she's as racist as he is. Either of you want to change your mind about tagging along?"

"I'm not afraid," Melanie said. "Why don't we go directly to his hunting cabin?"

"We'd have to drive onto his land and by his house to get there," Moorehead replied. "I don't think saying you saw your sister in a dream is sufficient 'probable cause' to justify a search warrant. Let's talk to Rogge first and then decide what to do."

We were riding in a well-marked sheriff's car, rather

than the unmarked unit that Moorehead normally drove. "Last year," Moorehead continued, "one of my deputies came across an abandoned car on the state road that passes through Rogge's property. It had a flat tire. When we ran the plates, we discovered it was registered to a young black woman from Jackson. Apparently she'd wandered off the interstate and gotten lost. We searched the area for weeks but never found her."

"You think Rogge grabbed her?" Melanie asked.

"I think he did something to her. Of course, he acted real concerned and called me several times with clues. You could tell he was just enjoying the hell out of sending me on wild goose chases. At the time, he was doing excavation work at his home. He told us he was building a concrete bunker for the race war that he says is coming. I've always wondered if that poor black woman is buried under his bunker's concrete floor."

The two-lane blacktop that we were riding on cut through seemingly endless acres of pine trees. Moorehead slowed when we reached a rusty steel bridge. The creek under it was about to overflow its banks because of last night's downpour.

"The turnoff to Rogge's house is exactly two-tenths of a mile from the center of this bridge," Moorehead explained. "It's not paved and it's intentionally not marked. He gets his mail in town because he doesn't want a mailbox on the road here signaling where he lives."

We'd already passed several tracks that broke away from the highway sporadically and disappeared into the woods. Some looked as if they hadn't been driven on in years. Moorehead had explained that the ruts had been made by heavy trucks as they followed logging teams into the forests to haul away timber. We hadn't seen another car on the asphalt for several miles. "It seems awfully isolated out here," I said.

"The interstate made this highway obsolete," Moorehead replied. "It used to be the only road that connected

Pushmataha and a tiny town forty miles north. Rogge and his relatives own several thousand acres of prime forest around here and this road jigsaws back and forth across their property."

"Racism and hatred must pay well," I said.

"Old man Rogge made a fortune extorting white businesses during the sixties when he ran the Klan. Everyone but the Peterman family kowtowed to him. Jeb and his wife run one of those Aryan hate sites on the Internet. I'm not certain how much they earn but they're obviously getting enough to get by very comfortably. No one has ever seen either of them work steady at a regular job."

Moorehead slowed the cruiser to a crawl when the odometer showed we had traveled exactly two-tenths of a mile. He gently edged off the highway onto a bed of still-wet pine needles. I was afraid we'd get stuck in the wet ground, but the needles covered a hard road that would have been impossible for motorists traveling the highway's speed limit to have seen. The cruiser entered the forest gingerly but didn't get far. A fallen branch blocked the path. Moorehead dragged the branch to the side. When he returned to the squad car, he flipped on its red and blue flashing lights. "Every time I've been out here, that branch is blocking the path," he said.

Another fifty yards into the forest, we reached gravel. Fifty yards farther, the cruiser's wheels rolled onto pavement again.

"Oh, no!" Melanie exclaimed.

Directly in front of us was a four-by-eight-foot plywood sign.

TURN AROUND!
PRIVATE ROAD!
TRESPASORS WILL BE SHOT!

"It gets better," Moorehead said. He called his dispatcher over the car's radio. "We're about two miles from Rogge's house. Give 'em a call and tell 'em to expect company."

A quarter of a mile farther down the road, we reached a second billboard.

NIGARS, JEWS, FAGOTS,
AND MIX BLOOD MONGRELS
TURN AROUND OR DIE!

It was obvious that none of the Rogges knew how to spell.

A few feet farther down the road was a smaller sign that read: AMERICA THE BEAUTIFUL, only the letter "c" in "America" had been replaced with a swastika.

Moorehead spoke into his two-way radio. "You get a response?"

"No one answered."

"Try again."

Moorehead slowed. Another two hundred yards into the forest, the trees thinned and we soon entered a clearing. I'd expected to see a shanty surrounded by junk cars and a barbed-wire fence. But Rogge's compound was striking. A two-story log cabin with a dark green metal roof sat in the center of this man-made meadow. The house had a wrap-around porch with four rocking chairs sitting peacefully next to its front door. There were red, white, and blue annuals in window boxes near the chairs, giving the house a patriotic flair. About twenty yards to the right of the main house was a smaller, one-story log home with a bright red metal roof and smoke drifting slowly from its chimney. A covered walkway and brick sidewalk linked the two cabins. Set a few yards back from the bigger cabin was a two-story barn, painted dark green. It had a satellite dish attached to its roof. A Mercedes-Benz ML 500 SUV and an ancient Willys Jeep were parked at the barn's entrance.

"There's his bunker," Moorehead said, pointing to the right of the smaller cabin. It took me several moments to spot because the bunker had been painted in camouflage and blended with the trees behind it. The aboveground portion was circular and rose about seven feet high. Narrow slits had been strategically cut to give its occupants a 360-degree view.

"Your sister might be locked inside that bunker," Moorehead said.

"No," Melanie replied. "Heather told me that she was under the floors of a 'hunting cabin' and there was water leaking in around her."

An American flag was flying from a pole in the front yard, but the Rogges had raised it upside down, a sign of distress.

Moorehead edged the cruiser toward the main house and switched on the car's siren, letting it whoop three times. Four Doberman pinschers bolted toward us. Two threw themselves against the driver's-side window, showing bared teeth. The third peered at Melanie, while the fourth locked its eyes on me.

Moorehead spoke through the cruiser's loudspeaker. "Jeb, this is Sheriff Moorehead. I need to speak to you." No one appeared, so Moorehead turned on the siren and let it whoop five more times, a move that drove the dogs into even more of a frenzy.

Still, no one showed themselves.

Moorehead sighed and then spoke again over the loudspeaker: "Either pen your damn dogs or I'll spray 'em!" He turned a knob on the radio and spoke to his dispatcher. "Anyone answer the phone?"

"Yep, someone picked up, but hung up as soon as I identified myself," the dispatcher said. "There's definitely someone inside the main house."

Moorehead decided to give Rogge one final warning over the loudspeaker: "I'm going to spray the dogs if you don't call 'em off."

He removed a canister of pepper spray from the glove box and slowly lowered his window about an inch. The Doberman there banged its head against the glass as it tried to push his snout through the opening. Leaning back to protect himself from any splash, Moorehead held the canister only an inch from the dog's teeth and shot a narrow stream directly into its nostrils. The Doberman yelped in pain and fell backward onto the driveway, startling the other three dogs. It whacked at its nose with its paws as it stumbled blindly toward the grass in front of the cabins. I saw a door in the smaller cabin burst open and a teenage boy run toward the howling dog. "He's gassed Midnight!" the youth screamed. A younger girl followed from the cabin and the other dogs joined them on the front lawn.

"Stay here!" Moorehead ordered. He opened his door and stood up. Speaking into the cruiser's loudspeaker, he said: "C'mon, Jeb. Let's do this the easy way!"

The three dogs turned to look at him, but none attacked. They were distracted by their whining cohort. A woman in her late forties stepped from the large cabin's front door onto the porch.

"She's wearing Laura Ashley!" Melanie exclaimed. I was just as surprised. I'd expected Julie Rogge to be a tough-talking, hardened slug. Instead, she was a tiny, neat woman who looked as if she could have been a school's PTA president.

"Jeb isn't here, Sheriff," Julie Rogge announced. "And there was no need for you to use pepper spray on my dog. I was about to have our son call them off."

"Where's Jeb?"

"I'm not sure," she answered. "He's out huntin'." She looked at her son, who was trying to soothe the Doberman. "If that dog is blind," Julie Rogge said, "the county will have to replace it, and trained guard dogs ain't cheap!"

"He'll be fine after the spray wears off. Wash him with a hose."

"I'm not talking about physical injuries," she snapped. "I'm talking about psychological damage."

Sheriff Moorehead ignored her complaint. "I'm going to take your word, Julie, and assume Jeb isn't hiding somewhere inside."

Moorehead climbed back into the car and began to back it away from the cabin. As he turned the cruiser around, the three dogs who'd been watching once again attacked the car. I watched Rogge's girl, who was probably eleven, as she gave me the finger.

Moorehead told his dispatcher: "Make a note in the log that I was forced to use pepper spray on one of their dogs after I warned their owners repeatedly to pen them. I'm certain Jeb will file a complaint."

"How can you be sure he wasn't hiding inside?" I asked. "Do you really trust that woman?"

"Rogge drives a white Ford Bronco and I didn't see it parked outside the barn," he replied. Moorehead spoke to his dispatcher again. "Also make a note in the file that Julie Rogge specifically told us Jeb was hunting. Based on that information, I've decided we have just cause to continue on and drive to his hunting cabin."

"Didn't it burn down a few years ago after it got hit by lightning?" the dispatcher asked.

"I'll let you know after we get there," Moorehead replied. He put down his radio microphone and said: "My dispatcher, the fellow who I was just talking with—he's Jeb Rogge's cousin. We played football together in high school. He hates Jeb even more than me."

At the edge of the clearing, Moorehead turned the cruiser north onto another barely visible path. The terrain was turning rocky and I again worried that the car would get stuck, but Moorehead pushed forward.

"How come you know where Rogge's hunting cabin is?" Melanie asked.

"Because my daddy built it and I helped him when I was a kid."

Melanie and I exchanged glances. "The Rogges hired your father?"

"He was the best craftsman in Pushmataha when it came to building log cabins. Besides, whites around here don't mind hiring blacks to do manual labor—as long as the whites are the ones in charge. My mama was against it, but my daddy thought he might be able to help educate Rogge and dampen his racist views."

"What happened?" Melanie asked.

"The Rogges tried to cheat him out of what they'd promised to pay. They claimed we'd done shoddy work."

"So you've actually been inside this cabin?" I asked.

"Inside, outside, on the roof, and, more importantly, I know where the trap door is to the crawl space. I used to hide down there whenever the Rogges came to see Daddy."

As we continued up a steep hill, I heard the bottom of the cruiser scraping against rocks and noticed Melanie's face had become pale and her forehead sparkled with sweat.

"You feeling okay?" I asked.

She shook her head, indicating that she wasn't.

"Do we need to stop?" I asked. "Are you going to be sick?"

"No," she whispered, and then, without warning, she clutched her chest, fell forward, and cried: "Aghhhhh!"

Moorehead slammed on the brakes.

I reached over from the back seat, grabbed Melanie by her shoulders, and gently pulled her upright. She was conscious, but she was breathing rapidly.

"It's Heather!" Melanie said. "He's hurting her! I can feel it! Hurry! Quick!"

Thirteen

ey, bitch! Nigger-lover," he yelled. "I'm letting your sorry white ass go! Come here. You're free to leave!"

There was no answer from under the hunting cabin's floor.

"I ain't gonna hurt you. I promise. I'm letting you loose."

No reply. No movement.

"Listen, bitch!" he exclaimed. "You need to get your dumb white ass over here or I'm going to lock this goddamn trap door and forget you're down there! Don't make me come get you!"

Only silence.

Continuing to spew expletives, the man dropped to his knees onto the cabin floor, switched on a flashlight, and, bracing himself with his left hand, ducked his head into the trap door hole to look for her.

Heather wasn't there.

He quickly scanned the crawl space with his light.

"Shit!" he shrieked. "What the hell?"

He dropped through the trap door. His boots made a *thuck* when they hit the mud. With his flashlight grasped in his left hand, he reached behind his back with his right hand and withdrew a .22-caliber, western-style revolver. He scanned the cabin's underbelly again, moving the light beam slowly in front of him as if it were a prison searchlight.

Nothing. She was gone!

The only items underneath the cabin were the plastic tub, empty water bottles, and the KFC chicken bucket that he had brought her. They were strewn on the mud about ten feet away from him. One bottle was on its side, the others were half buried in mud, and the paper bucket was upside down.

He used the discarded items as his starting mark and once again, he swept his flashlight beam over the mud and up and down the concrete footings, searching every inch of the crawl space.

How could she have escaped? It didn't make sense!

He moved the light methodically clockwise, and when he had gone full circle, he simply stared at the pile of trash, wondering what to do next. No tunnel. No opening in the footings. No broken floorboards. No way out! Yet she was gone!

Someone must've freed her! Who? Why?

He heard a vehicle outside.

Had his partner let her go? Had he gotten cold feet?

Still holding his pistol, he climbed from under the floor and stepped to the cabin's front door just in time to see a figure walking from the trees toward him.

Heather had been afraid to twitch. The entire time that he had been looking for her with his flashlight, she'd been within ten feet of him. Only she'd been invisible. Had he looked under the KFC bucket, he would've seen her mud-caked face. Unable to escape, Heather Cole had buried herself, much like an animal burrowing into the ground. She'd dug the hole during the night's rainstorm, carefully patting the mud in front of the hole into a slight incline.

When she'd heard him coming, she'd slid into her soggy

grave and frantically pulled the muck over her body. The incline had helped create an optical illusion. She'd used her teeth and head to flip the KFC bucket over her face. Everything else had been buried.

It worked!

She rose quickly now, a mud-splattered zombie rising from the ground. She crawled to the trap door. He'd not bothered to lock it. She didn't care that her body was still caked with grime. She glanced up, half expecting him to be waiting there for her. But he wasn't.

Mustering her courage, Heather slowly raised her head through the opening, and saw for the first time exactly what was above her. The trap door opened into the middle of a one-room cabin that was missing half of its roof. The shingles and rafters above her looked burned, like black spears of charcoal.

But above them was the blue morning sky.

The room was littered with discarded beer cans and charred wood that had fallen from the ceiling. Glinting in the debris were shards of green and brown bottles and spent red shotgun shell and brass rifle casings. There was a window to her left, but the glass was busted out. The front door—the only entrance and exit—was ten feet on her right and was shut. Because she'd been buried, she'd not heard the vehicle approaching the cabin. She assumed her kidnapper was searching outside for her.

Got to get out now, before he returns!

She climbed from the hole onto the wooden floorboards.

Keep moving! He'll be back!

She moved to the window and peeked outside. A white Ford Bronco was parked at the back of the cabin to her left but no one was inside it. *Voices! Men! Arguing! Outside!* On her right. Moving now. Heather stood, still naked, and tiptoed to the front door. She tried the knob. It turned.

"You crazy? I didn't drive out here and let her loose this morning!" she heard a stranger's voice declare.

"Well, the bitch is gone!"

"You sure?"

"Look for yourself!"

There was nowhere to hide in the cabin. She looked for a weapon. None. She could still hear them speaking, but couldn't make out the words. They were moving clockwise around the cabin, walking toward the white Bronco.

Go now!

Taking a deep breath, she jerked open the door and burst through it—falling face-first forward. The cabin's entrance was two feet above the ground and she'd missed the two cinder blocks that Rogge had stacked there for steps. As she fell, she heard a noise. A loud pop. Brown pine needles cushioned her fall, but she still hit hard, landing with her hands outstretched. Pain shot through her palms and rib cage, which was still sore from the beating he'd given her.

Got to run! Hurry!

She scrambled to her feet and ran toward the trees only a dozen yards away. Her bare feet sent the wet needles flying behind her as her toes dug into the moist soil. Clumps of mud fell from her still-damp skin. She was shedding her chameleon skin. She ran as she had never run before. And she didn't stop until she was fifty yards into the trees. Steadying herself against a tree's rough bark, she turned to see if anyone was chasing her.

No! Not yet!

She studied the cabin. The white Ford was still parked there. But she couldn't see either man.

Where am I? Does it matter? You're free! Run! Hard! Fast! Anywhere! Find a highway! Get a ride! Call the police! But for now: Run! Run! Run!

The miles she'd logged over the years jogging were paying off. Despite the pain in her abdomen, she kept at a steady pace. Her bare feet hit sharp rocks, but they didn't slow her. *I'm free!*

Her mind tried to make sense of what had happened. She'd heard the men argue. They had started toward the Bronco. She'd burst through the doorway. The sound. The popping noise. What was it? A gunshot. Yes, she was sure. But wait! There was more. Rewind the tape. What had she heard? His voice. That's it! She'd heard the stranger's voice before! She recognized it! Oh, God! She'd first heard it in Washington! Oh, God! It was him! How could it be? But it was!

Fourteen

"There's Rogge's Ford Bronco," Sheriff Moorehead said as he inched the cruiser toward the hunting cabin. No one was in sight outside the charred cabin.

"Can you tell if Heather is here?" I asked Melanie, who was still struggling to catch her breath.

"No!" she gasped.

Moorehead parked at the narrowest gap between two trees to prevent Rogge from fleeing down the makeshift road. "Let's see if we can rouse him," he said, opening the car door. "You stay put."

"No way," I replied, stepping from the car.

Using the driver's door as a shield, Moorehead spoke into the cruiser's loudspeaker. "Jeb Rogge, this is Sheriff Moorehead. Show yourself!"

Nothing.

The cabin door was closed. We were about thirty feet from it. Moorehead looked at me and asked: "Ready?"

"Almost." I raised my pant leg and removed a .38 short-barreled revolver from its ankle holster.

Moorehead seemed surprised. "I've got a permit," I explained.

"Does everyone from Washington, D.C., carry handguns?"

I wasn't certain what he meant by that remark but didn't want to waste time asking. Instead, we began moving forward toward the cabin. Because there were no windows on the front, Rogge would have to come through the door if he wanted to shoot at us. But if he was already hiding in the trees, we would be easy targets.

About ten feet from the cabin, we bolted forward and threw ourselves against its wall, one of us on each side of the door. Moorehead rapped on it.

"Jeb, come out!" he yelled. "This is the sheriff. We need to talk!"

Nothing. Moorehead tried the knob. The door was unlocked. He pushed it open a crack. "Jeb?" he called. No response.

He whispered: "I'll go through first. You back me up." Before I could reply, Moorehead shoved the door and bounded through. The cabin was empty.

"There!" he yelled, pointing toward the floor. I saw an open trap door. Moorehead aimed his shotgun at it.

"Heather!" I called. "It's Nick, Nick LeRue. Melanie is outside. Are you down there? Are you hurt?"

There was no answer, so I looked down through the trap door. I couldn't see anything. I dropped into the black hole. It took my eyes a few moments to adjust.

"No one's here, but someone's been digging," I yelled. I crawled toward a hole. There was something white sticking out. *Please God! Not Heather!* I reached down and tugged on the white material, half expecting to find a body under it. Instead, the material pulled free from the muck. It was a RACE FOR THE CURE T-shirt. A pair of women's underwear was buried there too. I took both, even though I knew this was a crime scene.

Moorehead was waiting for me. "These have to be Heather's," I said, flopping the wet and muddy T-shirt and panties onto the cabin's floor. "She definitely was being held hostage here. I pulled these from a hole big enough for a body. But it was empty."

"Let's look around outside."

We hustled out the door. "I'll go left," I said. "You go right. Don't shoot me when we meet at the back of the cabin by the Bronco!"

Moorehead darted around the corner. As I rounded the cabin, I thought again about how we were easy targets, especially for an experienced hunter hiding in the woods armed with a deer rifle. I was only a few steps away from reaching the Bronco when I heard Moorehead shout: "I've found him!"

Rather than backtrack, I raced around the back of the cabin. "It's me—don't shoot!" I yelled as I spun around the corner.

Moorehead was squatting next to a tree trunk, off to the side of the cabin. A man was sitting on the ground with his back leaning against the trunk. His head was hanging down. His unshaven chin was resting on his chest.

"Nick LeRue," Moorehead said, as he stood. "Say hello to the recently departed Jeb Rogge."

Although Rogge had aged, I still could see several features that resembled the child's face from the photograph of the lynching. He was wearing a red baseball cap with a Peterman Lumber Company logo on its front. There was a small hole on the right side of his head just under the cap's edge. Rogge was holding a .22-caliber revolver in his right hand. Although his pistol was not nearly as powerful as a larger-caliber handgun, it was an effective killer. During the 1970s, it was a favorite of Mafia hit men because it was quiet, ammunition was cheap and easy to find, and the slugs were often difficult to trace, especially hollow-point rounds which mushroomed upon contact.

"I don't think he's been dead long," Moorehead said. "Funny, it looks like he shot himself."

"Suicide?" I replied skeptically. "Why would Rogge shoot himself?"

"Maybe he finally realized what a miserable shit he was," Moorehead replied. "One thing for sure, he won't be missed by many around here."

"Melanie said there were two kidnappers," I replied.

Moorehead gave me a doubtful look and said: "Yeah, but that was based on a dream, not fact."

"Hey," I replied, defending her, "she was right about Heather being held under the floor of this hunting cabin. There could still be someone watching us from the woods. His partner."

"I don't see any footprints. And we didn't see any other vehicles when we came up the road. It's the only way up here."

I cupped my hands around my mouth and yelled: "Heather! Heather Cole! It's Nick LeRue! You out there? Rogge's dead! You can come out of hiding now!"

We waited for several moments, but there wasn't any response.

"Let's do a quick search," Moorehead suggested. We used Rogge's body and the tree stump as our starting point and walked around the cabin clockwise. I kept at the edge of the trees. Moorehead walked ten feet farther in. Near the end of our sweep, I spotted several clumps of mud that were the same color and texture as what I'd seen in the hunting cabin's crawl space.

"This came from someone who's been under the cabin," I said. I cupped my hands and yelled for Heather again.

"We're gonna need dogs," Moorehead replied. "Let's seal off this area before we contaminate it."

"How good is your forensic team?" I asked him.

"I got two deputies who attended one-week courses at the FBI Academy in Virginia," he replied. "But don't worry, I was going to call in the state boys. Still, if you want to make some calls to your people in Washington, be my guest."

"I'll use my cell. It's in the cruiser," I said. We started walking toward the car.

"I've got a pal at the Mississippi Corrections Department whose dogs can hunt down any living thing or person. If

Heather Cole ran off in these woods or her body was taken somewhere and hidden, these dogs will find her."

I suddenly noticed that Melanie wasn't in the cruiser's front seat.

"Melanie!" I hollered. I started running toward the car. "Melanie!"

"There she is!" Moorehead yelled.

Melanie was standing about fifty feet in front of us in the woods.

"You scared me!" I said, when I reached her. "Did you see something?"

She was looking up. Now she turned and stared into my eyes. Both of her still-pale cheeks glistened in the morning sunshine. They were wet with tears. She didn't speak, she simply turned her head and looked upward again. I followed her eyes, searching the tree limbs above us, wondering what she had seen. I finally saw it perched near the very top of the tree, peering down at us. A few moments ticked by before I recognized what I was seeing. A few more passed before I understood why Melanie was so upset.

"It's an owl," she said, "like in my dream! Heather's dead!"

Fifteen

Phillip Shurman, the FBI's liaison officer on Capitol Hill, and I were close enough friends that I had his number in my cell phone directory. I caught him just as he was about to begin running his Saturday morning errands.

"Heather Cole was kidnapped? Jesus Christ! This will be as big as the Chandra Levy case!" he gushed, referring to the former Capitol Hill intern who disappeared while jogging. For months, the media hinted that a married California congressman, who supposedly had had a personal relationship with her, was responsible for her disappearance. Her bones were later discovered in a park where a drifter had attacked and killed another young woman.

"We'll fly a team down today," Shurman promised. "Meanwhile, keep the locals from touching anything, and I do mean *anything*! I'll call our agent in Jackson as soon as we hang up and get him to Pushmataha."

While I was speaking to Shurman, Sheriff Moorehead was giving his dispatcher instructions over the cruiser's two-way radio. After we finished, Moorehead said: "I've got a deputy on his way to guard the crime scene. Another deputy is going to seal Heather Cole's two motel rooms."

"I don't want Jeb Rogge's body moved," I replied, "especially since we don't know whether or not this is a suicide."

Moorehead removed a roll of bright yellow police tape from his trunk and we roped off a fifty-foot perimeter around the hunting cabin and body. Melanie was out of earshot, smoking a cigarette.

"I don't want Melanie here when your pal's tracking dogs arrive, especially if searchers end up dragging Heather's body from the woods," I said.

"I'll have a deputy drive her back to town," Moorehead said.

"I'll ride back with her," I announced. Moorehead looked surprised, but I had several reasons for wanting to return to Pushmataha. The most important was questioning Lester Alfred before anyone else got to him. He was the last person alive who had participated in the 1955 lynching and, in my mind, he was still a suspect. There was a slim chance that he might know where Heather was. "Think you can get me a copy of Jeb Rogge's telephone records for me?" I asked Moorehead.

"You're still thinking someone else is involved in this," he replied. "Sure, I'll get his records, but I think you're wasting your time. I've got a hunch that Rogge kidnapped Heather Cole to scare her and when that didn't work, he murdered her. As soon as he realized how much trouble he was in, because of who she was, he took the coward's way out and shot himself."

I wasn't convinced.

Moorehead added: "There are lots of caves in these hills. They're actually crevices that drop hundreds of feet. If Rogge threw her body into one of them, we'll have a hell of a time finding it."

The deputy who arrived a short time later was clearly disappointed when Moorehead ordered him to drive us back to Pushmataha. He dropped us at the courthouse where our SUV was parked and then hurried out to the hunting cabin.

"You're going to confront Lester Alfred now, aren't you?" Melanie asked.

"Your sister told you there were two kidnappers," I replied. "It makes sense he'd be the other one."

"I'm going with you."

I didn't argue. We walked across the courthouse lawn to Alfred's pharmacy. Entering it was like traveling back in time. A soda fountain with eight round stools stood parallel to the store's left wall. All of the seats had red plastic covers. Along the right wall were four wooden booths. Retail shelves began at the end of the soda fountain. There were three aisles stacked with over-the-counter remedies and school supplies. The pharmacist's counter was at the very rear of the store.

A black teenager was washing Coca-Cola glasses when we walked inside. Since she knew Pushmataha's regulars, she recognized us as being out-of-towners. So did the two boys at the fountain and the four men nursing coffees at a table. I walked directly to the prescription counter at the back of the store, where a white-haired man, wearing a white jacket over an open-collared shirt, was dividing pills into vials. His name tag read: LESTER ALFRED. PROPRIETOR. He smiled, but his grin vanished as soon as he spotted Melanie coming up behind me.

"Ms. Cole," he said in a hushed voice. "You promised to leave me alone! I don't have anything more to tell you."

"Mr. Alfred," I replied softly, "I'm from the United States Senate Judiciary Committee. Jeb Rogge is dead. Is there somewhere we can chat?"

"Rogge's dead? Sure, ur, okay, Senate-what committee? Ur, just a moment." He hollered to the front of the store. "Felicia, keep an eye on the prescription counter for a few minutes, please."

Turning, he motioned us behind the counter and unlocked a door to his right. All three of us walked through it.

We had entered the pharmacy's storeroom. Alfred led us to a flight of wooden steps built against the building's back wall. There wasn't a door at the top of the stairs. Alfred had hung strings of multicolored glass beads from the doorframe. He separated the strands and we stepped into his spacious but spartan upstairs living room. Melanie and I sat on a fake-leather couch while he deposited himself into a sunshine-yellow vinyl-covered chair. The walls were painted lime green and were dingy. Although there was a window air-conditioner in the corner, it wasn't running, and the hot room smelled stale and was stuffy. Alfred was tall, about six feet four inches. He had wavy hair that he wore puffed up and carefully coiffured. His face was an unhealthy pasty white and dotted with brown age spots. But what I noticed most was that he was heavily perfumed. I recognized it as Old Spice, my father's favorite.

"Jeb Rogge was found outside his hunting cabin a short while ago with a bullet hole in his head," I announced. "The sheriff and I believe he kidnapped Heather Cole and had been holding her at his cabin. She's still missing."

"I'm Heather's twin sister," Melanie volunteered.

"Please, I need some water," Alfred said. "I'm feeling a bit woozy." He started to stand but his knees were giving. Melanie got him a glass from the kitchen. After he finished his water, he felt both of his cheeks with the back of his left hand. "I'm better now." He had thin, delicate hands, that were manicured. Alfred said: "I'm confused. You say you're a twin? That Heather Cole is your sister?"

"That's right," Melanie said.

"And Jeb Rogge kidnapped her and now Sheriff Moorehead has found him dead?"

"Yes," I replied. "We think Rogge had an accomplice."

"Oh, my, this is just awful," he said. Then he added: "Oh, my goodness, you think I knew about it! That's why you're here, isn't it? You think I helped him!"

"Do you know where Heather Cole is?" I asked.

"Heavens, no!" he replied, clearly alarmed.

"When did you last see my sister?" Melanie asked.

"Wednesday morning. She just showed up here."

"I assume she asked you about the lynching, correct?" I said.

He began to fidget. "Then you know about it?"

"We know you were in the park that night in 1955 with the Rogges. That you are the L initial carved on the trophy tree."

"Oh, my goodness, oh, my goodness!" he exclaimed. "This means more reporters will be coming here, doesn't it, because Rogge is dead and that young girl is missing? They're going to dig up that old mess!"

"Heather Cole is a renowned reporter and the media always comes down hard whenever one of its own is hurt or threatened," I said.

"I watch CNN," he replied. "I know all about that *Wall Street Journal* reporter who was murdered in Pakistan and how it was worldwide news. Oh, my goodness, this really is just terrible!"

"The reporters will ask you about the lynching," I said. "They'll want to know if you helped Rogge kidnap Heather. If you know anything, it'd be better to tell us now."

"I didn't have anything to do with this!" he shrieked. He looked scared. "When I met your sister, she said she was going to put my name in her book. I felt trapped. I didn't want to tell her anything. But if I didn't, I wouldn't be able to explain how my father and I were victims too."

"Victims?" Melanie asked.

"The Rogges forced my father to open the courthouse door that night and they made both of us go to the park and watch that dreadful incident."

"It was a lynching," I said, "and you didn't just watch. You took part in it. You struck Lamar Grant with a baseball bat, for God's sakes!"

"You—you know about that too?" he stammered. "But you've got to understand, the Rogges forced us. They'd have murdered us too if we'd tried to stop them!"

"When was the last time you talked to Jeb Rogge?" I asked.

"I'd not spoken to him for thirty years but after your sister showed up—I didn't know what to do, so I called him."

"When did you call?"

"On Wednesday, right after she left my store. I said, 'She's a reporter and she knows about us!'"

"Why'd you call him?" Melanie asked.

Alfred lowered his head and stared down at the floor. "I'm being totally honest here. I was terrified. I'd thought that dreadful night was behind me, forgotten, and forever going to remain in the past."

"Why'd you call him?" I repeated.

"The Rogges are bullies. I called because I thought he might be able to scare her into leaving town. But you've got to believe me! I never dreamed he would kidnap her."

"What did you think he'd do?" I asked sarcastically. "Invite her in for tea?"

"I don't know! It was stupid, but I was afraid. I told your sister that Jeb Rogge was a very dangerous man, but she went out and confronted him anyway. She shouldn't have done that! It was her own fault!"

"Where were you this morning?" I asked.

"Oh, my, you really *do* believe I was involved!" he replied. "But I've got witnesses. People saw me here this morning! I always open early on Saturdays because several old-timers come here for coffee. I had four gentlemen and four ladies in here at six o'clock. I can tell you their names if you want."

"You never left the pharmacy this morning?"

"No! Felicia can swear to that too!"

"We came by here last night and your lights were out."

"I went to bed at eight-thirty because I have a timid stomach. I've not slept well since your sister came to see me and asked all of her damn questions! I've tried so hard to put all that behind me and now it's going to come out again!"

Alfred pressed the back of his hand against both of his cheeks. "I'm sixty-five years old. I can't take this stress. You've got to understand that things were different in Mississippi back in the fifties. I tried to explain this to your sister. I asked her straight out: 'What's the point of picking at this old scab?' But she wouldn't listen! She just had to have her big exposé!"

He was becoming indignant. "The truth is, this is all your sister's own damn fault. You Yankees run down here all the time and lecture us about race. But I'll bet neither one of you has ever had a black neighbor or any friends who are African American! What do you know about race relations?"

He used his arms to push himself from his chair. "I don't wish to be rude, but you both need to leave now. This entire incident is going to ruin what's left of my life." Without waiting for us to respond, Alfred walked through the glass beads, down the wood steps, and to the storeroom door. By the time we joined him, he'd calmed down, but only a little.

"Young lady," he said to Melanie. "Please know that I'm truly sorry if my actions had anything to do with your sister's kidnapping, but you've got to understand that my life was going along fine until she arrived in town. And now I'm going to be publicly humiliated. I'm sorry if I sound insensitive, but I've spent nearly fifty years trying to make amends for that lynching. Damn Jeb Rogge and damn your sister for coming down here!"

He shut the door, leaving us in the pharmacy and him still standing in the building's storeroom. I heard him lock it. We walked to the front of the store. Everyone was watching us.

"Mr. Alfred," the young black woman said, "will he be coming downstairs soon?"

"He didn't say," I replied.

As soon as we stepped outside, Melanie asked: "What now?"

"I'm going back to the hunting cabin," I said. "Alone! You need to go into hiding before the media hits town." I thought she'd argue and insist on returning with me to Rogge's cabin. But she didn't.

"I want to go to the motel," she said. "I'm going to take a nap."

I didn't ask why. I knew. She was going to try to make contact with Heather.

Sixteen

"**D**o you think Lester Alfred helped Rogge kidnap my sister?" Melanie asked as we were riding in our rented SUV to the Holiday Inn. "He doesn't strike me as a violent man," she added.

"When I was in the FBI," I replied, "I investigated a murder. A man came home and found his wife stabbed to death in their bedroom, at least that was his story. Their two children were sleeping in another room during the attack. The husband claimed a burglar had killed her."

"You didn't believe him?"

"A pane of glass in the back door had been broken. The burglar had reached through it and unlocked the door. A few things were missing from the house, but nothing valuable. What made me suspicious was how the wife had been murdered. She'd been stabbed sixteen times."

"Yuck! But why'd that make you suspicious?"

"Stabbings are different from other murders. Shooting a person is an impersonal act—if murder can ever be impersonal. You pull a trigger. Stabbing is an up-close, in-your-face, intimate act. You can feel a knife blade pierce the skin, puncture vital organs, hit bones. And when you withdraw the knife, you feel the blood pushing up behind it ready to burst out. You hear your victim's breath. You see the shock as the last moments of life pass from them."

I suddenly realized that my vivid description was upsetting her. "I'm sorry," I said. "I didn't mean to get so graphic."

Melanie nodded.

"Anyway, our forensic guys determined the first blow had been fatal. Yet the killer had continued stabbing her. That told me it wasn't a simple burglary. It was a crime of hatred, of passion."

"It was the husband, right?"

"Yep, he told us that he'd entered the house through the front door and had gone directly upstairs to the bedroom, where he'd found his wife. He'd called the police from a phone there and had stayed with her until he let the cops inside, again through the front door. But when I examined his shoes, I found slivers of glass from the broken window that had been in the back door. He'd been clever enough to step outside and break the window so that the glass had fallen onto the kitchen floor—just the way a burglar would have done it. But then he had stupidly walked through the glass on his way upstairs to call the police. It turned out he'd discovered that afternoon that his wife was having an affair."

Melanie lit a cigarette as I turned into the Holiday Inn parking lot.

"The reason I told you that story is because no one suspected this guy was capable of murder," I said. "He was bright, articulate, handsome, personable. He'd never been in any trouble before. None. There was nothing in his background, no history of violence. He came from a respectable home. That's what you have to understand about murder. The people who do them in real life are not like the ones you see on television or in the movies where evil people always look evil and talk evil. In real life, even someone who appears to be a kindly old man, like Lester Alfred, is capable of killing. And Heather was definitely pushing Alfred's panic buttons."

I went inside the motel room to make certain no one was hiding in it. I was happy that I'd rented the room in my name. That would make it more difficult for the media to locate her. I told Melanie that I'd call her later and left for Rogge's hunting cabin.

Although Melanie and Heather were clones, I'd spent enough time with both to notice subtle personality differences. Melanie was more reserved. She also was married and marriage was a topic that Heather and I had argued about constantly. I wanted to tie the knot, but she'd always refused.

"I need to focus on my career," she'd say. Or: "Why bother getting married? It can ruin a love affair."

Those were excuses, not reasons. I thought about Heather and our relationship as I drove north from Pushmataha. I knew Heather loved me, at least she had in the beginning. We'd met shortly after I'd joined the Judiciary Committee. Back then, I was just an investigator. Windsor Hathmeyer was the chief committee investigator, but he was about to make a huge blunder. Everything happened quickly. Clarence Thomas had been nominated by the White House to fill an opening on the U.S. Supreme Court. Predictably, the Democrats and liberals had come out swinging because Thomas was a black conservative Republican. Still, the process had gone relatively smoothly. Our committee grilled him and then forwarded his nomination to the Senate floor for a vote. It was at that point that the train ran off its tracks. Anita Hill, a law professor in Oklahoma, accused Thomas of sexual harassment. Her charges blindsided the committee. The Senate was furious and demanded that my boss conduct a special hearing to investigate. The fact that no one had warned the committee in advance about Hill's sexual harassment charge is what cost Hathmeyer his head.

The committee's hearings were as lurid as anything I'd

ever seen. Hill claimed Thomas had described sex scenes to her from pornographic films that showed "sex with animals," "group sex," and "individuals with large penises," including an actor known as "Long Dong Silver." As expected, Thomas "unequivocally, categorically" denied that he ever "had conversations of a sexual nature or about pornographic material with Anita Hill." He went even further and testified that he had never had "a personal sexual interest in her."

About midway through the hearings, Heather had stopped me in the hallway of the Dirksen Building and introduced herself. I remember the exact day, because earlier in the afternoon, Hill had testified that Thomas had once picked up a soft drink at work and remarked: "Who has put pubic hair on my Coke?"

Heather said: "Can I ask you a question?" Without waiting for me to say no, she'd said: "I'm trying to obtain a list of the X-rated videos that Clarence Thomas rented and I've heard the committee has a copy."

"Sorry," I replied. "I'm not authorized to talk to reporters. You need to ask the committee's public information officer."

"Those guys are paid to keep information from us. Besides, I need a source on the committee and you're the cutest guy on it, so I've chosen you!"

Although I was flattered, her comment struck me as odd, since the committee was investigating sexual harassment. I should've walked away, but her smile kept me there.

"Why do you want a list of his porno movies?" I asked.

"Officially, the public has a right to know as much as it can learn about the moral character of a potential Supreme Court justice," she replied. "But the truth is that's bullshit my editors have conjured up, to justify publishing a list of porno simply because everyone in town wants to read what sort of smut he's been watching!"

"I could lose my job if I gave you a list," I said.

"That's a bit melodramatic, isn't it?" she said. "First of all, I'd protect your identity and, second, who'd really care? This isn't a national security issue."

"I take my promises seriously, especially when it comes to keeping secrets," I said.

"Secrets? On Capitol Hill?" she said, interrupting me. "They'd told me that you'd just joined the committee from the FBI. You really *are* naive, aren't you? President Roosevelt once said the only way to keep a secret in Washington between three people is if two of them are dead."

"Benjamin Franklin said that, not Roosevelt."

"I know," she replied. "I'd heard you're a big fan of famous quotations. I was testing you."

I couldn't tell if she had intentionally said Roosevelt or was simply good on the uptake.

"If you checked me out," I said, "then you know I'm a man of my word. And that means I'm not going to slip you a list of X-rated videos."

The next afternoon, Heather telephoned and asked if I'd meet her for a drink at a Capitol Hill pub. I declined. "We established yesterday that you love quotations," she persisted, "so let's make a deal. Why don't you ask me a famous quote right now and if I answer it correctly, then you'll have to meet me for a drink? If I'm wrong, you're off the hook. I'll move down my cutie-pie list and call some ugly guy on your staff."

"All right," I replied, intrigued. "Who said: 'Integrity without knowledge is weak and useless, and knowledge without integrity is dangerous and dreadful'?" I thought it was an appropriate quote, since she was trying to get me to leak a committee document.

"That's the best you can come up with?" she cockily replied.

I suspected she was stalling.

"Samuel Johnson," she answered. "If you'd really wanted to stump me, you should have picked someone more obscure than one of the most important English writers of the eighteenth century."

She was correct! It was a Johnson quote and I was stunned because it wasn't one of his best-known ones. Only months later did I learn that Heather had guessed. She'd chosen Johnson only because she knew from a college liter-ature class that—except for the Bible and Shakespeare—he is the single most quoted prose writer in the English lan-guage in dictionaries of quotations. That incident tells a lot about Heather. She wasn't afraid to take chances. She also thought she could talk her way in and out of any situation.

I'd met her later that same night at Mr. Smith's Restau-rant in Tysons Corner, Virginia, because I didn't want to be seen talking to her in Washington. She'd arrived nearly an hour late. She'd done that on purpose. When she found me still waiting there, she'd known then she had me hooked. Drinks had led to dinner, and by dessert, we'd learned enough to spark a friendship. At least, I considered it a friendship. Heather had simply been working me. In Wash-ington, reporters and foreign spies share similar skills: They become your friends first before they screw you. That's how they get your help.

Heather began calling me every day. When I still didn't slip her the X-rated list, she switched tactics.

"I got part of that movie list from someone else," she said, "but I'm not certain it's accurate. How about if I read you the names of several films and you tell me if they're on your list? You wouldn't want me to publish the wrong ti-tles, right? That would get me into hot water and also em-barrass Clarence Thomas and the committee."

She'd tried to make it sound as if I'd be doing the world a favor, but I saw through her ruse. "Nice try," I replied, "but I'm not biting. You didn't get a list from someone else. You're fishing."

She sounded hurt. Then she got tough. "Listen, Nick," she said. "Everyone on the committee knows I've been call-ing you every day for a week and when I print this list to-morrow, they'll assume you gave it to me. So you might as well help me because you're going to be blamed anyway."

I should've been furious. This was blackmail. But by that time, I liked her so much that I didn't get angry. "Heather, I'm not playing your reporters' games. Goodbye."

She didn't call me the next day and the *Tribune* never

did print a story about which X-rated videos Clarence Thomas may or may not have watched. In fact, I didn't hear from Heather again until after the Senate voted 52–48 in favor of approving him. Two days later, a package arrived. It came the same day that Hathmeyer resigned as the committee's chief investigator and I was promoted into his job. The package was from Heather.

"Congratulations, Nick! You're the only Capitol Hill staffer who has enough integrity to keep his word. P.S. I still think you're damn cute!"

Inside the package was an X-rated video called *Sex Freaks* starring Long Dong Silver, the "seventeen-inch-long" porno star whom Hill had claimed was a favorite of our newest member to the U.S. Supreme Court. I called Heather that night to thank her and we agreed to have dinner later that week. This time, she only kept me waiting fifteen minutes. She looked gorgeous in a black silk blouse held closed by a black string tied just under her bodice. Her skirt was knee-length and was a flashy zebra print. It was both eye-catching and edgy. Whenever she leaned forward or laughed, her blouse would gape open and I could catch a glimpse of her flesh-colored bra.

"You know," she told me after we'd ordered, "the latest Gallup poll shows that a majority of Americans believe Clarence Thomas told the truth and Anita Hill lied during your committee hearings. What do you think?"

"I don't know," I said, playing it safe. I didn't want to be quoted in tomorrow's edition.

"You still don't trust me," she replied. "You think I'm going to write something. Sorry, but the world isn't sitting around waiting breathlessly for Nick LeRue's opinion. You blew your chance at fame when you refused to leak me that list."

She took a sip of her wine.

"The committee never had a list," I said. "It was a rumor. Besides, Clarence Thomas insisted he never watched porno."

"I don't know of any red-blooded American male over

the age of seventeen who hasn't or doesn't watch porno—
except for priests and really old guys."

"Do you believe Thomas sexually harassed Anita Hill?"

"Of course, and time will prove me right. Sexual harassment is everywhere, especially in this city. Washington is a
city ruled by powerful men and sex is one of the perks of
being powerful. Your committee was stacked against Anita
Hill. None of its members wanted to believe her because
deep down, all of them probably felt some guilt. At one
time or another, they'd all done what Clarence Thomas
did. They'd made some sexual remark to see if an attractive woman would bite."

"You use your sex appeal to get what you want!"

"I flirted with you. But I'm not your boss, am I?" she
replied. "Besides, I'd be stupid not to flirt in this town. Answer me this: Would you have gone to dinner with me if I
had been a male reporter?"

"No."

We argued back and forth during every course. But ultimately, Heather was proven right. Within a year, a Gallup
poll showed that a majority of Americans had changed
their minds about our judiciary hearings. They'd decided
that Anita Hill had told the truth and Thomas had lied.

When it came time for dessert that night, Heather said:
"Let's skip the chocolate mousse and head back to your
place. You can put on the video I sent you. Call it follow-up
research."

That's how Heather was. If she wanted something or
someone, she went for it. In less than a year, she'd moved
into my place. We used to joke: Clarence Thomas, Anita
Hill, and Long Dong Silver were responsible for bringing
us together.

I spotted a line of sheriff's cruisers and other vehicles as
soon as I crossed the steel bridge near the turnoff to
Rogge's house. I didn't envy Sheriff Moorehead having to

tell Julie Rogge that her husband was dead. A deputy was standing guard at the tree line. Moorehead told him over the radio to let me pass. He was waiting when I reached the hunting cabin and he wasn't happy.

"LeRue," Moorehead declared, "we need to talk!"

He directed me away from the others, mostly men in blue overalls marked with various law enforcement insignias. I could hear tracking dogs barking in the woods.

"You just come from interviewing Lester Alfred?" he asked.

"Yes, I wanted to question him before we got overrun by reporters. Why? Did he call you and complain?"

"Hardly," Moorehead replied. "He hanged himself. They just found his body in the storeroom at his pharmacy!"

Seventeen

It was after midnight when I returned to the Holiday Inn. I rapped gently on the door, but Melanie didn't answer, so I unlocked it and slipped inside. It was dark. There was light peeking from under the bathroom door and I could hear the shower running. I walked over to it and said: "Melanie, I'm back. You okay?"

She didn't answer, so I turned the knob and pushed the door open just a crack so she could hear me. Steam drifted out.

"Melanie. It's me. You okay?"

I could hear crying. I peeked inside and saw her blurred image behind the frosted shower glass. She was sitting inside the tub with her legs pulled up against her chest and her face buried against her knees. I walked into the bathroom and sat on the floor with my back leaning against the shower stall so I was looking away from her.

"Melanie," I said softly, "what happened in your dream?"

"Heather wasn't there."

"You weren't able to contact her?"

"I tried, but she didn't appear. That's never happened before. Ever. Even when my dreams weren't about her, she was always in them, somewhere in the background."

"What's that mean?"

"I've never felt so lonely, so separated from her."

"Sheriff Moorehead had tracking dogs searching the woods all day. They followed Heather's scent from the cabin and into the woods, but they lost it there. They'll try again tomorrow. It's possible she escaped and could be wandering around."

"No," she replied firmly. "Don't you understand? Heather has always been with me. She was like my breath. You don't always see your breath, unless it's really cold outside, but you know it's there. It's just a part of you. Heather was like that. Only now I don't feel her. There's no breath."

"Moorehead is bringing in volunteers tomorrow to walk through the woods. He's even got a helicopter flying in."

Melanie didn't respond.

"I'm going to give you some privacy," I said. I shut the bathroom door and went to use the bedside phone. I wanted to rent another motel room where I could sleep.

"Sorry, we're sold out," the desk clerk announced. "It's because of all the excitement."

"What excitement?" I asked innocently.

"A reporter from Washington, D.C., was kidnapped and a local guy was found dead this morning, shot in the head. A bunch of FBI agents checked in here this afternoon and I've been turning away reporters who want rooms."

"Where are the reporters from?"

"Two came from the *Washington Tribune*. All the television networks have sent someone too. CNN was here first. The sheriff's asking for volunteers to search, and I'm going as soon as I get off work. I want to be on television!"

Melanie appeared at about the same time as I hung up. She was wearing her gray sweats and had a towel wrapped around her wet hair.

"Trying to find an empty room," I said.

"I want you to stay here with me tonight. I don't want to be alone." She sat down on the bed and began drying her hair with the towel. "It's okay. My husband isn't the jealous type. He understands how much you are helping me. I spoke with him earlier and he's making arrangements to fly out here." Switching subjects, she asked: "Did they find anything at the cabin?"

"The forensic team was still there when I left. The theory is that Rogge shot himself."

"But you don't believe that, do you?"

"No, I don't," I replied. "First off, Heather said there were two men involved. But the fact that there's only one way to drive up to the cabin has convinced Moorehead that Rogge was acting alone. Otherwise, the sheriff says we would have encountered someone on the road trying to escape." I paused and then said: "There's something else I need to tell you. After we left Lester Alfred today, he hanged himself."

"He's dead!"

"The teenager working behind the soda fountain is Sheriff Moorehead's niece. She got concerned when Alfred didn't come back down to work. She called his upstairs apartment and when there wasn't an answer, she called the sheriff's office. A deputy found him hanging on a rope in the storeroom. He'd climbed up on a chair and then kicked it over."

"Do you think Lester Alfred was Rogge's accomplice?" Melanie asked.

"No," I replied. "He had an alibi. It checked out."

Melanie stepped over to the desk and retrieved the photograph that the Reverend Carter had given me. It was the shot that showed five white men standing in front of a very dead Lamar Grant.

"The curse lives on," she said. She touched her finger on Robert E. Lee Rogge's face in the picture. "Old man Rogge is killed in a freak accident." She slid her finger sideways to the next smiling white face. "So is his son, Peyton." She moved her finger again. "Stanley Alfred is dead. And now Jeb Rogge and Lester Alfred are both dead too. My sister, Heather, is missing and the five men who lynched Lamar Grant are all dead. Who else is there now?"

I wasn't sure. "I know it sounds strange, but I've just got this gut feeling that Rogge wasn't acting alone. I think there was someone else at that cabin, someone we haven't identified, and just like the five men in this photograph, he doesn't want Heather or anyone else digging into the past."

"A 'gut feeling'! You—the man who doesn't believe in supernatural acts, ESP, hunches, or telepathic communication in dreams?"

I ignored her sarcasm. It was a fair shot. "Let's go back to the beginning and think this through logically," I said. "Why did Rogge kidnap Heather?"

"Because he wanted to scare her."

"I thought that too, at first. But he could have scared her without abducting her. It would have been easy for him to have left a threatening note on her rental car or to have forced her off the highway one night while she was driving. I think he kidnapped her because he wanted something. He wanted to find out what she had learned about the lynching."

"That doesn't make sense because Heather already knew who was involved in the lynching," Melanie replied. "Everyone did."

"Did she? Do they?" I replied. "What if Rogge kidnapped her at someone else's request. What if there was a sixth white man at the hanging—somebody who no one knows about?"

"If there's a sixth man, then why aren't his initials in the tree?"

"I'm not sure. Maybe we should take another look at the tree."

"Right now?" she asked.

"Yes. If we wait until morning, the park is going to be crawling with reporters."

Since she was already wearing her sweats, Melanie simply slipped on a pair of sneakers. Ten minutes later, I pulled the SUV into a parking spot near the historic marker along the town square. With a flashlight, we made our way across the deserted park to the trophy tree. Even in the darkness, it was easy to find.

"You hold the light," I said, handing it to her. She shined the beam onto the ten-inch-by-five-inch opening cut into the bark. I photographed the carvings from several different angles. Then I slowly ran my right hand over the cuts. When I reached the letter L at the bottom, I paused.

"You can feel the burnt wood next to the L," I explained. "It's where the lightning must have struck the tree. I'm guessing the bolt actually hit the initial A that Lester Alfred had carved there, obliterating it. Here, feel it."

Melanie touched the tree with her left fingers.

"If there was another man at the lynching, then he would have carved his initials directly underneath Lester Alfred's," I theorized. I rubbed my fingers against the trunk under the initial L.

"The bark here has been gouged out!" I announced. "The cuts are deeper than what's around it."

Melanie touched the same spot. "I feel the hole too!" she exclaimed. "The wood has definitely been cut away!"

She withdrew her fingers and I studied the area where the lightning had hit the trunk. The bolt's impact had caused a crack. "I think the wood underneath Lester Alfred's initials was gouged out before this tree was struck by lightning," I said. "Visualize this tree surface as if it were a sheet of paper. Now draw a line on that sheet and then tear the paper in half. If you put the paper back together correctly, that line will match up."

Melanie ran her hand along the crack, feeling both sides. "The gouge marks are the same," she said. "If you pushed this crack back together, the marks would match just like that line on your paper."

Melanie removed her hand. "Look," she continued, "there's only a half-inch gap at the top of this carving, between the bark and the words: 'Nigar Hung Here.' But there is a good four inches of space between the initial L and the bark at the bottom. They were making room for another set of initials."

"So our mystery man carves his name in the tree," I said, "along with everyone else. But after the lynching and before the thunderstorm, he has a change of heart and returns to the park to gouge out his initials."

"Why?" Melanie asked.

"He didn't want anyone to know that he had taken part in the lynching."

"But the other five would have known."

"That's right, and for some reason they agreed to keep quiet about him."

I heard a noise. It sounded like a person stepping on acorns. Melanie heard it too. I swept the flashlight beam in that direction but there was no one there.

"Let's get out of here," Melanie said. "This is getting creepy."

We walked back to our SUV.

"It was probably an animal we heard," I said. I flipped on the SUV's headlights and tried to use them as a spotlight as I backed from the parking space.

"Look!" Melanie screamed. "Someone's there! Behind that tree!"

I followed the line where her finger was pointing, but I didn't see anyone.

Slamming the car into park, I opened the door and began to step outside to investigate.

"No!" Melanie cried. "Let's just go! Now!"

I peered into the darkness. If someone had been lurking there, he probably was gone by now. I closed the door and put the SUV back in drive.

When we reached the Holiday Inn, I went directly to my desk and picked up the photograph of the five men at the lynching. "What can these dead white men tell us?" I said.

"Dead men tell no lies," Melanie replied.

"Actually, the quote is: 'Dead men tell no tales,'" I said, correcting her.

I looked again at the old images and suddenly I saw what we had been missing.

I held up the photograph so that Melanie could look at it.

"What do you see?" I asked.

"The same thing we've both been seeing since the Reverend Carter gave it to you."

"Try looking with fresh eyes. Describe the picture to me."

"A black man is hanging from a tree. Five white men are standing at his feet. They are all smiling."

"How many people are at the lynching?"

"I just said there are five white men and Lamar Grant. That makes six."

"Wrong! Try counting again."

She stared at the photograph and then at me and then back at it. "Oh, my God!" she exclaimed. "There were *seven* men there that night!"

"The photographer!" I exclaimed. "Someone had to take the picture. Someone was behind the camera. He's our mystery accomplice! He's got to be the guy who removed his initials from the tree!"

I turned over the photograph but there were no identifying marks written on its back.

"This photograph was taken with a flashbulb," Melanie said. "See how Lamar Grant is difficult to see. That's because his dark skin absorbed the light differently from the white-skinned men. They look washed out while he has faded into the background!"

"You seem to know a lot about photography," I said.

"My father was a newspaper editor. I grew up around darkrooms." She studied the print. "This is a good-quality print and that tells me that it was taken with an expensive camera, not a Brownie, which is what most families had in the 1950s. The negative couldn't have been enlarged into a crisp eight-by-ten-inch print unless it was taken with a good lens. I'm guessing this photograph came from a Speed Graphic—that's a camera that newspaper photographers often used in the 1950s."

"Would an ordinary person own a Speed Graphic?"

"Not unless they were very wealthy."

"The Reverend Carter said the local newspaper published a photograph of Lamar Grant hanging from the tree," I recalled. "I wonder if the newspaper's photograph of Grant was taken at night or the next morning when the body was discovered."

"Why would that matter?" she asked, and then she answered her own question. "Of course, if it were taken at night, then the newspaper photographer had to have been at the lynching. That would mean that he took both photographs: the one used in the newspaper and the one that old man Rogge handed out as souvenirs!"

"That's right," I replied. "He'd be our mystery man."

I suddenly realized how exhausted I was. I laid back on the bed even though I was still dressed. I was simply too tired to disrobe. "Let's go by the newspaper office first thing tomorrow," I said.

I'd fallen asleep by the time Melanie came to bed, but a few hours later, I woke up when I felt a weight pressing against my chest. It was Melanie. She had snuggled up next to me. It wasn't sexual. She didn't want to be alone. She really never had been. Heather had always been there. I gently closed my arm around her and thought about Heather.

I didn't want to be alone either.

Eighteen

Melanie's head was still resting on my chest when the phone rang at eight-thirty a.m. I slid from beneath her.

"Nick? Nick LeRue?" an unfamiliar voice asked.

"Who's this?"

"Andrew Middleton of the *Tribune*. You heard anything new about Heather?"

"Why don't you ask your reporters?" I replied suspiciously. The Holiday Inn clerk had told me the night before that there were two *Tribune* reporters in town investigating Heather's disappearance.

"I thought you and Melanie Cole might know something new. Is Melanie with you?"

So finding Melanie was the reason for this call.

"No," I replied, lying. "I haven't seen her."

I could think of several reasons why I wasn't going to help Middleton, but I only needed one: I hated his guts because of Heather.

"Do you know where Melanie is staying?" he asked.

"The desk clerk said there wasn't a Melanie Cole registered. I tried the other motel in town, but she wasn't registered there either."

"Why are you trying to find her?"

He ignored my question and asked: "Have you read my story in this morning's edition?"

"No, I don't think Pushmataha is in the *Washington Tribune's* circulation area," I replied sarcastically.

"It's on the Internet and the Associated Press sent it over its national news wire. The major newspapers in Mississippi are running it. I reveal in my story that Heather was in Pushmataha to investigate the 1955 lynching and that Jeb Rogge was involved in the hanging. Obviously, that's why he abducted her!"

"Congratulations! I'm happy you've found a way to profit from Heather's kidnapping."

"Listen, LeRue," he snapped, "I don't ever expect us to be friends, but we need to work together on this for Heather's sake. I've already gotten space for a page one piece tomorrow if I can get an interview with Melanie. Keeping this story in the national spotlight is the best way to put pressure on the locals in Mississippi and the FBI to find her. *Now* do you know where Melanie Cole is staying?"

I glanced at Melanie, who was hugging my pillow and still asleep.

"Nope, haven't seen her," I replied. "But you'll be the first to know if I run into her."

I hung up.

Melanie opened one eye. "Who was that?"

"Andrew Middleton wants to interview you. You're page one stuff."

"Why didn't you wake me?"

"Let's just say he's not my favorite reporter."

I ran an errand while Melanie got dressed. At a local combination gas station–convenience store, I bought a morning's edition of the Jackson *Clarion-Ledger* and a black baseball cap with an emblem on it of an open-mouthed bass chasing a lure. GOIN' FISHIN' was printed in red letters above the brim. When I got back to the Holiday Inn, I knocked on the motel door to warn Melanie and then stepped inside. She was on the telephone.

"Okay, darling," she said. "I love you too. Don't worry. It's okay. Goodbye."

I figured she was talking to her husband and based on the look on her face, it appeared that she had gotten bad news.

"My daughter, Kaitlyn, is sick," she said. "My husband isn't going to be able to fly down here right away. He needs to stay with her."

"Sorry," I said. But I really wasn't. I was happy that he wasn't coming. I handed her the fishing cap.

"Your disguise," I explained.

She gave me a confused look, so I held up the newspaper. Heather's photo was printed on the front page.

"We don't want anyone seeing you and thinking they've spotted Heather," I explained.

In addition to a locally written story about Heather's disappearance and Jeb Rogge's death, the *Clarion-Ledger* had published Middleton's exclusive under the headline: *Reporter Investigating Old Lynching When Kidnapped.* I scanned it and didn't see much new until I got to the final paragraph.

> One of the clues that Heather Cole had unearthed was a black-and-white photograph of five men. It showed them standing at the feet of Lamar Grant after he had been lynched.

I reread that paragraph and then read it aloud to Melanie.

"How in the hell did Andrew Middleton find out about the lynching photograph?" I asked.

"Maybe Middleton telephoned the Reverend Carter— you know, pulled his name from the phone book, just like you did," she suggested.

"I don't think so," I replied. "Middleton's article specifically says that Heather knew about the lynching photograph—that she'd actually seen it. That doesn't make sense. The Reverend Carter got his two copies from Lester Alfred. That leaves the three copies that the Rogges had and they sure didn't show them to Heather."

"You're forgetting our mystery man," Melanie replied. "If there was a sixth white man at the lynching, then he would have a copy too."

She was right. I'd forgotten about the mystery man's copy.

"How do I look?" Melanie asked. She had tucked her hair up under the fishing cap and put on sunglasses. "Am I disguised well enough?"

I glanced at her. It's amazing how some women can look sexy even when they are dressed in blue jeans, a simple top, and wearing a baseball cap. Of course, having a large-mouth bass on the cap helped.

"You've become a regular James Bond," I replied.

The *Pushmataha Record* newspaper office was one block off the town square. But its offices were closed because this was Sunday. I drove the SUV around to the rear of the building and parked. A few minutes later, a rusty blue Ford Pinto pulled up and a young man carrying several cameras got out and fumbled for a key to unlock the newspaper's back door.

"Hey," I yelled, stepping outside. "Hang on a second!"

"Paper's closed," he called back. "You'll have to come back tomorrow."

I whipped out my Senate identification card, which had an impressive seal embossed on it. "The Senate Judiciary Committee would like a copy of the photograph that your newspaper published in September 1955, of the Lamar Grant lynching," I explained.

"Everyone wants a copy of it," he replied. "Heather Cole's disappearance is making national news. I spent most of the night searching our files, but we don't have any pictures of that lynching."

"I was told that your newspaper published a photograph of him hanging from a tree with a sign strung around his neck."

"That's true but our files about Lamar Grant and that lynching are empty. There's no old clips, no photographs, not even any negatives."

"Did someone destroy them?"

"Who knows? Back in those days, our paper was a mom-and-pop operation, and the couple who owned it didn't do a very good job of keeping records."

"Do you know the name of the photographer who took the picture of the lynching?"

"Don't have a clue. And even if you were lucky enough to find a copy of the September 1955 newspaper, you still wouldn't be able to identify the photographer because the newspaper didn't credit them back then."

"Wouldn't you have some sort of records that would identify the photographer? How about old payroll accounts?"

"Like I said, this used to be a mom-and-pop shop. People brought in most of the photographs that were published. There was no staff photographer. Reporters took their own pictures to go with their stories. I've had every news organization in the country—ABC, CBS, CNN, NBC, Fox, even the *National Inquirer,* calling and offering me money for a copy of that photograph but there simply aren't any in our records and I don't know how to locate the photographer."

"How about old-timers? Anyone in town who worked for the newspaper in the fifties who might remember the lynching?"

"Naw, the Gannon newspaper chain bought the *Pushmataha Record* thirty years ago. Since then, most employees come here right out of journalism school. It's a good place to cut your teeth before moving up to a bigger-circulation paper. Our chain uses it as a training ground."

He unlocked the bolt on the steel back door and tugged on it but it was stuck. He needed both hands to jerk it open. "Our owners don't spend a cent more than they have to here," he complained. "That Ford Pinto I'm driving, that's the company car. It's got 165,000 miles on it."

He shut the door behind him and I returned to the SUV.

"Any luck?" Melanie asked.

"Nope," I replied. I was pondering what to do next when Melanie said, "Your friend is back."

I saw the young photographer I'd just spoken with approaching us.

"Hey, I thought of an old-timer," he said. "Only this guy might be more trouble than he's worth. He's a kook."

"What sort of kook?" Melanie asked.

"He sends us copies of our newspaper each week with all of our mistakes circled in red. No one pays any attention to him. His name is George something, uh, ur, McKinley, no, McKinney. He used to own the newspaper and lived in Pushmataha all of his life until his wife died and his kids stuck him in a Jackson nursing home. Someone's already thrown away the corrections that he mailed us last week. But a new batch should show up Tuesday. You could use them to track him down."

I was intentionally nonchalant. "Thanks, but no thanks. Doesn't sound like he's worth the trouble."

The photographer shrugged and headed back toward the building. As soon as he had disappeared inside, I said: "Let's find George McKinney!"

"You just said he was a waste of time!"

"That's what I wanted our pal to think. Otherwise, he'll be sending every reporter who shows up here to find him."

An hour later, I pulled off the interstate at a service station. While I topped off the SUV's tank, Melanie ripped the Yellow Pages listings of Jackson's nursing homes from a directory. She called them on my cell phone when I continued driving.

"I've found him!" she squealed after her fifth call. "He lives in Sunshine House."

Much to my surprise, Sunshine House lived up to its name. It was a modern nine-story building with a dome-shaped glass atrium. A cheery receptionist said she'd seen George McKinney walking outside behind the home carrying a stack of newspapers. We spotted him in a gazebo. He was sitting at a redwood picnic table with a week's worth of newspapers piled in front of him. I introduced Melanie and flashed my Senate credentials. McKinney had a water-melon belly that rested above his black trousers. He was wearing a short-sleeve pink shirt, a red bow tie, and red suspenders. He was chewing a cigar and his black-framed eyeglasses were so thick, they made his eyes look double their normal size. He was holding a red grease pencil that he'd been using to scribble on the newspapers. I guessed he was close to ninety years old.

"They won't let me smoke anymore," he groused. "Every Sunday, I come out here and chew on one of these and do what I did for more than seventy years. I read the papers and mark the mistakes. I mail the corrections out each Monday, but they keep making the same damned errors over and over again, so I suspect no one's paying much attention. You know, young people don't like to listen to us old geezers."

He jabbed a wrinkled finger at a paragraph that he'd circled. "This idiot has written that a Pushmataha woman was taken by ambulance to the hospital after she 'complained of having a temperature'! The last time I checked, everyone has a temperature unless they're dead." Pointing to another correction, he said: "And this story says a woman and her husband got into an argument 'over' money. The correct word is 'about.' You argue about things. You never use 'over' unless you're standing, flying, skipping, or jumping 'over' something."

He carefully placed the corrected sheet onto a stack of other red-marked pages.

"These damn newspaper chains have been gobbling up small-town newspapers for years and they turn them into nothing but advertising circulars," he declared. "No one cares about quality."

He peered through his thick lenses at Melanie and added: "I doubt there is anyone at the *Pushmataha Record* who even knows about the Sage of Little Rock."

Melanie blushed.

"Your last name is Cole, right?" he continued. "I'm assuming you're some relation to Heather Cole, who, I read in this morning's newspaper, is missing. I checked both the *Pushmataha Record* and the *Clarion-Ledger* and neither mentioned that Heather Cole's father was a Pulitzer prize-winning editor in Little Rock. The *New York Times* was the only paper who made that father-daughter connection."

"Heather is my twin sister," Melanie explained.

McKinney removed his cigar and grinned, sending a wave of wrinkles across his cheeks. "I greatly admired your father's courage. I wrote an editorial against the Klan myself, back when my wife and I owned the *Pushmataha Record*. The Klan is nothing but a bunch of white-hooded thugs. But the week after that editorial ran, we were only able to sell one advertisement. Only one damned ad. It was from the Peterman mill. Old man Rogge had ordered the merchants to boycott us and the Petermans were the only folks who weren't scared of him."

"How horrible for you," Melanie said.

"I'll never forget what happened. My wife went out on the back porch one night to investigate a noise. I thought it was the Klan and was getting my shotgun and hollering at her to get back into the house. Turned out someone had left us a bagful of collard greens. Black people, who barely had enough to eat themselves in those days, began bringing us food. Every night, someone left something. We never saw them. Never asked them to do it. They just did it on their own."

"Dad would have enjoyed that story and also enjoyed meeting you."

"I would've been too ashamed to have met him," McKinney replied. "I caved in. Without any advertising, our little paper was on the verge of going under financially, so I called old man Rogge and asked him to call off the boycott."

"Did he demand a payoff?" I asked.

"Five hundred dollars and a promise that I wouldn't write editorials against the Klan. That was his price and I'm sorry to say I agreed to it. The next week, our paper was full of ads. I'd saved the paper, but I'd sold my soul. That's why I admire your father. He didn't back down."

"No, and it cost him his life," she replied.

"I still remember exactly what I was doing on the day when I first heard that he'd been shot," McKinney said sadly. "I stopped and said a prayer for your family. They never did catch the shooter, did they?"

Melanie shook her head no.

"It had to have been the Klan. He was hitting it hard in editorials. How old were you when he was murdered?"

"I'd just turned six," she replied softly. "It was the day after our birthday—Heather's and mine."

I decided to get to the point of why we had come to see him.

"The *Pushmataha Record* printed a photograph of a black man, Lamar Grant, when he was lynched in September of 1955. Do you remember it? There was a sign hung around Grant's neck warning blacks against registering to vote."

"Of course I remember!" McKinney replied. "I'm old but I still recall things from the past, vividly. I also read Andrew Middleton's story today about why Heather Cole had gone to Pushmataha—to investigate the lynching."

I took from a file folder the photograph that the Reverend Carter had given us and handed it to McKinney.

"We think this photograph of the lynching was taken with a Speed Graphic camera because of the quality of the enlargement," I explained. "That's why we've come to see you. Did someone from your newspaper take it?"

"I've never seen this photograph before," McKinney said. "I read in Middleton's story today that Heather Cole had uncovered a copy of a photograph that showed five men at the lynching. This must be a copy of that same photograph."

"I'm sure it is," I said.

McKinney's sight was so weak that he was holding the print only a few inches from his nose. "Damn it," he complained, "if I'd known in September 1955 that this photo existed, I would've printed it on the front page. That way, everyone in town could've seen the cowards responsible for lynching Lamar Grant."

"Didn't most people already know who they were?" Melanie asked.

"Yes, especially since those miscreants carved their initials into that damn tree. But this picture shows their faces, shows them smiling! It's outrageous!"

"We think it was taken by the same photographer who took the one of Lamar Grant hanging in the park with the sign around his neck—the photo that your newspaper published," I explained.

McKinney scrutinized the front and the back of the glossy. "By God!" he exclaimed. "I believe you're right. I think this and the one we published were taken by the same person."

"Do you remember who that was?" Melanie asked.

"I sure as hell do!" McKinney gushed. "And for a very good reason! Ever heard the name Nehemiah Peterman?"

"As in United States Senator Nehemiah Peterman?" I asked.

"The very same! Granted, Peterman was just a pimple-faced teenager back then. He was still in high school in 1955, but he's got to be the photographer."

"Are you sure?" I asked. "What sort of camera did he use?"

"He owned his own Speed Graphic. He was rich enough to afford one," McKinney replied. "And this photo was definitely taken with that camera. I was a journalist too long not to recognize a Speed Graphic shot."

"What else do you remember about the picture you published? Are there other similarities that link the two shots?" I asked.

"They were both taken at night. I remembered it rained hard that morning, but the picture that we published was taken before that rain."

"How do you know that?" Melanie asked.

"Because the sign hanging around Grant's neck was legible. After the rain, the letters were so badly washed away that you couldn't read them."

"Was Peterman working for you at the newspaper?" Melanie asked.

"Yes, he was. His brothers all worked at the family mill, but he didn't want to do that. He wanted to try journalism, so I paid him to write stories about our high school football team and to take pictures around town. Turned out he was a lousy writer but a damn good shooter—good enough that I paid him ten dollars for every photograph of his that we put in the paper."

"And you're absolutely certain that he was the photographer who took your newspaper's shot of the hanging?" I asked.

"Jesus Christ!" McKinney thundered. "You don't forget something like that! I was home asleep when the sheriff called that morning. He told me the Klan had broken into the county courthouse and lynched Grant. I grabbed my camera and hurried to the park, but when I got there, the sheriff told me that Nehemiah Peterman had already taken pictures. In fact, he said it was Peterman who had called him to report the lynching!"

"Nehemiah Peterman called the sheriff?"

"That's right! I rushed over to the newspaper's darkroom and, sure enough, young Peterman was busy developing prints of Lamar Grant hanging from that tree."

"How come Peterman knew about the lynching before anyone else?" I asked.

"I wondered the same thing. He said one of his friends had been driving by the park and had noticed a commotion. His friend called him."

"Did this 'friend' have a name?" I asked.

"Peterman wouldn't tell me. Said the kid had snuck out of his parents' house and didn't need the trouble."

"How convenient," I replied.

McKinney continued: "Peterman claimed the Klan was gone by the time that he had gotten to the park. He saw Lamar Grant hanging there, took several pictures, and then ran over to the newspaper office and called the sheriff."

McKinney paused for a moment and then added: "Back then I didn't have any reason to doubt his story. In fact, I thought he was a damn brave kid for going to the park and taking those pictures. I gave him a twenty-buck bonus."

McKinney held the photograph up close to his face again and stared at the five white men in the photograph. "Now that you've shown me this picture, it appears that young Nehemiah Peterman deceived me. The only way he could have taken a shot of these five men posing in front of Lamar Grant was if he had been there at the park while the lynching was taking place!"

"Maybe he lied to you because old man Rogge had threatened him," Melanie volunteered.

McKinney chuckled. "Old man Rogge threatening a Peterman—now, that's a sight I'd have enjoyed seeing! The Peterman family has operated a lumber mill for more than a hundred years in Pushmataha County. That's a very tough, ruthless business. You'd be hard-pressed to find a family in all of Mississippi that has as much clout, money, and muscle as it has. I don't think that old man Rogge had enough gumption to threaten a Peterman."

"Do you think Peterman really found out about the lynching from an anonymous friend?" Melanie asked.

"Not now," he replied. "I'm guessing Jeb and Peyton Rogge tipped him off in advance. Hell, old man Rogge probably encouraged his sons to tell Peterman. Rogge was trying to scare blacks from registering to vote. What better way than to make certain a photograph of Lamar Grant appeared on the front page of my paper?"

"Why would Nehemiah Peterman, a rich teenager from the most prominent family in Pushmataha County, be associating with the likes of the Rogges?" I asked.

"Jeb and Peyton Rogge and Nehemiah Peterman probably had more in common than you might think. The Rogges' old man had everyone scared of him. Peterman's old man was Pushmataha's most powerful citizen. The fact they might have run around together doesn't surprise me. What *does* shock me is that Peterman apparently didn't try to warn anyone. I know we're speculating here, but what sort of kid allows a lynching to happen?"

"An ambitious one," I replied.

McKinney handed the 1955 photograph back to Melanie, who slipped it into our file folder.

He said: "This could be very embarrassing to Senator Peterman. Remember the heat Senator Trent Lott got when he made remarks that suggested he supported segregation? That fiasco would be minor compared to this. Here's a white senator taking snapshots at a lynching! And just look at those men in that photograph of yours. Why, they're proud of what they've done!"

"Do you think Peterman might have actually helped them lynch Lamar Grant?" I asked. "Was he a mean kid?"

"Whew!" McKinney said. "That's a hell of an accusation! This man is now a United States senator!"

"And that's part of the reason why I asked!" I replied. "Think about it. Senator Peterman had more to lose than Jeb Rogge or Lester Alfred when it came to having Heather Cole dig into their pasts. Everyone in Pushmataha already knew Rogge was a racist. For God's sake, he and his wife operated an Aryan Web site! Lester Alfred already had apologized to the black community. But nobody knows about Nehemiah Peterman's role in the lynching. If Heather Cole exposed him in her book, his political career would've been finished. That's why I'm asking: Do you think Nehemiah Peterman would risk kidnapping someone in order to protect his reputation and career?"

McKinney mulled over the question. "I'm afraid I can't answer you," he finally said. "The Nehemiah Peterman I knew as a teenager was a rich, spoiled kid but he was never violent around me. Too many years have passed since then for me to say whether or not he's now capable of kidnapping."

Once again, McKinney was quiet for a moment, and then he said: "A United States senator kidnapping a *Washington Tribune* reporter—wow, that's a real man-bites-dog story!"

"Can we trust you to keep quiet about this until we have some evidence that either proves Peterman was involved or clears him?" I asked.

McKinney stroked his shaven chin as if he had an imaginary beard growing there. "All of my life," he said, "I've loved scoops! There's nothing I like better than to expose corruption. I've always believed that journalists don't work for the newspaper's owners even though they're the folks who sign their paychecks. They work for the public. I know I'm an old man with idealistic principles, but that's how I think." He looked at Melanie. "I'd like to think your father thought that way too." His voice cracked. He was becoming emotional.

"I'll give both of you my solemn promise," he said, "that I won't say a word to anyone about Senator Peterman. I'll wait until you find more evidence. But then I want to write something about this. I want the world to know that he was there while Lamar Grant was hanged."

McKinney rose from his chair, reached out, and took hold of Melanie's hand. "You're such a pretty woman. Life goes by quickly, my dear. Before you know it, you're old and it's too late to correct all of the mistakes that you've made. I never knew your father, but I am honored to have an opportunity now to help you." He glanced at his pile of newspaper clippings on the table. "Let's leave these here. It's time for me to take an afternoon nap and I'd like you to escort me inside. Seeing me holding hands with a beautiful young woman will give everyone something to gossip about for days!"

After we left McKinney in the lobby and were driving back to Pushmataha, Melanie said: "Do you remember what the Reverend Carter told us about the lynching?"

"What are you referring to?" I asked.

"Carter said that when Lester Alfred confessed, he said everyone who was at the lynching had been forced by old man Rogge to hit Lamar Grant with a baseball bat. That way, they were all coconspirators. Do you think Peterman took a swing at Grant before they strung him up?"

"I doubt we'll ever know," I replied, "especially now. All of the other witnesses at the lynching are dead."

"What about the carving?" she asked. "Do you think Peterman carved his initials in the tree and then later gouged them out?"

"George McKinney just told us that the photograph in the newspaper was taken before the thunderstorm—so the timing fits. The Rogges and Alfreds bust Grant out of the jail and march him into the park. They hang him and old man Rogge has Peterman take a souvenir snapshot. In addition to that photograph, he takes a shot for the newspaper that only shows Grant hanging there with the sign around his neck. Peterman hurries over to the newspaper office, but before he calls the sheriff, he gets worried. After all, he's just put his initials in that tree along with everyone else—only Nehemiah Peterman isn't like everyone else. His family owns the lumber mill and his parents have made it clear that they're opposed to racism and the Klan."

"So he panics and runs back to the park and cuts out his initials," Melanie interjected.

"And," I said, picking up the scenario, "as luck would have it, it starts to rain and, completely by chance, a lightning bolt hits the trophy tree, further disguising his part in the lynching."

"The only men who know about him are the Rogges and the Alfreds, and because of the Peterman family's clout, none of them ever says anything about him."

"Maybe it was clout when it came to the two Alfreds, but I think took something more to keep the Rogges silent, especially if Peterman did smack Lamar Grant with that baseball bat."

"Blackmail?"

"Sheriff Moorehead said Rogge hadn't worked for years but he sure had a nice house, cars, and plenty of cash. The Rogges would have had the Petermans over a barrel."

"That would explain why Rogge kidnapped Heather," Melanie said. "He abducted her because Peterman needed to find out if she had learned his family secret. Rogge couldn't just scare her away."

Suddenly Melanie exclaimed: "Oh, my God!"

She didn't need to explain what she was thinking. I'd already reached the same conclusion: a long-hidden secret. Blackmail. The threat of an exposé. That was plenty enough motive for murder.

Nineteen

Before we reached Pushmataha, I called Sheriff Moorehead.

"Any luck?" I asked.

"I've got a hundred volunteers combing the woods, but there's no trace of Heather. How's her sister holding up?"

"As well as can be expected."

"Before I forget, copies of Jeb Rogge's phone bills are waiting for you at the courthouse in my office," Moorehead said. Then he warned me that reporters and television camera crews had staked out Rogge's hunting cabin and were milling around town. "Word's out that Heather Cole has a twin. They're asking where she is and if she's giving interviews."

I switched subjects. "Does Senator Nehemiah Peterman own a house in Pushmataha County?"

"He and his brothers and sisters all live north of town. Actually, they're fairly close to Jeb Rogge's place. Peterman's brother is Rogge's neighbor. The senator's acreage is next to his brother's spread."

"What's that mean in relation to Rogge's hunting cabin? How far is Senator Peterman's house from the cabin?"

"About four miles as the crow flies. Why?"

"Just curious. I saw the senator in Washington last week. How well do you know him?"

"Everyone here knows him. He gave a speech at the Pushmataha Elementary School Friday night. He comes home at least once a month. You won't find many folks who will say anything nasty about him or his family."

When I hung up, I told Melanie that Senator Peterman was in town Friday night. "That means he could have been at Rogge's hunting cabin early Saturday morning—just before we found Jeb Rogge dead," I added.

"Wouldn't we have seen him on the road that leads to the cabin?" she asked.

"Not if he came through the woods on an ATV—a four-wheel, all-terrain motorcycle. He could have cut across his brother's land. Let's find out if the FBI forensic team has found any ATV tracks at the cabin."

I telephoned Phillip Shurman in Washington.

"The team faxed a preliminary report to headquarters this morning," he said. "I'll check to see if there were any ATV tracks." He put me on hold. When he returned, he said: "They found ATV tracks at more than a dozen spots in the woods near the cabin. But no one paid much attention to them because Rogge and his son used ATVs when they went hunting."

"Did the forensic team make any moldings of the ATV tracks? It rained hard Friday night, so the ground would have been pretty muddy."

"There's nothing in the fax indicating they did. It's preliminary, but I think the team is going to conclude that Jeb Rogge and Lester Alfred both took their own lives."

"I don't believe Rogge killed himself. Did they check the trajectory of the .22-caliber slug?"

"Nick, do I tell you how to do your job?" Shurman asked. "We've got a top-notch forensic team investigating this. They've already reached several conclusions: The chicken bones found under the the cabin floor contained traces of saliva from both Heather and Rogge. That proves she was definitely being held there. It looks like Rogge was bringing her food and water. Traces of Heather's and Rogge's blood were found inside Heather's room at the Stars and Bars motel too. She must have scratched him while they were fighting. That's enough to show Rogge abducted her. But there's absolutely nothing that suggests anyone murdered Rogge at the cabin."

There wasn't any point in arguing. Instead, I waited and vented to Melanie. "Forensic evidence is the all the rage. DNA, trace evidence, fingerprints, gunpowder residue— everyone is convinced science and technology can solve any crime," I complained.

"I've read how DNA testing has led to dozens of innocent men being released from death rows," Melanie volunteered.

"Forensic analysis has absolutely revolutionized criminology, but all it can do is provide a detective with clues. You still have to understand what those clues mean and how they fit together, and you can't do that well unless you understand people and their motives. Sometimes there may not be any forensic evidence because the killer plotted out the crime with great precision and discipline. That, in itself, tells you much about the murderer. I'd rather have an investigator on my side who has a sixth sense when it comes to understanding people, than the FBI's best forensic team."

"Then we're really in luck," Melanie said. "Because Heather has been guiding us."

When we reached the Pushmataha Courthouse, I suggested that Melanie stay in the SUV to avoid reporters. I hurried in to get Rogge's telephone bills. When I returned, Melanie was gone. The file folder that she'd been carrying was on the front seat along with her purse. I scanned the town square and saw several people running into Rabbit Creek Park toward the trophy tree.

A gaggle of reporters and camera crews had encircled Melanie by the time I reached the tree. She had removed her fishing cap and sunglasses.

"Heather Cole is my twin sister," she announced in a calm and controlled voice. "As many of you know, she was abducted and the FBI has determined that she was held under the floorboards in a crawl space at Jeb Rogge's hunting cabin. What the authorities haven't told you is that Rogge didn't act alone. There were actually two kidnappers."

A voice inside my head began silently pleading with her: *Don't accuse Senator Peterman! Please, please, please! We don't have enough proof!*

"Was the second kidnapper Lester Alfred?" a reporter yelled.

"The second kidnapper is not Lester Alfred," Melanie replied. "But you're on the right track. My sister was abducted because she was investigating the lynching of Lamar Grant—a hanging that happened right here where I'm now standing. The second kidnapper was also involved in that lynching."

Now the voice inside my head was screaming: *Don't tell them about your dream! Don't tell them that you talked to Heather in your dream!*

"How do you know there were two kidnappers?" a reporter called out. "Has the FBI told you there were two men involved?"

"No. It wasn't the FBI. My sister, Heather, told me there were two of them."

For a moment, the reporters seemed confused. But their hesitation didn't last.

"How'd she tell you?" one asked.

"Are you saying you've talked to your sister since she was kidnapped?"

"No!" Melanie shouted above the harangue of questions. "Heather told me two nights ago that she had been kidnapped by two men. I talked to her in a dream."

Oh, damn! the voice in my head shrieked.

"Did you say 'dream'?" one of the reporters asked. "You talked to your sister in a dream?"

"Is this a joke?" another demanded.

"Not at all," Melanie said. "Heather appeared to me in

my dream. She told me that I had to come quickly if I wanted to save her. She told me there were two men responsible for her abduction. She told me she was being held under the floor of a hunting cabin. That's how Sheriff Moorehead knew where to look." She took a deep breath and then said: "I know the second kidnapper's name. I know exactly who he is. I've come here today to tell you that he will be punished. I am going to see to it. He will not get away with what he has done! Heather wants him punished and so do I!"

Melanie was immediately pelted with questions about her clairvoyance. Her impromptu press conference quickly degenerated into a freak show. The more Melanie tried to explain her simultaneous dream conversations, the more ridiculous she sounded.

But it made compelling television.

Here was the twin sister of a missing, and famous, Washington reporter explaining to the world on *CNN Live* that she had spoken to her missing sister during a dream. Incredibly, Melanie acted as if paranormal dream communication were an everyday occurrence—not just for her, but for everyone. I pushed myself through the throng and gently touched Melanie's arm.

"Time to go," I whispered.

"Hey, who are you?" one of the reporters yelled.

Ignoring the question, I gave Melanie's arm a tug. By this point, she realized she was being ridiculed. She slipped up next to me but we couldn't escape because we still were encircled by a ring of TV crews. I gently pushed one of the cameras out of the way so we could exit.

"You can't do that!" the cameraman screamed. "This is a public park, we've got a right to be here."

I leaned in close to prevent anyone else from hearing me. "You got a right to be here and I got a right to kick your ass if you don't get out of our way!" I said. He knew from my tone that I meant it.

"He just threatened me!" the cameraman yelled as he moved out of the way. The others cleared a path.

"If you can talk to your sister in dreams," a reporter snapped, "why not take a nap and ask her where she is right now?"

Much to my horror, Melanie replied in a sincere voice: "I plan to do that tonight."

Behind me, I could hear a reporter humming the opening bars from the old television drama *The Twilight Zone*.

"Melanie, don't say anything more," I whispered.

"Will you tell us tomorrow if you've reached Heather?" another reporter called out.

A cameraman said: "With a body like that, you can visit me in my dreams anytime, babycakes."

The news hounds followed us across the park to the SUV and kept filming as we drove away.

"They didn't believe me," Melanie said.

"Did you really expect them to?"

"I was hoping they might, but it doesn't really matter," she said. "I've accomplished what I wanted to accomplish."

"What the hell does that mean?" I said, clearly peeved. "Why did you talk to them? I thought we were a team here, working together, not simply deciding on our own to hold a press conference!"

"I wanted the second kidnapper to know I knew about him. I want him to believe I know his name."

"But we don't know his name!" I protested. "We have suspicions about Peterman, but we could be wrong. Are you trying to make yourself a target? What if Heather is still alive and being held hostage somewhere? How's he going to react? How's he going to treat her?"

"Heather's dead!" she said flatly. "I've known that since Saturday morning."

"You can't be certain. She could've escaped. She might be wandering around in the woods."

"No, Nick, Heather is dead and you're just going to have to accept that. As far as what I said today, I want you to know that Heather wanted me to say those things. She urged me to tell the world there was a second kidnapper and he's going to pay!"

"What are you talking about? Another dream?"

"No. Sometimes I know exactly what Heather wants me to say and do. It's been this way since we were little kids. We've always known each other's thoughts but this is even more than that. Now that I know she is dead, I can feel her becoming part of me once again, even stronger than before. It's as if her essence is moving into my body and my mind now. We are merging together."

"What are you saying?" I asked.

"When I was waiting for you in the SUV, I felt an urge come over me to talk to the media. I knew immediately it was Heather who wanted me to do it. She was moving me to brief them. So you see, I didn't really have a choice."

"You just told me Heather is dead!"

"Death doesn't matter. Death can't end our twin thing. Heather is still part of me and can work through me, you know, to do things for her."

She could tell from my expression that I simply didn't understand what she was saying. Either that or I didn't believe her.

"Listen, Nick," she said. "I can't explain it, okay? It's just how it is! Sometimes Heather takes control!"

When we reached the Holiday Inn, I made certain the room was safe and there were no onlookers and then dashed outside and hustled Melanie indoors from the SUV. I drove it around to the other side of the motel and parked it. Now that we had been shown on national television driving away from downtown Pushmataha, I didn't want the SUV parked outside our room.

"I'm going to take a shower," Melanie said. Moments later, I heard her sobbing in the tub despite the noise that the water was making. Only then, at that very moment, did I remember that Jeb Rogge's telephone records were still out in the SUV. I went outside and fetched them.

At least they were something real. They were something I could hold in my hand and examine for clues.

Twenty

I was beginning to examine Jeb Rogge's telephone bills when the motel phone rang.

"What the hell is this nonsense about Melanie Cole going on television saying she talks to her sister in dreams?" Phillip Shurman asked. Before I could reply, he said, "Nick, I put my ass on the line to get our finest forensic team down there for you and now this entire investigation is becoming embarrassing."

"Embarrassing? How's it embarrassing?"

"Because I'm being told your case is a simple kidnapping and suicide, and even though Heather Cole is a prominent *Tribune* reporter, we've got a triple homicide in Boston, and a mob hit in Brooklyn, and both cities want help from our forensic guys who are still tied up in Mississippi. Having Heather's sister appear on CNN acting like she's part of the psychic friends network isn't winning us any points here."

I tried to calm him. As soon as I put down the phone, it

rang again. This time it was my boss. "You were seen on CNN with Heather Cole's twin. Aren't you supposed to be on vacation?" Senator DeLong asked.

"It's a long story," I replied.

"Do you know whose home state you're in? For God's sake, you're in Senator Peterman's backyard. Now listen, he and I have patched up our little differences and I don't want you stepping into something down there and tracking it all the way back up here and causing a stink. You let those good old boys in Mississippi handle this. You understand?"

After we finished talking, I unplugged the phone and spread out Rogge's telephone bills on the motel table. The Rogge family had three separate phone lines. One was an 800 number that you could call to purchase various Aryan hate posters, books, T-shirts, and hats. You could also listen to recorded hate messages. Press one to hear how Jews controlled the media; press two if you were infuriated by interracial dating; three was reserved for gay-bashing; and so on. It appeared from the bills that a second telephone line was used as the family's main number. A third, private line had an unlisted number and it was registered solely to Jeb Rogge. He'd used it only a dozen times in the past thirty days. I started with it.

The first call that caught my attention was an incoming call that had been made from a local Pushmataha number to Rogge on Tuesday around noon. I'd seen that number before. It was Lester Alfred's at the pharmacy. Obviously, this was the call that Alfred had made after he was confronted by Heather. Alfred had admitted that he'd panicked and called to warn Rogge about Heather.

According to the phone records, as soon as Rogge had finished talking to Alfred, he had placed a call to a number in the 202 area code. I recognized 202 because it is assigned to Washington, D.C. The next three digits were 224, which is the prefix for the three U.S. Senate office buildings, including my own office line.

Interesting! Rogge had called someone on Capitol Hill

as soon as Alfred had warned him about Heather. I plugged in the motel's phone and dialed the complete number. After four rings, it was answered by a machine.

"You have reached the office of Mississippi Senator Nehemiah Peterman. We're sorry, but our offices are closed . . ."

This was almost too easy.

I reviewed what I had learned. Heather confronts Alfred. He calls Rogge and Rogge calls Peterman. It made sense since all three had good reasons for not wanting Heather to investigate the Lamar Grant lynching.

The telephone records showed that Rogge's call to Senator Peterman's office lasted less than a minute. Unless you're the president of the United States or a fellow senator, it usually takes more time than that just to be put through to a senator. I had a hunch that Rogge had simply left word with someone that he wished to speak to the senator.

I continued down the bill and found that twenty minutes later Rogge had received a telephone call from a Washington, D.C., prefix—289. That wasn't on the Capitol's grounds, so I dialed it and let it ring, one, two, three, four times. I thought an answering machine might pick up, but none did. I was about to hang up when someone picked up the receiver but immediately put it down, ending the call. I dialed the number again. This time, no one responded until the ninth ring.

"Hello!" I said. "Hello!"

But, as before, the line went dead. I dialed the number for a third time and let it ring and ring. When someone finally lifted up the receiver, I exclaimed: "Please don't hang up!"

"Whatdayawant?" a gruff voice asked, the words running together.

"Who am I speaking to?" I asked.

"Whoyacalling?"

"Who are you?" I asked.

"Whoyacalling?"

"I'd like to know who I'm speaking with?"

He hung up.

Once again, I redialed the number. Ten rings later, a woman answered.

"Stop calling this number or I'll put the police on your ass!" she declared.

"Wait," I said. "Could you please tell me who this is?"

"Ain't none of your business. You need to get yourself a job instead of smoking crack all day long!"

"I think I dialed the wrong number," I said. "Can you please tell me where I'm calling?"

"You trying to be funny?"

"No. I don't have a clue what you're talking about. I'm simply trying to find out if I dialed the right number."

"Well, this here is a pay phone at the train station in Washington, D.C., and it's right in front of my cash register at the Frank N' Stein and it rings all day and all night with peoples buying smack."

I began to ask another question but she hung up.

Although there are several subway stations in Washington, there is only one train station that has fast food restaurants inside its complex. That's Union Station, which is about a ten-minute walk from the Senate office buildings.

I looked at the timetable that I'd written out. Heather confronts Alfred. He calls Rogge. Rogge telephones Peterman's office. Twenty minutes later, Rogge gets a return call from a pay phone in Union Station. According to the phone records, that call lasts ten minutes.

I continued reading down the list of phone calls. The next day—Wednesday—at exactly six p.m., Rogge received another telephone call from the Union Station pay phone. At exactly six p.m. on Thursday, he got another call from that number.

"Find anything?" Melanie asked, as she stepped from the bathroom.

I showed her the sequence. "Senator Peterman's office on Capitol Hill is in the Dirksen Office Building, the same as mine. He could slip out a side door and walk over to the train station and back without anyone thinking anything odd was going on."

"Did Jeb Rogge get a call from Union Station on Friday at six?" she asked.

"No, there's none listed."

"That's the night when Senator Peterman came home to Mississippi and gave a speech at the elementary school," she noted.

"Look at this," I said, pointing to Rogge's Friday list of telephone calls. "Rogge began calling a number at seven p.m. and kept dialing it every half hour until ten o'clock when, apparently, someone answered." It was a local Pushmataha number.

"Let's dial it," Melanie suggested.

I did, and after seven rings, a man answered: "This is the Peterman house, how can I help you?"

"Sorry to disturb you," I said, "but this is Nick LeRue. I'm an investigator with the Senate Judiciary Committee. Is the senator available?"

"No," the man replied politely. "He and his wife returned to Washington early this morning. If it's important, I can telephone him at his house in Virginia and give him your number to call."

"I'll just call his office on the Hill tomorrow," I replied. "Thank you."

As soon as I had hung up, Melanie said: "Jeb Rogge used his private line to call Senator Peterman at his home in Pushmataha on Friday night, and the next morning, Rogge turns up dead at the hunting cabin and Heather has disappeared."

"Don't you think it's odd that Rogge called him at home?" I asked. "The only reason why Peterman would use a pay phone in Union Station would be if he wanted to hide his tracks. Yet, Rogge called him at home."

"It was raining hard on Friday night, remember," Melanie said. "Rogge may have been too lazy to drive into town to use a pay phone."

"So it's possible that Senator Peterman doesn't know

there's a phone record that shows Jeb Rogge called him," I said. "He might think that Rogge was using a pay phone. I wonder what the media would make of that call."

"Especially if we were to tell them that Senator Peterman was also at Rabbit Creek Park in September 1955, taking photographs of Lamar Grant being lynched," Melanie added.

I picked up the phone and dialed a Washington, D.C., number. On the third ring, a man answered, and I could tell from his voice that he'd been asleep. "Shurman," I said, "I need a favor. Can you get me copies of the telephone records from a pay phone at Union Station?"

"A pay phone at Union Station?"

"That's right. It's in front of the Frank N' Stein Restaurant. You know, hot dogs and beer."

"Are you drunk?" he asked.

"No. I'm very serious."

"And this isn't something that could've waited until morning?" he complained.

"I'm in a hurry, and I know how long these things can take."

"Every beat cop in Washington knows those pay phones are used by dealers peddling dope. There's probably a thousand calls made every day on them. That's a lot of paperwork."

"Start with last Tuesday and only give me the records for calls that were made between the hours of five p.m. and eight p.m. up to Saturday night. That should limit the number."

I read Shurman the pay phone number.

"LeRue," he said. "Don't call me again tonight."

When I finished the call, Melanie asked: "Why are you getting them?"

"I want to see if Peterman called anyone else in Mississippi from the train station after he talked to Rogge at six o'clock each night. I want to make certain there isn't another suspect in this daisy chain."

I looked at the clock. It was one a.m. No wonder Shurman had been angry. Melanie pulled back the bedcovers. "Ready for bed?" she asked.

I ignored several obvious sexual comebacks and instead walked into the bathroom to shower and brush my teeth. Melanie and I had been together almost constantly for three days. We had spent two nights sleeping in the same bed. With all of the drama unfolding around us, I'd forgotten to ask her about her husband and their daughter, Kaitlyn. I assumed that Melanie had telephoned them earlier when I had gone out to get us some carry-out food. I was curious how much longer I was going to have Melanie all to myself. I decided to ask, but when I stepped into the room, the lights were out and I could hear her breathing softly. We had slept in the same bed enough for me to know that she was already asleep. I crawled under the sheet that separated us and within minutes, so was I.

Twenty-one

Melanie was falling, looking up at a shrinking white stream of light that became smaller and smaller as she dropped until it became like a distant star on a clear night. She was surrounded by darkness. Silence. Solitude. She couldn't hear. Her ears were clogged. She reached up and used her fingers as pincers to extract the blockage. It was something dry, so dry that it cracked when she grabbed it. She tugged, but it wouldn't budge free until she jerked it hard. A plug of blood-soaked tree leaves popped from deep inside her ear but as soon as she'd removed it, another fell into her canal. She locked her fingers onto this plug too, and pulled until it came bursting out, only to be immediately replaced by another.

Now she was having trouble seeing. Her eyes were dotted with mud that fell from above like pigeon dung. She wiped her face, but her fingers only smeared the sludge. Undefined images flittered above her.

She tried to turn but her legs refused to obey her. She was trapped in a limp body. A noise. Followed by a piercing pain. Then another. And another. Stings, but with more punch.

The scene changed.

Melanie was drifting now under clear water. She didn't need to swim to the ocean's surface, but instead was able to breath beneath it, like fishes in the blue tropical seas. Where was she? Off an island? The Bahamas, perhaps, where black women troll the beaches offering to braid corn rows in vacationers' hair and gigolos gleefully splash oil onto the backs of wealthy divorcees who sun themselves on chaise lounges like beached whales with skin dimpled by cellulite.

She could see them on the shore, but she had no interest in joining them. She was free. Hundreds of fish surrounded her. Pale green swallowtail damselfish slithered to her right, followed by schools of yellowtail. She spied a blue-banded goby sticking close to the soft coral and sponges growing on the reef beneath her. There, darting over a jagged rock, was a red garibaldi with brilliant blue specks. It was circling the nest it had made, flashing its brilliant colors to attract females to lay eggs, willing to bite human divers if they ventured too close.

Melanie was nude, her skin pale white in this undersea world so vibrant with colors, an albino with warm water washing over her breasts, buttocks, and pubic area never before so openly exposed. She twisted, rolling over so that she could now look upward at the sun's yellow rays that pierced the invisible fluid ceiling, trickling down in splinters through a natural prism, creating shades of reds, purples, and pinks, as if she were swimming under the stained glass of a great cathedral's rose window.

A child appeared. It was neither male nor female, but a cherub with short curly locks of yellow hair, like gold spun from some underworld Rumpelstiltskin's wheel. The child motioned for her to follow and Melanie understood without speaking that this angelic guide had been sent specifically for her. She slipped in behind the child's tiny feet, following as they glided through curious fish, some racing

beside them toward an opening in the reef, a black hole—
spilled ink on white parchment. Melanie stopped, afraid to
enter the opening, but her child-guide dove headfirst into
the craggy darkness. Because she did not want to be left
behind, Melanie followed.

They were not alone. She could feel the presence of
other things. The fish here, however, were huge, fierce, and
dark. Gray sharks hovered above her, watching her every
move with dead eyes, inching through the still water which
had no current. She glanced below her and saw fish such as
none that she had ever seen. They were hideous, bumpy
creatures that would come rising up without warning, their
ugly faces appearing from the depths and then vanishing
beneath her. These fish had no eyes, for there was nothing
in their lightless world to see. She moved closer to the
child for fear of becoming lost as the tiny angel swam
deeper and deeper. The water was cold now, even frigid,
causing Melanie to shiver and wish that she was no longer
nude. Still, she pushed on.

She was afraid. She had traveled a long distance and she
realized she might not be able to find her way back. She
had to fight a growing urge to flee, to escape from this
frightening darkness and return to the clear surface where
she could gulp in mouthfuls of air. But the angel beckoned
her and she did not want to break away and be alone with
the fish wandering aimlessly beneath her, watching her.

Just as her exhausted arms were about to fail, Melanie
and her guide reached their destination, and the child
paused, allowing Melanie to move past her. It was Heather,
dressed in white, a full-length gown, and lying in a coffin
made of glass. Her eyes were closed, her hands motionless
along her sides. Her skin was translucent, as if there were
no skin, only a white presence, a ghost of what had been.

Melanie pressed herself against the sheer sarcophagus
and screamed Heather's name, and when the corpse inside
heard her, it opened its lids and stared at Melanie and tried
to smile but its lips were frozen and could not be moved.
Only Heather's liquid eyes could deliver any message,

only its eyes could show the love that it felt, only its eyes could tell Melanie that this shell of withering flesh that once had been Heather, had understood that she had come to be with her on this, her final journey.

Despite the repugnancy of the scene, Melanie clutched the casket and kicked wildly in a failed effort to pull it to the surface. It weighed too much. She searched for a tool to smash the enclosure, but there was none, so she pounded her fists on its smooth surface until she felt certain that she had shattered every bone in her hands. The child-guide came to her and motioned for her to follow, but she didn't want to go and she leaned forward and pressed her lips against the glass, tasting the salt in the water, but not caring. She cried, her tears mixing with the sea, and she suddenly heard the moaning of a giant whale as she stared at her sister's large pupils now devoid of light, having turned dead, like those of the fishes below them. As the clear container drifted down to depths where even the fish without eyes could not swim, Melanie heard another moan, hollow, sad, a bellow that reverberated through the water, bringing sadness to all who heard its pitiful wail.

The child-guide escorted Melanie back through the cave into the shallower water, where the tropical sun shone down and everything was bright. It left her there, disappearing behind a school of scythe-marked butterfly fish, all bright yellow and black, their scales flashing refracted sunshine as they scurried by.

Suddenly Melanie realized she was devoid of oxygen and this sent her scurrying toward the air. She kicked hard. *Hurry.* Her lungs felt as if they were going to burst. She was frantic, still too deep below the divide between the sea and surface to breath. She wasn't certain she could make it.

"Melanie! You're having a nightmare!"

She was gasping. Her body was wet with sweat. "Just . . . ah . . . give . . . ah . . . me a . . . ah . . . minute," she stammered.

"I'll get you some water," I said.

"No!" she shrieked. "Not water!"

I sat next to her on the bed and waited.

"Nick," she whispered, "it was Heather. She came to say goodbye."

I looked at the red digits on the motel radio. It was 6:58 a.m. I started to speak, but the telephone rang. It was Sheriff Moorehead.

"We've just found Heather Cole's body," he said.

"Where?"

"About two miles from Jeb Rogge's hunting cabin. In a cave that someone had stuck branches over. A search dog crawled in there about a half hour ago and when its handler went in after it, he spotted Heather's body. Someone had pushed her down into a crevice. Her body was resting on a muddy ledge about fifty feet down."

"Had she been shot?"

"Yes, once in the head at close range and then several more times in the chest. Small-caliber. I'm guessing it's the same pistol that Rogge later used on himself. The way I see it, Rogge shot her in the head once he got her to the lip of the cave, and then pushed her down into the crevice. Only I don't think she was dead, because the crew that climbed down to get her found signs that she had tried to move. She'd tried to brush leaves and debris off her face that he'd tossed down on her to hide the body. I think Rogge must have seen her stirring and fired the other shots to finish her off."

"Did you find any ATV tracks near the cave?" I asked.

"It looked like someone had driven by there recently on an ATV, but they must have been dragging branches or chains or something behind them to distort their tracks because the tire treads were completely chopped up."

He waited for me to comment but I didn't.

Moorehead said: "We're transporting her body to the Pushmataha County Hospital. She's nude, covered with blood and grime. After the crime-scene people get done, the nurses will clean her up and you can bring Melanie over to identify the body. You know where her sister's staying, right?"

"Yes, I'll tell her the news," I said.

I hung up and looked at Melanie. But I didn't need to say anything. She already knew.

Twenty-two

I stood at the back of the chapel inside Washington National Cathedral during Heather's funeral and watched the mourners. The president of the United States was traveling overseas, but had sent his press secretary. I spotted at least a dozen members of Congress, including my boss, as well as another dozen Georgetown socialites. Most of them were women, who used to bristle whenever Heather skewered their parties in the *Tribune,* but who always made certain she was invited to their next soiree. Every member of the Washington press corps who mattered was here. Two network anchors had flown in that morning. Famed investigative reporter Andrew Middleton was sitting next to Melanie. Although I had lived with Heather much longer than he had, Middleton was her most recent lover and that entitled him to center stage and condolences.

Heather would have been impressed by her send-off. It was a testament to her prominence. She had always relished her role as a media celebrity. During a eulogy being given by one of Heather's editors from the *Tribune,* my mind drifted back to that last day when Heather and I had lived together. No matter what you claim after someone leaves, you really do know in your heart why she deserted you. You can pretend that you were shocked and your friends—because they are your friends—will let that pass without correction. But even they saw signs that the end was coming even if you wanted to pretend that you never had.

Heather and I had been bickering, not about anything important, but about little irritants, like how I never made the bed when I was the last to leave the apartment in the mornings, or how she never bothered to replace the toilet paper after she had used the last of it. Looking back, I can now see that those spats were more important than I had first thought. We'd reached a point in our relationship where neither of us was able to overlook the trivial things that don't matter much when you love someone.

It was during our final few hours together that the gloves had flown off. That's when she'd announced that she really didn't want to resolve our differences, but instead wished to leave and make a fresh start with someone else.

"We're different people from when we fell in love!" she exclaimed.

"Please don't give me that 'we've grown apart' line—it's so cliché," I replied.

"It's more than that. You can't give me what I want from life."

What came next was a soliloquy by Heather that eloquently pointed out everything that I had done wrong during our relationship. Her critique was so well spoken that I half expected her to hand me a list of footnotes after she had finished, with the times of my sins carefully listed. I hadn't prepared a rebuttal. That's one of the advantages of being the one who leaves. You have time to rehearse your lines because you're the one who knows when you're actually going to end things. I can summarize her complaints in a these few words: I had become a noose.

"It may sound arrogant," she'd said, "but I've always known I'm special. I've always known my life matters."

Most people, she explained, live mundane lives in cookie-cutter suburbs where they watch their Gap kids playing soccer on Saturdays, parade off to church services on Sundays, and spend two weeks a year traveling in a minivan on a family vacation to a national park, a beach, or a mountain cabin. If there is any excitement in their lives, it comes vicariously, mostly through movies or gossip. Some of these drones might get wild during a drunken weekend in Las Vegas. If they are really adventurous, others might cheat on their spouses in a desperate effort to pump genuine emotion into their stagnant lives. But most humans die without ever leaving a mark.

"The rest of this country describes 'Potomac Fever' as a horrible curse," she'd said. "They accuse their congressman of being bitten by it. But I say, 'Thank God they've gotten it!' Everything really important in America happens in one of only three cities—New York, Los Angeles, and Washington, D.C. The rest of this nation is an intellectual and cultural wasteland."

It was an odd statement, because her father had become famous writing as an editor in Little Rock, Arkansas. But I hadn't pointed that out. I couldn't have, really, because she was still in the midst of delivering her speech.

"In New York City, power is defined by money. The Donald Trumps rise to the top. In Los Angeles, it's all sex and entertainment and youth. But here in Washington, it takes more than being rich or having big tits to emerge as a player. Washington is about power—pure unadulterated political power—the kind that absolutely terrifies people because you can reach out and crush them with it."

Heather then said something odd. She started spouting off a series of names: Sam Rayburn, Carl Albert, Ed Muskie, Claude Pepper, Jim Wright, Tip O'Neill, Sam Ervin, George Romney, George McGovern, Pat Schroeder, Geraldine Ferraro, Walter Mondale, Gary Hart. What any of these former members of Congress had to do with our relationship wasn't clear to me. But that hadn't slowed her down. Instead, she moved on up the political power ladder: Richard Nixon, Gerald Ford, Jimmy Carter, Ronald Reagan.

When she got to Bill Clinton, I interrupted: "What's your point? I don't recall inviting any of these politicians into our bed."

"All of them were once gods in this town," she'd replied. "Now they're has-beens. What's my point? Do you know who has outlasted every one of them?" Without waiting for my reply, she'd answered her own question. "The Fourth Estate! The media!" How many years has Barbara Walters been interviewing presidents and world leaders? How many presidents have been grilled by Helen Thomas at White House press conferences?

"I AM A JOURNALIST!" she'd declared. "And Washington is where the absolute best of the best reporters come."

It had been at this moment when Heather had explained to me in the simplest of terms how power in our nation's capital works. There are three categories of residents in the city, and only three: those elected or appointed to power, those without any power, and the media elite. "Of them, journalists dominate. Why? Because they can make a nobody into a somebody, and bring a somebody to his knees."

Continuing, Heather explained that Washington's elected officials and their subordinates flow through this city in an endless stream. Democrats. Republicans. Independents. It hardly matters. They arrive with a flourish, promising to change and improve the system, but as soon as they get settled in, it is the system that changes them. They get drunk on its power. The need to impress overwhelms them. They begin to sprinkle foreign phrases—*je ne sais quoi* or *joie de vivre*—into their casual conversations. They surround themselves with the accoutrements of power: expansive offices, stretch limousines, personal aides, and reserved booths at the fanciest restaurants. And having once tasted these perks, they hunger for more. This is when they learn Washington's most sacred truth. In the nation's capital, the perception of power can lead to the acquisition of more power. And that is the real key to understanding the power hierarchy in this city.

As masters of the print and air waves, journalists control perception.

Each morning, Washington's most powerful read the *New York Times,* the *Wall Street Journal,* and the *Washington Tribune* before they take a bite of breakfast. Why? So they can see who's being quoted, who's hot, and who's in charge. They hire professional coaches to prepare them for television interviews and depend on public relations experts to spin their points of view. They keep the home telephone numbers of media critic Howie Kurtz and the dean of political writers, David Broder, in their private Rolodexes. They go out of their way to court whoever is the hottest talking head of the moment: Don Imus, Bill O'Reilly, Rush Limbaugh. It's a dangerous game. Misspell "potato" and your presidential ambitions are ruined forever. Look straight into the camera and firmly deny that you "had sex with that woman" and polls will show that the nation will believe you until she produces a dress stained with your semen. And even then, someone will believe you because you seemed so damn sincere on television. The media has become the message.

"I'm going to be the next Sally Quinn, the next Benjamin Bradlee, the next George Will, the next William Safire, the next Tim Russert," Heather had assured me.

It was at this point that I had stupidly asked her what this diatribe about journalism had to do with our foundering relationship.

"You hate going to Georgetown parties!" she'd fairly shrieked. "You've got hundreds of sources on Capitol Hill, but they're all elevator operators and disgruntled staffers. You don't network with anyone who's on the 'A' list!"

"I've never stopped you from attending Georgetown parties or from networking with your precious elite," I'd replied.

"You want me to become your wife, the mother of your

children," she'd declared, as if I were asking her to commit some heinous crime. "You want me to move to the suburbs and become a stay-at-home mom."

"I do want you to marry me and have children," I answered. "Is that so horrible?"

"But you're a *nobody*!" she'd continued. "Even worse, you enjoy being one! You're happy to watch the game from the cheap seats. I need a quarterback."

In the end, it had come to this: I was being ditched with a sports metaphor. I had failed to make the first squad. I was a waterboy, and definitely not a quarterback.

I left the chapel before Heather's funeral ended and wove through the television cameras and photographers. No one asked me who I was. It was true what Heather had said. In a city of celebrity, I didn't mind being a nobody. I paused and glanced back as others now came streaming out of the church. The pallbearers carried Heather's burnished bronze coffin down the stone steps. I wasn't going to attend the graveside ceremony. I'd had enough, and so, apparently, had most of the other mourners. Having made their obligatory appearance, they were now scampering away, clutching cell phones to their ears as they raced like salmon hurdling upstream toward a black line of waiting limos.

"Have the Palestinians walked out of the peace talks?" one newsman barked into his phone.

"Is the mayor's news conference still on?" another demanded.

"Do we have footage?"

Washington prides itself as a city of great monuments to the nation's past, but it actually has little memory. Instead, it's a city of *what's next!* Like yesterday's edition of the *Tribune,* Heather Cole had become old news.

I strolled four blocks down a side street and flagged a taxi. During the ride, I thought of another newspaper editor who, like Heather's father, had once been called a "sage." William Allen White won two Pulitzer prizes for his small town Kansas editorials. I recalled one written in August 1901, called *What Is a Man Profited?*

> The longest funeral procession that has formed in ten years followed the Rev. John Jones three long miles in the hot July sun out to Dry Creek Cemetery. Now, a funeral procession may mean little or much. When a rich and powerful man dies, the people play politics and attend his funeral for various reasons. But here was the body of a meek, gentle little old man . . . It won't take twenty minutes to settle his estate in probate court. The reason so many people lined up behind the hearse that held the kind old man's mortality was simple: They loved him.

White went on to describe how when money "talks, it speaks a broken, poverty-stricken language. Hearts talk better, clearer, and with wider intelligence."

I remembered White's editorial because of my father. He used to keep a copy of it framed on the wall of his study in his church. Perhaps he secretly pictured himself as a much-beloved Reverend John Jones. But he'd never been that to me.

I usually don't feel sorry for myself, but I wasn't in the mood to return to work after the funeral, so I let the cab drop me at my apartment on Capitol Hill. It's a nice two-bedroom on the second floor of a red brick row house about eight blocks behind the Library of Congress in a neighborhood that is going through what Realtors call "gentrification." That's a code word that means whites are slowly moving into a neighborhood and pushing out poor minorities, but if you're white, you're still taking a risk buying property there because the tide sometimes swings back. At night, an occasional streetwalker can be spotted on my corner and if you venture out alone after dark, there's a good chance you'd encounter a gang of toughs who'll demand your billfold. I hadn't read that morning's edition of the *Tribune,* so I decided to fix myself a sandwich and thumb through it. Heather's photograph stared up at me from the bottom of the front page. The story was a wrap-up, the sort of life summary that newspapers publish as a tribute, whenever someone important on their news staff dies.

> *By Philip Dodge*
> *Washington Tribune Staff*

Washington Tribune journalist Heather Cole will be memorialized today at two o'clock during funeral services at the Bethlehem Chapel of the Washington National Cathedral. At four o'clock, the FBI and the Pushmataha County Sheriff's Office will hold a press conference to announce that they are ending their investigation into her abduction and murder. . . .

"Based on forensic evidence at the crime scene and interviews in Mississippi and elsewhere, we feel confident that Heather Cole was murdered by Jeb Rogge, a self-described racist, and that he acted completely on his own," a spokesman for the FBI said.

The story went on to rehash the facts about her murder: how she had gone to Pushmataha to write a book about the 1955 lynching, been abducted, held hostage, then shot and tossed into a cave. Near the end, there was a brief mention of Melanie and how she and Heather were identical twins. But it didn't mention anything about Melanie's impromptu press conference in Rabbit Creek Park or her claim that she could communicate clairvoyantly in her dreams with Heather.

I spread peanut butter from an old jar onto a slice of dry bread. I didn't have jelly. I added some stale chips and returned to the living room and read the paper. Thankfully, there was a knock on my door after my first bite. It was a Federal Express delivery. The FBI's Phillip Shurman had sent a package. It contained telephone records from the pay phone located in Union Station in front of the Frank N' Stein Restaurant.

I spread the documents out on the kitchen table. Based on copies of Jeb Rogge's telephone records, I already knew that someone—Melanie and I both suspected that it was Senator Peterman—had telephoned Rogge in Mississippi on Wednesday and Thursday nights at precisely six o'clock from the pay phone.

I ran my finger down the pay phone records until I came to six o'clock on Wednesday. Incredibly, the next number called was one that I recognized. It was the *Tribune*'s switchboard and the call had lasted eighteen minutes. Why had the caller telephoned the newspaper immediately after talking to Jeb Rogge?

I flipped through the pages until I found Thursday at six o'clock. Once again, I discovered that the caller had dialed a local number immediately after hanging up with Rogge.

I called Penny Polandick, a librarian at the U.S. Senate Library. Its primary function is to keep track of the hundreds of legislative bills that are introduced each year in Congress, as well as the transcripts of all Senate committee hearings. Over the years, however, I'd developed a friendship with Penny. She was incredibly skilled at finding obscure information.

"I need you to check a phone number in the crisscross directory," I explained. I read her the number. The crisscross matches telephone numbers with addresses.

"Mr. LeRue," Penny said (she is always formal), "that number belongs to a pay phone located in Georgetown."

That means the caller using the Union Station pay phone was calling a pay phone in Georgetown. "Where exactly in Georgetown is that pay phone located?" I asked.

"At the corner of Twenty-ninth and M streets," she replied. "My girlfriends and I go to a restaurant in that block and if I remember correctly, there's a pay phone just outside a liquor store at that corner. That's probably this phone."

For a moment, I wondered if I had stumbled on a drug dealer's telephone call and had made an error by assuming my six o'clock Union Station caller had placed the second call. But something in my gut told me that I was still on the right trail. I decided to play a hunch. "Penny, what's Andrew Middleton's address in Georgetown?"

A few moments later, she said: "Middleton has a listed home telephone number, but he doesn't list his street address in the directory. Guess he's afraid of fans showing up unannounced. You're in luck, though, because a friend of mine who works over on the Senate Intelligence Committee has been to parties in his house and she just gave me his address. It's on Olive Street Northwest."

"Do you have a map that shows how far his house is from the liquor store pay phone?"

She checked. "It's less than two blocks away."

I thanked her, hung up, and thought about what I'd just learned. My gut feeling was that after Peterman had spoken to Jeb Rogge in Mississippi, the senator had called Andrew Middleton. If I was correct, he'd called him on both Wednesday and Thursday nights. Why?

The trouble with circumstantial evidence is that you link your facts together with assumptions that you want to believe but which could be easily explained or flat wrong. An example: all those goofy similarities that people see in the Kennedy and Lincoln assassinations. Still, I felt I was on to something. And if I was correct, I felt what I had discovered was significant. Why were both men using pay phones? The obvious answer: They were covering their tracks. That meant they didn't want the public to know what they were doing. I scribbled some questions on a notepad:

Was Peterman trying to get Middleton to call off Heather and make her return to Washington? How are Peterman and Middleton linked?

Another thought popped into my head. It had been Middleton's idea for Heather to investigate the 1955 lynching. He was the one who had told her about the initials carved into the tree and had helped her get a juicy book contract. Senator Peterman had taken part in that 1955 lynching— he was the photographer who took the souvenir photograph of the five men. Somehow, Middleton knew about that photograph. He'd referred to it in the exclusive news story that he'd written about Heather's disappearance. So I wrote: *Had Andrew Middleton learned about that lynching photograph from Peterman? And, if so, why had Peterman told him about it?*

My phone rang.

"Can I come up?" It was Melanie.

"Sure, where are you?"

"Outside your building in a cab."

I was waiting with my door open. She was still wearing the black dress that I'd seen her in a few hours before at Heather's funeral. Her eyes were puffy. We sat in the living room.

"I didn't know where else to go," she said. "I'm staying in Heather's apartment at the Watergate and I just needed to get out of there!" Melanie surveyed my apartment and noticed I had a chessboard set up by the bay window. She walked over and examined the position of the pieces.

"I'm not very good at this. Heather was the real player, but it looks like a stalemate," she said.

"That was the last match that Heather and I were playing when she dumped me," I replied. "I'd move a piece each morning before I went to work. She'd move one at night before she went to bed. It was a ritual. I guess I thought it was ironic that we'd reached a draw—or stalemate—on the day when she left me. I never bothered to put away the set."

I decided to ask Melanie about her family. "When are you heading home to South Dakota?"

"My husband and children were supposed to fly out for the funeral, but Kaitlyn had a bad asthma attack. They took her to the hospital, but she's okay now. I feel guilty because I'm not there for her, but I told my husband that I'm not leaving Washington D.C. until we prove Senator Peterman murdered my sister."

I nodded toward the newspaper that I'd left on the coffee table. "According to the *Tribune,* the FBI says Jeb Rogge acted alone."

"Bullshit!" she said. It was the first time that I'd ever heard her swear. "Heather told me in my dream that there were two kidnappers and we both know that Peterman was at the lynching and he was last person Rogge called before he and Heather were murdered."

She reached into a black bag that she was carrying and removed a file folder. From it, she took a picture. It was the 1955 "souvenir" photograph of the Lamar Grant lynching. Someone had used a black marker to write the names of the five men—Robert E. Lee Rogge, Peyton Rogge, Jeb Rogge, Stanley Alfred, and Lester Alfred—above each man's head. There was a yellow sticky note attached to the sheet with the words: *This should be a big help! Love, A.M.*

"Where did you get that?" I asked.

"I found this hidden in the bottom of Heather's desk," she replied. "I think Andrew Middleton gave it to her."

"How the hell did Middleton get a copy of this photograph? The only prints were given to the Rogges and the Alfreds—"

"Peterman must've had one," Melanie interrupted. "After all, he was behind the camera. He would have been given the sixth copy by old man Rogge."

"But why would Peterman hand over an incriminating photograph to the country's leading investigative reporter?"

Melanie shrugged. "You're right, it doesn't make sense."

"Was there anything else in Heather's file folder?" I asked.

"Yes," she replied. She gave me several sheets. "It's all information about Senator Peterman," she said. "It looks like Heather downloaded it from his congressional Web site on the Internet."

I examined each page. The first was Peterman's official biography. It was a gushing public relations release that described how he'd grown up in Pushmataha, been an excellent student and athlete, graduated from the University of Virginia (UVA), and then earned a law degree from American University, Washington College of Law, in downtown D.C. After that, he'd returned to Mississippi, where he'd been a successful prosecutor before entering state politics. His bio listed a dozen state laws that he was credited with getting enacted before he ran for the U.S. Senate. It also described how he was a committed family man who was still married to his childhood sweetheart. I didn't notice anything peculiar.

Besides the bio, the file contained recent press releases. One of those caught my eye. It said Peterman had been given an award by a UVA secret club: the IMP Society, which was described as one of the oldest secret societies at the school. The IMP was organized in 1913, after the administration disbanded a group called the Hot Feet. Its members had gotten into trouble for taking a moose, kangaroo, polar bear, Bengal tiger, and other mounted animals from the school's science department and putting them in front of several professors' residences, the press release noted.

I suddenly had another one of my hunches.

Picking up the phone, I called Penny Polandick at the Senate library. "I need you to find out what college Andrew Middleton attended."

It took her a few moments to check. "He graduated from UVA," she announced. "Then he went directly into the military. Did you know that Middleton studied acting and drama in college? He didn't take a single writing class, which seems funny now that he's such a famous journalist."

"Does his biography list any college organizations that he belonged to?"

"Just a sec while I check." When she returned, she began reading a long list. I stopped her when she reached the IMP Society.

Hanging up the phone, I said: "Peterman and Andrew Middleton both attended UVA."

"They couldn't have been there at the same time," Melanie said. "Senator Peterman is in his early sixties and Middleton is younger than that, so their paths couldn't have crossed."

"That's right," I continued, "but they both were members of the IMP Society, one of the school's secret societies."

"What's a secret society?"

"They're like fraternities. They're very elitist. The only reason why I know about them is because of the Judiciary Committee."

Melanie gave me a puzzled look.

"A few months ago," I explained, "an attorney from Yale was nominated to become a federal judge. He was a member of a secret society called the Skull and Bones, and I read quite a bit about it so I could assure the committee that there wasn't anything wrong with him being a member. The Skull and Bones meets in a building that looks like a crypt."

"Do these secret groups do anything?"

"It's all hush-hush, but some details have leaked out. They have parties, cement friendships, but their main function is to establish connections that they use later on during their lives. One of the initiation rites of the Skull and Bones was that each potential member had to present his autobiography to the group. They were required to reveal something very personal about their past—usually something embarrassing."

"Like what?"

"Some childhood horror story or something illegal that they'd done. It had to be something intimate, because sharing potentially damaging information made the members bond. They had to trust one another."

"Sort of like, 'I've got something on you and you've got something on me, so neither of us better rat the other guy out'?" Melanie said.

"Well, I don't think George Bush and other famous secret society members such as William F. Buckley and Garry Trudeau would describe it that way."

"Do you think the IMP Society at UVA requires its members to confess?" she asked.

Both of us pondered that thought for several moments. Then I said: "This is total speculation, but what if Peterman talked about the 1955 lynching when he was required to reveal something incriminating about his past?"

"That would have been a big confession," she replied.

"It might seem so now, but you've got to remember that he was attending UVA between 1956 and 1960. UVA is in the South and telling other inductees that he had been present at a lynching might have seemed pretty cool to him at the time."

"But that still doesn't explain how Middleton would have gotten a copy of the souvenir photograph," she said. "Remember, he didn't attend UVA at the same time as Peterman."

"I think I know the answer. These secret societies keep scrapbooks that identify all of their members. It's part of their tradition and it also makes it possible for members to network with each other later in life and make certain that an imposter doesn't claim to be a member when he's clearly not one."

"So Peterman reveals that he attended a lynching—" she said.

"Even better than that," I interrupted. "He tells the story and also shows the other inductees copies of photographs that he took—including the souvenir picture."

"And ten years or so later, Andrew Middleton shows up at UVA," she continued, picking up the story.

"Right," I said. "Middleton looks through the scrapbook to familiarize himself with other IMPs and, bingo, he comes across the souvenir photograph and story."

"And he steals the picture," she said.

"That's how he gets the sixth copy—the one that he later gives to Heather, the one that you found in her desk with all of the men's names now written in marker above their heads."

"But why would Andrew Middleton hold on to that photograph for several decades without doing anything, and then suddenly tell Heather about the lynching?" she asked. "Especially if he knew it could result in her discovering the truth about his IMP Society pal Senator Peterman?"

"Let's ask him," I said. "Let's go see Andrew Middleton right now in Georgetown and ask him what the hell is going on."

Twenty-three

In the eighteenth century, Georgetown was a tobacco port on the northwest tip of Washington, D.C. It received cargo by way of the C & O Canal, which still runs through it, although today bikers, joggers, and nature seekers have replaced mules pulling barges. Georgetown has always been a posh neighborhood. It's where John and Jackie Kennedy first lived as a couple and where one of the wives of former Washington Redskins owner Jack Kent Cooke caused a sensation by leaping onto the hood of a fleeing Jaguar sports car being driven by her much younger male companion during a raucous night out. Scandal, history, dignitaries, and the wannabe-famous—all packaged inside a few historic streets. Secretaries of State Henry Kissinger, Cyrus Vance, and Madeline Albright all chose Georgetown addresses. Movie star Elizabeth Taylor lived here during her marriage to husband number seven, U.S. Senator John Warner. Other well-known residents include: former CIA spook William Colby; media heavyweights Katharine Graham, Ben Bradlee, Britt Hume, Rowland

Evans; five-time Grammy winner Mary Chapin Carpenter; tell-all biographer Kitty Kelley; and novelist Herman Wouk. Georgetown has appeared in the movies *True Lies, St. Elmo's Fire, Enemy of the State,* and, of course, *The Exorcist.* A Georgetown address represents power, prestige, and money. Mostly money, and lots and lots of it.

As our taxi parked in front of Andrew Middleton's 1860s-era brick rowhouse built in the then-popular Queen Anne style, I noticed a bumper sticker slapped on a bright red Ferrari 360 Spider convertible parked nearby. Its message seemed fitting: ANYONE WHO SAYS MONEY CAN'T BUY HAPPINESS JUST DOESN'T KNOW WHERE TO SHOP!

A plump Irish housekeeper with a thick brogue and silver hair answered the door. Middleton appeared moments later and invited us into a library to the right of the foyer. Floor-to-ceiling cherry bookcases covered each wall. The shelves contained at least a thousand books. Middleton instructed his help to bring coffee. He then offered Melanie condolences, once again. He sounded sincere. But I remembered several stories Heather had told me about him before she had abandoned me for his bed.

She'd described him as being the most "calculating" individual she'd ever met. At one point, the *Tribune* had wanted to interview a woman who was refusing to talk to the media. Middleton was already famous and he used his notoriety to persuade the subject to meet with him and another *Tribune* staff writer. Before they arrived, Middleton gave the other reporter instructions. He was told to be pushy, even rude, during the interview. Middleton, meanwhile, would stay quiet and play with the woman's dog. After a few minutes, Middleton would become upset with his cohort's conduct. He'd intervene, reprimand the junior guy, and send him to wait in the car. Then Middleton would apologize to the interviewee and gently begin asking her questions—not as a coldhearted reporter, but as a sympathetic and concerned listener.

Middleton's tactics had worked and the target had fallen for his good cop/bad cop routine. The woman trusted Middleton and during the coming days he became her closest confidante. All the while, he sucked information from her like a giant sponge. After he had gotten what he needed, he wrote a brilliant but personally devastating story about the woman.

"Andrew Middleton," Heather had told me, "is a seducer. He becomes whatever he needs to be, says whatever is required, does whatever must be done to entice you into trusting him. It's only after you have confided your innermost secrets to him that you realize that his loyalty is entirely to the story, not you, even if telling that story means watching you bleed."

She had considered that description a compliment. Not me.

Middleton certainly didn't look threatening. He was in his late fifties, thin and towering—well over six-feet tall. He was dressed in what passes for the unofficial uniform in this town: an expensive gray wool suit, light blue oxford shirt with white collar, and a dark red silk tie. He had a dimple in the center of his chin and a nasal tone to his voice. Like Heather, he used his eyes to reach out and touch you with sympathy, concern, compassion. For a moment, I wondered what it would be like to be Andrew Middleton: famous, rich, powerful.

As far as I was concerned, it had all come to him with relative ease. Reared in southern California, the son of a wealthy banker, Middleton had gone directly from UVA into the Army. It was during a time when many soldiers were being sent to Vietnam, but he had been assigned to teach in the foreign language school at Fort Bragg, North Carolina. He'd applied for a reporting job at the *Tribune* as soon as he was discharged, but a major newspaper like it didn't hire inexperienced reporters even if they were fluent in Russian, Spanish, and French. An editor there suggested that Middleton get a job at the *Louisville Courier-Journal* in Kentucky, which was a training ground at the time for the *Tribune.* Legend has it that Middleton telephoned the *Tribune*'s metropolitan editor every morning for three straight months. In each call, he pitched a news story that he'd written about Louisville. The editor bought several of his stories because they were so cleverly written. In each call, Middleton reminded the editor that he wanted to work for him. The editor later joked that he had hired Middleton to stop calling because the *Tribune* was publishing more stories about Louisville than it was about the Washington, D.C., suburbs in its own circulation area.

Middleton had been assigned the night police beat. It was a frustrating position, because the next morning's paper was already being printed by the time he arrived at work. He was simply there overnight in case something traumatic happened. If something newsworthy did occur, his job was to alert the *Tribune*'s editors and the paper's best reporters. But Middleton was not to be denied. After his night shift ended, he continued working. Sometimes he'd stay at his desk twenty hours straight. No one could remember any reporter more intent on succeeding.

His chance at stardom had come shortly before the presidential election in the early 1970s. The incumbent was a sure winner but he was paranoid. Just to make certain that their man would win, the president's reelection staff decided to sabotage his opponent's campaign. They pulled a number of dirty tricks and then sent in a team of burglars to hide listening devices inside their opponent's national political party's headquarters. They got caught. The D.C. police thought it was a simple break-in, but Middleton discovered that one of the burglars had once worked for the CIA. From that moment on, Middleton had clamped on to the story like a pit bull. But despite his hard work, he had soon been stymied. Enter an anonymous source: the Wizard. It was a nickname that Middleton gave his source because of the movie *The Wizard of Oz*. Much like the movie's fictional character, Middleton's source preferred to pull strings from behind a curtain. With the Wizard's guidance, Middleton had traced the dirty tricks and burglary all the way into the White House. Ultimately, Middleton had proved that the president himself had been involved in a cover-up. The leader of the free world was forced to resign or face impeachment.

If this all sounds familiar, it's probably because Middleton's story was memorialized by Hollywood in a made-for-TV movie that was the second highest watched program that year. Only the Super Bowl drew more viewers. The drama not only turned Middleton into an instantly recognizable celebrity, it also caused the Wizard to become the talk of the nation. Middleton absolutely refused to name his secret source, which made the mystery man even more intriguing. The only clues to his identity could be found in a best-selling book that Middleton wrote. He described the Wizard as a quiet, humble, high-ranking civil servant who believed passionately in the U.S. Constitution and free press. Middleton went on to explain that he had first thought of the pseudonym for his source one afternoon after federal agents arrived at the *Tribune* with a subpoena. Not wanting to be served, Middleton had slipped out a side door and hidden in a neighborhood theater that happened to be showing *The Wizard of Oz.*

For more than twenty-five years, a number of journalists had tried to identify the Wizard. The University of Illinois journalism department had spent three years using computers to compare Middleton's book with likely sources. Still, no one had ever been able to unmask the Wizard, although several prominent Washingtonians had been scrutinized by the media as possible suspects. Among them: former White House speech writers and presidential assistants Patrick J. Buchanan, David Gergen, Jonathan Rose, Raymond Price, Stephen Bull, and Fred Fielding. Other White House operatives, such as Alexander Haig and John Sears, also were named. For a while, the most popular choice was the FBI's former number two official, W. Mark Felt. Some even insisted the Wizard was Henry Kissinger.

Each time Middleton was asked, he refused comment. But he promised that he'd reveal the Wizard's identity eventually—after the Wizard had died. Until then, Middleton's lips were sealed.

Having unseated a president, Middleton could have easily spent the rest of his career basking in the spotlight and lecturing at universities. Instead, he continued writing exposés. He tracked down Nazis in South America, was the first to report the Iran "arms for hostages" scandal, uncovered cheating inside the savings and loan industry, and revealed that India, Pakistan, and Korea each had developed nuclear weapons.

He was everywhere, it seemed.

Middleton knew when the Berlin Wall was about to come down before German leaders. He predicted the collapse of the Soviet Union. He identified a Russian KGB mole who had successfully burrowed inside the FBI. He wrote about congressmen who were cheating on their wives with young interns. He detailed the horrors of the Taliban and insisted Saddam Hussein was not stockpiling chemical weapons when every other reporter wrote that he was. But it was his Washington, D.C., scoops that proved just how well he held Washington in his palm. He seemed to know about the most intimate conversations uttered in secret inside the most sacred federal temples of power. Often it appeared as if he had actually been present during top-secret sessions. He lunched with foreign leaders, vacationed with movie stars, appeared on Wall Street business round table discussions. Little wonder that Heather had been mesmerized by him.

"I regret now that I ever encouraged Heather to go to Mississippi," Middleton told Melanie in a sad voice. "I never should have suggested that she investigate the trophy tree."

I'd kept my mouth shut since we had arrived. I'd been lost in my own thoughts. But now I jumped in, and I was blunt. "We were wondering how you got a copy of a photograph that was taken during that 1955 lynching," I said. "It's a picture of five white men standing at the feet of Lamar Grant. You gave it to Heather."

Middleton looked surprised, as if he hadn't noticed earlier that I was in the library with them. "I didn't give that photograph to Heather," he said. "She showed it to me."

I didn't believe him.

"Then why is there a yellow sticky note attached to it that says: *This should be a big help! Love, A.M.*?" I asked.

"I just told you that Heather showed *me* that photograph. I was impressed, so when I returned it, I added that note. I knew the photo was going to make it easier for her to track down the men who had lynched Lamar Grant."

His explanation came out smoothly, as if it were rehearsed.

"The names of the five men were written on that picture. I know Heather's writing and it wasn't hers. Did you write those names on there?"

"There weren't any names written on the copy when she showed it to me," he replied.

Again, I didn't believe him. I was convinced that he had given Heather that photograph with the men's names already written on it. I had a hunch that he had wanted her to find Jeb Rogge and Lester Alfred. But since Heather was dead, there wasn't any way for me to prove it.

"Why'd you send Heather to Mississippi?" I asked. "You had to know it was going to be dangerous for her."

"Mr. LeRue, I realize you're bitter because Heather left you for me. But you're making this sound sinister when there's nothing sinister about it. The idea for the book about the trophy tree actually came from my New York publisher. An editor there heard about the lynching and was intrigued that five men had carved their names into the tree trunk. He asked me if I would be interested in writing about it."

I glanced at Melanie. She was listening intently. I knew she was silently comparing his explanation to what Heather had written to her in a letter that she'd mailed just before she'd gone to Mississippi. Melanie had mentioned that letter to me when we first met, and she had stated emphatically that Heather had said it was Middleton's idea for her to write the book. He and Heather had then contacted his publisher with the idea.

Middleton continued: "At the time, I was too busy to

look into the trophy tree lynching, but I thought my publisher was on to something, so I mentioned the idea to Heather and she jumped at it. So you could say that I *gave* her the idea. But the real concept for the book came from my publisher. Again, there is nothing sinister about any of this!"

I still didn't believe him. He was clearly skirting responsibility. But was he simply embarrassed because Heather had been murdered while researching the book or was there another reason why he was intentionally distancing himself from the project? I decided to try a different line of questions.

"Are you and Senator Peterman close friends?" I asked. I looked for a reaction, but his eyes remained steady.

"Not really," he replied. "Why do you ask?"

"When was the last time you spoke to him?"

His eyes narrowed. "I didn't realize you'd come here to interrogate me, Mr. LeRue. May I ask why you are so interested in Senator Peterman?"

I was thinking about how I wanted to reply when Melanie blurted out: "Because we think Peterman might have helped murder Heather!"

Middleton slowly put his coffee cup down on the table next to him. "Why would Senator Peterman want to harm Heather?" he asked. "That seems a bit dramatic."

I didn't want Melanie to tell him what we had learned about Peterman, so I took charge. "We don't know. That's why we wanted to ask you about that 1955 photograph of the lynching." I was being careful because I didn't want Middleton to know that we had figured out that Senator Peterman had been at the lynching and had taken the picture. I said: "We thought you might have heard about the lynching from him, you know, since the two of you both attended UVA. We thought you might have seen the photograph there."

I thought Middleton was becoming irritated, although he certainly didn't show it outwardly. I wanted him to know that we had been investigating *his* past as well as Senator Peterman's.

Without a trace of emotion in his voice, Middleton said: "Senator Peterman attended UVA several years before I did, so we never met there."

"But both of you were IMPs, weren't you?" I asked.

For the first time, I sensed that I had surprised him. He leaned forward in his chair. "I'm a bit confused," he said, although he didn't look confused at all. "What does Senator Peterman have to do with the lynching and Heather's death? And how does the fact that he and I both graduated from UVA have anything to do with any of this?"

"The senator's from Pushmataha," I replied. "The lynching occurred in Pushmataha. Heather learned about the lynching from you. And you and Peterman both went to UVA. It seems logical that he might have told you about the lynching."

"No, those are merely coincidences that you are trying to make into something insidious," he replied.

He looked at Melanie and forced a smile. "I know Senator Peterman and, yes, we both graduated from UVA, but the truth is that I don't have many friends," he said, "and that's especially true when it comes to politicians. It's the price I pay for being an investigative reporter. I can't risk getting too close to a senator, because I might have to investigate him someday. Heather understood that and I think that's one of the reasons why she felt so comfortable with me. As journalists, we connected in a way I don't think others could fully appreciate."

I was fairly certain that Middleton was taking a verbal jab at me, since Heather had dumped me for him, but I was determined not to react. Just the same, I said: "I heard Heather had moved out of your house before she left for Mississippi. Was your relationship over?"

Middleton stood and walked over to an antique rolltop desk. He returned carrying a small black box. Inside was a diamond engagement ring. "I had planned to ask Heather to marry me as soon as she returned from Mississippi," he said, "so the answer to your question is: No! *Our* love affair was not over."

I was wondering if Middleton just happened to keep engagement rings handy for use in such occasions when we were interrupted by a loud bang that came from outside the library. Middleton's maid yelled: "Clover! Stop!" Seconds later, a dalmatian burst into the room, the nails on her paws making a clicking sound as they attempted to dig into the cherry hardwood floor for traction. The hound ran directly at Melanie and jumped. Its paws landed on her lap and its tongue licked Melanie's face.

"Clover, get down!" Middleton ordered. He grabbed the dog's blue collar and pulled her to the foot of his chair. "She's rambunctious but perfectly harmless," he said. "I'm not surprised Clover went right for you. I bought her for Heather. They used to run every day together. Because I was at the funeral, I haven't had a chance to take Clover out today for a walk."

"She's beautiful!" Melanie said. "How old is she?"

"Less than a year. Heather named her Clover because she eats it." He chuckled and seemed to be lost momentarily in a memory. As I watched, a single tear traced down his cheek. "I don't wish to be rude," Middleton continued, "but this has been an emotional and difficult day. I'm also afraid I have other business that I need to address."

Melanie and I stood, just as the Irish housekeeper appeared with a leash. She pulled Clover from the library. We followed Middleton into the foyer, where he gave Melanie a hug and then turned to face me. He didn't offer to shake my hand.

"Please let me know if you find out anything more about Senator Peterman," he said. "Meanwhile, I'll contact Heather's publisher and see if her editor there has any idea where that copy of that old photograph came from."

Neither of us felt comfortable discussing Middleton during the cab ride back to my apartment, although I did manage a few hushed editorial comments, such as, "He's lying!" We didn't want the taxi driver to eavesdrop. Instead, we made small talk and I noticed that Melanie's black dress was covered with white hairs from Clover. She picked several off. "Dalmatians shed year-round," she explained, "and if you don't exercise them daily, they can turn destructive."

"Something you picked up in a Walt Disney movie?"

"No, Heather and I had a dalmatian named Blue when we were growing up."

"Blue was the name of your black-and-white-spotted dog?"

"Yes," she said, without offering an explanation. "I'm not surprised that Heather wanted another dalmatian. She liked animals and babies too!"

"Whoa! Heather never showed any interest in children the entire time we were together," I said. "She told me she never wanted kids."

"Maybe you didn't know her as well as you thought," Melanie answered. She opened her purse and removed a cigarette. For a moment I felt as if she were giving me a hint about Heather, telling me something about her that I didn't know, some secret in her past.

"No smoking in cab!" the driver growled, interrupting my thoughts.

Melanie stared out the window and I thought about Andrew Middleton and Heather. Then I thought about Melanie and her paranormal ability to communicate with Heather. I said: "I read a magazine story once about a boy whose arm got cut off in a piece of farm machinery. Years passed, but he still felt as if that arm was attached and he was genuinely shocked when he woke up each morning and saw it wasn't there. You and Heather were once joined together. She was part of you and you were part of her. I'm just wondering: Is she still there? Is that what you were trying to tell me the other day when you said that Heather sometimes takes charge of you?"

"I came home once unexpectedly after my father was murdered," she said, "and my mother was standing in the dining room talking. I went to see who she was talking to and no one else was in the room with her. She told me that my father had appeared to her. That she had just seen him sitting at his seat at the table. He just wanted her to know that he was okay. At the time, I was worried that my mother was going nuts. But now I believe he actually was there—at least to her. They'd been married a long time and knew each other so well. Maybe he was a ghost. Maybe she alone could see him—somehow in her mind. I can't explain it. But she was absolutely convinced that he was there and talked to her."

When we reached my apartment, I paid the cabbie and walked around the taxi to open the door for Melanie. But she didn't get out.

"I'm going back to Heather's place," she explained. "I going to try to contact her."

Twenty-four

There is no light. Only darkness. Not like at night, when the stars and moon are still bright enough, even on a cloudy night, so you can see your hand in front of your face. No. This is pitch-black. As if you'd awakened inside a sealed box eight feet under.

Whoosh!

Melanie is running, hard, chased by an unseen demon.

Whoosh!

Melanie is inside her sister's Watergate apartment now. She is watching Heather, who is sitting at a desk scribbling furiously on a legal-sized yellow notepad. Heather doesn't look up, doesn't acknowledge Melanie.

"Heather?" Melanie says.

No reaction.

"It's me, sweetie, Melanie, your sister. Can you hear me?"

No reaction.

Melanie steps forward and reaches out, but when her fingers touch Heather's shoulder, there is nothing there. Melanie moves back.

"Heather, I need to ask you some questions."

No reaction.

Melanie walks forward again, but this time doesn't try to touch Heather. Instead, she glances over Heather's shoulder. Her dead sister is writing the same two words. A name.

Jason Simon.

Jason Simon.

Jason Simon.

Melanie says: "Jason Simon."

Whoosh!

Melanie is flying, above the trees, over pastures, horse farms, with white wooden fences. A two-story farmhouse appears and she glides down in its backyard, landing gracefully beside a weathered barn with a decaying John Deere tractor parked by its side door. The tractor is a faded green with bright yellow wheels and hard black rubber tires buried in knee-high weeds. The barn was once red but the sun has caused the pigment to turn brown and flake, revealing gray splinters. There is a wooden plaque next to the side entrance: JASON SIMON.

Whoosh!

Melanie is in the Watergate apartment. Heather is back at her desk, but this time she is reading.

"Heather? It's me!"

No reaction.

Melanie glances over Heather's shoulder to see what she is reading. It's a Holy Bible.

"What are you trying to tell me?"

No reaction.

Peering over Heather's shoulder, Melanie reads out loud: "Second Book of Samuel, Chapter Eleven."

Heather closes the Bible and turns her face to the right so she can look up at her sister, who is standing directly behind her. Melanie glances down at her sister's face. The left side is infested with maggots. Bits of white bone poke through rotting flesh. Melanie screams and scratches her own cheeks. She wakes up in pain from her own fingernails. She grabs the telephone and dials.

* * *

"Heather was in my dream!" Melanie exclaimed.

"Jesus!" I replied. "It's four a.m. You okay?"

"Her face was being eaten by maggots!"

"Melanie, it was only a dream."

"No, Nick. It's happening. Right now. I can feel them."

"Did you ask her any questions?"

"Heather didn't speak. I don't think she could. But she gave me two clues. A name: Jason Simon. Ever heard of him?"

"No. What's the other?"

"A Bible story. Old Testament."

"Which book, what passage?"

"Nick, the left side of Heather's face was being eaten."

"You said that. It was a dream, Melanie, a dream! Did you see what verse she was reading?"

"Second Samuel, Chapter Eleven."

"I'll get a Bible and read the verse. Stay on the phone."

Several moments later, I returned. "Heather was reading a story about King David. He was a powerful—"

"I know who King David was," she replied.

"According to Second Samuel, King David went out on his balcony one afternoon and saw a nude woman bathing in a pool at a nearby house. He wanted to have sex with her. Her name was Bathsheba. Only she was married."

"I remember that name—Bathsheba—but not the story."

"David sent for her, had sex with her, and then sent her home. Her husband didn't know. The next day, David sent for her again. Eventually, Bathsheba got pregnant."

"I'm sorry, but I can't concentrate. I can't get the image of Heather being devoured by maggots out of my head. I think I'm going to be sick."

I heard the sound of the phone fall. Footsteps. In the background, I could hear Melanie heaving and then the sound of a commode flushing. A few moments later, she picked up the phone.

"I'm back."

"Bathsheba's husband was a soldier named Uriah. He was out of town leading troops in battle. David called him home to the royal palace and twice tried to send him to his own house so Uriah could have sex with Bathsheba. That way, Uriah would think the baby was his. But Uriah spent the first night guarding the palace because he was loyal to King David and didn't want any harm to come to the king. The second night, he got drunk and fell asleep before he could have sex with his wife." I paused. "Are you sure you're up to this?"

"No. I still feel sick, but go ahead."

"Time was running out, because Bathsheba was beginning to show. So David ordered one of his generals to take Uriah to the front lines where the fighting was the most fierce. He told the general to watch and when Uriah was surrounded by the enemy, the general was to order his other men to pull back so that Uriah would be killed. And that's exactly what happened. Uriah was murdered, but no one knew it. They thought he had simply died fighting in combat. Bathsheba mourned him for a few days and then moved into the palace with David and gave birth to their son."

"That's the story Heather was reading in my dream?"

"There's more in the next chapter. David thinks he has gotten away with it, but God knows what David's done and kills their newborn son as punishment."

"What does this have to do with Senator Peterman?"

"I'm not sure. But we can discuss it later this morning. You need to sleep," I said.

"I may never sleep again. I don't want to see my sister like that. I don't want to be alone. Can you come over?"

A half hour later, I arrived at Heather's apartment. She was wearing her now-familiar gray sweats as pajamas.

"I've been using Heather's computer to search for Jason Simon," she announced. "There are fifteen Jason Simons in the Washington D.C. metropolitan area. But I don't think any of them is our man."

"Why not?"

"In my dream, I was flying over horse country. I eventually came to an old house and a red barn with the name 'Jason Simon' on a little sign hanging next to the barn's side entrance. It was like one of those signs that kids make—you know, a wood-burning. The Jason Simon we need to find lives in horse country."

"Try Middleburg, Virginia. That's horse country."

She typed Jason Simon into an Internet people-search. There were two. One lived in the actual town of Middleburg, but the other had a rural address. "It's on Smithe's Farm Road," she said. "That sounds horsey." She wrote down the information and announced: "I can be ready in fifteen minutes. Fix yourself some breakfast while you wait."

"You want to leave in fifteen minutes?" It wasn't even five a.m. yet.

"By the time we find the place, I'm sure Jason Simon will be doing his farm chores."

Traveling west, still waiting for the morning sun to rise behind us, I watched the headlights of eastbound commuters on Interstate 66. They were driving from the Virginia suburbs: formerly tiny towns, such as Clifton and Centreville, that were now part of one sprawling development of shopping centers, parks, and cul de sacs. I thought of Thomas Jefferson. Whenever I travel in Virginia, I often find myself thinking of him and how much he loved this state and how strange it would be if he were suddenly transported from the 1700s to today and could see what's happened since he rode on horseback through these same hills. Would he think we did a good job setting up his democracy?

"Everything in this world is a matter of calculation," Jefferson once wrote. "Advance then with caution, the balance in your hand. Put into one scale the pleasures which any object may offer, but put fairly into the other, the pains which are to follow, and see which preponderates."

I glanced at Melanie, who was beside me in the car look-ing straight ahead. *"Put into one scale the pleasures which any object may offer . . ."* I thought.

When we got to Middleburg, I asked the foreign-born clerk at a gasoline station for directions to Smithe's Farm Road, but he didn't know where it was and didn't care whether or not I found it. Continuing into town, I spotted a café.

"Not this again." Melanie winced. "The last time you and I went into a café, in Mississippi, it wasn't exactly an enjoyable experience."

"I'm not ordering chitlins or any other food I've not eaten before," I said. I pointed to one of the trucks parked nearby. It had a white magnetic sign slapped on its driver's door that said: RURAL MAIL CARRIER. The café smelled of greasy bacon, eggs, coffee, and cigarettes. There were probably thirty customers inside, mostly grizzled older men. I asked a waitress to point out the mailman and she yelled, "Hey, Gilbert, someone wants to see ya!" A rotund bald fellow waved us over. I asked for directions.

"The horse writer?" he asked. "Is that the Jason Simon you're after? The one who lives in an old farmhouse?"

"A two-story white farmhouse with an old red barn be-hind it," Melanie said.

"That'd be him."

A half hour later, we were traveling along a gravel road west of Middleburg when Melanie pointed to a clump of trees and declared: "His place is right over there."

A two-story white farmhouse came into view. I pulled onto a dirt road and said: "This looks deserted."

"There'll be a green and yellow John Deere tractor parked behind the house next to the barn. It will have lots of weeds growing around it."

As we came around the back corner, I saw the tractor. She'd described it perfectly. "This is all exactly how I saw everything in my dream," she said.

I parked and Melanie led me to a side entrance. A sign

with Jason Simon's name burnt into the wood was nailed next to a door. I pounded on it with a clenched fist.

"Hang on!" a man's voice called from deep inside.

Moments later, a bearded man answered.

"Jason Simon?" Melanie asked.

"You've found me!"

"I'm—" Melanie began.

"I know who you are. I saw your photograph in the *Tribune* when I read about your sister's funeral. Please come in."

He led us through the barn. Its main floor was divided into wooden stalls that now housed rusted farm machinery and cardboard boxes stacked haphazardly—some open, others taped shut, as if someone had been searching through them and simply stopped once he found whatever it was he wanted. Simon's office was in a corner. It had a wood wide-plank floor built on top of two-by-fours to hold it above the barn's dirt floor. His office walls were made of Sheetrock panels nailed into joists. None of the wood or Sheetrock was painted. There were two metal folding chairs inside the office. Both faced Simon's desk. Both had stacks of magazines and newspapers on them.

"Just push that junk on the floor," he said, motioning toward the chairs, "and have a seat."

The room was a catastrophe. Simon had built wooden shelves along one wall, but they sagged under the weight of books, magazines, and rainbow-colored reports that had been piled on them seemingly at random. Along another wall leaned gray file cabinets, many with their drawers half opened, all crammed with too many papers. Cardboard boxes, like the ones I'd seen scattered throughout the barn, were stacked behind the two folding chairs. Simon's computer rested on the right corner of his desk and had a distracting screen saver that showed a frantic mouse trying to escape through an endless maze. His desk itself was a tribute to clutter. I counted three partially filled coffee cups, several half-filled wax packets of saltines, and two crushed Coke cans perched on top of an unsteady tower of papers and notepads. Directly behind his desk, he'd tacked a poster of a Thoroughbred racehorse named Spend-A-Buck, winner of the 1985 Kentucky Derby.

"How'd you hear about me?" Simon asked.

"My sister gave me your name," Melanie said.

He didn't seem surprised. "Only a few days ago, Heather was sitting in the exact same chair you're sitting in now," he said. "She was just getting ready to leave for Mississippi. Did you know we once worked together at the *Tribune*? Our little reporter cubicles were only a few feet apart."

"You're a newspaper reporter?" I asked.

"Not anymore. I write puff pieces for horse magazines now and freelance. A year ago, I ghost-wrote a book for the president of a local bank who's full of himself and wanted the bank's history documented—as if anyone really gives a good goddamn about it. But there was a time when Heather and I were both ambitious and on the *Tribune*'s fast track."

"Why'd Heather come see you?" Melanie asked.

"For the same reason, I'm guessing, that you're here. She wanted to ask me about Andrew Middleton." Simon smiled, revealing crooked teeth yellowed by too many cigarettes, too much coffee, and too little dental care. "You see, I'm the world's foremost expert on Andrew Middleton, or should I say, on his dark side." Simon waved his arms toward the cardboard boxes and files scattered around us. "There's more than a decade of research in this room into that son of a bitch's life."

"Are you writing a book about him?" I asked.

"I should! I've got enough. But no publisher would touch it. They'd be too afraid because the *Tribune* would retaliate by never reviewing another of that publisher's books. Trust me, with what I know, I could cut Middleton's balls off." Simon lit a cigarette, the last from a soft-pack, which he squeezed and tossed toward an already overflowing waste can. It hit and bounced off onto the floor.

"What's odd about all this," Simon continued, "is that Andrew Middleton was my hero when I was in journalism school and later when he hired me to work at the *Tribune*. I wanted to be just like him."

"What happened between you two?" Melanie asked.

"At first Middleton was complimentary and supportive. Then I got my big break. Do either of you remember the Year of the Spy in the 1980s?"

"It was 1985, wasn't it?" I replied. "A dozen Americans were caught spying, mostly for the Russians."

"That's right. Before then, our country hadn't really had any major espionage cases, at least not since the Rosenbergs. Then all of these modern-day Benedict Arnolds began coming out of the woodwork," he said. "I convinced one of the worst spies to talk to me for a book. Of course, before I began writing it, I went through all the correct channels at the *Tribune*. I applied for a one-year sabbatical and I went out and wrote a hell of a book. It hit the *New York Times* best-seller list and was made into a television miniseries."

"Did Middleton help you?" Melanie asked.

"Hell, no!" Simon said. "I never asked him for anything. But when it came time for me to return to the newspaper, he screwed me! And he did it with a big grin on his face. You ever been to his Georgetown house?"

"Yes, just yesterday," Melanie replied, "after the funeral."

"When it came time for me to return to work, Middleton invited me over to his house for breakfast. He told me that he wanted me to join his investigative staff. I was excited. We were just making pleasant conversation and he brought up my book."

Simon finished his cigarette, but instantly cracked a fresh pack and fished out a new one. Melanie got one of her own from her purse as Simon picked up his story: "Middleton asked me how I had gotten a spy to talk to me and I told him the truth: I'd split my book royalties with the spy in exchange for his exclusive cooperation. I knew Middleton wouldn't like that, because most journalists are against 'checkbook journalism'—paying for interviews. But this was a book. It didn't have anything to do with the newspaper, and besides, I'd already disclosed my financial ties with the spy to all of my editors before I took my leave of absence."

"Did Middleton object to what you'd done?" Melanie asked.

"No, that's the odd part. He didn't really seem to care. He just dropped the subject. He said: 'Because we're going to be working closely together, I want to ask you a few questions about some of our coworkers. It's important for me to know how you really feel about them.' I should have smelled a trap, but I trusted him, especially when he said: 'Now our conversation is completely off the record, just between you and me, because I want you to be brutally honest.' The first person he asked me about was the newspaper's new executive editor. A few months earlier, this guy had just gotten the job that Middleton himself had always wanted."

"I'm getting confused," Melanie said.

"Sorry, let me put it as simply as possible," Simon said. "Andrew Middleton's ultimate goal was to become executive editor at the paper and it looked as if he was going to get it after he forced a president to resign and became famous. But then he blew it."

"How'd he blow it?" she asked.

"A young black reporter who worked directly for Middleton wrote a story about an eight-year-old black kid who, she claimed, was turned into a heroin addict by his junkie mother and her boyfriends. It was a heartbreaking story that outraged Washington. The reporter won a Pulitzer prize for it. But a short time later, she was forced to admit that she'd made up the entire story. There was no eight-year-old heroin addict. The complete article was one big lie. The *Tribune* had been duped. It was the most embarrassing moment in the newspaper's history!"

"What did Middleton have to do with that?" Melanie asked.

"An internal investigation by the newspaper's ombudsman revealed that several experienced reporters had privately warned Middleton and his underlings that there was something fishy about the story. But Middleton had stuck with it."

"How'd he react to the news?" I asked.

"The funny thing about Andrew Middleton is that he is a genius at getting other people to reveal their innermost secrets. But it's damn near impossible to get him to reveal any of his," Simon replied.

I wanted to get Simon to hurry up on his story, so I prodded him. "You mentioned that Middleton had asked you to tell him your opinion of the new executive editor—the guy who got the job that he had lost."

"That's right. The executive editor had just taken charge and I was truthful. I said that I really didn't like the new editor. I can see now how stupid I was. But Middleton had promised that we were talking off the record and, like an imbecile, I believed him. I kept thinking: *This is the most famous reporter in America. He has refused to reveal who the Wizard is! He will protect me if I tell him the truth.*"

"Let me guess," I replied. "Middleton told the new editor every nasty thing you'd said about him."

"That's exactly right! That same morning. Middleton went directly to that editor and told him what I'd said. He accused me of being unethical because I'd paid the spy for his story in my book too. He said I had tried to hide the payoff from him."

"Were you fired?" Melanie asked.

"When I learned what Middleton had done, I raced downtown and confronted him. I asked him why he had betrayed me. I said, 'You told me that we were talking completely off the record! You broke your word!' And do you know what he told me? He said: 'My loyalty is to the *Tribune* and you're naive if you don't understand that.' He said the executive editor deserved to know my true feelings about him. That's when I knew my career at the *Tribune* was over."

I was having trouble feeling sympathy for Simon, even though it was clear that Middleton had deceived him. One of the first lessons you learn in Washington is never to say anything behind someone's back that you wouldn't say to his face. In this town, it will *always*, and I mean *always,* get back to them. Of course, the second rule of survival is *to* never trust a reporter, even someone with a reputation like Middleton's, especially if he tells you that your conversation is off the record. If anyone should have known that, it should've been another reporter!

"I'll tell you why I have never forgiven Middleton," Simon continued. "I could have moved on and forgotten him except for one thing. When I left his house that morning, he reached over and put his arm around my shoulders, like a father would do to his son, and he said: 'Not only are we going to have a good time working closely together, we're going to become great friends.' I *believed* him. I thought he was sincere. And at the very time he was putting his arm around me, he was plotting my firing. That's sick, man. He played me for a fool!"

"That is sick," Melanie said.

"I'm not the only reporter whose career he's ruined. Middleton undermines reporters who are successful, especially those he thinks are threats. He's jealous."

"What did Heather ask you about him?" Melanie asked.

"When they were living together, your sister learned something spooky about his past and she was trying to determine if it was true."

"What was it?" I asked.

"I'm not entirely sure, because she refused to tell me everything. But I know it involved the Wizard. She asked me if I knew who the Wizard was."

"Do you?" Melanie asked.

Simon finished his sixth cigarette and dramatically lit his seventh. "I've spent decades doing research on Middleton," he said. "No one has studied him as much as I have. The answer to your question is yes. I know his secret." He stood and walked over to a box marked: MIDDLETON: FIRST BOOK: THE PRESIDENT RESIGNS. He lifted the lid. "I've done a sentence-by-sentence study of Middleton's first book—the one in which he describes how he brought down the president's inner circle. I've spend hours poring over his claims. And I'm going to share with you now what the evidence shows."

I looked at Melanie. This was exciting. We were both eager to learn the Wizard's identity. But Simon was not about to simply blurt out a name. He'd worked too many years to do that.

"First," he said, "some background. When Andrew Middleton wrote his book, he explained that he and the Wizard had developed a secret way to contact each other without the White House catching them. If he wanted to ask the Wizard a question, Middleton put his red ten-speed bicycle out on his apartment's balcony. He explained that his apartment was on the route that the Wizard took to work each morning. If he saw the bicycle, he knew Middleton wanted a meeting. Now, if the Wizard wanted to get in touch, he'd draw a happy face on a specific page of Middleton's morning edition of the *New York Times*—the one that was delivered to Middleton's apartment. He'd indicate the date and time under the face when they should meet. Most of their rendezvouses took place in remote areas of Rock Creek Park."

"I remember those scenes from the movie," Melanie gushed. "They were scary. You never saw the Wizard's face, only a shadow figure."

"Yes, it was all very dramatic," Simon said. "It also never happened!"

"What?" she replied.

"There were no secret signals."

"How can you be sure?"

"Because I went to the apartment complex where Middleton lived before he became famous. He lived in a sixth-floor apartment and when I went up to see it, I discovered that his balcony faced an interior courtyard. The only way anyone could have seen a red bicycle sitting on that balcony was if you parked your car outside the building, walked inside, and entered the courtyard. Even then you still had to crane your neck back and look up to the sixth floor. There were eighty apartments in that complex. Do you think a high government official parked his car outside Middleton's building each morning and walked into that courtyard to see if there was a red bicycle sitting on Middleton's balcony?"

It did sound a bit far-fetched.

"Middleton fabricated that story. And that's not the only one," Simon continued. "While I was in Middleton's apartment complex, I asked the building superintendent how the *New York Times* was delivered. He said the newspaper wasn't delivered door-to-door. A stack of newspapers was dropped in the reception area and the people who subscribed were responsible for coming down and claiming a copy. There was no way the Wizard could have known which newspaper Middleton was going to grab when he came down to get his copy. There is no way the Wizard could have drawn a happy face on a certain newspaper telling Middleton when to meet him. Again, Middleton invented that story."

"The red bicycle and happy face are embellishments?" I asked.

"Andrew Middleton made them up for dramatic effect," Simon replied. "I can give you other examples. He wrote that he nicknamed his anonymous source the Wizard because of the movie *The Wizard of Oz,* which he said was playing at a local theater. Well, I checked the listings and that movie hadn't played in Washington that entire year!"

"Why would Andrew Middleton feel the need to embellish and create things?" Melanie asked.

"Because he wanted to juice up the story and make it even better than it was. That's what motivates reporters—getting on page one—not politics or their own prejudices. You asked me earlier who the Wizard is? Everyone wants to know who was his secret source! You want to know the answer?"

Simon paused to add a bit of unnecessary drama.

"The answer is: There is no Wizard! He doesn't exist

and never did! Middleton created him to add drama to his story."

"There is no Wizard?"

"There's no all-knowing single source," Simon replied. "If you dig far down, you'll find that Middleton was feeling pressure from his publisher and Hollywood scriptwriters. They wanted him to make the story more entertaining—a mystery!"

"If there is no Wizard," I said, "then who provided Middleton with information about what was happening inside the White House?"

"I'm not saying that Middleton didn't have any sources. He did. Lots of them, and most of what he wrote in his first book has proven to be accurate. But there never was a single, deep source. If anything, the Wizard is a composite character he made by merging two or three actual people together."

"I guess it really shouldn't matter that he combined sources," Melanie said.

Her remark made Simon visibly angry. "Andrew Middleton fashioned a fictional character—just like that young *Tribune* reporter who fabricated an eight-year-old drug addict! He broke the rules just like she did! Only she was run out of journalism, while he's still revered as a hero!"

"Why haven't you exposed him?"

"I'm not alone here—other reporters have said there's no Wizard. But how can you prove that a person doesn't exist if, in fact, he never did exist? There is no way to prove Middleton wrong because he has told a lie that can't be double-checked."

"Didn't Middleton say that he'd reveal the Wizard's name after the Wizard died?"

Simon slapped his hand against his desk. "That's what makes this fable so damn brilliant! All Middleton has to do is wait until a former high-ranking government official dies. Then he can announce that the dead guy was the Wizard and no one will be able to prove him wrong. That's the wonderful thing about secret sources, especially fictitious ones. No one can ever prove you wrong!"

"What did Heather think of your theory?" I asked.

"She told me that Middleton was hiding something—something specifically about the Wizard. But she wasn't convinced that the Wizard was a composite character. She asked me if I'd ever run across the Scarecrow Report."

"The what report?" Melanie asked.

"Scarecrow Report. It's something only die-hard Middleton-watchers know about."

"I've never heard of it," I said.

"After the president was forced to resign, his vice president was sworn into office. By this time, everyone had heard about Middleton and his inside source. Now, just think for a moment about what you would do if you were the new president. The last thing a new president wants is some unidentified, high-level government employee leaking information. So the new president ordered the FBI to quietly identify the Wizard."

"That makes sense," Melanie said. "A new president would want to know who he could trust."

"Over the years, both the White House and the FBI have refused to confirm or to deny that such an investigation was ordered," Simon continued. "But the FBI supposedly called its search Operation Scarecrow because of the *Wizard of Oz* movie. Remember: The Scarecrow is the one who wanted a brain. It was an inside joke: The 'brain' was going to catch the Wizard."

"Did the FBI determine the identity of Middleton's source?"

"I don't know," Simon replied. "Heather came to see me because she had found someone who said he was willing to provide her a copy of the Scarecrow Report. She wanted to pick my brain so she could make certain that what she was being offered was authentic and not part of a hoax."

"Did she tell you who was offering her the report?" I asked. "Was it someone in the White House or in the FBI?"

"She didn't say, but I'd give my left nut to know!"

Simon took a long drag on his cigarette. "I've got to admit that I was suspicious of Heather when she first knocked on my barn door. I hadn't spoken to her in years and I thought maybe Middleton had sent her to spy on me. But when I mentioned my suspicions, Heather told me that she had ended her relationship with Middleton. Then she said Middleton didn't even remember who I was. Can you imagine the nerve of that cocksucker? That son of a bitch ruined my career and he tells Heather that he doesn't even remember me! I was like a speck of dust that he simply brushed off!"

Simon glanced around his office. "I'll show you more examples of his fabrications."

"Sorry," I replied, "but we've got to go."

On the drive back into Washington, Melanie asked: "What do you think of Jason Simon?"

"Very bitter. Very angry. Very frustrated. Very obsessed. But I believe what he said. I don't believe the Wizard is an actual person. It's been too long since the president resigned."

"What do you mean?"

"Washington is a city of stupendous egos. If there were a Wizard, why hasn't he stepped forward and taken credit? After all, it's been more than twenty-five years. He'd become famous and he'd make a million bucks telling his life story in a book. Money, fame, history—that's too much for anyone drawn to this town to walk away from. That's why I believe there is no Wizard."

Melanie didn't reply. She seemed to be thinking about something else. Finally, she said: "Heather led us to Jason Simon in my dream. He told us about the Scarecrow Report. That's got to be what Heather wants us to pursue."

"If there is a Scarecrow Report," I replied, "then my buddy at the FBI, Phil Shurman, should know about it. I'm going to give him a call."

"Good," Melanie said, "but that still leaves us with the other clue: Why did Heather show me the Bible story about

King David and Bathsheba? What does it have to do with any of this?"

"I'm not sure."

Without warning, she asked: "Nick, why are you still helping me?"

Her question surprised me. "I like to think of myself as one of the good guys who wears a white hat," I replied. It was supposed to be funny, but it didn't seem all that funny. I had helped Melanie in the beginning because I was still in love with Heather. I had wanted to rescue her. *Why was I still helping?* The most obvious answer was that I wanted Heather's killers brought to justice. At least that's what I told myself. Was there something else? I looked at Melanie. She was wearing blue denim jeans and a cream-colored blouse. Simple. Yet stunning. I wished, at least for a moment, that she hadn't told me in Mississippi that she was happily married and had two kids.

Twenty-five

Phillip Shurman suggested I meet him around noon when I called about having lunch.

I arrived early at the J. Edgar Hoover FBI Headquarters Building on Pennsylvania Avenue and while I waited in the lobby, I thought about the first time that I'd reported to work here as a young agent. The rectangular building is architecturally deceiving. People walk by it every day without realizing it's the closest thing to a fortress in downtown Washington. There are no windows on the street level and the second floor is completely missing. There are elevator shafts, enclosed stairways, and concrete pillars which rise up from the base to support the remaining floors but the second floor is an open gap. The design is supposed to make it difficult for an angry mob to break into the building. There's even a concrete moat on one side.

Shurman suggested we walk to one of his favorite hangouts, the Old Ebbitt Grill, an elegant pub near the White House. As soon as we settled into a booth at the back, he ordered a shot of Jack Daniel's and asked: "Who's going to be the source today?"

The FBI requires its agents to pay for their own lunches unless they're interviewing confidential sources. The same is true about the Senate Judiciary Committee. But like many other federal bureaucrats, Shurman had devised a way to beat the system. Whenever it was his turn to buy lunch, he identified me on his expense account as a congressional source. That way, he got the FBI to pick up the tab. Shurman assumed that I did the same when it was my turn to pay. And I let him believe it. But the truth was that I never stuck the committee for our lunches. I understood how Shurman rationalized his minor expense account larcenies. After all, the FBI never paid him overtime for all of the extra hours that he put in. He was in his second marriage, paid alimony, and had kids to support. But I always felt uncomfortable sticking taxpayers for our beers and burgers. It just seemed petty.

Often the information that we exchanged was useful. I usually did my best to warn Shurman about what the committee was doing when it came to the FBI, and he tipped me off to potentially embarrassing tidbits that my boss needed to hear. Most lunches, however, were just excuses for us to socialize and complain about our jobs. I've always suspected that most of Washington's pricey restaurants would go bankrupt if government employees, lobbyists, politicians, and reporters suddenly had to pay for their own meals.

We were about halfway through our entrées when I asked if he had ever heard of the Scarecrow Report. The question surprised him enough to make him pause just as he was about to take another bite. He lowered his fork.

"Assuming there is such a report, and I'm not saying there is, are you asking about it for yourself or is the committee interested?"

"This is personal."

"I thought so. If you'd said it was for the committee, I'd have known you were lying."

"Why?"

"Because no one on the Hill has the balls to ask about it. No one wants to become the target of an Andrew Middleton investigative news story."

"What can you tell me about the report?"

"Nothing."

I folded my arms across my chest and glared.

"Does this have something to do with Heather Cole's murder in Mississippi?" he asked. Before I could reply, he said: "I knew you'd continue digging, even after we closed our investigation."

"Jeb Rogge wasn't the only kidnapper involved," I said. "There's at least one other person." I lowered my voice. "And it could be a U.S. senator. I'm trying to figure out how Andrew Middleton fits in—if he fits at all."

"Jesus Christ!" he said quietly. "You'd better have more than just conjecture to back up accusations like that."

"That's why I need to know about the Scarecrow Report."

Shurman leaned close. "Nick, as a friend, back out of this."

"I'm not afraid of the senator or Andrew Middleton or the mighty *Washington Tribune*."

"You should be."

He didn't say anything for several moments. Instead, he took several mouthfuls and finished his drink. He waved to our waiter and told him to bring another shot. "There's something you apparently haven't considered," he finally said, his voice but a whisper. "Maybe Andrew Middleton isn't as high as this goes. Maybe he's not really pulling the strings."

I didn't get it. What was he was implying? And then it hit me. Who else would care about the Scarecrow Report? The *Wizard*! If he was an actual person and was still working in the government, he might not want his identity uncovered. I still didn't have a clue how any of this tied in to Heather's murder. But she had been pursuing the Scarecrow Report before she had gone to Mississippi and it was important enough for her to tell Melanie about it in her dream.

"Are you suggesting that I need to be wary of the Wizard?" I asked. "I thought he was a composite figure, made up by Middleton for dramatic reasons to sell books."

"What I'm suggesting is that you walk away from all of this, now."

By this point, we'd finished eating and neither of us said anything as the waiter cleared our plates. Shurman ordered several scoops of macadamia nut ice cream and when we were alone again he asked: "You aren't going to take my advice, are you?"

"No. You knew Heather. You know I loved her. How can you sit there and tell me to turn a blind eye to her murder?"

"Our best forensic guys say Heather was killed by a single kidnapper. If that's good enough for the bureau, it should be enough for you."

"It's not. I want to know about the Scarecrow Report."

Shurman glanced around the crowded restaurant to make certain that no one could hear him, and then he said softly: "Okay, but you're the one who's putting his nuts in a bear trap." He leaned as close as he could to me. "The White House asked the bureau to identify the Wizard after the president was forced to resign. Our director handpicked ten of us to work on it."

"You were one of them?"

"Yes, otherwise I never would've known what happened. None of us was told the names of all the suspects. We each were assigned an individual target and after we completed our investigation, we turned in our individual reports and our job was done. I investigated a White House speechwriter who's now a well-known newspaper columnist and sometime presidential candidate."

"Was he the Wizard?"

"No, I proved it couldn't have been him."

"Did any of your coworkers finger the Wizard?"

Shurman paused. "I can't be sure."

"You're lying," I said. "One of you had to have identified him, if he exists."

"You don't understand. No one in the bureau ever found out the results because another federal agency intervened and took over our investigation."

"Another agency took charge? Which one?"

"Think about it," he whispered. "We were told to back off because of national security."

"Langley? The CIA took over?"

He moved his head slightly, giving me a nod. "Two guys showed up, collected all of our files, and a few hours later we were told to erase everything about the Scarecrow investigation from our computers and files. It was odd."

"Why would the CIA take control?" I asked. But as soon as that question left my lips, I knew the answer: *The Wizard had some CIA connection.* I looked Shurman directly in the eyes and said: "CIA cover-up?"

"I should've had a piece of apple pie with my ice cream," he replied, an obvious signal to me that he was done discussing the Scarecrow Report. "There seems to be something almost patriotic these days about ordering apple pie for dessert."

I decided to walk back to Capitol Hill rather than hailing a cab. As I did, I dialed Jason Simon on my cell phone. He was in his barn office. "Why would a certain agency in Langley be interested in the Scarecrow Report?" I asked.

"The CIA?" he replied in an excited voice. "Did you get a copy of it?"

"No," I said. "But I learned that they took charge of the investigation."

Simon let loose with a set of expletives. "I've filed dozens of Freedom of Information requests with the FBI and CIA about the Wizard and those Langley bastards claimed they never spent one minute investigating him!"

"Why would Langley care?" I asked.

"There's always been speculation that the Wizard was a

top CIA guy," he replied. "Former CIA Director William Colby was a prime suspect because he was appointed director shortly before the president was forced out."

"I thought the agency and president were on the same conservative side. Why would Colby do anything to help Middleton?"

"Colby was called the last 'gentleman spy.' The theory is that he was trying to protect the CIA's image and distance it from the petty corruption at the White House. You've got to remember that the CIA director before him—Richard Helms—was fired by the president after he refused to use the CIA to aid in the White House cover-up. A person such as Colby would have been personally appalled by the president's dirty tricks. Colby also was in a high enough position to have known the information that ultimately was leaked to Middleton. There are other reasons why someone in the CIA might have been Middleton's source."

"Such as what?"

"Andrew Middleton went directly into the Army after UVA. He's always claimed that he taught foreign languages at Fort Bragg. But when I tracked down several guys who were assigned to that same school, they said Middleton never worked there."

"What's that mean?"

"You figure it out! A UVA graduate goes directly into a military job where no one sees him. Sounds like a cover to me."

My mind was whirling. Was it possible that Andrew Middleton had worked for the CIA while he was in the service?

"Has anyone ever suggested that Middleton was CIA?" I asked.

"He's strongly denied it and no one has ever taken the charge seriously," Simon replied. "But it would explain why a reporter who had only worked at the *Tribune* on the police beat for a few months had such high-level sources at the White House—wouldn't it?" Then Simon said: "Did you know that in April 1996, Colby disappeared while canoeing on the Potomac River? He was missing for nine days before his body was found in a tributary. He was seventy-six and an autopsy suggested that he had suffered a stroke or heart attack before falling into the water and drowning."

"What do you think happened?"

"Those who tend to believe in conspiracies have always wondered if his death was an accident. Some claim it was the Russians, but I've never believed that. Why kill him? They had nothing to gain. Neither would any terrorists. But his own agency—now, that is another story."

"What exactly are you suggesting?"

"What if the agency had a secret that it didn't want out? What if Colby had found out about it?" he said. "Did I mention that his widow said after her husband's death that there was no way that he had been a newspaper source? Nor was he the sort of man who would tolerate such disloyalty."

"In other words, his wife was saying that he wasn't the Wizard," I said.

"That's right."

My call to Simon had sparked more questions than it had answered. I went over the facts in my mind. Heather had found out something disturbing about Middleton's past. He had suggested she investigate the trophy tree lynching and gotten her a lucrative book contract so she could pursue it. Senator Peterman had taken pictures at the lynching and had tried to keep his role in it a secret by gouging his initials out of the tree trunk. Heather had been abducted by Jeb Rogge and then murdered. Peterman and Middleton had been talking to each other over pay phones before she was killed. Peterman had also talked to Jeb Rogge. Heather had told Melanie in her dream about Jason Simon. He had told us about the Scarecrow Report. Phillip Shurman had said the CIA had taken charge of the Scarecrow investigation. Jason Simon said Middleton might have been a CIA agent while he was in the Army. The Wizard. William Colby's death. The Old Testament. King David. Bathsheba. How did they all fit together? Or did they? Were they pieces of a jigsaw or simply unrelated events, speculation? Middleton had accused me of taking coincidences and trying to make them sinister. Was I doing that? Was my hatred of him blinding me?

My cell phone rang.

"Hello?" I said.

"Nick," a cheery voice replied. "This is Andrew Middleton."

"Funny," I said, "I was just thinking about you."

"I'm calling about yesterday," he said. "I want to apologize. It was a difficult day for me, as I'm sure it was for you. Anyway, I'd like to help you and Melanie, especially if you're right about someone else being involved in Heather's murder. I've got a lot of connections with a lot of important people in this town. That could be helpful."

"It sure could," I answered, playing along.

"Great! Tell me what you know about Peterman and the lynching. What did you discover in Pushmataha? Do you think he is trying to cover up something about his past?"

"Listen," I said. "I don't feel comfortable talking about this over my cell phone. I also happen to be walking down the sidewalk right now."

"Sure," he replied. "I understand. Maybe we can meet later at my house again."

"Sounds good," I said.

"I'm glad we're going to be working together on this," Middleton said. "As a team. I think we may even end up as close friends someday."

As I politely ended the call, I remembered what Jason Simon had said about his last encounter with Middleton. Just before the investigative reporter had stabbed Simon in the back, Middleton had gushed about how much he was looking forward to the two of them working together as a team.

Why did I suddenly feel that I was being set up?

Twenty-six

Whenever my boss, Senator Leslie Homer DeLong, wishes to discuss something with me, he generally stops by the Judiciary Committee offices in the Dirksen Building, plops down in front of my desk, and begins telling me one of his legendary LBJ yarns. Eventually, he'll get to the point. In all of the time that I've worked for him, there have been only a handful of times when he has summoned me to his Senate office. He has never sent his administrative aide, Clarissa Poe, to fetch me. Never. So when I got to my office and found a message marked UR-GENT from Ms. Poe, I knew something extraordinary was in the works.

Poe had left explicit instructions. I was to meet her at precisely 2:30 p.m. at the Abraham Lincoln sculpture in the U.S. Capitol. The Lincoln bust was made by Gutzon Borglum, who became famous as the sculptor of Mount Rushmore. Within the close-knit world of Capitol Hill employees, the bust of Honest Abe is well known because the work has only one ear. Legend has it that Borglum chipped off Lincoln's left ear by accident and, rather than trying to repair it, simply assumed most people wouldn't notice. Few did.

It was 2:15 p.m., so I hurried over to the Capitol's ground floor, where the Lincoln statue is displayed. Poe was already nervously pacing even though both of us were five minutes early.

"This way," she said sternly, spinning to her right and entering a narrow passageway. Although she'd not offered any explanation, I knew where she was taking me. I'd first heard rumors about "secret offices" shortly after I had gone to work for the committee. But it wasn't until I'd read a story about them in the *Washingtonian* magazine that I knew they actually existed. The rooms are located behind the cascade of stone steps that visitors see when they first approach the U.S. Capitol from Pennsylvania and Constitution avenues. There's only one hallway that leads into the maze of hideaways and it's guarded by a succession of uniformed Capitol Hill police officers. According to the magazine, the secret places are divided up among the most senior members of Congress. They are supposed to be quiet hideouts where a senator can contemplate world affairs without being interrupted. But through the years, it's been suggested they are frequently used for much less momentous duties. In the late 1970s, there were reports about sexual liaisons in the private chambers.

Poe and I were asked to produce our Senate ID badges at the first checkpoint. The officer compared them to names on a clipboard and then let us pass. At the second guard post, which was only a few yards away, Poe handed the officer a handwritten note from Senator DeLong. The officer disappeared into an adjoining alcove, where he apparently telephoned our boss. After he hung up, the officer said: "Mr. LeRue, please follow me." That was his not-too-subtle way of telling Poe that she wasn't going any farther.

The officer led me around a corner to where another officer was waiting. This new one escorted me down a short stairway and into a hallway where none of the doors was marked by a number. He stopped at one of them and knocked. Senator DeLong opened it.

Based on all of the rumors I'd heard, I'd expected to see red-flocked wallpaper and a heart-shaped water bed. But my boss's secret office was neither exotic nor erotic. It contained a mini-refrigerator, five muted televisions all playing at once, and a nearly bare green felt-topped poker table stacked with old copies of *Congressional Reports*.

DeLong noticed me eyeing the table. "This used to be LBJ's private office," he said. "I specifically requested it after he left Congress for the White House. Can you imagine how many deals were cut here over hands of five-card stud and cigars?" He motioned me toward an overstuffed chair. "Kick off your shoes," he said. "Get comfortable." I noticed that he was wearing a worn pair of moccasin slippers. "I'm having something with a little punch to it, but there are diet sodas in the refrigerator if you prefer." I popped open a Diet Coke. While DeLong always had been friendly with me, he wasn't the sort of boss you ever really felt completely comfortable with because you never knew exactly what he was thinking or what his agenda might be. Our secure setting made me believe that he wanted to discuss something extremely sensitive and I wanted to make certain that my thinking wasn't blurred by booze.

As expected, he began by telling an LBJ story. This one was about how a rival of LBJ's had once rented a helicopter during a heated congressional race in Texas. "Because this old boy could hippy-hop from town to town, he could cover more ground than LBJ, who was stuck driving across the state. One afternoon, both of them arrived at an outdoor chicken barbeque at a county fairground and after LBJ's opponent finished giving his campaign spiel, he hopped into his whirlybird and took off."

DeLong grinned. "Now, this young fellow couldn't leave well enough alone. While he was leaving, he looked down and spotted LBJ standing on the back of a pickup truck just beginning his speech, so this youngster tells the pilot to hover directly over LBJ for a few minutes. He figured the noise from the chopper would drown out LBJ's speech. It must have been a hilarious sight. There was old string bean LBJ holding on to his cowboy hat while that thing circled overhead. Yep, that kid was pleased as pie with himself. But when election day finally rolled around, LBJ got one hundred percent of the vote in that county. *One hundred percent!* Do you know why?"

I didn't, but wouldn't have said anything even if I had known, because it would have ruined his story.

"Because that smart-ass trick in the helicopter backfired. The copter's blades had whipped up the dry Texas topsoil and deposited dirt into everyone's eyes and onto their barbeque plates. Those voters weren't electing LBJ as much as they were voting against his cocky opponent who'd ruined their chicken dinners."

DeLong laughed loudly at his own story. Then he took a sip of his bourbon and said: "Is this Melanie Cole as attractive as her sister?"

"They are, ur, were identical twins."

"Huh, lots of men fantasize about having sex with twins. You sleeping with her?"

"She's married, Senator, happily so."

"That wasn't my question."

I didn't reply.

"Nick LeRue," he said. "I've always watched your back. There have been times when some members of the judiciary have been after your ass and wanted you fired, but I've always protected you."

"I know, sir, and I appreciate it." But I really didn't know. I couldn't remember a time when the committee wanted me fired. Just the same, I might not have known, so I assumed he was telling me the truth.

"I called you here to give you some friendly advice: Forget about this woman. She's not worth your job."

"My job? Is my job in jeopardy?"

"You've been around long enough to know you never pick a fight with anyone who buys ink by the barrel."

I recognized the phrase. He was referring to the *Washington Tribune*. "Did Andrew Middleton call you?"

DeLong looked at me and I could tell that he was pondering how much he wanted to say. "Yes." he replied. "Of course, he asked me not to tell you, but he specifically asked me—no, let me rephrase that—he strongly suggested that I fire you."

"Are you going to?"

"It depends. Middleton knows too many secrets about people on the Hill who don't want their dirty laundry hanging on the *Tribune*'s front page."

"Including several on the committee?"

DeLong took a long sip and then gently shook his glass, causing the ice cubes to clink against the sides of the crystal. He didn't respond. So I said: "I think Andrew Middleton might be involved in Heather Cole's murder. I can't simply walk away from that because one of the committee members is being threatened."

"Wouldn't that depend on *who* is being threatened?" he asked.

Suddenly I understood. Middleton wasn't threatening to expose some faceless committee member. He was threatening to expose him. DeLong took another sip, finishing his drink. He set down the glass and asked: "Do you know what the downfall of most great men in the U.S. Senate and the U.S. House of Representatives is and always has been, historically speaking?"

"Blind ambition? Greed? The abuse of power?"

"No," he replied quietly. "Pussy. Good old American pussy. Wilbur Mills made a fool of himself chasing a stripper. Wayne Hayes kept a secretary on his payroll who didn't even know how to type. And everyone knows about Jack Kennedy and his women." He glanced away from me and let out a sigh. "It's a supply-and-demand problem. Most men love pussy. Hell, they can't get enough of it!

And women happen to own one hundred percent of all the pussy in this entire country."

I was stunned. I had no idea that my boss was having a sexual affair—if that was, indeed, what he was implying.

"Even good old LBJ had trouble with his zipper on occasion. It's just so damn easy here. Power is such a turn-on." He looked back at me. "Let's just say it would be prudent for you, and this unnamed committee member, if you dropped your interest in the Cole murder and decided to take an indefinite leave of absence. You could go on a much-needed vacation, perhaps, visit your father in the Midwest. If I recall, you're estranged from him."

"How long is indefinite?" I asked.

"Three or four months, but with pay, of course," he replied. "What I'm suggesting is an opportunity for you, really."

"What exactly do you mean?"

He suddenly looked angry. "Damnit! I shouldn't have to explain this! Forget about the murder and leave town or you're fired! That clear enough?"

I knew better than to ask my next question, but I couldn't stop myself. "Is that what's best for me, or what's best for you?"

I thought he might erupt, but as I watched, I saw what seemed to be embarrassment and disappointment wash over him. He was quiet for a moment and then he said: "Clarissa Poe brought you over. A lovely young girl. Young. What's she, thirty-five? She's married, you know, with two children in elementary school. Her husband's a lawyer over at the SEC. I pulled some strings. Nice couple. Perfect children. Her kids call me Grandpa. Shit! Thirty-five. She's younger than my daughters."

"What can you tell me about the Scarecrow Report?" I asked.

My question hit him cold but he was good on his feet. He had been in politics too long not to be. "Did you enjoy my story about LBJ and the helicopter?" he asked.

"Like all your LBJ stories, I found it entertaining."

"But I'm not sure you understood the moral to this one."

"Don't throw dirt into voters' barbeque chicken if you expect them to elect you?"

"LBJ didn't put it so delicately. He used to say, 'Never shit where you eat.'" DeLong stood and poured himself another bourbon. "I gave you the job you have, didn't I?" he asked.

"Yes," I replied.

"Then don't shit on me. You can't bring back Heather Cole. She's dead. Forget about her sister."

"Because I respect you, I'll take a leave. But I'm not going to stop digging. I'm not running away from Andrew Middleton."

"Nick, you're an idealistic fool!"

This was the first time in memory that he called me only by my first name.

He continued: "You don't have a choice here. You can't take a leave and continue to dig. Give up your manhunt or you're fired!"

For a moment, I thought about the cell phone conversation that I'd had less than an hour before with Andrew Middleton. He'd said we were going to work together as a team. Yet, at that point, he'd already called my boss and threatened him.

I stood up. "If that's the case, then I'm out. I'll have my desk cleaned out by tomorrow night."

"No need," he replied. "Clarissa is boxing it up now. I knew your answer before you arrived. But I was hoping to talk some sense into you. I hate to lose you, especially because of something as trivial as this."

"Trivial? A woman's been killed. Murdered. A senator and a famous journalist might be involved! That's not trivial."

He rubbed his forehead. "Do you know how many times I've voted on actions that have resulted in young Americans being sent into combat? Do you realize how many decisions I make every day that affect this country's future and the world's safety? And you dare to waltz in here and tell me that Heather Cole's murder is so significant that I should risk everything I've accomplished and everything I do so that you can keep investigating it? What can you really prove?" he asked. "Do you know how many murders were committed in this city alone last night? I don't see you getting upset about any of them. The only reason you care about this one is because Heather Cole dumped you and you want revenge on Andrew Middleton! You make it sound noble, but revenge never is."

"You're wrong," I said. "This isn't about revenge. It may have started out that way, but it's not anymore. It's about justice. It's about people who think they are above the law because they are rich and powerful. I can't do anything about all of those other murders which happened in this city last night. But I can about this one. And the fact that Andrew Middleton is blackmailing you to fire me is proof that I'm on the right track."

"Everyone loves *Mr. Smith Goes to Washington*," DeLong replied. "But that's Hollywood. It's fiction. Life isn't fair. And justice? Nick, you're making a big mistake. Dig all you want. You'll still never get Middleton. As a friend, not as your boss or as a senator, I'm urging you, don't do this. It's not worth it. Once you leave this office, it will be too late to ever change your mind."

"Thank you, Senator," I said. I stuck out my hand and shook his. Then I turned and walked out the door.

Melanie called while I staring at the chess pieces on the board in my apartment near the bay window. As it happened, I had made the last move. It had been Heather's turn to go next, but she had walked out before she had taken it.

Melanie sounded frightened.

"Meet me at the Freer Gallery of Art in a half hour," she said.

"Why not just come here?" I asked.

"No! I can't. I'll explain when I see you—in the Peacock Room."

"The what?"

"Ask a guard at the museum."

The Freer Gallery is one of the lesser-known Smithsonian museums that line the National Mall, the grassy strip between the U.S. Capitol and Washington Monument. The art gallery is in a stone building west of the Air and Space Museum, which draws the most tourists. While there were still tourists milling around the aeronautical museum's front doors, the Freer Gallery was almost deserted. A guard pointed toward a door and I stepped inside a room whose walls and ceiling were painted green and decorated with bright gold peacocks. I didn't see Melanie, so I pretended to be a tourist and read the description of the Peacock Room that was in a pamphlet. The reason why it was so small was it had been an actual dining room that had been disassembled board by board from the London home of Frederick R. Leyland, a wealthy shipowner from Liverpool, England, and rebuilt in the gallery. Leyland had commissioned the American-born artist James McNeill Whistler to decorate the dining room. The shipping magnate wanted the decor to complement an extensive porcelain collection that he owned, as well as a painting called *The Princess from the Land of Porcelain* that Whistler had completed earlier. It had taken Whistler two years to paint the Peacock Room. As I waited, I pondered why it had taken him so long and why a rich 1800s shipowner from Liverpool had started collecting porcelain in the first place.

"This room is a favorite of mine," Melanie said, stepping up to me. "My father introduced Heather and me to it. He loved fine art. I've always felt safe from the outside world here in this beauty."

"You sounded frightened on the phone."

"It was a pay phone," she said. "A few blocks from here. Something odd happened this morning."

"You okay?"

"Just very scared," she replied, "and even more confused. Heather's probate attorney called and insisted I meet him. I did and then he insisted that we have lunch. It took a long time and I got the impression that he was intentionally trying to keep me occupied."

"Maybe it's because you're beautiful and he was hitting on you?" I said.

"Nick, he's nearly seventy years old!"

"Ever heard of Viagra?"

I hoped my humor would help her relax, but it didn't.

"This is serious," she said. "When I finally broke free and returned to Heather's apartment, I went directly to her desk where I'd been working. And that's when I knew something was wrong."

"What do you mean, wrong?"

"I'm right-handed but my ink pen was on the left side of my writing pad. I studied the desktop and it struck me that everything that had been on the right side of the desk was now on the left side."

"Are you certain you weren't just confused?"

She gave me an exasperated look. "Last night I noticed there was a lot of dust on the bookshelves directly behind Heather's desk. I was going to clean them today. But I didn't have time and when I looked this afternoon, the dust was gone." She reached over with her right hand and gently touched my left arm. "I'm sure someone searched Heather's apartment. That's why the lawyer was keeping me preoccupied for so long."

"Was anything missing?"

"No, nothing. In fact, I didn't notice anything different except for the dust and the fact that the items on the desktop were the opposite from where they had been."

"I think I know what happened," I said.

Another couple came into the Peacock Room, so I moved Melanie away from them. "When I was at the FBI training center in Quantico, Virginia, I took a course on clandestine searches—how to search a room without leaving any tracks. The first step is photographing everything in the entire room so you can put everything back exactly as it was."

"But things weren't like they had been," she said.

"And I know why," I said. "During our training, one of the students made a mistake. He photographed a desktop but was in such a hurry that he printed the negatives with their dull side facing up, rather than their shiny side. That made everything in the photograph reversed. When we used his pictures, we ended up putting everything back in the wrong spot."

"That would explain why my ink pen was on the wrong side of the pad," she said. "And the dust was wiped away when the books were taken out and examined. That means Heather's apartment was searched! But by whom? Who would take the time to photograph everything?"

"The CIA. They use the same search techniques."

I glanced around. The other couple in the room had gone, so we were completely alone. "You were smart to suggest that we meet here."

"Why?"

"If the CIA searched Heather's apartment, then it probably is watching you. It might have even known in advance that we were meeting here. But the Smithsonian would never allow anyone to hide any listening devices in these walls because the entire room is a work of art, a canvas. You chose the one spot in Washington the CIA couldn't bug!"

"Heather wrote an article about how the CIA had gotten into trouble during the 1970s," she said. "And I distinctly remember that it said the CIA was prohibited from spying on U.S. citizens. It can only spy outside the U.S. So why would the CIA risk searching Heather's apartment or spying on us?"

Just then another couple entered the Peacock Room. They made me feel uneasy. He was wearing an off-the-rack suit and she was dressed in a gray woman's business suit. That's not your typical tourist outfit, but it was the sort of clothes you might be wearing at the CIA when your boss suddenly ordered you to rush over to the Freer Gallery to eavesdrop on a conversation. I motioned Melanie toward the exit.

"Up until the mid-1970s, the CIA did about anything it wanted to do in this country. That includes trying to hire the Mafia to kill Fidel Castro," I said, as we exited the gallery. "But after Senator Frank Church exposed all of the agency's antics, the CIA got muzzled, especially when it came to domestic spying."

"So what's changed from then and now?"

"September eleventh. The Bush administration took off the muzzle. Hell, they cut the leash too. The CIA is running wild now. All the agency has to do is claim it's conducting surveillance for reasons of suspected terrorism and it has a free hand to break into anyone's home or tap their phones."

We got into my car and neither of us said much until after I made an illegal left turn off Jefferson Drive and entered the westbound traffic on Independence Avenue. At that point, we were stalled in the nightly commuter traffic.

"Where are we going?" she asked.

"I think we need to take a ride in the country," I replied cryptically. "I hear horse country is pretty this time of year."

The traffic inched along during the next hour and by the time we reached the outskirts of Middleburg and turned onto Smithe's Farm Road, I had told Melanie that Andrew Middleton had gotten me fired—after he had played nicey-nicey to me on the telephone.

"I'm sorry," Melanie said. "I'm sorry I dragged you into this mess." Her voice cracked with emotion. She was starting to cry. "But if I hadn't—if it weren't for you—I couldn't have survived. Now I understand why my sister fell in love with you."

"Yeah, I'm a real hero," I replied sarcastically. "An unemployed hero, but a hero just the same." I laughed, but she didn't. Then I said: "Just remember, I do have some faults. I mean, Heather dumped me for Middleton."

"She made a mistake," she replied softly. "You're a very special man." I took my eyes off the road and turned to look at her, but she was staring out the passenger-side window. I dialed Jason Simon's telephone number on my cell, but no one answered and his machine didn't pick up. It didn't matter. We were less than a mile away.

"Oh, my God!" Melanie shrieked.

I saw it too, off to my right. Simon's barn was engulfed in flames. Two Middleburg fire engines were in the gravel driveway. Water hoses were shooting streams at the inferno. We parked and ran toward the old barn, which crackled, sizzled, and spit, as its sun-dried planks burned like kindling, shooting millions of hot sparks into the darkness as if they were tiny fireflies circling high above, and then drifting slowly down.

I spotted Simon watching his barn burn about sixty yards from the old John Deere tractor. The tractor's frame looked black and forlorn as the flames licked around it.

"They think it started in my office," he said. "Probably a cigarette."

"Are you okay?" Melanie asked.

"I'd run out of smokes and had driven into town to get what was supposed to be my last pack. I was going to quit tomorrow, you know. The place was already raging by the time I got back."

Although it didn't seem like the best time, I asked him: "How certain are you that Andrew Middleton worked for the CIA while he was in the Army?"

"Does it really matter now?" he said. "All my research is gone. Years of interviews—poof—up in smoke. I can't prove it even if it's true."

"Didn't you have any of your research backed up on computer files?" Melanie asked.

"That was something else I was going to do tomorrow."

"But you still have what's in your mind," I said. "You can retrace your steps, rebuild your files."

"Why bother? No one cares that Andrew Middleton fabricated the Wizard. He's written so many books since that first one that he's become legitimate. He's a national icon. He's won the battle and the war. I quit. I'm through."

"Nick and I care," Melanie replied.

Simon shook his head in disgust. "All I can tell you is that no one at Fort Bragg ever saw him in the foreign language school. They all assumed his job was a cover. Do you know who else trains there? The CIA's special paramilitary teams. Those guys are impossible to trace. And Middleton's past is just as impossible to pin down. With him, there's never any smoking gun—just suspicions and unanswered questions."

Suddenly Simon began laughing. "I just said smoking gun. We're watching all of my research burn and I just said there was no 'smoking' gun. What a farce!"

The blaze was so intense, I could feel the heat against my face and my eyes were beginning to swell with tears from the smoke. Melanie and I left Simon standing, watching the inferno, and returned to my car.

"You think someone started that fire on purpose?" Melanie asked.

"That barn was a hazard waiting to happen," I said. "But it was rather convenient how it began while he was out running an errand. And a CIA special ops team would know how to make a fire look like an accident."

Melanie began to cry. "I'm sorry. I've been in tears almost all day. I'm responsible. I just know it. Simon could have been killed. You've been fired. Heather is dead. I'm so, so tired of all this. I just don't know who to trust anymore. I thought Andrew Middleton loved my sister, and now the CIA may be watching us. . . ." Her voice trailed off.

"You can trust me," I said, although I knew it sounded sappy.

"I just want all of this to end, so I can go back home."

I had become so accustomed to having Melanie with me that I'd forgotten, once again, that she would be leaving at some point. I offered her tissues from the glove compartment.

"Most of what we know is based on conjecture and supposition," I said. "It's time for us to stir the pot by confronting people. Maybe we can get them to make a mistake."

"The CIA?" she asked.

"No, let's go back to when this was a simple murder investigation. Let's pay a visit on Mississippi Senator Nehemiah Peterman."

Twenty-seven

S enator Nehemiah Peterman lived in a pretentious new development in Vienna, a Washington suburb in Virginia. His house was one of a dozen $950,000, Colonial-style homes built on lots that appeared from above as if they had been laid out by a pizza maker. Each was sitting as far back as possible on its individual wedge of land. The tips of the lots met in a cul-de-sac at the center. I entered the long, concrete driveway that snaked toward his house and parked behind a Cadillac Escalade bearing a congressional license tag that said: MISS-ONE. It was next to a red Jaguar XJ-8, also with a vanity plate. I hate personalized licenses. Most of the time, I don't have a clue what the jumble of letters and numbers are supposed to mean, although the tag on the Jaguar was obvious: ALL-MINE.

An adolescent boy with jowls still thick with baby fat invited us inside the marble foyer without even asking our names and moments later Senator Peterman appeared wearing a black dinner jacket.

"Oh," he said, obviously surprised. "I thought you were

from the limousine service. I'm scheduled to leave for a charity event in Georgetown."

I stuck out my hand and introduced myself as the chief investigator for the Senate Judiciary Committee.

"I remember who you are from when you humiliated my good friend Daniel Hertell at his judicial nomination hearing," he snapped. He ignored my outstretched hand and looked at Melanie. "I recognize you from the photographs in the *Tribune* about your sister's murder in my hometown. I don't usually accept visitors in my home without invitation, but since you're here, come into my study. My wife is cleaning up after dinner and the kids are busy with homework."

"I didn't know you had small children," I said, trying to show an interest in his family.

"They're grandkids," he said curtly, without offering any more explanation.

Rather than sitting behind an ornate mahogany desk, he leaned against its front, a signal that he didn't plan on staying long to speak to us. There were two black leather chairs in front of the desk, but neither of us sat. I noticed that behind him, hanging on the wall, was a six-foot-long, twelve-inch-wide pine plank with the words PETERMAN LUMBER COMPANY carved into it.

"My sister was investigating the lynching of Lamar Grant in Rabbit Creek Park for a book when she was killed," Melanie began.

"I know, I know," he said, rushing the conversation. "I can't say I was thrilled that she was digging into that event. Race relations have come a long way since then. Our new county sheriff is an African American. You both met him when you were in Pushmataha—Jacob Moorehead. A hell of a guy! And a good friend of mine! But, unfortunately, all Washington reporters ever want to do is dig up dirt."

I decided to get right to the point. "We have copies of Jeb Rogge's telephone records and they show you spoke to him several times just before Heather Cole ended up dead."

"Listen, LeRue," he said firmly. "I don't care one bit for

you. I didn't like how you bushwhacked my friend at his confirmation hearing and I don't appreciate you and Ms. Cole showing up at my home unannounced." He paused for emphasis. "Furthermore, I don't like what you're implying here: that I somehow colluded with Jeb Rogge. Nor do I like how you just lied to me when you introduced yourself as the committee's chief investigator. I heard this afternoon that you were fired by Senator DeLong and no longer represent the committee in any fashion."

Peterman was turning the tables by launching a full-scale attack. It was a smart move. A good defense. Before I could reply, he added, "The only reason why you two are still standing in my house is out of respect for Ms. Cole here and her deceased sister." He looked at Melanie. "I don't know what sorts of lies Mr. LeRue has been feeding you, my dear, but I'll be happy to explain why Jeb Rogge and I spoke several times on the telephone. Mr. Rogge was a constituent of mine. A rather pesky one, as a matter of fact. He was a racist and a horrible man who hated nearly everyone and everything. Among them, the Internal Revenue Service. I was trying to help him resolve a complaint that the IRS had filed against him. That's why you'll find my telephone numbers listed on his phone bills. Obviously, I also have a thick file about the IRS feud. So you see, there is nothing secretive or sinister about my communications with him. I was simply trying to help him. That's my job— helping my constituents."

"How noble," I said sarcastically. "You never discussed Heather Cole with Jeb Rogge? You never told him that her investigation might result in his being charged with murder because of the lynching of Lamar Grant?"

"I don't think your question is even worth answering," he replied coldly. "I just explained why I spoke to Jeb Rogge. Now I think we're finished here."

"What about the telephone calls from Union Station— the pay phone in front of the Frank N' Stein Restaurant?" I asked.

"I don't know what you're talking about."

I decided to lie. "We have a witness who identified you from a photograph as the person who made calls from that public telephone at precisely six o'clock each night during the week when Heather was kidnapped and being held hostage."

Melanie shot me a puzzled look that, thankfully, Peterman didn't notice. My lie caught him unprepared. "You have a witness who claims he saw me making phone calls from a pay phone—where?" he repeated.

"Union Station. Frank N' Stein Restaurant. C'mon, Senator," I said gruffly. "The FBI has provided us with telephone records from that pay phone that show you and Rogge talked several times. If it was just about an IRS dispute, then why were you calling him from a pay phone?"

Before he could answer, I added: "We also know why you were just as eager as Jeb Rogge to make certain that Heather Cole didn't pry into the lynching."

I thought I saw a nervous glint in Peterman's eye, but he quickly regained his composure.

"You're lying," he snarled. "There's no such witness because I never used that pay phone." Again, he looked away from me at Melanie. "No one in Pushmataha is proud of what happened in Rabbit Creek Park," he said. "None of us wanted your sister to write a book about it, but that doesn't mean any of us wanted her harmed!"

"Really?" I sneered. "Jeb Rogge kidnapped her. That's how badly he wanted to keep his name out of her book. And you had more to lose than he did!"

Peterman glowered at me. "What the *hell* are you talking about?"

"You were there on the night Lamar Grant was hanged! You took part in it!"

Peterman's eyes bore into mine. He was trying to tell if I was bluffing. He was trying to intimidate me. He said: "You'd better have proof if you plan on making an accusation like that against me."

I opened the file folder and took out the photograph of

the lynching—the one that showed five white men standing under a swinging Lamar Grant. I thrust it toward him.

He studied it as if he were seeing it for the first time. "I'm not in this picture. Why are you showing it to me? On the night of the lynching, I was camping in the woods with my brothers and they'll corroborate that."

"That's not true!" Melanie blurted. "You *called* the sheriff!"

"The sheriff's been dead for years," Peterman said. "But even if he were alive, I'm sure he'd back up my story—not your accusation."

"You aren't in that photograph," I said calmly, "because you were standing behind the camera. You took that photograph!"

Peterman was quiet for several moments as he thought about his answer, and then he said: "The men in this photograph are all dead. They're the only ones who can say for certain who took it!"

"You're wrong, Senator," I replied. "We have a witness who says you took it. We also know that old man Rogge made everyone beat Lamar Grant with a baseball bat—and that includes you!"

For the first time, Peterman looked shaken.

"There is no such witness," he said, "because I was not there!"

It is scientifically impossible to tell if someone is a murderer simply by looking at him. I know that. But at that moment, watching Peterman, I knew that he was involved both Heather's kidnapping and her murder. Call it a sixth sense. Perhaps it's like the survival skills that a man in prison develops whenever he meets a new inmate and he must decide within seconds whether or not the cellmate's a threat. For whatever reason, I knew Peterman had been helping Jeb Rogge and, I strongly suspected, had later murdered him and then staged his death to look like a suicide. At that same moment, I also realized that the only person who could testify that Peterman had been at the lynching was George

McKinney, the retired Pushmataha newspaper editor now living in a Mississippi nursing home.

"Where'd you get this photograph!" Peterman demanded. "And who is this liar who says I was there?"

For a second, I didn't know how to respond. I wasn't going to tell a man I suspected of two murders the name of the only witness who could send him to prison. And then another name came to me.

"Our witness told us all about this photograph," I said, "and he's planning on exposing you in the newspaper. He's simply waiting for the right moment."

Melanie gasped. She was obviously afraid that I was going to identify George McKinney. Peterman noticed the terror in her eyes.

"The person who gave us this photograph and told us that you were at the lynching," I said with much drama, "is Andrew Middleton."

Peterman was visibly stunned. The skin on his neck stretched taunt across his blood vessels as if it were being pulled across a drum. I'd scored a direct hit. I decided to push my luck. "Middleton told us that you were both members of the IMPs at UVA. He seems to know an awful lot about your past!"

"If Andrew Middleton told you that I was in Rabbit Creek Park that night, then he is mistaken," Peterman replied. "My initials aren't carved in the trophy tree and I've already told you that I was with my brothers camping. As far as that photograph goes, I don't know anything about it or who took it! Now get out of my house!"

He'd said what I'd expected him to say, but his words had sounded unconvincing and he knew it.

I followed Melanie as she walked from the study. "By the way," I said, "did you know that it was Andrew Middleton's idea originally to send Heather Cole to Pushmataha? It wasn't her New York publisher's. Middleton was the one who told her about the trophy tree and urged her to investigate it. He's been setting you up from the start."

Peterman's face had turned blood red. "I hope you and

Ms. Cole have very good attorneys," he said, "because if you utter one sentence of this nonsense in public, I'll sue you for everything you own!"

As if on cue, the doorbell rang. It was Peterman's driver. We slipped by him. As we walked toward my car, Melanie said: "What the hell are you doing? What just happened in there?"

"We scared him," I replied.

"I was afraid you were going to tell him about George McKinney!"

"I wasn't going to say anyone's name, but then I decided to finger Andrew Middleton just to see how he'd react. And it worked!"

"You're trying to turn them against each other?"

"Absolutely."

"What do we do now?"

"We stir the pot even more," I said. "Let's pay a visit to Andrew Middleton." I looked at my watch. It was 6:45 p.m.

Twenty-eight

Think King David. Bathsheba. Heather studying the Old Testament. Bathsheba's husband slaughtered at the front lines. Heather murdered in Pushmataha. Jeb Rogge. Senator Peterman. Andrew Middleton. Telephone calls between all three of them. The 1955 lynching. Back to King David.

As Melanie and I rode into Georgetown, I thought about Melanie's dream. Why had Heather been reading about King David? How did that biblical character's actions tie in to Heather's murder?

It hit me! By the time that we crossed the Potomac, I understood.

Middleton answered the front door on my first knock. It appeared as if he'd been expecting us. When we entered the foyer, I heard the clicking of Clover's toenails as the dalmatian raced across the hardwood floor. The dog skidded around the corner with its tail wagging and leapt at Melanie.

"Down, Clover!" Middleton commanded. But she ignored him. Clover stood on her hind feet with her paws pressing against Melanie's waist. Middleton grabbed her collar, jerking her back. He pushed the dog behind the double doors of his dining room. I could hear whimpering as Middleton led us into his library.

"You two have been busy today," he said. "A very angry Senator Peterman just called here."

"You've been busy yourself," I replied. "You had me fired!"

I thought he might be flustered, but he wasn't. "I've heard you like presidential quotes," he said. "Here's one: 'If you can't stand the heat, get out of the kitchen.' "

I had never wanted to smack someone in the face as much as I did at that moment. But the timing wasn't right. We needed to talk to him. He said: "One of the reasons why I'm so successful is because I know how to cut through the B.S. and separate facts from opinions. Based on what the senator just told me, you both seem to believe that he and I were involved in Heather's murder. What facts do you have?"

"We've got telephone records that show the two of you were calling each other on pay phones when Heather was kidnapped and killed," Melanie declared. "I thought you loved my sister!"

An injured look washed over his face. "I did love your sister," he said tenderly, "and I didn't have anything to do with her abduction *or* murder. The fact that you are questioning my devotion to her is very disappointing. That's why I'd like to clear the air."

"Are you denying that you and Peterman talked over pay phones?" she asked.

"Ms. Cole," he replied softly, as if he were lecturing a child, "I'm an investigative reporter. It's my *job* to talk to politicians and sometimes I call them from pay phones because they ask me to. I might have spoken to him while Heather was in Pushmataha. In fact, I'm certain I did. But that doesn't mean I was plotting to harm Heather!"

"Then you won't mind telling us what you and Peterman discussed?" I interjected.

"I'm not going to tell you a thing about our conversations," he replied. "My reputation is based on the fact that I keep my word about confidentiality."

"That's not what Jason Simon told us," I said. "He claims you ruined his career at the *Tribune* after you had promised to keep his comments off the record."

"Jason Simon is an unethical reporter," Middleton answered. "I'm sure he blames me for his failed career, but he self-destructed completely on his own."

Our verbal jabs weren't getting us anywhere. Middleton realized it too. "Let's get specific," he said. "The truth is that neither of you has any facts that link me to Heather's death. I can say this with certainty because there aren't any facts to be had."

"You lied to us about your role in sending Heather to Mississippi," I said. "You said it was her publisher's idea, but in a letter that Heather wrote, she said that you were the one who came up with it."

"We've been over this before," he replied. "The publisher told me. I was busy, so I passed it on to Heather. It's semantics."

"You lied about the photograph," I continued. "You claimed that Heather had found it on her own and had showed it to you. But that's not true, is it? There were only six copies of that photograph made. Each of the Rogges got one. That adds up to three. Then there were the two copies that Stanley and Lester Alfred received. That's five. The final one belonged to Peterman. Somehow, you got his photograph and you gave it to Heather!"

"Does it really matter where that picture came from?" he asked.

I decided to play along. "You're right. It doesn't matter

where it came from. Just the same, how did you get a copy of it?"

"You're the detective here," Middleton replied. "You tell me."

"At UVA. That's where you found it."

Middleton considered for a moment whether or not he wanted to confirm my answer. He was experienced enough at interviewing techniques to know that the prudent thing to do would be for him to stay quiet. Otherwise, he might inadvertently offer us additional clues. But like most people who believe they are smarter than anyone else, he couldn't resist. He said: "When Peterman joined the IMPs, he told his fellow inductees about the lynching. He showed them several photographs that he had taken for the local newspaper. It was 1956, and rather than being repulsed, his buddies were impressed that he had actually witnessed a hanging."

"You found the photograph of the five men in a scrapbook?" Melanie asked.

"No. There is no scrapbook. But the IMPs keep a file on each member and Peterman's account of the lynching and several of the photos that he took were in that file. When I joined the IMPs, I heard about the hanging, read the file, and liberated the photo."

"Why?" Melanie asked. "Why'd you take it?"

"You've seen that picture," he replied. "It's a compelling piece of American history. Five white men standing in front of a hanging black man."

"So Peterman didn't know that his copy of the lynching photograph had been 'liberated' from the IMPs until we showed him a copy earlier tonight?" she said.

On some perverse level, Middleton was enjoying this. "Peterman's a fool. He called me when Heather first arrived in Pushmataha. I told him that a New York publisher had told Heather about the initials carved in the trophy tree and it had sent her to investigate. He never suspected that the book was my idea—until you put that idea in his head today!"

Middleton leaned forward, put his elbows on his desk, clasped his hands together as if he were going to pray, and said: "Congratulations! You've just gotten me to admit that I took the lynching photograph from UVA and gave it to Heather to help her investigation. You've just gotten me to admit that investigating the trophy tree was my idea. So what! The last time that I checked, it wasn't a crime to give a reporter a good story idea!"

"You're wrong!" I replied. "What you did *is* a crime. You ever read the Bible?"

Middleton gave me a puzzled look.

"There's a fascinating story in the Old Testament," I continued. "Since you like facts so much, you can find it in Second Samuel, Chapter Eleven, and read it for yourself after we leave. The first time I read it, I didn't understand what it had to do with Heather's murder. But now it's all fallen into place."

"Are you telling me that you think a Bible story links me to Heather's murder?" he asked incredulously.

"Yes, especially this story."

I could tell from Melanie's expression that she didn't have any idea how Bathsheba and King David helped to explain it.

"The chapter describes how King David coveted another man's wife—Bathsheba—a woman he quickly got pregnant," I explained. "King David decided to kill her husband. But because David was the king, he couldn't simply murder him. You following this so far?"

"I'm certain I didn't attend Sunday School as often as you did," he replied, "but I get the picture."

"King David solved his problem by arranging for Bathsheba's husband to be sent to the front lines during a fierce battle. Of course, the husband was killed—just as King David knew that he would be. King David thought he'd committed the perfect murder, since he wasn't anywhere near the battle lines. It was murder by proxy."

I paused to make certain the story had sunk in. "You wanted Heather dead," I continued. "But you couldn't do it yourself. You just couldn't shoot her, or stab her, or poison her. Why? Because you're famous, you're a goddamn national hero: the hardworking investigative reporter who drove a corrupt president out of the White House. And that put you in the same fix as King David. You had to find a way to kill her without anyone suspecting you. That's why you showed Heather the photograph and encouraged her to go to Pushmataha."

I waited for a reaction, but Middleton remained stone-faced.

I continued: "You and Peterman were both in the IMP, so you knew all about his role in the 1955 lynching. Even better, you had his copy of the photograph. You'd been holding on to it for decades. Now you saw a way to use it."

Again, Middleton didn't react.

I said, "Peterman had worked hard to get elected and you knew that if his secret ever became public, his political career would be finished. I'm guessing you'd done enough sleuthing on your own to know that Jeb Rogge was still alive, and was still living near Pushmataha, and was still a violent racist. That gave you two pawns: Peterman and Rogge. And you played both well."

I paused to give him an opportunity to jump in, but he didn't try to rebuff me.

"You intentionally dug out that snapshot and showed it to Heather. You knew she'd bite. You got her a hundred-thousand-dollar book advance and urged her to hurry down to Pushmataha to investigate. All the while, you knew that you were sending her into harm's way. You were sending an innocent to be slaughtered. Heather tracked down Jeb Rogge, just as you suspected she would do. Rogge panicked and telephoned Peterman. Again, that was something that you had anticipated. And then the senator called you. Did he ask you to call off Heather? I'm guessing he did. The two of them were like puppets on strings and they didn't realize that you were choreographing the entire scenario. I'm sure you were reassuring to the senator at first. You probably told him that you'd get Heather to come home and forget about the entire book project. Is that what you said?"

Middleton didn't respond, but Melanie was near tears. It was all coming together in her mind.

I said: "Then you gave Peterman the bad news. Heather wasn't going to beg off. She wasn't going to stop digging. Did you tell him how relentless she was? That she wouldn't give up until she had identified everyone who'd been at the hanging?"

As before, Middleton stayed stoic, but Melanie was clearly shaken.

Continuing, I said: "You'd already figured out what Peterman would do. You knew he'd be forced to ask Rogge for help. I'm guessing they probably discussed different ways to scare her. But you kept pushing Peterman, didn't you? Did you tell him that Heather Cole couldn't be intimidated? You made certain that Peterman was running scared. And he was. He couldn't take the chance that Heather might already have discovered his secret. And there was only one way he could be absolutely certain that she never would. Jeb Rogge had to murder her. Of course, that opened up another can of worms for the good senator, didn't it? I'm guessing the Rogge family already had been blackmailing the Peterman family for decades because of the senator's role in the lynching. But now Peterman sees a way to kill two birds with one stone. No more Heather, no more Rogge." I paused and then said: "Giving a reporter a good story is not a crime, but conspiring to commit murder is."

Middleton lowered his head and for a moment he seemed to be seeking divine guidance, but he was simply gathering his thoughts. He looked up at us and said: "You've just accused me of engineering two murders. You have no proof. You have only theories. But even if you were able to somehow convince a jury that your King David conspiracy plot is true, you're still missing a elemental component for a murder case: What possible motive would I have for wanting her dead, especially since I was in love with her?"

"She'd dumped you!" I replied. "Jealousy. Anger. Revenge. Those are the oldest motives in history. You were a jilted lover."

"If that were the case," he replied, "then you had just as much of a motive as I did to murder her. You've never really gotten over her, have you?"

He was right. But I wasn't about to admit it. I said: "You could've wanted Heather to die because she'd found out a secret about your past."

He grinned, as if I had just told a joke. "You're reaching," he said, "but tell me: What dark secret from my past would that be?"

"That the Wizard—the source for your book—doesn't really exist. Heather discovered that you made up the Wizard for dramatic reasons. You fabricated him and you didn't want anyone to know. You didn't want your career to end like the career of that young reporter who fabricated the story about the eight-year-old drug addict!"

Middleton forced out a laugh. "Mr. LeRue," he said in a patronizing voice, "do you have any idea how many people have accused me of fictionalizing the Wizard? Dozens of reporters have theorized that the Wizard is a composite character. If I were some crazed killer, then why are all of *those* journalists walking around alive today?"

"Heather learned something that those others didn't," I replied.

"Oh," he said. "And what could that possibly be?"

"She'd gotten a copy of the CIA's Scarecrow Report."

Middleton's cocky smile vanished. He looked directly at Melanie and said: "Even though your sister moved out of my house, I still loved her. I wanted her back—regardless of what you two may now think." He returned his gaze to me. "I'm done answering your questions. You've stopped amusing me."

I said: "There's one fact that you've forgotten. There's one fact—not rumor, not a theory, but a fact—that links you directly to Heather's murder."

"You're bluffing," he said, "but, unlike Senator Peterman, I don't fall for bluffs."

"You're the only person Heather called from Pushmataha. We've got her cell phone records to prove that. That makes you the only person who knew that she had rented two motel rooms but was sleeping only in one: the Stars and Bars. Jeb Rogge knew exactly where to find Heather because you betrayed her. You told Peterman that she was at the Stars and Bars and he passed that information along to Jeb Rogge. That's the link that will tie you to her abduction and murder, and will eventually put you behind bars."

Middleton and I glared at each other as if we were schoolkids in a playground getting ready for fisticuffs.

I said: "The senator now knows that you manipulated him by giving that photograph to Heather. He's angry now because you used him. Trust me, if we can find evidence that also ties him to Heather's murder, Peterman will flip over on you in a heartbeat. And if he testifies against you, you're going to be found guilty. That's a fact, not a theory."

Melanie had heard enough. "You bastard!" she screamed, lunging forward at Middleton. "I hate you! You'll pay for what you've done!"

He grabbed her wrists before she could strike him. Strangely, a smile appeared on his lips. "Lots of people in this town hate me. And smarter people than the two of you have tried to bring me down. I'm not going to lose any sleep tonight worrying about you and your 'biblical' theories."

Melanie's hands were still trembling as we drove from Middleton's house. "That smug, superior son of a bitch!" she exclaimed.

"He's got good reason to feel smug," I replied. "Despite what I said, we really don't have enough yet to go to the police. We don't even know why he wanted Heather dead."

"It has something to do with the Wizard and the Scarecrow Report," Melanie replied. "The only time he looked worried was when you mentioned it."

"The fact that the CIA searched Heather's apartment tells me a copy of that report is definitely missing," I said. "I'm wondering where she hid it before she left for Mississippi."

"I'll ask her," Melanie replied. "Tonight. I'll contact her in a dream. Drop me off at Heather's apartment. I'm going to take a hot bath, drink some wine, and then get into a pair of her pajamas and crawl into her bed and think about where that report might be hidden. If she possibly can, she'll tell me!"

I was mentally debating the odds of Melanie contacting her dead sister again in a dream when my cell phone rang.

"I'm trying to reach a Mr. Nick LeRue," a woman's voice said.

"You've found him. Who's speaking, please?"

"My name is Doris Brown, I'm the head nurse at the Sunshine House in Jackson, Mississippi, and I'm calling because one of our residents, George McKinney, identified you as someone to call in case of an emergency."

The image of the old newspaper editor and the afternoon when Melanie and I had interviewed him in the gazebo flashed in my mind. "Is something wrong?" I asked.

"I'm afraid I have bad news," Brown said. "Mr. McKinney passed away this afternoon from a heart attack. I'm terribly sorry."

I hung up and told Melanie.

"George McKinney was our only real witness," I said. "He was the only person who could've testified that Peterman was at Rabbit Creek Park taking photographs on the night of the lynching. Without him, we really don't have anything that links Peterman to the hanging. And without Peterman, we lose Andrew Middleton."

By this time we had reached the curb outside Heather's Watergate apartment. "I've got to contact Heather tonight!" Melanie said with determination. "She's got to tell me where the Scarecrow Report is hidden."

"Without it," I said, "there's a good chance that Andrew Middleton will get away with what he's done."

"No, he won't!" Melanie said. "I'm not going to let that happen. I'll kill him if I have to!"

I watched her enter the building and then checked my watch: 8:05 p.m. A bit early for bedtime. On the drive home, I stopped at a liquor store. Diet Cokes weren't going to be enough to get me through tonight.

Twenty-nine

I couldn't sleep. I thought about Melanie. Was she dreaming? Had Heather appeared to her? After an hour of watching the red digits on my bedside clock mark time, I turned on the television. A John Wayne western and an infomercial about an all-purpose kitchen knife so durable it could cut through concrete blocks and still slice tomatoes were followed by a Canadian television sex-advice show whose seventy-something, gray-haired granny-host discussed acts of fornication with such deftness that I wondered if I was the only person left on the planet who still had more fingers than I'd had sex partners.

At six a.m., I gave up and went into the bathroom to shave and shower. I'd just lathered my chin when someone knocked at my door. I peered through the security peep-hole and saw Melanie. She was wearing a pair of sky-blue silk pajamas.

As I let her inside, I asked: "What happened?"

"I'm not sure!" she said in a frightened voice. "Hold me, please!"

She hugged me. I could feel her body trembling.

"How'd you get here?"

"Cab. I didn't have any money to pay him. He picked me up in Georgetown. He thought I was sleepwalking. I asked him to bring me here."

"Is he still waiting?"

"I don't think so."

I led her into the kitchen, sat her in a chair, got her a white terry-cloth robe that her sister had once worn and had left behind along with a pair of slippers.

"Did you contact Heather in your dream?"

"I don't know. I can't remember."

I heated some water in the microwave to make her tea. She ran her hand through her tangled hair. "My God!" she said. "I must look a mess!"

I handed her the cup of hot water, two tea bags, and a spoon. She held the ceramic cup in her hands, feeling its warmth.

"I remember taking a hot bath, drinking a couple of glasses of wine, and then I found these pajamas and put them on and went to bed. I must've fallen asleep, but after that . . ." She shook her head.

"Nick," she said, "I don't have any idea what happened! Nothing! The cabbie said I was talking crazy, but I don't know why I left Heather's apartment or where I went in Georgetown or why or what happened after I got there. It's all one big blank!"

"Drink some tea. We'll figure it out together."

She took a sip and there was another knock at my door. I glanced at my watch. It was only 6:20 a.m. I looked through the peephole and saw two men and a woman in the hallway. The men were dressed in suits; the woman wore a D.C. police officer's uniform. I opened the door and the men introduced themselves as homicide detectives.

"A taxi driver called us," Detective Gerald Humbolt said. "He said he brought a woman named Melanie Cole here. We've been searching for her."

I mentioned that I was a former FBI agent and ex-chief

investigator for the Senate Judiciary Committee. "Why do you want to talk to Melanie Cole?" I asked.

"You her attorney?" Humbolt replied.

"Does she need one?"

Melanie emerged from the kitchen. "I'm Melanie Cole. What's wrong, Officers?"

"You need to come with us," Humbolt said.

"Why? What's happened?" she asked.

"Do you know Andrew Middleton?"

"Yes. What about him?"

Humbolt said: "He's dead."

"Dead?" I echoed.

"Yes. In his house. He was shot."

"A robbery?" I asked.

"No," said Humbolt, who hadn't taken his eyes off Melanie.

Melanie said: "I'm not dressed."

"You got a change of clothes here?" the female officer asked.

"No, my clothes are at my sister's apartment. The Watergate. It's where I'm staying."

"We'll drive you there and I'll stay with you while you change," the woman said.

Detective Humbolt's cell phone rang. He grunted "Yes" and "Okay" several times and then hung up. "Ms. Melanie Cole," he said, "an arrest warrant has been issued for you. I'm going to inform you of your Miranda rights now."

"Oh, my God!" Melanie gasped. "Nick, help me! You've got to help me! You'll be my attorney, right? You'll represent me? I don't trust anyone but you!"

"What's the charge?" I asked, although I was pretty certain I already knew.

"The murder of Andrew Middleton," Humbolt said.

"No, no, no!" Melanie exclaimed, covering her face with her hands.

"It'll be okay," I said, although I wasn't really certain that it would be. "I'll represent you until we can get you an attorney who specializes in criminal cases." I turned to Humbolt and said: "I'd like to go with her to the station."

Humbolt glanced at what I was wearing: an old T-shirt and pair of baggy gray sweatpants. "You can't ride with us or her," he said. "And it will take a while for us to process her." He handed me his card, which had the address of the D.C. police headquarters on it. "You a member of the D.C bar?" he asked.

I was. I had passed the bar exam after finishing law school here. "Melanie, listen to me very carefully," I said. "Don't say anything to these detectives about Middleton or last night! Not one word. I'll come down to be with you as soon as I get dressed. Tell them you have nothing to say until your attorney is there. Tell them that you do not want to speak to anyone unless I'm in the room. Do you understand me?"

"Yes," she said. She glanced at Humbolt. "You heard what he said, right?"

The detective nodded and handcuffed her. They led her out.

I ran into the bedroom and stripped. As I was dressing, I flipped on the television. A reporter appeared on the screen standing outside Middleton's row house.

"Investigative reporter Andrew Middleton was found shot to death late last night in his Georgetown home," the newswoman announced. "D.C. homicide detectives found his body after an anonymous tipster reported hearing gunshots coming from inside Middleton's house. The caller told a 911 dispatcher that he'd seen a woman bolting from the house. The caller gave police a detailed description, including the fact that the woman was wearing only blue pajamas when she fled.

"Middleton, who is a bachelor, became famous in the 1970s when his investigative work at the *Washington Tribune* forced the president of the United States to resign from office . . ."

I hurried downstairs to my car. An all-news AM station picked up the story.

"The first officers at Middleton's house found his dog, a pet dalmatian, standing guard over his dead master's body. According to a police source, a nine-millimeter handgun was on the floor near the body. Police believe it's the murder weapon. A spokesman at the *Washington Tribune* said they were not certain what stories Middleton was currently investigating. He always worked independently and disliked discussing his stories with other reporters and editors. A police source, however, said that detectives do not believe his murder was related to his job. While no motive has been made public, sources said it appeared that the shooting involved a personal or possible romantic dispute."

Good, I thought. The police hadn't told anyone that Melanie had been arrested. As I drove, I used my cell telephone to call Stanley Slanafall, an attorney who used to work for the Senate Judiciary Committee before he opened up his own criminal defense practice. Not surprisingly, his specialty was defending members of Congress and other Washington celebrities. I called him at home and he promised to meet me at D.C. police headquarters. Next, I called my FBI pal, Phillip Shurman, at home and asked him to snoop around for me. I turned the radio volume back up just in time to hear the announcer breathlessly declare that one of the station's reporters was at D.C. police headquarters with an update on the Middleton murder.

"Homicide detectives have arrested a suspect. She has been identified as Melanie Cole, who, I've been told, is the twin sister of Heather Cole, a well-known *Washington Tribune* reporter who was murdered only days ago in Pushmataha, Mississippi. According to knowledgeable sources, Heather Cole was romantically involved with and lived with Andrew Middleton before she went to Mississippi, where she was abducted and murdered by a white supremacist. A police source said her twin sister, Melanie Cole, is believed to be the woman who was spotted by an eyewitness running from Middleton's house last night wearing only a pair of blue pajamas. The police source did not know if Melanie Cole was romantically involved with the murder victim."

A mob of reporters was clustered around the entrance of D.C. police headquarters. I pushed my way through without anyone asking who I was and went directly to the booking office.

"They've not brought her in yet," a sergeant told me. "I think they've taken her directly to the D.C. jail to avoid the media." The D.C. jail is located in Southeast Washington, several miles away from police headquarters. I began driving to the jail and called Slanafall again.

"Turn around!" Slanafall exclaimed. "They're trying to keep you from finding her. Trust me, if you drive down to the jail, someone there is going to send you to a precinct house. Every minute they can keep you away from your client is another minute they can use trying to interrogate her." Then he added: "Jesus Christ, you've never practiced criminal law, have you?"

"I warned her not to talk to anyone," I said. "They shouldn't even be talking to her."

"I can guarantee you they are," he replied. "Let's just hope she listened to you and has enough backbone to keep quiet. My guess is they're putting the squeeze on her right now inside one of the precinct stations."

Slanafall was correct. He called me twenty minutes later and declared: "I've found her up in Georgetown but I've raised so much hell they're taking her to the D.C. jail now. I still haven't seen her, so you need to get down there ASAP!"

Someone had tipped off the media. Camera crews were already set up outside the jail's main entrance by the time that I parked. Moments later, three D.C. squad cars with flashing red and blue lights raced up to the gate. The convoy slowed as the automatic chain-link gate opened, giving the camera crews plenty of time to film Melanie, who was sitting in the back seat of the second car. She couldn't raise her hands to shield her face because her handcuffs were attached to a "belly chain" looped around her waist.

By chance, one of the television cameramen happened to be assigned to Capitol Hill and he recognized me after the squad cars had entered the complex. Within seconds I had ten microphones stuck in front of me.

"You used to date Heather Cole, didn't you?" one of the reporters asked. "Why was her twin sister at Middleton's house in her pajamas?"

"I have no comment," I said as I tried to maneuver through them.

"Were Melanie Cole and Middleton lovers?" another yelled.

"Is that why she left in her pajamas?"

"Why'd she shoot him?"

When I finally got inside, the receptionist said: "You've got to show me your D.C. bar card before you can see Ms. Cole."

"I don't have it with me."

"Then how do I know you're an attorney? She's got to sign a release to see you too! You can't just come running in here and demand to see her! We've got rules and procedures."

A half hour later, Slanafall arrived. I was still standing in the lobby. He marched up to the receptionist and within five minutes we were sitting in an attorney-client conference room waiting for Melanie. It was a ten-by-twelve-foot room with a metal table and three chairs. Two officers brought her to see us. She was now dressed in a bright orange D.C. jail jumpsuit. Her eyes were nearly scarlet from crying.

I quickly introduced Slanafall, who gave her his pitch about how many criminal cases he'd tried and won. Then he warned her that he would prefer that she not say anything to him about the crime or her alibi until he had a chance to see what sort of evidence prosecutors had gathered against her. That way he could help her "formulate your defense"—a polite way of saying: *develop an alibi*.

"Did you say anything to the police or sign any typed statements?" he asked.

"I almost did," she replied. "They were so nasty. They

kept asking me questions about Middleton and my sister, Heather, and about where I was last night. But I told them that I wouldn't say anything until Nick got here and was with me. One of the detectives became really hostile and accused me of trying to hide something. He said I was going to spend the rest of my life in prison if I didn't tell him what happened. It was just horrible."

A few minutes later, Slanafall announced that he was going to see what he could learn about the charges against her. He left us alone.

"Nick," Melanie said, reaching over and grabbing hold of my hand. "Some of what happened last night has come back to me. I've started remembering bits and pieces!"

"Did you go to Middleton's house?"

Melanie looked down at the metal table between us, clearly embarrassed, and held my hand even tighter.

"Yes, I did," she said quietly. "I remember now—getting out of bed, putting a coat, and hailing a taxi. I don't know what happened to the coat. Maybe it's still at Middleton's house or I lost it somewhere in Georgetown. I just don't know. I can't remember!"

"Do you remember anything that happened at his house? Did you see him?"

"I'm not sure."

"Melanie, why did you go there last night?"

"I had to!" she declared. "I didn't have a choice!"

"Did Heather tell you something in a dream about Middleton or about the Scarecrow Report?"

Melanie looked up at me. There were tears flowing down her face. "I didn't shoot Andrew Middleton! I didn't murder him! But I know who did!"

"You know!" I nearly shouted. "Who? Who did it, Melanie? Tell me, so I can get you out of here! Did you walk in on his murder?"

"It was my sister, Heather!"

I wasn't expecting that. After the initial surprise wore off, I said, very calmly: "Melanie, you know that Heather's dead. She couldn't have shot Andrew Middleton. You must still be in shock. Dead people don't come back from the grave to shoot people!"

"I know exactly what I'm saying. I'm not in shock. You've got to listen to me. I know exactly what happened," Melanie firmly replied. "Heather did come to me in my dream last night, just as she has hundreds and hundreds of times. She told me that Andrew Middleton was going to get away with manipulating her two kidnappers. She said there was nothing any of us could do now to prove that he pulled their strings and had her killed. Then she told me that she was going to shoot him. After that, I don't remember much more. It was like she pulled me into the background and she took control over my body."

Melanie squeezed my hand hard.

"Nick, you've got to believe me," she said. "If you don't believe me, no one will! You know Heather has talked to me in my dreams. She told us where she was being held captive. She told us there were two kidnappers. She told us about Jason Simon and the King David story. Please don't doubt me now! She did it! She killed him—only she used my body to do it."

She was near panic. "I wasn't in charge," she said. "Heather was! You've got to believe me!"

I didn't know what to say. I'd heard of murder suspects who claimed they were sleepwalking, in hypnotic trances, delusional, or suffering from multiple personality disorder, but I'd never heard of a murder defense where the defendant claimed she had been possessed by a dead person! I looked at Melanie and the last words she had said to me after I'd dropped her off last night suddenly popped into my head. I'd just warned her that there was a chance that Middleton was going to get away with Heather's murder unless we could find the Scarecrow Report and decipher his motive for wanting her dead.

"I'm not going to let that happen," Melanie had declared. *"I'll kill him if I have to."*

Thirty

They've got a helluva lot of evidence against your client," Phillip Shurman said. We were in a booth at a Denny's Restaurant in Fairfax, Virginia. It was his choice. He didn't want to be seen talking to me. I didn't care and didn't have an appetite, but he'd ordered the "Grand Slam," scrambled eggs, pancakes, bacon strips, and hash browns.

"To begin with," he continued, "there's the Walther nine-millimeter found lying on the floor near Andrew Middleton's body. It was registered to Heather Cole. Apparently, she'd bought it only a few days before she'd left for Mississippi."

"Any fingerprints on it?"

"No, it had been wiped clean, but ballistics identified it as the murder weapon. Detectives also found the box that it had been purchased in and a receipt for it in Heather's Watergate apartment where Melanie was staying."

Shurman poured more warm maple syrup on his pancakes. He was enjoying playing detective. It'd been a while since either of us had actually investigated a case.

"Besides the nine-millimeter, they recovered a black cashmere woman's coat lying on the porch near the front door of Middleton's house. Forensics found trace evidence—hairs on the coat that match the suspect's hair. It looks like she was at his house last night and left the coat behind."

"Anything else?"

"Yep, unfortunately for you, there's plenty more," he replied. "The police have two witnesses, both neighbors, who identified Melanie Cole from photographs." He fished a notepad out of his pocket. "One neighbor, a Miss Virginia McClanahand, said she saw your client arrive at Middleton's house in a taxi a few minutes before nine-forty p.m. She felt confident about the time because she had just finished watching her favorite comedy on television at nine-thirty p.m. and was about to go to bed when she realized that she hadn't gotten her mail that day. She went outside to get it and that's when she saw your client climbing out of the cab. When she went back inside, she noticed it was nine-forty."

He flipped a page in his notebook and then continued. "The other witness is a young man who was walking home from dinner. He actually spoke to your client. His name is Alex Andre and he said he first saw her while he was walking south on Twenty-eighth Street toward Q Street. She was wandering between graves inside the Oak Hill Cemetery and he thought it was odd because she wearing pajamas. He looked at his watch. It was ten p.m. He knew the graveyard was closed and he asked her if she needed any help."

"What'd she say?"

"He said that she ran deeper into the cemetery."

"Has the coroner's office fixed a time of death?"

"Sometime before ten o'clock," Shurman replied. "However, the cops are claiming that they know the exact time of the homicide based on an anonymous phone call."

"Someone called? Someone other than the two witnesses?"

"Yes," Shurman replied. "The caller said he was walking his dog past Middleton's place when he heard three loud pops and saw a woman in blue silk pajamas come running out the front door. He looked at the time and saw it was exactly nine-fifty-five p.m. He walked to a nearby pay phone and called 911."

"That's very precise information. Who was this caller?"

"The cops don't know and he hasn't come forward or volunteered to testify. The call was traced to a pay phone about two blocks south of Middleton's house—at the corner of Twenty-ninth and M streets."

"It's outside a liquor store, right?"

"That's right. The caller refused to give his name to the dispatcher. He said he lived in the neighborhood and didn't want his neighbors to think he was a snoop if his tip turned out to be nothing. That's why he was using a pay phone rather than calling from his house."

"What about the taxi driver who picked up Melanie and drove her to my apartment? Have the cops interviewed him?"

"Yes," Shurman said, once again referring to his notepad. "He's a driver for Liberty Cab Company. He first noticed Melanie around three o'clock that morning after he dropped a passenger near 28th and Q streets. He remembered her because she was only wearing pajamas and was wandering through the graveyard. He told detectives that he stopped near the cemetery after he discharged his passenger. He was doing some paperwork and he saw your client inside the wrought-iron fence. He watched her for several minutes. At one point, she got down on her knees in the grass. He got another call and left Georgetown. Later, he saw your client walking along M Street toward downtown at five-forty-five a.m. That's when he pulled over and asked her if she was lost. He drove her to your apartment without charge. He assumed she had mental problems."

"Let's go over those times again," I said. "Melanie arrives at Middleton's house, according to the first witness, near nine-forty that night. Now, the anonymous witness claims he was walking his dog past Middleton's house at nine-fifty-five when he hears gunshots and sees Melanie come bolting out. She is next seen wandering through the Oak Hill Cemetery five minutes later at ten p.m. She runs away when the witness calls out to her. She is still meandering around the cemetery at three a.m. when the cab-driver spots her and then at five-forty-five a.m. he finally picks her up as she's strolling down M Street."

"That's what the cops say."

"That means Melanie was in Georgetown from nine-forty p.m. until five-forty-five a.m., or for nearly eight hours, still walking around in her pajamas."

"Apparently she wasn't in a hurry to get out of there," Shurman said, as he finally finished the last bit of eggs on his plate and put down his fork. "Tell me something, Nick," he said. "How much do you really know about Melanie Cole?"

"I know she and Heather were twin sisters and that she lives in South Dakota, with her husband and two kids."

"Really?" he said. "She told you that she has a husband and two kids?"

Suddenly I had a queasy feeling in my stomach.

"Melanie Cole is not married," Shurman said. "I checked into her background for you. She doesn't live in South Dakota and she doesn't have any kids either."

I suddenly realized why her family had not appeared at Heather's funeral or why her husband hadn't contacted me after Melanie was arrested.

She'd lied to me!

Shurman continued: "Your client is a secretary in Loveland, Colorado. She works for a small advertising firm there: Poovey and Casynn." He glanced up at me to see if he should continue. I nodded.

"Obviously," he said, "when I realized that she'd lied, I did more research, and I'm sorry to tell you this, but your client has quite a few skeletons. She dropped out of college during her senior year. The school was reluctant to say why, but I tracked down a classmate and learned that Melanie Cole had suffered a mental breakdown. She was admitted to a state psychiatric hospital in Pueblo, Colorado, and later went into a private treatment facility in Arizona."

"What sort of treatment program?"

"Your client is suffering from bipolar disorder with possible schizophrenic affective disorder. The doctors weren't sure of which."

"Did she suffer from delusions or just extreme highs and extreme lows?" I asked.

"She suffered delusions—the normal stuff, feelings of grandiosity, hearing voices, couldn't sleep—there was only one thing that was really different. Her records show that unlike other delusional patients, who always think the CIA is after them, she thought her sister Heather could take control of her body."

I couldn't believe what he'd just said. Shurman had no idea that Melanie had told me the day before that Heather had seized control of her body and had murdered Andrew Middleton. Obviously, if Shurman had discovered that Melanie had a psychiatric record of delusional behavior, so would the prosecution.

Shurman flipped shut his spiral binder. "If I were you," he said. "I'd start preparing an insanity defense. Based on what I found in her past, you'd probably be able to show that she was out of her mind when she shot Middleton."

"*Allegedly* shot Middleton," I corrected.

"Oh, sorry, Counselor," he said.

I left the Denny's parking lot en route to the D.C. jail and as I drove south onto the outer loop of the Capital Beltway, the wide highway that encircles all of Washington, D.C., I thought about Melanie and how she'd deceived me. How could I have been so stupid? I'd never believed in any supernatural mumbo-jumbo but I'd let her talk me into believing all this twin nonsense. I had another thought. If I'd been blind to Melanie, was I also being blind when it came to Senator Peterman and Andrew Middleton? What evidence did we really have? The FBI found no evidence of two kidnappers. What if Jeb Rogge had acted alone? What if Peterman had talked to Rogge simply because he was a constituent? Was it possible that Andrew Middleton didn't send Heather to Mississippi knowing that she would be kidnapped and killed? I was confused. No! Some of what Melanie had said had proved to be absolutely true, hadn't it? She was right about Heather being kidnapped. She had told me that, before we knew that Rogge had abducted her! She was right about where Heather was being held hostage too! And what about her dream? How else would she have known about Jason Simon? How else would she have been told about King David and Bathsheba? Wait! How much of that was real and how much was because I wanted to believe it—like a horoscope that you fit to your own situation? There was no question that she had lied to me about being married, lied to me about having children, lied to me about living in South Dakota. Why had she lied? How could I trust her now?

My cell phone rang, interrupting the mental argument that I was having with myself. It was Slanafall calling from his cell phone. He'd just left Melanie at the jail.

"Our client just told me who she thinks murdered Andrew Middleton," he said.

"Yes, she believes her sister, Heather, did it," I replied.

"You do realize that Heather is dead, right?" he asked me.

"Yes."

I was about to tell him what I'd learned about Melanie's mental history when he said: "I've already called a psychiatrist to examine her. What's funny is that she asked me if she could take a polygraph test. She's absolutely convinced that she can prove that it was Heather who pulled the trigger and shot Middleton. She said it was because they were twins."

"Is having her take a polygraph a good idea?"

"As long as the other side doesn't know, it's okay. There's something else we need to consider. If you're representing her, you can't be called to testify. The question is: Who's going to explain this convoluted story she told me about your investigation of Senator Peterman and Andrew Middleton?"

"Having me testify wouldn't be wise," I said. "You don't want the prosecution asking me questions about comments that Melanie made on the night of the murder."

"Okay," he said after a short pause. "This sounds like something we need to discuss in person, not over cell phones." We agreed to meet later that night for dinner.

Melanie was all smiles when they brought her into the attorney conference room. "I did it!" she gushed when the two correctional officers left us alone. "Last night—I contacted Heather. I talked to her in my dream!"

"Melanie," I said quietly. "Why did you lie to me about your past? You told me you were married. South Dakota. The Black Hills. A husband. Two children. Remember? Little Kaitlyn and Matthew?"

Her face became flushed. "I'm really, really sorry, Nick, but I had a good reason to mislead you. I needed you to go with me to Mississippi and I knew you were still in love with Heather. I didn't want things to get complicated."

"What do you mean, get complicated?"

"Nick, you were in love with my sister. We're identical twins. When Heather and I were teenagers, the first thing our boyfriends did whenever we broke up with them was make a play for the other twin. I didn't want to risk having that happen."

I considered acting offended, but thought better of it. The truth was that I *was* attracted to her. I said: "What other lies have you told me?"

"Nothing else," she answered. "Everything that I've shared with you about Heather and my dreams happened just like I said. I only lied to make certain we didn't get romantically involved. But now that Heather is dead, things are different." She reached across the table and touched my hand. "Surely you know I've developed strong feelings toward you."

Without thinking, I jerked back my hand.

"Melanie, you've lied to me about more than your fake marriage and nonexistent children!"

"What are you talking about? Why are you being so cruel?" she demanded. "I just explained why I misled you."

"What about your mental breakdown? How about the time you were institutionalized in Colorado and the private treatment center in Arizona? When were you going to tell me about your diagnosis—bipolar disorder? When were you going to tell me about the delusions you've had—about how you've been convinced before that Heather had taken control of your body?"

"She has!" Melanie replied. "Jesus Christ! Am I supposed to confess everything horrible that's ever happened to me? What's next: a list of every man I've ever had sex with?"

"It's not the same!" I shot back. "You've got a mental disorder. You should've told me that up front! I had a right to know!"

"Why? Why did you have a right to know? Am I supposed to wear a sign around my neck proclaiming that I have bipolar disease and have had delusions? What are you saying? That you can't trust me now because of my illness?"

"For God's sake, you've had episodes when you haven't known what you were doing! What do you expect?"

She recoiled back in her chair with a pained look on her face. "Two days ago, you believed me. But now all of the trust that I earned is gone. Poof! I've worked for years to understand and control my illness. I take my medicine religiously. Those delusions took place years ago! When am I forgiven? When do I suddenly become trustworthy again?"

"Never," I replied coldly.

Visibly shaken, Melanie struggled to find words.

"This isn't fair. I'm not crazy. I'm not suffering from delusions. I *can* talk to Heather in my dreams. She *can* take control of my body. And I'm *not* psychotic because I believe that! I don't care what you or any doctors tell me."

"Are you taking your medicines now?"

"No," she replied. "I've not taken them today. I've not taken them since they arrested me. I was afraid to tell anyone because I didn't want the prosecution to find out. I thought they'd react just like you are. But it's okay. I can go for several days, even weeks, without anything happening. The medicine is built up in my system."

I switched subjects. "Why were you wandering around in Oak Hill Cemetery on the night of the murder?" I asked. "You were there nearly eight hours."

"I was searching for Heather's grave," she replied.

I should've figured that out earlier. Heather was buried in Oak Hill.

Melanie leaned forward with a hurt look in her eyes. "Nick, don't turn your back on me now!" she pleaded. "Heather did this, not me."

"Do you know how crazy that sounds? Do you think anyone on the jury is going to believe that your sister took possession of your body?"

"Give me a polygraph! I didn't kill Middleton!" She looked directly into my eyes and then released a loud sigh, because she realized that I wasn't buying it. Melanie's shoulders slumped. "I was so happy when I first came into this room to see you because I had great news. I wanted to tell you that Heather appeared to me in my dream last night. But now I don't even want to tell you, because I know you no longer believe me."

I didn't reply. She was right.

Melanie continued: "I didn't ask Heather about the murder. I could feel that she didn't want to talk about it."

"I bet!" I snapped sarcastically.

She glared at me. "Listen, Nick, at some point, you must decide: Either you are going to have faith in me and accept my explanation or reject me."

"What makes you think I've not already decided?" I asked.

"Fair enough," she replied. "I'll understand it if you want to walk out of here and never talk to me or see me again. I'll understand that. I mean, you've lost your job over this. But I genuinely thought you were a bigger man than that."

"Melanie, you could be having a delusional spell right now and not even recognize it. That's what happens with bipolar victims. I've read enough to know that. I'm sure you genuinely believe that Heather took control of your body last night. But that doesn't mean it really happened! Dead people don't come back and possess live people's bodies! It doesn't happen—even with twins!"

"How can you be so damn sure?" she asked. "When did you become God? But because you need proof, let me give you a way to test me. I know where Heather hid the Scarecrow Report. She told me where to look."

I didn't know what to say. She was obviously sick, and yet I wanted to believe her. I wanted to accept that she and Heather had talked in her dream. Now I was the one who lowered my head and looked down at the table. I said: "I'm sorry, Melanie, but I just don't know if I can go along with any of this telepathic twin stuff anymore. It doesn't make sense."

"You're so arrogant," she said. "When did God begin confiding in you about the mental abilities that He gave us? Would you have gone to Mississippi if I'd told you that I have a mental illness and was taking medication to keep me from having delusions? Of course you wouldn't have gone. You didn't have a clue before this morning that I even had an incurable mental illness. You were perfectly willing to believe me then! But *now*—now that I've been labeled as being crazy—you're treating me like I'm a stranger whose every word should be mistrusted. And you have the gall to sit here and demand to know why I lied to you about my past!"

"That's not fair," I said.

"Oh, yes, it is!" she replied. "You've stigmatized me, when it's your own limited imagination that's the problem! You want proof that I'm not nuts—that Heather and I talk to each other in our dreams? Okay, I'll tell you exactly where she hid the Scarecrow Report and then I'm going to tell you something else that you need to know."

During the next several minutes, she told me where the report was hidden. After she finished, she stood up from the table and rapped on the steel door, signaling the officers outside that she was ready to be taken back to her cell.

"You said there was something else that I needed to know," I reminded her.

"Bipolar disorder is passed on genetically," she said. "Do you know what that means? It means your perfect love, the woman you lived with all those years, the woman you adored and wanted to marry—my precious sister, Heather—was just as bipolar as I am. Remember, Nick? We have the exact same genes! That means, she lied to you too! She deceived you just as I did. She never told you about her own delusional episodes, did she? She took medicine every day and hid it from you and never let you in on her secret. And do you know why she hid it from you?"

Melanie didn't wait for me to answer. "She didn't tell you the truth because she knew that you couldn't handle it. You'd put her on a pedestal. You wouldn't have been able to deal with the fact that she was flawed—that she was psychologically damaged goods. That's the real reason why she never agreed to settle down with you, get married, and have kids! That's the real reason why she finally decided to leave you! You kept talking about the whole white-picket-fence trip, and she knew, deep down, that she couldn't give you what you wanted. She knew you didn't love her enough to accept her as she was. You never would have forgiven her for something that she never asked for, never wanted, and couldn't do anything about! It wasn't her blind ambition that made her leave. It was your narrow-mindedness!"

Thirty-one

A decade ago, I would have put Melanie on the witness stand and let her explain how her sister had taken possession of her body and murdered Andrew Middleton," Stanley Slanafall said as our waiter slipped a slab of filet mignon in front of him. We were eating at his favorite D.C. steakhouse. "A jury would have found her not guilty by reason of insanity and she would have been sent to a Saint Elizabeth's and eventually released, once she'd gotten better. But there's no way I'd risk an insanity plea now."

"Why not?" I asked. "The cabdriver who brought her to my apartment thought she was mentally ill and she'd just spent eight hours wandering around a cemetery in her pajamas. Besides, she has a medical history of a mental illness and has been diagnosed as suffering from bipolar disorder."

"So what? Chances are, she'd still be found guilty of murder and sent to prison for life without parole," Slanafall replied. "People are meaner now—no, wait, that's not really true—it's more that they're frustrated and afraid. I still remember when schizophrenics and manic-depressives were warehoused out of sight in insane asylums. Horrible things happened back in those days."

"I remember watching the movie *One Flew over the Cuckoo's Nest*," I said. "Conditions did look bad."

"Exactly, but I'd argue that even that old state mental hospital system was better than what's happening now across America to the mentally ill and I've got only lawyers like myself to blame."

Slanafall was one of the most brilliant attorneys in Washington, a city where nearly everyone you meet seems to have a law degree. He was a partisan Democrat, a card-carrying member of the American Civil Liberties Union, and a feisty, red-haired Jewish New Yorker who'd been married four times and loved nothing better during dinner than a good argument. Modesty was not an adjective that anyone ever used when describing him. We'd been friends for years and during all of that time, I'd never heard him admit that he was wrong or accept blame for anything.

"What are you talking about?" I asked.

"In the 1980s, I joined other ACLU attorneys in launching a full-scale attack on state mental hospitals. Our mission was to close them down forever. They were warehouses and weren't necessary anymore. The pharmaceutical companies had developed promising new drugs, such as lithium, that made it possible for mentally ill patients to live normal or close to normal lives. We were determined to change the system and we did. We used civil rights laws to make it nearly impossible for anyone in this country to be forcibly committed, even if they are stark-raving mad."

"I remember reading about 'deinstitutionalization,'" I said. "Getting people out of the state facilities and returning them back into their communities."

"Oh, we put them back into their communities, all right," he said. "And most are worse off now than ever before! Look around this city. We live in the richest and most advanced country in the world. Yet we have people freezing to death in the winter because they're sleeping on steam grates."

"The homeless?"

"A large percentage are homeless because they are mentally ill patients who have stopped taking their medications and have nowhere to go. Their families, if they have them, can't intervene because it's against the law. No one can force them to take their drugs. That's what's insane about what we did. We were so worried about protecting these patients' individual civil rights that we made it against the law for anyone to rescue them, even though they're in no mental condition to help themselves. They could be living normal lives, but we're letting them die in rags in the name of civil liberties!"

"I don't see what this has to do with the insanity defense," I said.

"There's nowhere for the mentally ill to go for help. If one of them hears voices that tell him to push a woman in front of an oncoming subway train, like what happened in New York, we lock them up. We didn't 'deinstitutionalize,' we 'transinstitutionalized' the mentally ill. We've moved them out of state hospitals and into jails and prisons. Do you know what the single largest public mental health facility in the United States is today?"

"No," I said.

"It's the Los Angeles County Jail!" Slanafall said, slapping the table with his open palm. "That's why I wouldn't risk using the insanity defense. First of all, I don't think Melanie is psychotic. But even if she were, a jury wouldn't want her walking the streets, so they'd vote to put her in prison. It's a national disgrace!"

Slanafall had become so impassioned that other diners had stopped eating and were staring.

"I'm sorry," he said, lowering his voice, "but this is personal to me. My brother sleeps under bushes outside the Department of Commerce Building. Every night I drive by there to make certain he's alive. Once he was brilliant, and now he thinks there's a hole in the North Pole that leads to the center of the earth and aliens fly in and out of there."

"I didn't know about him."

"It's not something I tell most people."

"There's nothing you can do to help him?"

"That's the irony here. I'm partly responsible for the laws that prohibit me from forcing him into treatment." Slanafall cleared his throat. "I helped put my own brother under that hedge."

Slanafall raised his knife and jabbed at the steak on his plate. He cut it into a dozen pieces.

"If you don't use the insanity defense," I said, "what defense will you use for Melanie?"

"Blaming her dead sister, Heather, isn't really an option," he replied. "Although I did notice last night some fool on television who claims he can talk to the dead. That means we need to find someone who is alive as a possible suspect. Any ideas?"

"Actually, I do."

For the next several minutes, we discussed Heather's murder, Jeb Rogge's death, and Senator Peterman's possible role in both. I explained the confrontation with Middleton that Melanie and I had had, our search for the Wizard, and how we were convinced that the CIA had searched Heather's apartment looking for a missing copy of the Scarecrow Report.

"I'd love to accuse the CIA of killing Middleton," Slanafall said. "But this isn't the 1970s and our nation is in the midst of a patriotic surge. No one is going to believe he was snuffed out as part of a CIA conspiracy."

"How about Peterman?" I asked. "He was furious when he learned that Andrew Middleton was behind the 1955 lynching photograph and Heather's decision to write a book."

"All you have on him is conjecture and speculation," Slanafall said. "Besides, you can't really prove now that Peterman was ever at the lynching. All of the witnesses are dead, including Middleton. No, I think we'll have to try a different defense."

"What do you have in mind?"

"Let's be practical here. Every bit of forensic evidence points toward our client. So why fight it? Instead, we change the focus of the trial. We admit that Melanie shot Andrew Middleton."

"You want her to admit that she murdered him?"

"That's right, and then we argue that the rotten son of a bitch got exactly what he deserved."

"You're losing me here, Stan."

"Middleton used to live with Heather Cole, correct? They were lovers. The police have witnesses who saw Melanie running from Middleton's house late at night wearing only a pair of skimpy silk pajamas. This is salacious stuff that we can capitalize on. We have Melanie testify that Middleton telephoned her earlier that evening and invited her to come over. Maybe he offered her dinner. Maybe he just wanted a soft shoulder to cry on. The guy was grief-stricken and he wanted to tell Melanie how much he loved and missed Heather. Two grieving souls—sounds plausible to me!"

"It makes sense if you don't let any of the facts get in your way."

"Fuck the facts," he replied. "Okay. Middleton and Melanie have dinner and reminisce about Heather. It gets late and he suggests that she spend the night at his place. It's all perfectly innocent. She's been sleeping in Heather's apartment, but that's beginning to creep her out. She's having weird dreams—seeing her sister's ghost—stuff like that. Again, this all sounds plausible to me. Anyway, Melanie accepts his invitation and he gives her a pair of silk pajamas to wear that used to be Heather's."

"I don't like where you're going with this."

"Well, you should, because it's downright brilliant. We've got Melanie, an identical twin, in her dead sister's pajamas, spending the night at Middleton's house. She testifies that she's about to go to bed in the guest room when Middleton comes barging in and comes on to her sexually. She grabs her sister's gun, which she has started carrying with her, and runs downstairs to escape. But he chases her into the library. That's where she shoots him—just as he is about to rape her!"

"You're going to claim it was self-defense?"

"Melanie is a beautiful woman. Middleton was desperately in love with her twin sister. Not only does it sound plausible—it's got great media appeal! The public is going to love this. Court TV will air it live. The tabloids and the major newspapers will be enthralled, especially since Middleton was one of their own. If we're lucky, we can find some of Middleton's old girlfriends. Maybe he was kinky. Maybe he has a history of slapping them around. Who knows?"

"Am I being naive here?" I asked.

"Yes, especially if you start harping about how none of it is true. This trial isn't about ferreting out the truth. No trial is. Trials are about winning and losing. My job is to save Melanie's life. If you march into court and tell a jury that long story about King David and Bathsheba and Senator Peterman and Middleton and the Wizard and the Scarecrow Report—then Melanie is going to get convicted. I'll guarantee it! But my explanation is something that every juror can comprehend. It's ripe with scandal, real soap opera stuff. It's what you'd see on television and that makes it seem real."

Slanafall was on a roll.

"Jurors don't like to be bored or confused by too many facts," he continued. "They want to be entertained, titillated, and most of all, they want to believe they're doing the right thing. I'm going to give them that opportunity—a chance to save an innocent young woman who was being attacked by a famed investigative reporter, a man with power, money, influence. And the best thing about this defense is that Middleton can't complain because he's dead!"

"You'll going to destroy his reputation?"

Slanafall put down his fork. "Based on everything you've told me tonight, Middleton was a ruthless, lying lout. Suggesting he was a rapist would be a fitting punishment."

Despite his rationalizations, I still wasn't comfortable with his plan. "If you want to prove that someone else murdered Middleton," Slanafall said, "be my guest. But until you can bring me the murderer's head on a silver platter, I'm sticking with the self-defense scenario. It's the most credible and it may be Melanie's only chance for an acquittal."

He stabbed another bite of steak. "You've got to admit," he said, "it makes more sense than having Melanie tell everyone that Heather pulled that trigger!"

At my request, Melanie had signed a notarized letter that authorized her landlord to allow me to enter Heather's Watergate co-op and remove any personal items that I wished. I drove there after Slanafall and I finished dinner and I handed the property manager a copy of the letter.

He balked. "Melanie Cole is not the unit's leaseholder. She can't tell me who I can and can't let in."

"But she is the executor of Heather Cole's estate and Heather owned that property," I replied.

"I don't care," he said. "I don't believe that I am obligated to let you inside unless I want to and, quite frankly, I don't want to!"

He was being so difficult that I suspected he was hiding something from me. Slanafall had heard rumors that several tabloid reporters were offering cash for personal photographs of Melanie and Heather. I wondered if the property manager had slipped inside her place and lifted a few.

"The best way to resolve this is by calling the judge handling Ms. Cole's murder trial," I said. "Of course, he'll want to know your name, especially after I explain how you are arbitrarily preventing us from retrieving evidence that could help exonerate her. He might even be angry enough to slap you with an obstruction-of-justice charge. At a minimum, I'm sure he'll call your boss."

I was bluffing, but it worked. The manager considered the consequences and then handed me a spare key. "The police already have been through everything, so if there's anything missing, such as pictures or stuff, you need to take it up with them," he said.

I'll bet, I thought.

I expected the rooms to be in shambles, but except for a few drawers left open, everything appeared undisturbed. I did notice that a photograph of Heather that had been taken during a White House press conference while she was asking the president a question was missing from its frame on her desk.

In her latest dream, Melanie had seen Heather sitting at her desk. Heather had opened the top right desk drawer and removed a gold key ring with a small canister of pepper spray attached to it. There were nearly two dozen keys on the ring, Melanie said. Most were probably for locks that Heather no longer used or had been lost or discarded long ago. Heather had selected a brass key with the words DO NOT DUPLICATE imprinted on it.

I opened the right drawer, spotted the key ring, and found the brass key. I slipped it off the ring. Where better to hide a key than in plain sight on a key ring?

I checked the apartment to see what other photographs might have been taken. Two more were missing from the bedroom. When I returned the spare key to the manager, I said: "There're several photographs missing. I'll check with the police to make certain that the detectives didn't take them. But I'm warning you right now, if they show up on the front page of some supermarket tabloid this week, you'll be hearing from me and the police."

He scowled but didn't say a word.

I glanced around as soon as I stepped outside the Watergate. A couple was walking toward me on the sidewalk and there was a taxi double-parked a few feet away. I knew from my FBI training that when a government law enforcement agency tails someone, it does it by flooding an area with agents. The only time a single agent follows you is if you're in a Hollywood movie. The last time that I had been involved in an FBI surveillance, we'd had thirty agents on the ground and a helicopter circling the area. The more agents, the more difficult for the person being followed to slip away or to identify who might be watching him. Despite my schooling, I couldn't tell if I was being watched.

I strolled down the sidewalk and entered a late-night convenience store. I kept one eye on the front door and waited, but I didn't notice anyone come inside. Still. I had a nagging feeling that I was being shadowed. I left the store and drove back to my apartment on Capitol Hill, where I changed clothes, turned off all of the interior lights, and then crept out into the hallway, down a stairway, and out into the backyard. I climbed over the fence, dropped into my neighbor's yard, and exited between the buildings onto a side street. I jogged several blocks until I reached the Capitol South subway station, where I caught a westbound train. I got off at the next station and crossed over to the eastbound side. I caught the next train and rode it one stop beyond Capitol South. Then I got off and checked to see if anyone was watching me. I waited several minutes and then boarded another westbound train. I rode this one to Metro Center. When it arrived, I hurried upstairs to the street, where I hailed a cab.

I couldn't be certain if my subway antics had worked, but I knew that at the very least I'd caused anyone tailing me a bit of heartburn. I instructed the cabbie to drive me to Mail Boxes Etc., a franchise operation that specializes in packaging items, mailing them, and offering its customers private mailboxes. The store was only two blocks away from Heather's apartment. I told the driver to wait while I dashed inside.

Because it was late and well after the store's regular hours, a steel gate had been pulled down from the ceiling to divide the store in half. Behind the gate at the rear of the store were packaging supplies, a cash register, and copying machines. The front half contained a wall of mailboxes to which customers could have access twenty-four hours a day. The key that I'd taken from Heather's apartment was for Box 355. I spotted it near the center of the wall of private boxes. It was in clear view of anyone standing outside on the street. I positioned myself so that I was standing between the mailboxes and the store's front window, blocking the view from outside with my body. While someone spying on me from the street would know that I was opening a mailbox, that person couldn't be certain which one it was.

I slipped Heather's key into number 355, turned it, and reached in with my left hand. There was a manila envelope inside. At the same time that I was drawing it out of the box, I lowered my right hand down in front of me and unbuttoned the waist-long black leather jacket that I was wearing. With my left hand I stuck the manila envelope into my coat, tucking it under my right armpit. I squeezed down hard with my right shoulder and pinned it against the side of my chest. I then used my right hand to remove a similar manila envelope that I had brought with me from my home. I had been carrying it under my coat, in my left armpit. It only took me a few seconds to make this switch, so when I turned around and faced the store's front window, it appeared that I had simply removed a manila envelope from one of the mailboxes.

I carried the dummy envelope, which was now in plain sight, outside to a blue United States Postal Service box on the sidewalk directly in front of the store. I deposited the decoy package down the hatch, and jumped into the waiting cab and told the driver that I wanted him to take me to Capitol Hill.

If anyone had been observing me, they would have thought that I had taken a package from a private mailbox and immediately mailed it.

When the cab reached Constitution Avenue, I announced that I'd changed my mind and wanted to return to the Mail Boxes Etc. He turned the car around. We were about a block away when I spotted a black sedan double-parked in front of the store and four men in black suits circled around the blue USPS mailbox.

"Let's not stop," I said. "I want you to take me to Virginia. I'll give you directions as you drive. I'll also throw in another fifty as a tip!"

I wasn't certain if any of the black suits milling around the mailbox had noticed my cab. But my curiosity—about whether or not I was being followed—had been satisfied. I assumed it was the CIA. By the time the cab had crossed the bridge and reached the George Washington Parkway, I'd come up with a plan.

I told the cabbie to drive me to Great Falls, Virginia, via Georgetown Pike Road, a two-lane blacktop that winds its way along the Potomac River through multimillion-dollar houses buffered by acres of trees and hills. It would be difficult for anyone to follow us without me noticing, especially this late at night, because the area is residential. Several times, I pretended that I was lost and had the cabbie turn down side roads and then double back. It was well after midnight when we finally entered a narrow lane that disappeared into the woods by the river.

"You can just drop me off here," I said. "I'll walk the rest of the way."

"Here? You sure?" the driver asked. There were no houses in sight.

I paid him and watched his taillights disappear. Then I walked briskly into the woods and ducked behind a tree. A few minutes later, I heard the sound of a car engine but didn't see any headlights. I watched as a black Chevrolet sedan slowly cruised up the road. I guessed its occupants were wearing night-vision goggles. I hoped they weren't using heat sensors or monitoring me from the air.

The car passed without stopping. I counted to five hundred and then hurried back onto the blacktop and began jogging. When I reached the second mailbox on my right, I hurried up a gravel path to a modern house sitting deep in the trees. I pounded on the door and stood back so that Stanley Slanafall could see me when he flipped on his outside lights and answered the door.

"What the hell is going on?" he demanded. A miniature schnauzer was yapping nonstop behind him.

"I'm being followed and it won't take them long to figure out that I'm headed here," I said, stepping inside. "I need a car."

"What?" he said. His dog was making such a ruckus that he couldn't hear me. He spun around and lifted up his arm as if he were going to slap its nose and it ran out of the room. "Don't tell me who's following you," he said, scooping a set of keys off a hook. He handed me a Washington Redskins cap. "A disguise."

"You can always claim your car was stolen," I said.

There was a Mercedes CLK 430 parked in the circular drive. Ten minutes later, I was riding north in it along Route 7. I was headed to a bed and breakfast in Harpers Ferry, West Virginia, at the confluence of the Potomac and Shenandoah rivers, a favorite spot for Civil War history buffs because it's where abolitionist John Brown was caught during a botched attempt to raid a federal arsenal and lead a slave uprising. Heather and I had loved the scenery and history of the rivers and bluffs. We'd always stayed at the family-owned B&B and over the years had befriended the proprietors, which was good, since I woke them up. I parked Slanafall's car in a garage behind the main house.

When I was finally alone in a guest room, I opened the manila envelope. Across the top in bright red letters were the words TOP SECRET. Directly below that heading was a single line: SCARECROW REPORT.

Thirty-two

When I was fourteen, I read *Of Human Bondage* by W. Somerset Maugham. My father, the minister, hated the novel because it described a man's search for meaning in his life and Maugham concluded there really isn't any. We're born, we live, and we die, and that's pretty much it. There's one particular passage I memorized. It's near the end of the book when the main character finally understands that life is meant to be enjoyed and there is no hidden master plan to it.

It was like one of the puzzles which you worry over till you are shown the solution and then cannot imagine how it could ever have escaped you. The answer was obvious.

This is how I felt after I read the Scarecrow Report. The reason why Andrew Middleton had decided that Heather was a threat to him became clear. All I had to do was step back and look at his career to see it. He was guilty of orchestrating her murder and I now knew why.

Of course, figuring out Middleton's motive was only part of this puzzle. I was dealing with two murders: Heather's and Middleton's. I believed now that Melanie was innocent. The question was: How to prove it?

I took a long shower. I like to think in the shower. The quiet. The heat from the water. The steam. I mentally revisited everything I had seen and done since I'd met Melanie Cole and she'd convinced me to join her in helping find Heather.

At the FBI Academy, one of our instructors told us that there is no such thing as an unsolvable crime. No matter how careful or how smart a killer is, he always makes a mistake. He always leaves a clue behind. *Where is the clue in Heather's murder? What am I missing?* Standing naked under the pelting water, a thought came to me. *The murder weapon.* And then another thought. *Animal DNA.*

After I dressed, I drove to a gas station and used a pay phone to place a call to Pushmataha, Mississippi.

"I'd like to speak to Sheriff Jacob Moorehead," I said. "Tell him it's Nick LeRue from the Senate Judiciary Committee calling."

"I've been thinking about you ever since I heard that Melanie Cole has been charged with murder," Moorehead said when he came on the line.

"She's innocent and you can help me prove it," I replied. "Do you remember the Saturday morning when the three of us drove to Jeb Rogge's hunting cabin looking for Heather? You said something to me right before we went to search the cabin."

"What'd I say?"

"I took my .38 snubnose from its ankle holster—do you remember what you said when I did that?"

"Sorry, but I don't," Moorehead replied. "Let me think. I remember I was carrying my shotgun and I was pretty keyed up because we thought Rogge might shoot at us. But I don't remember my exact words."

"It's important. Try."

"Oh, wait, now I remember. I asked you if everyone in Washington D.C. carried guns. I was making a joke, but you didn't seem to get it."

"Why'd you ask me that?"

"Because Heather Cole had a gun too. When she first came to Pushmataha, she showed me a handgun she was carrying in her purse. She wanted me to know that she owned one and had brought it with her."

"That's what I thought!" I exclaimed. "Now do you recall what brand of handgun she owned?"

"She made some comment about how she didn't actually know much about handguns, so she'd walked into a Virginia gun shop and asked them to sell her the same gun that Dirty Harry used in the Clint Eastwood movies. She thought that's what she'd bought."

"She owned the same gun as Dirty Harry?"

"No. The gun dealer had actually sold her a much smaller gun. Dirty Harry used a .44-caliber magnum. That's a huge caliber. The handgun that Heather Cole showed me was a Walther nine-millimeter."

Like most law enforcement officers I've known, Moorehead considered himself somewhat of an expert at identifying different models of handguns.

"It was a nine-millimeter?" I asked. "You're certain?"

"I know the difference between a Walther nine-millimeter," he declared, sounding a bit insulted, "and a .44-caliber cannon."

"Then answer this question for me, Sheriff," I said. "If Heather Cole had her Walther nine-millimeter handgun with her when she was in Pushmataha, Mississippi, then how did it end up being the handgun that was used in Georgetown a week later to murder Andrew Middleton?"

Moorehead thought for a moment and then asked: "You sure we're talking about the same weapon here?"

"Ask the FBI," I suggested.

"Let me think about this," he replied. "I know she had a handgun because I saw it and my deputies found a box of nine-millimeter ammunition in Heather Cole's room at the Stars and Bars. But I've got to admit that we never did find her Walther."

I said: "Here's what I think happened. I think Jeb Rogge saw the Walther when he first slipped into Heather's motel room. Maybe she had it on the nightstand or on a table."

Moorehead interrupted: "Rogge grabs it and takes it with him."

"A Walther like hers would cost more than a thousand dollars and that's not something that Rogge would leave behind."

"I'm with you so far," he said, "but that still doesn't explain how the gun got from Pushmataha to Washington, D.C. Rogge's dead, remember? He sure as hell didn't take it up there!"

"That's right. That means someone else took the gun away from him at some point. I think it was on the Saturday morning when Heather was murdered and Rogge was killed."

"The FBI forensic team concluded that Rogge killed himself!"

"What if the FBI's wrong? What if there were two kidnappers—just like Melanie said there were? What if that second kidnapper rode an ATV to the cabin? That's how he got there without us seeing him on the road. What if he murdered Rogge and staged his death to look like a suicide?" I asked.

Picking up on my train of thought, Moorehead said: "Only the second kidnapper made a mistake. He took the Walther nine-millimeter with him back to Washington."

My next call on the pay phone was to Penny Polandick at the Senate Library.

"I need you to call Senator Nehemiah Peterman's personal secretary," I said, "and ask her for a schedule of his most recent public appearances. Say you want it for some sort of study the library is doing."

"Mr. LeRue, are you asking me to lie?"

"I really need his schedule," I replied. "Do this as a favor for me."

"I heard you got fired. If I do this and the senator complains, I could get fired too!"

"Please, Penny! This is extremely important!"

"Call me back in an hour," she said.

I bought breakfast at a McDonald's fast food restaurant to kill time. Finally, the hour passed and I used more quarters and dimes to call her from the pay phone. I didn't want to use my cell phone in case the CIA was monitoring it. Polandick told me that Senator Peterman had two appointments on his schedule on the night when Andrew Middleton was murdered.

"He attended a charity auction from seven-thirty p.m. to nine-thirty p.m.," Polandick said. "Then he went to a Capitol Hill fund-raiser being given by the Republican Party. It started at eight o'clock, but it wasn't expected to end until after midnight."

I remembered that Peterman had been dressed in a tuxedo and had been waiting for a limousine when Melanie and I had surprised him at his house.

"Where was the charity event?" I asked.

"Inside an art gallery on M Street between Thirtieth and Thirty-first streets in Georgetown," she replied. "It was being given to benefit the Washington Children's Hospital, you know, kids suffering from cancer. Peterman's secretary said he was supposed to take a turn as a celebrity auctioneer from nine p.m. to nine-thirty p.m."

That was only a few blocks from Andrew Middleton's Georgetown house.

"Is the name of the limo service listed on Peterman's schedule?" I asked.

"He was picked up by Presidential Limousine. His secretary gave him the company's number, in case the driver was late or there was a problem. Do you want it?" She read it to me.

"Now I need you to find one more thing for me," I said.

"This is very important. Call the National Republican Party and ask them if they have any pictures of Senator Peterman shaking hands at the fund-raiser with the party's chairman or other dignitaries. Tell them it's for your library archives. And listen, I don't want just any photograph. I need a full-length shot—from his shoes to the top of his head. Understand?"

"Full-length. Call me back later this afternoon," she said. "This is exciting!"

I had just enough coins left for one more telephone call. I dialed information and asked to be connected to the *Georgetowner*, a tiny newspaper that covers social events in Northwest Washington, D.C. The receptionist gave me directions to its editorial offices. Two hours later, I parked outside a brick office building on the fringes of Georgetown. As I suspected, the *Georgetowner* was a small operation whose few employees handled any number of jobs. I told the woman who greeted me at the front desk that I was from the Senate Judiciary Committee and asked her if I could see photographs that the *Georgetowner* had taken at the Washington Children's Hospital's charity auction.

"Senator Peterman is on our Senate committee," I explained, "and we'd like to publish a photograph of him in an internal newsletter that we put out. You know, showing how he helped out the hospital and kids with cancer."

The woman sauntered over to a filing cabinet and removed a thick envelope that contained black and white glossies taken at the art auction. She dumped them on the counter and began fingering through them.

"Here's a good one of him smiling," she volunteered. Peterman was wielding a gavel behind a podium and pointing toward a painting of a floral arrangement.

"Yes, that's nice," I replied, "but I'm looking for a full-length shot of him."

She continued sorting until she found a picture of him standing between an attractive couple. The photograph showed all three of them from their shoes to their heads.

"This is perfect," I said. But the woman seemed skeptical.

"They're holding wine glasses," she noted. "Most senators don't like shots published that show them drinking liquor. Are you certain he isn't going to complain if you use this shot?"

"No, it's just for our internal newsletter," I said. I lifted it gently from her hand.

"Maybe I should call him and the couple he's posing with," she said. "They're prominent local residents and I don't want to irritate them by releasing this to you without their permission."

"You look busy," I replied. "Why not let me call them?"

She wrote out the couple's name and telephone number.

"Did you go to the auction?" I asked.

"Yes, and Senator Peterman was simply delightful as an auctioneer. I wish he could have stayed longer, but he said he had to go to another function and left as soon as his turn ended."

I examined the photograph more closely as soon as I got outside. It was just what I needed. I got change, found a pay phone, and called Presidential Limousine.

"I'm from Senator Peterman's office," I said. "The senator used one of your cars the other night and he was so impressed with the driver that he wants to send him a photograph signed by the president. Can you tell me the driver's name so I can pass it along to the White House?"

The limo manager put me on hold and then returned moments later. "The driver was Tony Kang."

"Are you certain?" I asked. "I don't want it to be autographed wrong."

"Mr. Kang picked up the senator at his house in Vienna at six-forty-five p.m. and drove him to an art gallery in Georgetown," the manager said.

"That sounds like our man," I said. "But just to make certain, was Mr. Kang the driver who drove Senator Peterman home after the Republican Party fund-raiser later that night?"

"No one drove him home," the manager replied. "Mr.

Kang was scheduled to take the senator to the fund-raiser, but after they got to the auction in Georgetown, the senator told Mr. Kang that he could go home. He said he wasn't going to need our service to carry him to Capitol Hill later or to drive him home in Virginia. He'd use cabs."

I checked my watch. It was three p.m. I drove the Mercedes that Slanafall had loaned me to Capitol Hill and pulled into the parking garage at Union Station. When I got inside the train terminal, I called Penny Polandick.

"Any luck getting me that photograph of Senator Peterman at the Republican fund-raiser?" I asked.

"I've got five different shots of Senator Peterman shaking hands with other Republicans. What should I do with them?"

"Bring them to Union Station. I'll buy you lunch. Meet me in the food court."

"The food court?" she said, sounding disappointed.

"You deserve better than a Big Mac or slice of pizza," I said. "But I can't take the time today. What if I make an appointment at the Senate Dining Room for next week?"

"Weren't you fired?"

"I'll pull strings."

"Can I bring my boyfriend?"

"That's fine. Anyone else?" I asked, half joking.

"Well, my mom's visiting. She's from Iowa. How about her too?"

"Just bring me the photographs," I said. Thirty minutes later, Polandick handed me an envelope. Three of the pictures inside showed Peterman from the waist up, but the other two were full-length shots.

While Polandick took a bite of a mushroom pizza slice, I compared the photograph that I'd gotten from the *Georgetowner* with the one of Peterman taken later that night at the Republican fund-raiser.

"Penny," I exclaimed, "as far as I'm concerned, you can

invite *all* of your relatives to lunch next week! You've just solved a murder!"

She smiled and I noticed that she had pizza sauce next to her lips.

It was showtime!

I hurried over to the closest pay phone, which just happened to be the one in front of the Frank N' Stein. I thought of the irony of using this phone as I called Senator Leslie Homer DeLong's private cell phone number.

"It's Nick LeRue," I said, when my former boss answered. "I need your help. I need you to arrange a meeting. I have proof that Melanie Cole is innocent."

Thirty-three

I tossed Stanley Slanafall the keys to his Mercedes as he walked toward me at the Union Station parking garage.

"Nice wheels," I said. "Thanks for the loan!"

I'd asked Slanafall to accompany me tonight. If things didn't turn out as I planned, I was going to need a criminal defense lawyer.

"Where're we going?" he asked. "You were mysterious on the phone."

"The Dirksen Senate Office Building—the Judiciary Committee hearing room," I replied. "My home turf."

As soon as we entered the building, two men in dark suits approached and flashed their CIA internal security identification badges. They led me into a nearby office and ordered Slanafall to stay outside. They patted me down and asked me to empty my pockets.

"No safe-deposit keys, bus locker receipts, nothing," one of them said into a microphone attached to his lapel. "All he's carrying is his billfold and two black and white photographs in an envelope."

"I'll tell you where the Scarecrow Report is hidden as soon as I'm finished in the committee room," I said. "I'll keep my promise as long as you've kept your part of our bargain."

The agent relayed my message and listened to a reply in the receiver tucked in his ear. "The people you wanted brought here tonight," he said, "have been *persuaded* to attend. I've been asked to remind you that what you have in your possession is a top-secret government document."

"I have a top-secret clearance," I replied.

"No, you *had* a top-secret clearance," he said, correcting me. "It's been rescinded. You are currently violating the law if you have that report in your possession."

He opened the door and fell in step behind Slanafall and me as we walked down the corridor into the committee room. Melanie was the first person I spotted. She was sitting in the front row, handcuffed and wearing a leg chain. Detective Humbolt was sitting on her left. Phillip Shurman was on the opposite side of Humbolt. Both men scowled when they saw me. I assumed both were furious that they'd been pressured into coming here. The CIA could be persuasive when it wanted.

"I'm telling you right now, LeRue," Humbolt said, "nothing you say is going to change a damn thing about this case!"

"Glad you're keeping an open mind," I replied. No one laughed.

Melanie said: "Nick, why are you doing this? We both know who killed Middleton."

Before I could answer, Senators DeLong and Peterman walked in.

"What the hell!" Peterman exclaimed as soon as he saw me. He shot a suspicious look at DeLong.

DeLong said: "Senator, these folks have raised questions about you and the Middleton murder. I thought it would be prudent to resolve them here in private before anything leaks to the media." He made it sound as if he had done Peterman a favor by tricking him into joining us in the hearing room.

Peterman quickly regained his composure. "I've certainly got nothing to hide," he proclaimed. "Let's get this nonsense over with!" He sat down in one of the committee members' chairs so he now faced us in the audience. Out of habit, DeLong sat in the chairman's seat.

"Senator Peterman," Detective Humbolt volunteered, "I want you to know that none of this was the D.C. Police Department's idea! The evidence speaks in this murder case for itself and it says loud and clear that Melanie Cole killed Andrew Middleton."

Peterman nodded appreciatively.

"Let's look at that evidence," I said, seizing the opening. "Ballistics matched the bullets in the victim's body to the Walther nine-millimeter pistol that Heather Cole owned. Tell me, Detective, were there any fingerprints found on that handgun?"

"No. It had been wiped clean."

"Doesn't it strike you as odd that Melanie Cole would go to the trouble of wiping off her fingerprints and then would drop the murder weapon on the floor, knowing it was going to be traced back to her?" I asked.

Humbolt said: "Murderers don't always think rationally. Besides, the gun's only one piece of evidence. We found your client's black cashmere coat outside the front door of Middleton's house. She was seen there by witnesses too. One saw her running from the crime scene after he heard gunshots!"

"This witness who claims he saw Melanie Cole running from Middleton's house, that's your anonymous witness . . . a man who called 911, but whom you still haven't identified—isn't that right?"

"Yes, but it's not unusual for witnesses to be afraid to testify in homicides," Humbolt replied.

"Didn't that witness call you from a pay phone at the corner of Twenty-ninth and M streets?" I asked.

"Yes, he did. He was out walking his dog when he saw your client fleeing Middleton's house. He telephoned our 911 dispatcher at exactly ten-fourteen p.m.," Humbolt said.

"How long did he stay on the telephone?"

"Four or five minutes. Does it really matter?"

"Did you ever canvas taxi companies to learn if any cabs picked up a passenger at the corner of Twenty-ninth and M shortly after that call was made?"

"No, why would I bother?" Humbolt replied. "The anonymous caller was walking his dog. Besides, he said he lived in the neighborhood."

"And you believed him," I said sarcastically. "What if I told you that a driver for the Yellow Cab Company reported picking up a passenger at the corner of Twenty-ninth and M streets that night at ten-twenty p.m.? He remembers the passenger because he was dressed in a black tuxedo and he told the driver to take him to the Republican Club on Capitol Hill."

I looked directly at Peterman and said, "You were wearing a tuxedo that night and needed a ride from Georgetown to the Republican Club, isn't that right, Senator?"

Peterman rocked back in his chair. "I took a cab from Georgetown to the Republican Club that night," he answered. "But the last time I checked, that wasn't illegal."

"Where did you catch your cab?" I asked.

"I don't recall," he replied with a smirk.

"Just so we're all clear on this," I said, "let me ask you directly: Senator Peterman, did you place that anonymous call to the police?"

"No," he replied. "I certainly didn't."

"Detective Humbolt," I said, "are your emergency 911 calls automatically tape-recorded?"

"Yes, they are."

"If you were to do a comparison of the anonymous

caller's voice and, say, the Senator's voice, you'd be able to determine if he made that call, wouldn't you?"

Peterman rose from his chair. "I'm not going to sit here while you conduct a witch hunt!" he snapped.

Detective Humbolt intervened. "Senator Peterman, my department would need to have probable cause to conduct a voice comparison and let me assure you, sir, that nothing Mr. LeRue has said has made me the least bit suspicious of you!"

Peterman sat back down.

I continued. "The first eyewitness in this case is the neighbor who stepped outside her house to get her mail. She saw Melanie Cole arrive at Middleton's house at nine-forty p.m. Is that correct, Detective?"

"That's when she saw your client," Humbolt replied.

"The next witness was the anonymous caller who claimed he'd seen Melanie Cole come running out of Middleton's house at nine-fifty-five p.m., just after three gunshots were fired."

"That's right," Humbolt said.

"There was a third witness too, wasn't there? He saw Ms. Cole five minutes later—at exactly ten p.m.—wandering around at Oak Hill Cemetery?"

"We were lucky," Humbolt explained, "because each witness said they looked at a clock or watch when they saw your client. That's how we know such exact times."

"Detective Humbolt, how far is it from Andrew Middleton's front door to the Oak Hill Cemetery?" I asked.

For the first time that night, Humbolt broke into a huge grin. "I thought this might come up," he said, "so I personally walked the route. It's one-third of a mile from Middleton's front door to the intersection of Twenty-eighth and Q streets, which is where our witness said he was standing when he first spotted Melanie Cole at the cemetery."

"How long did it take you to walk that distance?"

"Just under five minutes. I've checked with experts and the average person can walk a mile in fifteen to twenty minutes. The murder happened at nine-fifty-five p.m.

Melanie Cole was seen at ten o'clock at the cemetery. She had plenty of time to flee after she shot Andrew Middleton and get to the cemetery by ten."

"I walked that same route today," I said loudly, "and I'm afraid, Detective, that you've overlooked something rather elementary."

"I doubt it," Humbolt replied.

"The Oak Hill Cemetery is enclosed by a six-foot-tall iron fence and your witness was standing on the sidewalk that runs outside of that fence, according to his statement. Melanie Cole, however, was seen wandering around inside the graveyard grounds, which means she was on the other side of that iron fence."

Humbolt's cocky grin vanished.

"Do you know where the entrance to Oak Hill Cemetery is located?" I asked Humbolt. The detective didn't reply. "The gate is located at Thirtieth and R streets," I said. "That's the closest gate, if you are coming from Andrew Middleton's house. It's exactly a half mile from his front door. It took me seven minutes to get to the entrance and another eight minutes to make my way through the cemetery to the spot where your eyewitness saw Melanie Cole that night."

I paused so that everyone in the room would understand what I was saying. Then I said: "Your anonymous source couldn't have seen Melanie Cole bolting out of Middleton's house at nine-fifty-five p.m., because there is no way that she could've walked to the cemetery gate at Thirtieth and R, entered the grounds, and gotten to the spot where she was next seen. It would have taken her at least fifteen minutes to make that trip, not five minutes!"

Once again, I looked directly at Peterman. "The anonymous telephone caller knew when the murder had taken place: nine-fifty-five p.m. But he didn't have any way of knowing that Melanie Cole was going to be seen at ten p.m. meandering through the cemetery."

Peterman drummed the fingers of his right hand against the committee's curved dais and looked a practiced bored.

"On the night of the murder," I continued, "Senator Peterman was scheduled to attend a charity auction in Georgetown. The limo driver dropped him off shortly after seven p.m. at the art gallery. The driver had been told beforehand to wait, because he needed a ride after that event to go next to the Republican Club on Capitol Hill, where he was scheduled to attend a second fund-raiser." I paused to see if Peterman wished to correct anything that I'd said, but his eyes stayed fixed on space.

"However, records show that the senator sent his driver home shortly after they first arrived in Georgetown for the charity auction," I explained. "You said you'd take a taxi to Capitol Hill, didn't you, Senator Peterman?"

"I considered it a waste of money to have the limo wait for me," Peterman replied. "The driver was being paid by the group hosting the charity auction and I didn't want to take money out of its coffers that could be better spent helping children fight cancer."

"How noble!" I sneered. "But were you really worried about penny-pinching? Or did you want to make certain that the limo driver was gone so he couldn't watch you?" Before Peterman could reply, I said: "The very moment you finished your turn as the celebrity auctioneer, you dashed out of the gallery's back door. You then ran to Andrew Middleton's house! It took me three minutes today to walk from the gallery's back door to Middleton's place. You would have gotten there, Senator, several minutes before Melanie Cole arrived outside in her cab at nine-forty p.m."

Peterman's face was lobster-red. He was boiling. I continued my attack: "By the time that Melanie Cole knocked on Andrew Middleton's front door, you were already inside the house arguing with Middleton, weren't you? I'm guessing you both looked outside to see who was there. But neither of you wanted Melanie to see you together, so Middleton didn't answer her knock. After several minutes, she left for the cemetery."

I asked Melanie: "Do you know why you left your black

cashmere coat outside the front door of Middleton's house?"

"No," she said. "I remember taking it off, but that's all."

"The only person who knows what happened inside Middleton's house between nine-forty p.m. and ten p.m. is the killer!" I declared loudly. I turned so that I was now facing Peterman. I now had my back to everyone in the chairs behind me. "Why don't you tell us, Senator? Why'd you kill Andrew Middleton? Was it because you knew he'd betrayed you? Because you knew that he'd sent Heather Cole to Pushmataha?" I intentionally raised my voice so I was now shouting at him. "That's why you shot him and then wiped your fingerprints off the handgun and left it by the body. That's why you slipped out a back door again and made your way to M Street to catch a cab."

Peterman was so angry that I thought he'd explode, but he didn't respond.

I continued: "But you couldn't leave well enough alone, could you? You wanted the police to find Middleton's body while Melanie Cole was still in Georgetown. So you stopped to use the pay phone on M Street to call 911. You posed as a neighbor out walking his dog. You knew she was wearing her blue pajamas because you'd seen her when she knocked on the door. You gave the cops her description. Then you hailed a taxi and had it take you to Capitol Hill."

The hearing room was completely silent. Every eye was focused on Peterman. He slowly raised his hands and clapped them together three times. The noise echoed through the chamber.

"Congratulations," he said smugly. "You should have been a screenwriter. Unfortunately, you've overlooked several holes in your far-fetched drama. The murder weapon, for instance. How did a handgun owned by Heather Cole end up in my hands?"

"Actually," I said, smiling, "I'm glad you reminded me of that." During the next several minutes, I recounted my telephone call with Pushmataha Sheriff Jacob Moorehead. When I finished, Peterman shook his head in obvious disgust.

"You've not only got me murdering Andrew Middleton," he said angrily, "you've got me taking part in Heather Cole's murder *and* killing Jeb Rogge!"

"They're all related," I replied. "You had to kill Heather to keep her quiet about your part in the lynching. You had to kill Rogge because he had a big mouth and was probably already blackmailing you about the lynching. That's how he could afford that fancy Aryan compound of his, isn't it? And after you killed them, you had Andrew Middleton on your back. You knew you'd always be under *his* thumb, didn't you?"

Peterman jumped from his seat. "I've heard enough! You're insane! Where's your evidence? You can't prove any of this and you sure as hell can't put me at Middleton's house because I've never been inside it! Never! Ever! You can 'assume' and 'speculate' as much as you like, but you've got nothing that links me directly to any of those murders!"

This was the moment that I'd been anticipating. I opened the envelope that I'd brought with me and removed the two black and white photographs of Peterman. I walked to the front of the hearing room and held them up so that Peterman could see both of them clearly.

"Here's my evidence!" I said.

"What? Two pictures of me? What's that prove?"

"One is from the charity art auction," I said. "The other was taken at the Republican Club fund-raiser later that night. You're wearing the same tuxedo in both shots."

"So what?" he snorted.

"Notice anything different in these photographs?"

"Yes," he replied. "In the first one, I'm standing between a very influential Georgetown couple who happen to appreciate the fact that I'd donated my time to help raise money for Children's Hospital. In the second one, I'm shaking hands with a fellow senator who happens to think that I'm a damn good public official, and not a triple murderer!"

I carried the pictures over to Detective Humbolt. "How about you, Detective? Do you see anything different?"

He looked hard and said: "There's no difference that I can see."

I showed them to Melanie. After a moment, she exclaimed: "I see it! I see the evidence!" She tried to lift up one of the glossies but her handcuffs and the chain attached to them stopped her short. I plucked the glossies from her fingers and held them up so that everyone in the room could compare them.

"The photograph on the left," Melanie gushed, "shows Senator Peterman at the art gallery auction early in the evening. Look at the trousers of his tuxedo."

Everyone did. "Now look at the second picture!" she declared. "It's the one that was taken later that same night at the Republican Club fund-raiser. Look at his pant legs!"

Everyone peered at the second image.

"There's something on his cuffs," Senator DeLong said.

"I see it too," Phillip Shurman said. "It's white stuff."

"That's *dog* hair!" Melanie shouted. "It's Clover's dog hair! She's Andrew Middleton's dalmatian. Clover always leapt on me as soon as I stepped into his house. I was wearing a black dress the first time we went to see Middleton. It was after my sister's funeral and I had a horrible time trying to get those white hairs off of it. It was nearly impossible, even after I'd sent it to the cleaners."

"Dalmatians shed all year long," I explained. That's something Melanie had told me earlier.

"That's *why* I took off my black cashmere coat at the front door!" Melanie exclaimed. "Even though I was disoriented, I knew that I didn't want the dog to get on my coat when I went inside. I remember that now!"

Peterman bristled. "You're suggesting that because I have dog hair on the legs of my pants that I was inside Middleton's house?"

"You didn't have dog hair on those same pants when you were at the charity auction," I said. "The first photograph proves that! But you were covered in it when you showed up at Capitol Hill and posed for the second picture."

"Those hairs could have gotten there any number of ways. I could have brushed against someone who owns a white dog, for God's sake! You haven't proven a damn thing—except that you're an ass!"

"Animal hair," I said, "just like human hair, contains DNA. It can be traced back to a specific pet. In this case, a sample from your formal wear should tell us whether or not the hair came from Middleton's dog. And if those hairs are from Clover, then you were in Middleton's house on the night that he was murdered!"

Peterman started to leave through the hearing room's side exit only a few feet behind him. "I've been insulted enough!" he snarled.

"Senator Peterman!" Phillip Shurman shouted. "I don't think you should be going just yet!"

"Are you threatening me?" Peterman demanded. "I'll have you fired!"

"Then you'll have to me fired too," Detective Humbolt declared, in a surprise show of backbone. "Because if the FBI isn't going to have a forensic crew check your tuxedo, I can guarantee you that the D.C. Police Department will."

For a moment, Peterman looked as if he were going to return to his seat. Instead, he jerked open the side door and bolted through it.

"He's escaping!" Shurman shouted. He and Detective Humbolt each grabbed their cell phones.

"I'll get a search warrant for his house!" Humbolt yelled.

"I know several agents who live in Vienna," Shurman replied. "I'll get someone over there before he can get rid of the evidence!"

I walked over to Melanie. "Heather didn't shoot Middleton and neither did you!" I said. "Peterman killed him."

"What made you think of Clover's hair?" she asked.

"On the morning when you were arrested, Slanafall and I went to the police station to look at the evidence, after we'd left you at the jail. There wasn't any dog hair on the pajamas you were wearing. I knew Clover always jumped on you every time we'd been inside Middleton's house. That's when I knew that you hadn't been inside the house that night. Unfortunately, I didn't think until this morning about checking Peterman's tuxedo."

"Lucky for us," she said, "that he liked having his picture taken." She paused and then said: "That night seems like a bad dream now. I really thought Heather had taken control over my body."

"Maybe she had, but instead of having you kill Middleton, she simply wanted you to be with her at her grave."

I noticed the two CIA security officers walking toward me from the back of the hearing room. "It's time for you to keep your end of our deal," one said.

"Hey, Stan," I said, motioning to Slanafall, "give me your car keys for a second." He reached into his pocket and handed them to me. I removed a key that had the words DO NOT DUPLICATE stamped on it.

"Try Box Three-fifty-five," I said handing it to the CIA agent. "I think you already know where the Mail Boxes Etc. store is located."

"Cute," the agent replied.

I'd driven there earlier that morning and tucked the Scarecrow Report back into the same mailbox where Heather had originally stored it. I knew the CIA had already searched there and didn't think they'd look a second time.

"You tricky son of a bitch," Slanafall said. "You slipped that key on my key ring so they wouldn't find it when they searched you."

The CIA agent spoke to Phillip Shurman. "I believe you were given orders earlier today that need to be carried out now," he said.

Shurman glanced at me. "The agency has demanded that the FBI arrest you for taking control of a classified document without having the proper clearance. I'm supposed to place you under arrest."

"Just a minute," Senator DeLong bellowed. "Nick LeRue is the chief investigator of the U.S. Senate Judiciary Committee and, as such, is authorized by Congress to review top-secret documents."

"Senator, we were under the impression that Mr. LeRue had been fired," the CIA agent said.

DeLong put his arm around my shoulder. "Why would I fire the smartest chief investigator the committee has ever had?" he asked. "Are you saying that I'm an idiot? Before you answer, you might want to consider the fact that I'm close friends with the chairman of the Senate Intelligence Committee, which oversees your agency."

"No, sir," the agent said. "If you're vouching for Mr. LeRue, I'm certain my bosses at Langley and the FBI director will not wish to pursue this."

"You tell your bosses they should be damned glad that Nick LeRue recovered this report for them," DeLong said, dismissing the agents. He noticed Melanie was still handcuffed. "I'll see to it that you are released from jail ASAP, young lady," he promised.

"Thank you, Senator," she said.

Suddenly he laughed. "My God!" Senator DeLong exclaimed. "I just realized that Nehemiah Peterman is going to go down in history as the first United States senator ever accused of murder because of the hair of a dog!"

Thirty-four

The next afternoon, Sheriff Moorehead received a telephone call from Phillip Shurman, who was calling from FBI headquarters. Shurman got right to the point. "Last night, Senator Peterman fled the Washington metro area after he was questioned about the Andrew Middleton murder," he explained. "After further investigation today, the FBI has issued a warrant for the senator's arrest, charging him with unlawful flight to avoid prosecution. Because of his status as a member of Congress, we're trying to keep this quiet until we locate him."

"Senator Peterman is wanted by the FBI?" Moorehead asked, clearly stunned.

"Yes, and we're afraid he's trying to flee the country, if he hasn't already. There's a chance that he might return first to Mississippi. He was last seen driving a black Cadillac Escalade bearing a congressional license tag that says: MISS-ONE. We're sending an agent from our Jackson field office to assist you in case the senator shows up."

A short while later, Sheriff Moorehead called an emergency meeting to brief his deputies. "I don't want any of you trying to apprehend the senator on your own. This is an FBI case. If you see him, we'll let them make the arrest," he explained.

Deputy Clark Shades stuck around afterward. "I've known Peterman and his family all of my life," he told Moorehead. "Someone's making a mistake here."

"Like I said," the sheriff replied, "stay out of this. If you spot his Caddie, call me first. Is that clear?"

Just before eleven o'clock that night, the two-way radio in Sheriff Moorehead's study crackled. "Sheriff?" a faint voice said.

Moorehead happened to be balancing his family's checkbook, otherwise he might have missed it.

"Shades?" he replied.

"Officer down!"

Moorehead tried to get Shades to answer again, but his deputy didn't respond.

Although Pushmataha County was a relatively poor county, Sheriff Moorehead had persuaded the county commissioners to install tracking devices in all of the sheriff's squad cars, because many of his deputies worked alone and often traveled miles from town. Moorehead raced to the courthouse and used the computer there to locate Shades's cruiser. He cursed silently when he saw that the car was stopped just outside the turnoff that led to Senator Peterman's estate. Moorehead called for an ambulance as he drove north in his unmarked car. He also called the Holiday Inn and asked to speak to the FBI agent who had checked in earlier that night. But the agent wasn't in his room. Moorehead would have to handle this on his own.

About a mile from the Petermans' property, a black Cadillac Escalade shot out of the darkness and roared by Moorehead in the southbound lane. It was running without its headlights. Moorehead fought the urge to turn around and chase it. Instead, he continued toward Deputy Shades's abandoned cruiser. He spotted it moments later on the left side of the state highway. Moorehead made a U-turn to come up behind it. Clutching a flashlight, he hurried toward the car. Shades was lying in a roadside ditch about ten yards from the rear tires. Blood was splattered on his pants and shirt. He was panting softly in rapid bursts.

"My vest [breath] saved me!" he said. "But the bastard [breath] got me on my side [breath]. Can't move." Moorehead opened Shades's shirt. A small fist of shotgun pellets were embedded in the Kevlar. Because they were clustered tightly together, Moorehead knew the shotgun had been fired at close range.

"Didn't cuff [breath] the son-of-a-bitch," Shades gasped. "Trusted him [breath]. I saw him drive [breath] into his driveway [breath]. Followed him [breath]. He said the warrant was [breath] big misunderstanding [breath]. I asked him to ride to [breath] the courthouse and he got right in [breath]. Had a briefcase [breath]. Said he had something to show me [breath]. Pulled out a sawed-off shotgun [breath]. I'd just pulled onto the highway [breath]. Lucky I turned sideways to look at him."

While the vest had caught the brunt of the blast, at such a close range it couldn't prevent all of the pellets from doing damage. Blood was oozing from Shades's abdomen.

"Peterman must have run back to his house on foot and gotten his Escalade," Moorehead said. He could hear the ambulance siren wailing. It was getting close.

"Sorry, Sheriff," Shades blubbered.

Two paramedics arrived and ran up to them. "We've got him now!" one exclaimed. Moorehead hurried back to his car and sped onto the highway. As he drove, he began rousting his other deputies, all of whom were at their homes. He told them to converge on Pushmataha. Unless Peterman intended to drive his Escalade off-road, he'd have to pass through the town to escape. Moorehead pushed the gas pedal of his Mercury Marauder against the floor and listened as the car's 4.6-liter V8 engine screamed. He knew the car's 300-horse power plant hadn't come from the factory with as much pickup as the standard 345-horse, 6.0-liter V8 in Peterman's Escalade. But Moorehead had tinkered with the Mercury's engine, adding 60 more horsepower. He also knew that the Marauder weighed about 4,100 pounds, and that had to be at least 1,500 pounds lighter than Peterman's bulky SUV. Finally, because he was a sheriff, he'd modified the computer settings that normally restricted how fast the Marauder could be driven. As he thundered down the highway, the speedometer went as far to its right as possible, registering 140 miles per hour.

Moorehead was about three miles from Pushmataha when he spotted the SUV's taillights in front of him. Peterman had turned on his vehicle's lights and apparently had slowed so he wouldn't attract attention. Moorehead switched on the red and blue flashing lights hidden in his car's grill and unleashed the siren. Peterman hit the gas.

The highway leading into town was relatively straight and easy to navigate at high speeds, but the old road curved as it entered Pushmataha and both men nearly lost control as they swerved to stay on the blacktop. Pushmataha's town square had been designed to accommodate horses and wagons, not high-performance vehicles. As Peterman's SUV entered it, he jammed on his brakes and spun the steering wheel in an attempt to complete a sharp left turn. But he was simply going too fast. The SUV careened out of control, twisted completely around, slammed into the street curb, and flipped over, smashing against the historical marker at the entrance of Rabbit Creek Park. Moorehead also jammed his brakes as his Mercury entered the square. The car's rear tires screeched. Gray smoke filled the air and he could smell burning rubber. Although his sedan did not flip over, it skidded sideways, also out of control over the curb, flying up onto the lawn of the courthouse. Moorehead watched as Peterman climbed outside the SUV from behind an airbag. Boxed in on three sides by storefronts, the senator scrambled into the park. He was carrying a briefcase in one hand and a single-shot sawed-off twelve-gauge in his other.

Moorehead stepped out of the Marauder, drawing his

nine-millimeter Glock as he crossed the street and entered the park.

"Stop, Senator!" he yelled. "You can't escape!"

But Peterman kept running.

Younger and faster, Moorehead began closing the gap, but as he neared the park's pavilion, his left foot landed on an uneven patch and the sheriff heard a loud crack and fell forward. If there was any doubt in his mind about what had just happened, it disappeared when he looked down at his left hip. His upper femur had broken in half near where the bone meets the hip joint. It was a compound fracture, which meant that the bone itself had burst through his skin and was now jutting out of his pant leg. Blood was squirting from the opening—and it was the rhythmic bursts that scared him most. He'd broken his leg in the exact same place in a college football game years ago and doctors had warned him about running. But the wound hadn't bled like this when it had snapped the first time. Sprawled on his stomach in Rabbit Creek Park, Moorehead was afraid that his broken femur had somehow severed his femoral artery when it had torn through his muscle and skin.

Peterman had heard Moorehead collapse behind him. He darted behind a tree for cover and stopped to look backward and to catch his breath.

"We're both too old for this," Peterman gasped loudly.

The pain in his leg was excruciating, but Moorehead managed a lighthearted reply: "You've got that right, Senator!"

"Listen," Peterman yelled, "I've got a half million dollars in this briefcase. I'll bring it to you. It's yours. I've got a private airplane waiting for me in Jackson. Just let me walk out of this park."

Moorehead had dropped his Glock as he was falling forward. He'd needed his hands free to help him break the fall. The handgun lay three feet away. It was out of reach and without it he was defenseless. Just the same, he yelled: "You know I can't let you walk out of here, Senator!"

"Why not?" Peterman asked. He sounded weary. "A half million dollars! That's more than you'll earn in ten years.

And no one will ever know. Think of what you can do with that money. You could send your kids to college. Buy a new house. All you have to do is let me walk away."

Moorehead replied: "I don't understand why you're doing this! You're destroying everything that's important to you—your family, your career, your reputation."

"I don't have a choice anymore," he replied. "That goddamn Washington reporter ruined my life."

"You murdered Heather Cole?"

Peterman was silent for several moments and then he said: "I rode my ATV to Rogge's hunting cabin that Saturday morning. We'd arranged over the phone on the night before to meet. Rogge went inside to get the woman and then, all of the sudden, he comes running outside in a total panic. He says the girl has escaped."

"How'd she do that?"

"I don't know how she fooled him. We decided to split up and search for her. Rogge said: 'You'll need a gun.' He got me a Walther nine-millimeter from his pickup. I said: 'I've never shot a nine-millimeter, so he handed me his .22-caliber pistol and says: 'Take whichever one you want.' That's when I realized that I had *both* handguns."

"You shot Rogge?"

"At that very same second, we heard a noise. It was Heather Cole. She'd been inside the cabin all along, only now she comes flying out its door. Rogge was just sort of standing there in shock, so I stepped up beside him and shot him in the head with the .22. He dropped instantly. I leaned him up against the tree stump. Then I walked into the woods where I'd left my ATV. It didn't take me long to catch her. I shot her and she went down just like any other animal. I loaded her on my ATV, drove her to a cave, and dumped her body down into it. Only she wasn't dead, so I had to shoot her a couple more times. Then I went back to the cabin, wiped my prints from Rogge's gun, stuck it in his hand, and fired it into the air to make certain there was gunshot residue on his fingertips. Like I said, I'm in too deep now."

"My deputies are on their way," Moorehead yelled. He tried to lift himself up on his elbows so that he could crawl toward the Glock but a jolt of intense pain shot through him and nearly knocked him out. He paused and collected himself.

"I'm going to bring you the briefcase now with the money—your money—your half million dollars in it!" Peterman yelled. "Don't shoot me!"

As Moorehead watched, Peterman stepped into view from behind the tree. Because the moon was behind Peterman's back, Moorehead could only see the senator's silhouette. Peterman was holding the briefcase by its handle in his left hand, which he raised shoulder-high. He kept his right arm glued to his side. Peterman took a step forward and Moorehead heard a click. It was the sound that a metal hammer on an older-model, single-round shotgun makes when it is cocked.

"Don't come any closer!" Moorehead screamed. "I'll shoot you if I have to! I know you got a shotgun!"

Peterman stopped. "I'm just bringing you the money," he said. "That's all. No reason to shoot. We're friends, remember?"

Moorehead looked at the Glock. He dug his elbows into the dirt and used them like ski poles to push forward. His crippled left leg was throbbing and he was losing blood so rapidly that he was beginning to have trouble focusing. He felt light-headed, as if he were going to drift off to sleep at any moment.

"I'm thinking you've broken your leg," Peterman said. "I heard you fall." The senator began walking forward once again. "You broke it in three places in college, right? I remember that football game! Such a shame!"

Because of its short barrel, the blast from a sawed-off shotgun would spread over a wide area. Peterman would only need to aim it in the general direction of Moorehead for its pellets to do their deadly chore. The senator was now less than fifteen yards away.

"Stop right there!" Moorehead screamed. "Or I'll

shoot!" He was bluffing, because his right arm was still a good foot from the Glock. Just the same, Peterman stopped.

"Relax," the senator said. "I'm going to throw you the briefcase. It's all yours. Just let me go and take the money!"

At that instant, Peterman lowered his left hand and swung the briefcase back behind him as if it were a bowling ball about to be unleashed. He swooped the case forward and threw it. It flew upward into the blackness toward Moorehead. At that exact same time, Peterman swung his right hand up from his side. He was bringing the shotgun to waist-level, where he intended to fire it as soon as his now-free left hand could grab the weapon's shortened barrel—a move that would allow him to use both hands to brace the stumped gun.

Although he was woozy from the loss of blood and in agonizing pain, Moorehead's brain still comprehended what was unfolding. He could not reach the Glock in time unless he lurched forward by rolling onto his left side, a move that would send his compound fracture smack into the ground, causing the protruding bone to be pushed back against his skin. As the briefcase came flying toward him, Moorehead did just that. He jerked forward with all of his strength and grabbed the Glock. He screamed in agony as his broken leg dug into the soil. With his pistol now in his right hand, he looked at the outline of Peterman and began firing.

Before the briefcase hit the ground, Moorehead released three rounds, but the pain from his leg proved to be too much, and he blacked out while squeezing the trigger a fourth time. The last sound that he heard was the deafening roar of Peterman's twelve-gauge shotgun.

I'd won! I had gotten my happy ending! Melanie and I had proven that Senator Peterman had murdered Heather, Jeb Rogge, and Andrew Middleton. Melanie had been released from jail the next afternoon. It was finally over. And yet, I didn't feel any sense of completion. Instead, I felt sad. I still had the bottle of Jack Daniel's that I had bought a few nights earlier, so I got it out and poured myself a shot. Because I rarely drink whiskey, I really have never learned how to drink well. You're supposed to nurse bourbon, in regulated and enjoyable sips, not knock it down in gulps. I poured another. Then another. Then another. Too much, too fast. But I didn't slow down. I welcomed the caramel-colored Prozac.

Soon I felt my mind slipping into the twilight between reality and confusion. At some point, I looked down at my glass and noticed it was empty, and when I glanced up, she was standing in my kitchen.

She smiled. I smiled back. Or, at least, I thought I did. My lips felt as if they'd been starched. Was she really in my apartment? I hadn't heard her come inside. Maybe it was my desire for Melanie and my regrets about losing Heather that were causing me to see what I wanted to believe was real.

She reached down to where I was sitting and touched my cheek with the palm of her hand and I closed my eyes and focused entirely on the tips of her fingers. No, this was happening. I could feel her touch. But even if it had been a drunken illusion, I wouldn't have cared. All I wanted was her.

"Nick," she whispered.

I opened my eyes and she was holding out her hand, urging me to follow her. I was like a man repeatedly crossing through a room where a television was playing. I was conscious of fragments, bits and pieces of what was happening during my treks back and forth from lucidity and drunkenness, but not fully aware of what was happening each moment.

I forced myself to focus. We'd moved into the bedroom and she was slowly undressing me. I'd never been undressed by a woman and she did it with much care, as if my body were a present that she was unwrapping at Christmastime. As the layers of clothing came off, I again felt her soft caress. I was in heaven! I tried to force my brain to fight the booze-induced dullness that I had initially sought. *Concentrate. Stay alert.* I wanted to feel each touch, memorialize every scene, record every sensation. *Do not hurry. Slow down, time!*

Having stripped me, she rose from the bed and disrobed gracefully, her every move a seductive gesture that excited me. Now I regretted the alcohol and, for a brief moment, worried that it might curb my sexual urges. It is every man's secret fear, isn't it? At least those above age forty. A beautiful woman, a limp dick.

But as she moved onto my bed, a surge rushed into me and all fear vanished. Little LeRue was feeling quite frisky, thank you!

She did not climb on top of me, but instead slid next to me and for a second she simply laid there holding me. I wasn't certain why she thought it was necessary, but she apologized. "I'm sorry about the deception. I'm sorry I never told the truth. I'm sorry I never shared my secret with you."

"You were right about me," I replied. "I wouldn't have understood. I'm the one who is sorry."

She turned onto her side and when she did, her breasts came together, and I felt another visual jolt. She was perfect. I followed her neck upward and looked up into her eyes and was surprised because there was a sense of sadness in them. But before I could ask her why, she pulled me close, and I entered her. I'd never made love as we did. It was multistaged, filled with lust, sweat, naked skin pounding against naked skin, and yet there was a tenderness there. It was lovemaking fueled by tremendous longing. It seemed to last hours and when I finally felt my thigh muscles grow tight and I could no longer control the urge, I exploded, and in those few seconds, I felt her orgasm too. It was as tremendous as mine, and I knew that we had become one, not two separate perspiring individuals, but one rapturous soul.

Exhausted, I shut my eyes. I don't know for how long but when I opened them, she was crying. She wasn't sobbing or weeping, but was crying simple tears that ran slowly down her face. I started to apologize, to ask what I had done and how I could repair the damage, but she covered my lips with her finger and said: "No!"

She rested her damp cheek against my chest and held me tight, and I fell asleep.

When I awoke the next morning, she was gone and I had the worst headache of my entire life.

I had never felt so happy.

Thirty-five

I knew from the sound of the knock that it was Melanie outside my apartment door. I'd heard her knock enough by now to recognize it. It was nearly noon. I opened the door without bothering to peep through the security hole. She was angry.

"Have you seen the *Tribune* this morning?" she asked, slapping a copy down onto my coffee table.

"No," I replied, trying to ignore the pounding in my head. "Did they catch Senator Peterman?"

She scooped up the newspaper and held it in front of me so I could read its front page. A photograph of Andrew Middleton took up one-third of it. Next to the picture was the headline: *Famed Reporter Remembered as "Champion of Truth."*

"They lionized him yesterday at his funeral!" she exclaimed.

"That's what funerals are for," I replied.

"But he was a horrible man! All he cared about was getting a scoop. It didn't matter how many lives he ruined.

They make him sound like he was the best goddamn reporter who ever lived! It's not right!"

I read the first paragraph. The service had been at the National Cathedral, the same as Heather's funeral. However, Middleton's service had been held in the sanctuary, where only Washington's most elite are eulogized. The president and his Cabinet had all attended, as had a long list of dignitaries, many of whom had been profiled in the best-selling books that Middleton had written. A former secretary of state had called him "the most influential reporter in America for more than three decades." Another had praised him for his unwavering dedication to "ferreting out the truth." I noticed in the fourth paragraph a reference to the Wizard.

> With Middleton's death, one of the nation's most hotly debated mysteries will remain just that throughout all of history. The investigative reporter died keeping his promise to his anonymous source. He had vowed never to reveal the identity of the Wizard, the pseudonym that he had chosen for a government official who had provided him with key information during his investigation of a corrupt president. . . .

"Middleton is responsible for my sister's murder," Melanie shrieked. "He caused Rogge to be murdered, and made Peterman a killer. But the newspaper is turning him into an American hero!"

"Welcome to Washington," I said. "Look, I really don't want to sound like some cynical curmudgeon, because there are thousands of really good people in our government and in this city. But you've got to understand that this is the capital of illusion. Do you know who the most effective president in recent times has been?"

I knew Melanie didn't need a lecture, but I really wanted her to understand why the *Tribune*'s tribute to Middleton was predictable. I said: "It wasn't President Jimmy Carter, a man of conscience and deeply held religious beliefs. It wasn't LBJ, who was the shrewdest political wheeler-dealer in recent memory. And it sure as hell wasn't Bill Clinton, who was a Rhodes scholar and had climbed from an Arkansas trailer park to the White House. The most effective president was Ronald Reagan and do you know why? Because he was a skilled actor. He knew how to act presidential! His own relationship with his children was horrible, but he stood for family values. My point is simply this: What matters most in Washington is appearance. It's all show! And Andrew Middleton, thanks largely to a Hollywood movie that transformed him into a bigger-than-life figure, is an example of that. I'm sorry, but there's nothing you can do to correct it."

"Why did he have Heather murdered?" she asked. "What's in the Scarecrow Report? What was so damn important that it was worth her life?"

"The CIA made me sign a written statement stating that I would never reveal its contents."

"Goddamn it, Nick, that's not fair!" she protested. "Heather was my sister!"

I thought for a moment and then I said: "Do you enjoy playing games?" Before she could answer, I said: "Someday I'm going to write a novel and when I do, the main character is going to be a famous investigative reporter."

Melanie looked puzzled but as I continued, she realized what I was doing.

I said: "I think my novel's main character will attend UVA and be a member of a secret society—maybe the IMP. Of course, I'd have to pick a time period for my novel. I'd pick the late 1960s, because there was so much going on then: the Vietnam war, the Cold War, protests in the street. Did you know that the CIA was an unchecked agency in those days?"

"Unchecked?" she said. "What do you mean?"

"It could do anything it wanted. And it did. It was involved in plots to assassinate foreign leaders, especially Cuban dictator Fidel Castro. The FBI, meanwhile, was spying on Dr. Martin Luther King, Jr., and keeping secret files on radicals."

"And your novel's main character—would he be a radical?" Melanie asked.

"Absolutely not," I replied. "In fact, he'd enlist in the Army right after he graduated from UVA."

"Just like Andrew Middleton did," Melanie said.

"Exactly," I replied, giving her a knowing wink. "And he'd be assigned to teach language at Fort Bragg. But that would be his cover. The truth is that he'd go to work for the CIA. And he'd be the sort of guy who does well working undercover. He'd be good at keeping secrets and he'd be blindly ambitious."

"Just like Andrew Middleton," she repeated.

"Yes, my novel's main character sounds a bit familiar, doesn't he?" I replied. Continuing, I said: "When it's time for him to leave the Army, he wants to go to work at Langley. But the boys there have thought of a better use for his talents. They want him to work as a 'deep cover' agent. Do you know what that is?"

"No," Melanie replied.

"A deep cover agent is sometimes called a sleeper. Only a select few know that he works for the agency. He is sent out into society and lives what seems like an ordinary life with no obvious connection to Langley. The Soviet Union sent out thousands of sleepers during the Cold War. Some went years without hearing from the KGB. Only, in my novel, my main character is going to be more than a sleeper."

"What do you mean?"

"There's a twist. You see, the CIA specifically orders him to take a job as a newspaper reporter."

"Wait a minute," Melanie said. "It's illegal for CIA and FBI agents to pose as members of the media. Heather told me that!"

"That's right," I said. "But that's the law *now*. In the sixties, the CIA and FBI routinely had their agents pose as reporters, especially at civil rights rallies. That's why the media finally insisted they stop doing it. But what I'm talking about is even more devious than that. In this case, the young man from UVA doesn't pretend to be a reporter. He actually becomes one."

"I'm not sure I understand what you're saying," Melanie said.

"As soon as our main character is discharged from the Army, he applies for a job at the *Washington Tribune*. However, he's rejected because he doesn't have any reporting experience. So he works for a Kentucky newspaper but he keeps pestering the *Tribune* and eventually he's hired there. Just imagine what that means for the CIA. It suddenly has a sleeper working as a legitimate journalist in the most influential newspaper in Washington, D.C. That reporter can travel anywhere in the world. He can get access to world leaders, influential members of Congress, and the White House, even the generals at the Pentagon. He can write stories that affect world events."

"And no one would ever know that he was a sleeper agent," Melanie said.

"That's true, but even the CIA couldn't have predicted the jackpot that it was about to win. Not long after our man gets hired, there's a break-in at the Democratic Party's national headquarters and, bingo, the sleeper gets assigned to the story."

Melanie said: "Let's see if I can predict what happens next. The investigative reporter in your book begins unraveling a White House cover-up that leads him directly into the Oval Office and the president of the United States."

"That's a great idea!"

"And he breaks that story with help from an anonymous source, right?"

"That's right," I said. "He has a secret source who feeds him information—juicy, inside stuff about the president and the White House. Stuff no other reporters can get. And do you know why the information is so accurate? Because it's coming directly from the CIA. There's no individual, anonymous source. It's the CIA who is channeling him facts. Only the agency is hiding behind the facade of a cute pseudonym."

Melanie was quiet for a moment. She wanted to think about what I'd just told her. Then she said: "Nick, I think you're trying to tell me in your novelistic way that Andrew Middleton was a sleeper agent. I think you're also trying to tell me that the CIA fed him information about the Democratic Party break-in and what was happening at the White House during the cover-up. I think you're trying to tell me that it was the CIA who helped Middleton bring down a sitting U.S. president."

"I think you've caught the gist of my plot line," I said. "Of course, something unexpected happens. After the president is forced to resign, a new president takes charge and he quietly asks the FBI to identify our reporter's secret source."

"And that's something the CIA couldn't let happen," Melanie said, interrupting, "so it intervenes by playing the national security card and takes charge of the Scarecrow Report. It's got to protect its sleeper agent."

I said: "You got it! In the mid-1970s, Senator Frank Church conducted a series of Senate investigative hearings into the CIA's clandestine actions. The nation was so outraged by what Church uncovered that Congress stepped in and enacted tougher rules. But neither Church, nor Congress, nor the White House, nor the American public ever was told that a famous *Tribune* investigative reporter was a CIA shill. To protect itself, the agency erased all its history of the reporter being a sleeper, and he went back into deep cover status."

Melanie said: "But someone made a mistake, didn't they? They didn't destroy every copy of the Scarecrow Report. And somehow Heather obtained one. She read it and then she confronted Middleton. He would have been horrified. He was going to be exposed as an agent. He must've begged her not to print the story. Knowing Heather, she probably agreed to hold off until after she'd gotten back from Mississippi."

"I think that's exactly what happened," I said. "What she didn't know was that Andrew Middleton already had begun orchestrating her murder."

Melanie wiped her eyes. Then she stepped over to me, wrapped her arms around me, and put her face against my chest. "Thanks," she whispered. "I needed to know. It doesn't change anything. But I needed to know."

Phillip Shurman called, interrupting us. Melanie waited while I spoke to him.

"Did they catch Peterman?" she asked, as soon as I had hung up.

"Peterman was chased last night by Sheriff Moorehead. They both crashed their cars in Pushmataha's town square. Moorehead ran after him and they exchanged gunfire."

"Oh, my God!"

"Apparently, one of Moorehead's rounds hit Peterman in his thigh just as he was pulling the trigger of a sawed-off shotgun. The impact from Moorehead's bullet knocked Peterman backward, causing him to jerk his hands upward just enough that his shotgun blast missed Moorehead by mere inches. The sheriff's in a hospital. His leg is busted up, he severed an artery, and lost a lot of blood, but he's expected to fully recover."

"Good! And Peterman?"

"Moorehead got off three rounds before he passed out. Like I said, one hit Peterman in the thigh. Then another missed entirely. But one got him in his chest. He crawled about a hundred yards away from Moorehead before he collapsed and died."

Melanie said: "There's something else, isn't there?"

"Peterman's body was found near the riverbank in Rabbit Creek Park," I said. "It was lying directly under the limb of the trophy tree."

* * *

Although Melanie knew that I didn't like her smoking in my apartment, she lit a cigarette. "I was going to stop, but it doesn't seem like a good time right now," she said. She walked over to the bay window, near my chess set, and said: "Secrets. Andrew Middleton's and Senator Peterman's lives were destroyed because they were trying to hide a secret from their past. So was Rogge's life and Lester Alfred too. All of us have them, don't we, and we try to keep them hidden, but they're always there, haunting us, no matter what we do or how we change."

"Melanie," I said, "I want to talk to you about last night and what happened between us."

She spun around slowly and shot me a puzzled look. "What about last night?"

"About us, you coming over here," I said.

"Nick," she replied, "I didn't come to see you last night. I got out of jail yesterday and went directly to the Watergate to begin packing."

"You weren't here?"

"Heavens, no!"

"We didn't make love?"

Now Melanie really looked surprised. "That's not something I would have forgotten, Nick," she replied. "What's this all about?"

It had to have been the whiskey. I felt foolish, embarrassed, and disappointed.

Melanie finished her cigarette and said: "I had a powerful dream last night. I saw Heather. It was summer and we were living in Little Rock, Arkansas, and it was hot, and I was outside of our house standing in the backyard. When we were little, maybe five, my father built us a treehouse there. At the time, I thought it was terribly high up in the limbs and I was afraid to climb the wooden planks that he had nailed into the tree for us to use as a ladder. Of course, when I was older, I realized it was only five feet above the ground."

She turned her back to me and stared outside the bay

window. She said: "Heather was never afraid, and when Daddy finished building the treehouse, she scampered up and looked out the window and called out: 'C'mon, Melanie, you can see so much from up here!'"

Melanie fumbled with her purse and found another cigarette. I noticed her hands were trembling as she lit it. "In my dream last night, I heard a child singing. The song was coming from the treehouse. I went to check it out and when I reached the bottom of the tree, Heather popped her head out of the treehouse's window that my dad had cut in the boards. Only it was Heather as a child, not as an adult. She was five and giggling and truly carefree and she looked down at me and she said, 'Melanie, you can see so much from up here!' And then she darted her head back inside the treehouse and I heard her singing again and I knew she was happy—truly happy. It was the best time of our lives. My father was still alive back then and we were so young and innocent. I wish you could have heard her singing. Heather was really, really happy! Then I heard her say in a clear voice: 'I'm waiting for you, honey. I'll be here waiting for you! But you take your time!'"

I wondered if there was any more to her dream, but Melanie had finished. I said: "What do you think your dream means?"

"Heather was telling me that she's okay. She's happy. She wanted to tie up the loose ends. She wanted to say goodbye because she knew that I loved her. She wanted me to know that she would be waiting for the day when I join her in our treehouse. She's gone now. And I don't think she will ever come again in one of my dreams."

I walked over to her and gently pulled her close to me. Neither of us spoke for several moments and then she said: "Nick, I'm going home. I came here this morning to say goodbye."

When I released her, she said: "There's something else I need to tell you. I'm moving in with someone."

"W-what?" I stammered.

She took my hand, led me into the hallway and down the stairs to the front of my building. Parked at the curb was a U-Haul rental truck and sitting on the passenger side staring at us through the window was Clover, Andrew Middleton's dalmatian.

"I rescued her from the animal shelter earlier this morning," Melanie said.

Clover barked and scratched at the closed window. Melanie took my other hand into hers. "There are direct flights to Denver from Washington, D.C., every day," she said. "I've already checked."

We kissed and when she released me, we walked together to the U-Haul. Clover began jumping excitedly in the front seat as Melanie climbed inside the cab and started the engine. She leaned across the seat and rolled down the passenger-side window. "When you're ready," she said, "let me know. I'll be waiting."

I watched as the U-Haul pulled into the traffic. Clover stuck her head out of the window and sniffed the air. They were beginning a new adventure.

I returned to my apartment. I needed to shower and get dressed for work. But as I walked across the living room toward my bedroom, I stopped. Something was different. Something had changed. It took me several minutes before I realized what it was. Someone had moved the chess pieces on the board by the bay window. I stepped over to examine it. The rook was in a different location. The positions of the chess pieces had gone unchanged from the time that Heather had dumped me. Not a single move had been made and I had thought that the game was stalemated. But in a dazzling twist, the rook was now in a new space and, in moving the rook, the contest had been radically changed in a way that I had never imagined. My king was now in check. No! *I was checkmated!*

How? Who? Melanie? No, she didn't play the game well, and moving the rook had been a stroke of genius. Who else? A bizarre thought came to me.

Melanie had denied that she had come to my apartment last night. She'd denied that we had made love. I believed her. She had not been playing coy. I assumed that I had been simply drunk and had imagined her being here. It had been an alcohol-fueled sexual fantasy.

Or had it been?

What if the impossible had happened? What if Melanie had been correct about her sister's powers? What if Heather had taken charge over her mind and her body last night? What if it had been Heather who had come to see me? What if she had come to say her final goodbyes, come to tie up our loose ends? I thought about what I had seen, felt, and what she had said to me.

I'm sorry about the deception. I'm sorry I never told the truth. I'm sorry I never shared my secret with you.

Heather? Melanie? My imagination?

I stared down at the chessboard and its black and white game pieces. Heather had always made her next move before we went to bed.

How often in our lives do we think we are seeing events clearly, and yet we later discover that we did not fully see or understand them, not at all?

I picked up the rook. The match was over. She had won.

I didn't want to be alone, so I got dressed and walked to the Dirksen Building. I still had unpacking to do in my office. I had just emptied a cardboard container when Senator DeLong walked in, plopped down in a chair, and put his feet up on my desk.

"Did I ever tell you about the time—"

I interrupted him: "Why do I feel a long story coming on?"

DeLong looked hurt. "I'll cut to the chase, if you want. Years ago, I was with a senator when a bunch of kids from his district arrived to tour the Capitol. One of them asked: 'What's the most important quality that a senator must have? Is it courage or intelligence?' The senator thought for a moment and said: 'A man who is courageous but doesn't use his courage intelligently is a reckless fool! And a senator who is brilliant but is afraid to act with courage is merely an educated fool!' The student seemed confused until the senator said: 'It's good to be courageous and it's good to be intelligent but it's even better to have a big heart, because if you have a big heart, you can always go out and find someone with courage, and find someone with intelligence to help you. But if you don't have a big heart, all you'll ever care about is yourself, and you'll squander your talents.' "

I liked his story but I didn't have a clue why he was telling it to me.

"Nick LeRue," he said, "I'm trying to pay you a compliment. You were willing to give up your job in order to help Melanie Cole. That shows me you've got courage. You figured out who the real killer was, which shows you've got brains. But the fact that you got involved in the first place, that tells me that you've got a big heart."

He started to leave.

"Was LBJ the senator in your story?" I asked.

"No," he replied. "The truth is I just made up that entire little yarn. But I like it, don't you?"

He laughed. And so did I.

Acknowledgments

Thanks first go to Heather and Melanie Brown, my twin nieces, for allowing me to use their first names in this book and for making me curious about the unique experiences that twins often share. Next, I'd like to publicly thank my loving wife, Patti Brown Luzi Earley, who never doubted that I could write a novel. You are the best!

For advice about the U.S. Senate Judiciary Committee, I turned to Mary DeOreo, the committee's veteran investigator, and Mimi Devlin, its public information officer. Both were generous with their time and insights.

Several friends were kind enough to read early versions of *The Big Secret*. I appreciated their enthusiasm and suggestions. They include: Jay and Barbara Myerson, Keran Harrington, George and Linda Earley, and my parents, Elmer and Jean Earley. My mother read to me when I was little, first instilling in me a love of stories. Thanks, Mom.

In addition, I wish to thank Reis Kash, a fellow writer; Georginia Atkins Havill, for running her sharp editing pencil through early drafts; and my longtime friends, journalist/author Walter Harrington and novelist Nelson DeMille.

Thanks also are due my literary agent, Robert Gottlieb of Trident Media Group, for encouraging me to write a novel in addition to my nonfiction books, and my editor, Robert Gleason, at Tor/Forge Books, who really gave me top-rate editorial advice.

In addition, I want to acknowledge family members and friends who cheered me on. They include: Gloria Brown, James Brown, Ruey and Ellen Brown, Phillip and Joanne Corn, Donnie and Dana Davis, Marie Heffelfinger, Don and Sue Infeld, Richard and Joan Miles, Kendall and Lynne Starkweather, Lynn and LouAnn Smith, and Elsie and Jay Strine.

Finally, thanks to my children: Stephen and his wife, Michelle; Kevin, Tony, Kathy, Kyle, Evan, and Traci, who remind me daily of what really brings joy and gray hairs into my life.

Please visit the author's Web site at www.peteearley.com for information on his other books.

Look for:

LETHAL SECRETS

by Pete Earley

Available June 2005

One

Er, uh, would you like to go for coffee?" he asked, lingering near the door of their college economics classroom.

"Not today," she said. "But maybe some other morning."

She stepped by him into the crowded hallway. He was an American, and although she had lived in Brooklyn for five years, she still felt uncomfortable whenever she socialized with non-Russians. Still, he was handsome and seemed polite. He sat behind her every Tuesday and Thursday morning in the lecture hall. It was an easy class for her. She'd always been good with numbers.

It had taken him several days to screw up his courage. There'd been clumsy attempts. Once, he'd rushed to open the lecture hall door but was too timid to speak. Another time, he'd borrowed a pencil. It was innocent. She was nineteen. He appeared to be about the same.

Perhaps she was making a mistake. What harm would there be in going for coffee? He wasn't a stranger. But her stepfather expected her earlier than usual today. Their restaurant hadn't been open for very long. Her parents and uncle had invested everything in it.

She left the building. The sun felt warm. There were no clouds. Blue sky. It was mid-October and the trees in the park across from the NYU library were dropping their leaves. Despite the sunshine, the air was crisp. She thought about Moscow. She missed her friends there. She missed her older brother. But she didn't miss the city. It reeked of decay, stagnation, the past. New York was electric. It was her future.

Because she was preoccupied, she didn't notice the U-Haul truck edging up the street behind her as she walked to the subway. But even if she had, it wouldn't have mattered. There was nothing odd about rental trucks in Manhattan. The driver hid behind sunglasses and a navy blue baseball cap with white stitching. New York Yankees.

"That her?" the driver asked.

"Da, da, da," snapped Victor Manakov, the passenger sitting beside him.

The truck eased by the girl and slipped into a no parking zone four car lengths ahead. The driver kept the engine running.

Speaking into his cell phone, Manakov said, "She's the skinny one wearing a white blouse, black pants, carrying textbooks." The description was hardly necessary. The only other people on the sidewalk were a black youngster riding a skateboard and an elderly Hispanic woman walking with the aid of a cane.

Manakov climbed out of the truck's cab. It's rear cargo door jerked upward. Three men crawled out. Each was wearing blue overalls. They appeared to be moving men about to deliver furniture.

"Olga! Can that be you?" Manakov exclaimed in Russian.

She stopped, examined his face, but didn't recognize him.

Stepping closer, he said, "I'm a friend of your brother, Vladimir! We were fighters together in Afghanistan!"

The other men quietly encircled her, yet she didn't sense any danger. She was trying to match his face to a memory. He opened his arms, as if he were about to embrace her. That's when the others sprang into action.

One grabbed her left arm, the other her right, while the third reached around her waist and easily lifted her from the sidewalk. Manakov snatched her legs. Caught completely by surprise, she dropped her books and tried to struggle. But her reaction came too late. They tossed her into the truck. The door slammed down. The vehicle lurched from the curb.

"Shut up! Bitch!" Manakov yelled. He slapped her hard across the cheek. Olga was shoved onto her chest. Her hands and feet were pushed together and bound with gray duct tape. A torn strip was slapped across her lips. It all happened in a matter of seconds. One moment she had been recalling Moscow and daydreaming about the friendly American boy in her class. Now she was being abducted in the darkened rear of a rental truck.

Why?

Her body began to tremble. She couldn't control the shaking. Her face burned.

How had they known her brother's name? What did they want?

Most of all: *Why me?*